# TRACI STEAD

## THE SPIRIT SERIES

# *The* Doctor *of* Dunstable Plains

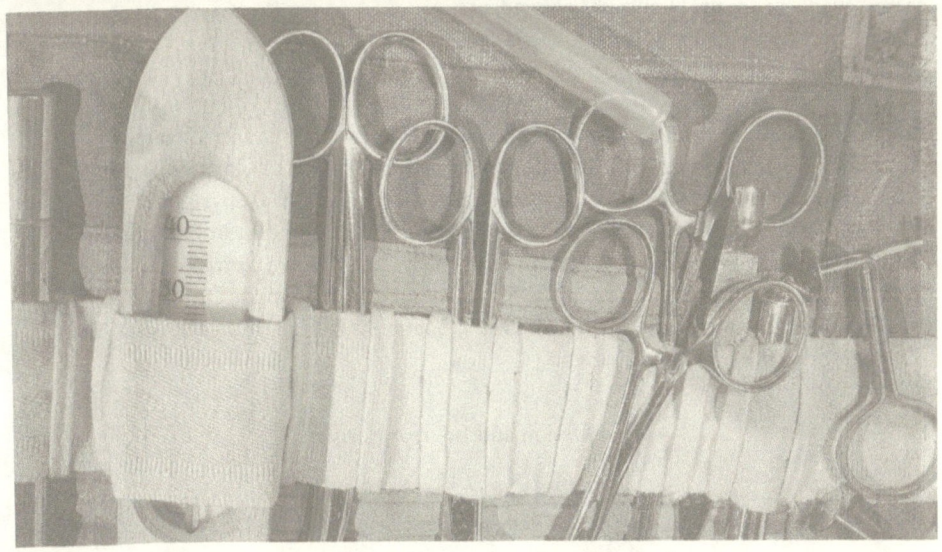

Cover Design and Interior Format

# DEDICATION

POOR AGRICULTURAL AND ECONOMIC OPPORTUNITIES in the last half of the nineteenth century caused many Quebecois to move south to the United States. By 1890, roughly as many Franco-Canadians lived in all of New England as the total population of New Hampshire. Poor farmers sent their sons and daughters to live in row houses overseen by matrons. They worked long hours in often dangerous conditions. Mill bells called them to work at 5:45; being tardy meant fines. They worked all day in cotton mills, wool factories, shoe shops, and lumber mills so that they could send money back home to their families. Besides dangerous working conditions, long hours, and homesickness, they also suffered from religious and ethnic discrimination. This story is for all of the people who learned to live in the midst of death.

# Acknowledgements

EVEN WORKS OF FICTION REQUIRE a lot of research. I want to recognize the Nashua Public Library and their fabulous local history resource room. The reference librarian was exceptionally helpful.

The Lowell National Historical Park is a national treasure with many personal stories about working in the mills. The Industrial Revolution was integral to the settlement of the area, and immigration of many ethnicities occurred. The town of Lowell is still a place of shelter for the immigrant and refugee.

The Country Doctor Museum in Bailey, North Carolina, houses excellent samples of medical equipment and pharmaceutical plants. The men who served rural America as physicians and the women who attended the first nurse training schools worked in primitive conditions. They often received chickens and other gifts as payment. They are to be commended for their service to the poor of our country.

I am not a physician for a reason. My family has been patient and encouraging as I have processed this story: watching amputations, learning how to reset bones, researching herbal remedies, and discovering the amazing advancements of the ancient Greeks and Romans. Did you know they performed cataract surgery? Still amazes me. Thanks, Matt, Jonathan, and Amos, for listening to my trivia and for sharing some of your own.

I must always acknowledge the Holy Spirit who moves in me and around me to show the story the Father would have me tell. Suffering and death are not pleasant topics, but they are crucial to the Christian faith. I hope I have told this tale well.

# PSALM 30

I WILL EXALT YOU, LORD,
for you lifted me out of the depths
and did not let my enemies gloat over me.
LORD my God, I called to you for help,
and you healed me.
You, LORD, brought me up from the realm of the dead;
you spared me from going down to the pit.
Sing the praises of the LORD, you his faithful people;
praise his holy name.
For his anger lasts only a moment,
but his favor lasts a lifetime;
weeping may stay for the night,
but rejoicing comes in the morning.
When I felt secure, I said,
"I will never be shaken."
LORD, when you favored me,
you made my royal mountain stand firm;
but when you hid your face,
I was dismayed.
To you, LORD, I called;
to the Lord I cried for mercy:
"What is gained if I am silenced,
if I go down to the pit?
Will the dust praise you?
Will it proclaim your faithfulness?
Hear, LORD, and be merciful to me;
LORD, be my help."
You turned my wailing into dancing;
you removed my sackcloth and clothed me with joy,
that my heart may sing your praises and not be silent.
LORD my God, I will praise you forever.

*To live is to suffer, to survive is to find some meaning in the suffering.*
*~Friedrich Nietzsche~*

# CHAPTER I

*Boston, Massachusetts: 1898*

A CHURCH BELL CHIMED THE TIME in the distance. Annie's light brown hair cascaded around her face as Increase bent over his wife, checking her vital signs.

*Even in labor she's beautiful,* thought Increase.

"Hold my hand," she said. "It'll still be awhile, I expect. What do you think it is, a boy or a girl?"

"There's only way to know for sure." Increase frowned. "And that time will be here very soon. You're nearly ready for the hard part."

"No," she replied. "The hard part comes after this. The diapers, the sicknesses, the colic. The hard part is living." She gasped with a contraction. "Living requires pain. I think beautiful, exciting pain is my favorite."

Annie relaxed her head against the pillows and a soft smile played on her lips. Light from the fireplace flickered on her cheeks. Soon her face twitched with discomfort. The contractions were getting stronger.

"Increase, I need you." Annie bent over, bracing herself against the flood of anguish that every mother has known since the very first birth. "It hurts." She panted.

"I know, Love," Increase whispered as he stroked her hand. "It will pass soon."

"Send for the dressmaker," Annie commanded with a new urgency. Sweat broke out on her forehead and her delicate hand trembled in Increase's own grasp.

"The dressmaker?" Increase laughed. "Are you planning the child's wardrobe already?"

"Not for the child—for my coffin, you murderer!" Annie raised herself from the bed, pointing, accusing Increase. Then she fell in spastic tremors that shook the house. As quickly as it began, it was over.

Moments later Increase looked at his wife lying motionless in the bed, two babies at her side. He fell on his knees, sobbing and clutching at her body, holding her face, begging her to speak. Annie never moved, but the tiny forms swaddled in soft blankets rustled in their cocoons.

Tentative, Increase pulled aside the blanket from the first child. His tiny fist waved and a whimper caught in his throat. Increase's tears flowed unchecked, the salty taste catching in the corner of his mouth.

Suddenly the second child wailed, demanding attention. Increase pulled away the cover and stared into his own face. The ugly child pointed at Increase with a deformed finger. "You did this," it accused. "You killed his mother—your wife!"

A knock at the door caused Increase to turn. There stood the dressmaker—with Annie, clothed in black funeral robes.

"No … no, wait," Increase said. "This can't be right. You're fine. It's just a dream."

But Annie turned and followed the dressmaker out.

"No!" he shouted. "Don't go. I'm sorry. I'm sorry. I'll do better. I'll save you. Please!"

His imploring did no good; they floated from the room.

A bell echoed through the streets. Increase sat up, alone in his sweat-soaked bed. The dream always ended with the same living nightmare. He was a widower with a young child to care for and raise without a mother. He had no companion by his side to share his pain and suffering, his sorrow and aching. The house would come alive in another hour, but now, before the rising sun softened the room with the pink glow of morning, Increase sat alone in his bed and mourned again the loss of his wife. He rose and stole to the decanter on the small corner table. The brandy shook in his hand as he tried to ease the agony of memory.

"Good morning, Increase," Lively murmured as she entered the dining room. "I see you didn't sleep well again last night." She nodded toward the empty brandy glass that sat next to his morning coffee cup.

Increase frowned at his sister. "No. It's always the same. Annie's dying and I can do nothing to help her. It's all my fault." He sighed with aged grief.

"You know that isn't true." Lively sat down next to him at the long table. "Sometimes women die during childbirth. Life is hard, but you have to keep on going."

"That's what she says in my dream: 'The hard part is life. Living is pain.'" He shook his head and then cleared his throat. "Well, she's right about that."

"No," Lively said as she took her brother's hand. "Existing is pain. When you were with Annie, you were living, but now you only exist. You need to live again, Increase. David needs you to live. We all do. It's been six years."

"I am living," Increase growled. "I'm living in a nightmare, a doctor who kills."

The sound of David's singing on the stairs set Increase further on edge.

"I have to get to the hospital," he said, choking on dry toast and emotion.

Rising from his chair he stormed from the room, a black cloud rumbling into the hallway.

"Good morning, Daddy," called David from the bottom stair, his chubby hand resting on the newel post. "Rebecca says we can go to the park today and ride the carousel."

Increase stopped to stare at the small frame of his son. Annie's presence never left the house as long as David was near. He was the lifeline that buoyed Increase from his darkest despair.

"That sounds wonderful," Increase said as he tousled the boy's hair. "Which horse will you ride?"

"The black one," David said. He smiled. "Aunt Lively says Mama had a black horse." His eyes twinkled as he stared up at his father. "Did you know Mama had a black horse?"

The light faded from Increase's eyes. "Yes, some say it was me," he muttered as Lively entered the stairwell. He grabbed his coat off the hook and twirled it about his shoulders. "I have rounds today. I'll be gone until late."

"Yes." Lively sighed. "Have a good day."

The late frost bit Increase's lungs as he charged down the stairs of the brownstone. Green budding oak leaves glittered in the morning light as the trolley clanged at the corner. Increase didn't have an automobile like most of the doctors at the hospital. He felt it was too showy, too boastful. The trolley was good enough for his patients, and it was good enough for him. He scrambled aboard as the car lurched forward, its bells warning pedestrians to stand aside.

Increase had not grown up in Boston. His family came from the middle classes of Concord, where style and wealth were stifled by a history of benevolence and education. It was there that Increase began his studies under the local physician before attending medical school in Boston. His schooling had gone well, and as one of the brightest students, he was asked to join the hospital staff. But his heart had stayed in Concord with a brown-haired beauty. Annie had been his faithful friend, sending letters of encouragement through the long years of work and study. She agreed to come to Boston as his wife.

After her death Increase had thought about returning to Concord, but he knew the childhood memories of friendship would be worse than the stuffy social life of Boston, so he stayed. His sister, Lively, moved to be with him soon after Annie's death, and took over the duties of mother and lady of the house. It was a practical arrangement that was working even if it wasn't satisfying.

The trolley stopped at the hospital and Increase shook himself into the present. Life or existence, whichever it was, called for his attention. He jumped to the brick walkway just as the car moved forward in its unending cycle of stops and starts.

The hooks lined on the wall for doctors' coats and hats were already full. Increase was running late.

Dr. Shevenell greeted him in the hallway. "The frost is nipping this morning. You look as if it might have bitten quite a lot."

True, Maurice Shevenell was one of the auto-owning doctors, but Increase had only been impressed by his genuine concern and care for his patients. Dr. Shevenell had helped train Increase during his intern days, and Increase had often thought the good doctor was the reason the hospital had taken on such a young physician as himself.

"It was a long night," Increase said. He placed his coat and hat on the chair back in the pharmacy closet.

"You're still thinking of your Annie," the older gentleman stated matter-of-factly.

Increase furrowed his brow at such a blunt prognosis. "Yes. Dreams—nightmares, I suppose—haunt me."

Frowning, Dr. Shevenell nodded. "They'll never stop. But they'll grow less intense and will visit less often. How long has it been?"

"Six years." Increase sighed, his shoulders slumping. "How long until I can inhale again?" The tears stung his eyelids. He blinked to stifle his weakness.

"I still dream of my Adelaide. It has been twenty-two years." Dr. Shevenell breathed deeply. "She comes to me when the days are hardest, when I push myself too much. Then I know that I need some relief, a distraction." He waited for Increase to look at him. "Come to dinner tomorrow night. Mariette's back from Paris. We'll eat and play bridge. Bring your sister too. You both need a change of scenery, I imagine." He offered Increase a warm smile.

"I'll ask Lively. Perhaps." It was all Increase could manage. Pleasurable pastimes were no longer a part of his world.

*Out of suffering have emerged the strongest souls;*
*the most massive characters are seared with scars.*
~Edwin Hubbell Chapin~

# CHAPTER 2

*Philippi, Macedonia: AD 50*

I CRINGED AS PATER'S COUGHING ECHOED down the hallway. His breathing was more labored since I last visited. His letters to Rome had disguised his true state, and I, as the child, had assumed all was well. Pater had been a strong soldier in the emperor's army. I adored him and couldn't imagine him weak.

Thus Casper's letter encouraging me to return home had been a shock. The manager of the house had always been trustworthy; if he felt that Pater needed me, then I would hurry home.

Casper had been right.

"Loukas, come here." The coughing continued like the crackling of autumn leaves on the forest floor.

I hurried down the dim hallway. Most of the servants were gone for the day, tending to their own families.

"Yes, Pater?"

I stepped into the coolness of his chamber. He lay on his bed with cushions piled under him to raise his lungs.

"I need more of Jehan's tea, the bitter one."

"Yes, Pater."

I turned on my heel and hurried to the kitchen. Pater's medicines were stored in the corner cupboard, dried herbs for teas and broths stacked in small pottery jars on the shelves. I searched through them for the special tea from the doctor.

I scooped out the leaves and put them in a cup. Water was always kept on the fire, and I poured it over the dusty green leaves. There wasn't much left in the jar. *I'll go see the doctor tomorrow.*

I stirred the strong tea while it steeped, my mind wandering back down the Via Egnatia. Many travelers walked the road to Rome these days. Life under Claudius was safe and stable. Asclepius had blessed me to study medicine in Athens and then to travel to Rome. Dionysus might be my patron god, but Asclepius was my hero.

"Loukas." Pater hacked and wheezed.

"Coming," I called and started down the hall with the hot cup of tea in my hands.

I stopped inside the room. Pater was wiping blood from his beard. He quickly wadded up the linen cloth and closed it in his fist. He tried to smile, but the coughing started up again.

I took the tea to him and sat on the edge of the raised pallet. He took the cup in his fine-veined hands and inhaled the strong vapors. His skin was pale death; the time was approaching.

During my time in both Athens and Rome, I had seen phthisis patients. A common ailment, it struck its victims without partiality. Pater was soon to be ranked among its conquests.

"I'll go see your doctor tomorrow," I said. "The tea is almost gone."

Pater nodded.

"I'm not sure what he puts in it. The smell is different than the prescriptions in Rome."

Pater spoke with the cup held close to his face: "Jehan is a good doctor. … He left Gaul after the final round of battles and visited Rome." He struggled to speak. "He was … the personal physician to … the centurions and tribunes." He sipped the hot liquid.

"No more talking. You need to rest." I pulled the cover tighter over his chest. "The doctor … Jehan, you said?"

Pater nodded.

"He can tell me all about it tomorrow."

I left the room, but the sound of suffering followed me like a dark shadow hiding the sun.

The herb garden could be smelled before it was seen. Tucked in behind the last of the houses, it grew near the base of the Pangaion hills. Snow still rested on the peaks, blending into the white clouds of spring that blew across the pale sky.

A low stone wall outlined the garden, with a bronze Nehushtan wrapped around the gate post. The gate was open and bid me enter the fragrant patch of poison. I smiled as I caught myself using my old teacher's phrase. *"You can either heal or kill. And you can do both with the same prescription."*

I entered the garden and spotted an old man digging roots near the wall.

"Hello. I'm Loukas, Aegeus's son."

The man looked up and smiled. He braced his hands against the stone wall and raised himself. Mud wetted his robes, and he brushed his hands off on a towel tied at his waist.

"Hypíaine—Good morning! I'm Jehan." He walked toward me and extended his arm. "And how is Aegeus this morning?"

We shook hands. I was surprised to notice that the old man was still strong.

"He's close to the end, I think. The skin is pale, the breathing erratic. The lungs are bleeding, though he tried to hide it from me." I pursed my lips in a forced smile. "The inevitable end of us all."

"Hm. What brings you here? Casper told me you should arrive soon, but I didn't expect you to come here."

"Pater is out of the tea you made for him. I would make it myself, but I'm not sure what herb you're using. The smell is hard to place, a bit unpleasant though not pungent." I tried to soften my reaction to his new medicine. "Pater says it helps."

The old doctor smiled and motioned me toward another section of the garden. We walked through the rows of green shoots. The growing season was only a few weeks begun and already tall, leafy stalks dotted the acre or so inside the wall.

"It's called 'bourse de pasteur.' It's especially good for bleeding ailments." We stopped next to a cluster of leaves spreading on the ground. "It can be dried, but it's best fresh."

"Looks like mustard." I examined the slightly elongated leaves. "Where did you find it?"

"Grows naturally back in Gaul. I brought it with me when I left there." He bent down and snapped off a few leaves. "You're right; it's related to mustard. It isn't as potent as mustard when you need a decongestant, but it helps clear the lungs a little. The main use is as a coagulant."

I smiled at the old man. "Pater said you're a good doctor."

"Epainō—Thank you. That's kind of him to say." He smiled and turned toward the small cottage. "Come on in and I'll get the tea together."

Dried plants and flowers hung from the rafters, and settled over the room like a fragrant dust. Small particles floated in a sunbeam near the door frame.

I sneezed and laughed. "You've brought the garden indoors."

"Yes. The garden's goodness isn't finished when it's done growing. In death the plants do some of their best work. I ..." He paused to look around the dim hut. "I help the death to be productive."

He mixed several leaves and dried flowers together and placed them in a small pouch. "This should be enough for a week. I'll be over to see Aegeus in a couple days. Unless ... Aegeus said you are a doctor. Perhaps he doesn't need me any longer." He looked in my eyes as he passed me the medicine bag.

"Pater needs you. I studied in Athens and in Rome, but I haven't worked alone yet."

"You should join me, then. You'll get some good experiences with the local ailments that way. I'm headed to check on some of the veterans in a couple hours. Would you like to join me?"

"I would, but let me talk to Pater and Casper first. I haven't been back long, and I don't know how much I can be spared."

"Of course. I'll be in front of the public baths at the fourth hour. Join me if you're able."

I walked back into the bright sunlit morning. A gray cuckoo startled from the wall and lifted into the air, its barred underbelly reflecting like the last of the snow on Mount Pangaion.

Pater had been pleased that Jehan invited me to join him. *"The men will hold you in high regard,"* I could still hear him say as he smiled ear to ear. Then another coughing fit had taken his breath and the moment was over. It was an awful sickness, this wasting away, waiting for death.

I looked ahead to see Jehan jump down from the wall around the baths. He waved in the air, motioning me to cross the street and meet him near the road. I weaved in and out of the bustling crowd. Philippi was a busy city these days, nothing like Rome, of course, but it definitely had changed in status and atmosphere.

"You came," Jehan said as he clapped me on the back. "Good. Good. We'll be visiting the new veterans today. Claudius has sent another group of them. They heal in Rome long enough to become a burden to the city and then they are shipped here." Jehan grimaced.

"How did you end up here?" I asked.

"I was needed." He shrugged and walked down the stone roadway.

We turned from the main road and started climbing the hill toward the city wall. A pebble slid between my sandal and foot, pinching the tender skin. I leaned against the wall and shook my leg to free the rock.

"Thank you for the tea for Pater. He was happy to hear I'll be accompanying you. Pater thinks highly of you." I smiled at the old man as the rock slipped back onto the ground. "You've made an impression on him."

"Aegeus is a good man. I shall see if he has managed to raise a good man." Jehan kept walking toward a low hut near a grove of oak trees. "It won't be easy, what you are asked to do."

I hurried after him. "What do you mean?" I asked as I took long strides up the hill. My breathing was heavy and a trickle of sweat dribbled down my temple.

Jehan raised a finger and kept walking. He stopped at the hut and knocked on the door before entering. I followed behind into the dark coolness of the one-room cottage. A curtain was pulled aside to reveal a bed in the far corner. A fire burned in the small grate, heating a pot of water.

"Good morning," Jehan said as he walked into the house. "I'm Jehan and this is Loukas. I've been assigned to care for you. Let's see what we have here."

The putrid scent of infected flesh rose from the bed. A feverish man raised his hand, acknowledging our presence. He was aware, alert, but in obvious pain.

"Good of you to come."

"Get some water, Loukas." Jehan motioned toward a cup on the table.

I retrieved the cup and filled it with tepid water from the fire. Jehan poured a bit of blue oil into the mug and then put the vial back in his pouch. He motioned for me to stir the liquid while he checked the patient.

The bandages around an amputated leg were wet with the draining infection. Jehan pulled them away and cleaned the wound. Then he wrapped the leg in feathery leaves of yarrow and covered them with a clean bandage.

He lifted the man's shoulders and held him while I slowly poured the warm liquid down his throat. Jehan nodded his approval as the last of the medicine was drained.

"We'll come back tomorrow," Jehan said—whether to me or the patient, I wasn't sure.

We left the house and headed up the hill toward another patient.

"It would be better if he died," I said. "He'll have no life without a leg."

"He's more than a leg, Loukas. He's a man with ideas, loves, plans." Jehan stopped walking so I could catch up. "For a while his body will tell him the leg is still there. A struggle will ensue. He'll wonder who he is without a leg." Jehan looked over at me. "The struggle will convince him that he is more than a leg."

"But he's suffering so much," I said. "Death would give him relief."

Jehan shook his head and turned back up the hill. "Your response to his suffering makes you a poor doctor, Loukas. He needs compassion, not relief. Not your kind anyway."

*Every man must do two things alone;*
*he must do his own believing and his own dying.*
~Martin Luther~

# CHAPTER 3

DARK DESCENDED BEFORE INCREASE ARRIVED home. Rebecca drew the nursery door shut. The long day in the park assured David a restful sleep. He barely made it through his lisping prayers for "Daddy and Aunt Lively and my dear Mama in heaven" before his little head nodded off to sleep. It made Rebecca's heart ache to know the sweet cherub would never know a mama's love. Her mistress, Miss Lively, did her best, but she was certain to be moving into her own home soon, and then what would happen to little David?

The front door blew open with the spring breezes as Increase stomped inside and removed his overcoat. His cheeks burned red with cold or fever; it wasn't clear which.

"Are you feeling well?" Lively asked. "Rebecca made corn chowder for dinner. I saved some back for you on the stove. You look feverish, though."

"Tired is all," Increase answered. It had been a long day at the hospital. A factory boy crushed his arm in one of the machines and the surgery to save the arm didn't look promising. *At least he didn't die yet.* "A bowl of chowder sounds good. Let me sit by the fire a minute first."

Increase entered the parlor and poured a glass of whiskey, then sat in his favorite reading chair, resting his head in his hands. Lively brought a bowl in to him and sat down in the opposite chair. He took the bowl and slurped it down, noticing the emptiness in his stomach for the first time.

"Increase," Lively said, "I'm worried about you."

"I'm fine, sister," Increase said. "Nothing a bowl of warm soup and a good night's rest won't cure anyway."

"And a bottle of whiskey?"

"Now don't start that again," Increase snapped.

Lively eyed him. "I'm just concerned, Increase. You never go out, nor do you ever have anyone in. The friends you had have given up on you, and now you can't go a day without a drink. ... You have to do something. You're not helping David with the life you're living."

Increase sat back in his chair. It was more than Lively ever said. Maybe she had a point.

"Actually Dr. Shevenell invited you and me over for dinner tomorrow evening. A game of bridge is to follow for the four of us—Oh, his daughter Mariette is back in town."

Lively's eyes lit up and she smiled. "Really? You told Dr. Shevenell that we would come to dinner?"

"Well, I was polite enough to say I needed to ask you first, but I don't know if I'll go after the accusations you just threw at me."

Increase turned toward the fire, pouting, but Lively just smiled.

"I'm sorry, brother. I just hate to see you so lonely and troubled. I'm happy we're going to the Shevenells'. Mariette must have so much to share about her time in Paris. I'll send a note to them while you finish your dinner."

"It isn't as formal as all that, Lively. Just use the phone."

Increase sighed. The phone had been a hospital requirement several years ago, but he had been reluctant to use it for personal business. Everything seemed to be changing, and he didn't like it.

Annie and Increase had been to Dr. Shevenell's home a couple of times after they were married, but he hadn't visited since her death. Lively was right that he had lost his friends. It wasn't his intention to shove everyone away, but he didn't want to be the lone man out, and he certainly didn't want to talk about Annie. It was just easier to send regrets than to regret going. After a year or so, the invitations ceased.

Lively was so excited that she glowed. *It isn't fair to expect her to care for me and David ... but she agreed to help as long as she's needed.* Increase looked hard at her standing there in the dusky light and wondered if he would sacrifice so much for her. The Shevenells' door opened. A young woman in a blue silk gown, with long black hair pulled into loose ringlets at the back welcomed Increase and Lively. Dr. Shevenell's daughter had grown up since Increase had last seen her.

"Good evening," she said, smiling. "Papa said you would be here soon. I'm Mariette, and you must be Dr. Graves and Miss Lively Graves."

Lively extended her hand to the young lady. "That's right. Thank you so much for inviting us to visit. Increase tells me you're recently back from Paris. I hope you'll tell us all about it." She entered the foyer and turned her back to Increase so he could help with her coat.

Increase stumbled into the lit hallway and muttered his own thanks. He was startled by Lively's sudden social grace and charm. He hadn't seen her in many social situations, not since they were in their teens. Now at thirty-two it seemed impossible that this was his quiet, dutiful twin sister.

A servant came by and took their wraps and coats. Mariette led the two into the parlor and invited them to sit by the fire. "Papa had to return to the hospital, but he promised to be back soon. I hope he doesn't leave me too often alone in this city. I don't seem to have any friends left in town after my time abroad."

Lively nodded. "I spend a lot of time alone myself. Increase is always at the hospital as well. We'll have to make fast friends and keep each other company." She laughed. "Tell us about your time in Paris, please."

Mariette flushed with pleasure. "My grandparents live there, and Papa thought it would be good for me to stay with them while I studied art. Would you like to see some of my paintings? I had to leave the sculptures at Grand-père's, but I was able to bring several paintings home to Papa."

She stood and invited them to follow. Off the small parlor sat a larger room, probably meant as a ballroom. Canvasses were lined haphazardly along the wall. The unpacking was incomplete and most of the pictures were unframed. Opened trunks and scattered items touted the owner's recent arrival.

"Please excuse the mess," Mariette said. "I haven't managed to get everything in place yet."

"Ah, you're here. Good," Dr. Shevenell said from the doorway. "Has Cook announced if dinner is nearly ready, Mariette? I'm famished." His peppery hair looked wild from the storm that threatened outside, and the odor of fresh dirt and rain hung heavy in the air.

"Dinner is ready as soon as you are, Papa." Mariette laughed. "I was just showing our guests my artwork. We'll wait for you."

Dr. Shevenell excused himself to change for dinner, and the three turned back to the paintings displayed on makeshift easels or leaning against the wall on top of bookshelves. Mariette had tried reproducing the styles of the great French artists, and to Lively and Increase's untrained eyes, they looked impressive.

"Your brushstrokes are so gentle and perfect," Lively said. "I could never get mine to flow so easily."

"Thank you," Mariette said. "I worked long and hard to perfect my skills, but my teachers never seemed to see much talent. I was dying inside, so I came home to Papa. Perhaps I can take care of him better than I can paint."

"Your pictures all have mothers and children," Increase said.

"That was my teachers' complaint." Mariette blushed.

"Oh, I'm not complaining, just noting. Why do you paint them so often?"

"I can't say for certain," she murmured and tipped her head. Then, staring at one of the portraits, she added, "I suppose it's because it was the thing I missed most as a child. My mother died giving me life. Such a paradox, don't you think?" She looked at him. "I feel connected to her in ways I can't explain."

"I'm sorry. I shouldn't have pried." Increase burned with embarrassment.

"Oh, no fear," Mariette said. "I'm not sad to have lost my mother, not anymore at least, but I know the loss has affected me nonetheless. ... Papa still grieves for Mama in ways I can't understand or ever grieve."

"Good evening, Lively. Good evening, Increase," Dr. Shevenell called from the partition. "Come to dinner. Come, Mariette."

Dinner was a simple menu intended to satisfy and warm the soul as well as the body. The talk centered on the sights of Paris and work at the hospital. Dr. Shevenell showed particular interest in the orphanage opening in Boston for the victims of the flu epidemic.

"There're so many children who need a family, but there aren't enough families to take them in. I can't do it myself, not with my work at the hospital, but I believe I can make a difference by helping with the orphanage."

"Papa always helps others," Mariette said. "Even as a child I knew he was a man of faith."

Dr. Shevenell blew on his soup while his cheeks tinged red with modesty. Mariette passed the rolls to Lively and then handed her the butter.

"Which church do you attend?" Mariette asked Lively.

"I go to St. Leonard's occasionally," Lively said. "I'm not a regular church attender, but I've taught David to say the Lord's Prayer. I went to the Easter service this year."

Mariette turned toward Increase. "Then you don't attend either? Such a shame. I can see sorrow in your eyes."

Dr. Shevenell cleared his throat. "How about that game of bridge now?"

Mariette's eyes went wide. "Of course," she said. "And I'm so sorry if I said too much."

Lively's gracious smile spoke forgiveness as they rose to enter the parlor, but Increase couldn't quite abandon the conversation. He walked into the parlor with the others and stood in front of a large portrait over the fireplace. A mother and child stood hand in hand watching a sailboat across a lake in the style of Georges Seurat. A father stood at a distance watching the scene.

Increase let out a deep sigh. "I believe in God, but I cannot worship a God who is so cruel." His voice vibrated with years of anguish.

"God is kind, not cruel," Dr. Shevenell said, placing his hand on Increase's shoulder.

"Is it kind to kill a woman who has done nothing wrong? Is it kind to sentence a child to a life with no mother? I'll acknowledge your kindness to orphans, but I see none in God." Increase's voice softened in defeat. "I don't think I'm feeling well enough for games," he said. "Please, excuse us."

"I overstepped the boundaries for polite company," Mariette said. "I'm sorry. Please stay and we'll speak of it no more."

"You've done nothing wrong. I'm overly tired is all. Please, our coats," Increase said.

The door closed on the bright lights of the house as Lively looked back to wave good-bye. Increase took her arm and guided her down the front stairs into darkness that enveloped them like a cold, midnight lake.

Increase rose early to get to the hospital. He wanted to check again on the boy injured in the factory. New instruments had been purchased by the hospital, and he was hopeful they had repaired the arteries in the boy's arm. If only infection could be staved off, the boy would have a chance to regain partial use of his arm and hand.

"Dr. Graves," a nurse greeted him at the desk, "you're being requested in Administrator Boyles's office."

*What did I do?* "Did he request me right away or should I complete my rounds first?"

"I think he'd like to see you first thing," the nurse said.

The hallway was quiet as Increase knocked on the closed door and waited for the reply. His insides were flopping like a fish at the end of a line. Perhaps the staff had finally realized what a poor excuse for a doctor he was. "Dr. Graves" was certainly an appropriate name for him, he mused as he snorted to himself.

"Come in," a muffled response called through the door.

Increase entered the sparsely furnished office. The hospital was founded in order to help the sick who couldn't afford more expensive facilities. The administration took costs seriously and promoted spending money on new technologies rather than comfortable office seating.

Administrator Boyles looked up from his paperwork and rose at the sight of Increase. "Good morning, Dr. Graves. I'm glad you could stop by."

*Well, that seems promising.* "The nurse said you wanted to see me before rounds."

"Yes—well, I suppose it could have waited until after, but since you're here, have a seat." Mr. Boyles pointed toward a chair across from his desk. "Dr. Graves, I have the pleasure of informing you that the hospital directors have taken note of your recent work. The directors and lead doctors agree that you should be named head surgeon. It comes with a lot of responsibility and work, but I'm sure you're the man for the job. There is a pay raise of course with the extra work. What do you say?"

"I'm … stunned," Increase said. "I really did not expect this."

"Well, you can take time to think it over. I know you'll want to talk to your sister. It will mean more time away from home and your son, but they've been so accommodating already. I'm sure they'll want to see you promoted."

Increase hadn't thought about David and Lively. His initial reluctance was lack of confidence, not concern for others. But the administrator was correct: he should talk it over with Lively.

His rounds flew by. Everyone seemed to be in the same happy state as Increase. The young boy was progressing well, and so far Increase found no sign of infection. The boy even felt up to talking with Increase.

"Feeling better today, I see," Increase said, looking over the boy's chart.

"Yes, sir," the boy answered. "My arm's doing right fine. That other doctor with the funny accent says I can go home real soon."

"You must mean Dr. Shevenell." Increase grinned. He listened to the boy's lungs; no fluid. "Yes, you should be able to go in a week or so. We just have to keep our eye on it for a while to make sure there's no infection." He began unwrapping the arm.

"Oh, I ain't worried about infection. My mother taught me how to cure fever ailments. I just have to get my hands on the right plants."

"Your mother takes care of fevers herself?" Increase asked. *Thank goodness the mill had sense enough to bring him to the hospital.*

"Not anymore, sir. She died in the flu epidemic a couple years ago. That's when I started working in the factory. My little sister takes care of the babies while I work. I have to get out of here soon, though, or she won't have no money for food," he said. "That funny-sounding doctor said this here bill will be all paid for, though. That sure put my mind at rest."

"You don't have any parents?" Increase asked.

He studied the wound. The incision was clear. He began rewrapping the arm.

"No, sir. They's both gone. But we children look after each other just fine."

The boy stiffened his chin and rubbed his bandaged arm. Increase nodded and turned for the door. *A kind God, indeed. How could Dr. Shevenell be so gullible?*

He finished his rounds and left the hospital early for a change. He needed to see Lively and discuss the promotion with her. And he needed to see David, to assure him that he would never be left alone.

Laughter rang out from the parlor as Increase entered the warm house. A bitter wind was blowing in from the northeast, and the cheery atmosphere was a welcome embrace.

"Hello," called Increase, placing his things on the coat tree.

"Increase! You're home early today." Lively swished into the hallway with a rustle of skirts. "Is anything the matter?"

He shook his head. "No. Actually I have good news and wanted to discuss it with you."

"How wonderful! Good news is always welcome," Mariette said from the doorway.

Increase startled and turned to see the guest. "I'm sorry," he said. "I didn't know we were expecting company."

Lively ignored the implied reprimand and said, "Mariette brought over a cake that was meant for dessert last night."

"Our cook is an excellent baker," Mariette said, "and I hated for you to miss the special treat."

"That's very kind of you," Increase said, meaning it sincerely but at the same time thinking, *Why does this girl's kindness annoy me so much?*

"You're quite welcome," Mariette said. She smiled at him and asked, "Now what's the good news?"

"I need to discuss it with Lively before I say anything," Increase said. "Where's David?" he asked, turning toward Lively.

"Here I am, Daddy." David giggled as he jumped from behind Mariette's wide skirts. "I was here the whole time. Mariette was playing hide-and-seek with me." He beamed at his father.

"Miss Shevenell," Increase corrected his son.

"Oh, he tried that at the start, but I told him 'Mariette' was best if we're going to be friends," Mariette said with a tousle of the boy's hair. "I hope we can all be friends." She looked up at Increase.

*How can she be so sophisticated and so naïve at the same time?*

"Your father has always been good to me. I'm sure you will be no different, but 'Miss Shevenell' is the proper address," Increase said, looking with disapproval at David.

"Yes, Daddy," David said, dipping his chin to his chest.

"I suppose I better go so you can discuss this good news." Mariette dismissed the tension with a flip of her hair and grabbed her wrap.

"What? No!" Lively looked at her brother. "Surely you won't make Mariette walk back in this weather, Increase."

"I'll be fine. George was to pick me up at five o'clock. I'm sure I'll meet him along the way. Have a good evening, and I'll talk with you soon, Lively. Good evening, *Dr.* Graves," Mariette said, emphasizing the formal title.

"Good evening, Miss Shevenell," Increase responded, missing the scorn in her delivery.

The door closed behind Mariette's burgundy jacket. Lively pursed her lips but only said she would let Rebecca know that Increase would be home for dinner. Then she turned toward the kitchen with a great deal of swishing of skirts and sighing. When she returned, Increase was throwing back a shot of whiskey.

"So it is good news worth drinking to," Lively mumbled as she settled into her chair.

"No preaching, Lively. I have good news, and yes, it is worth drinking to. I've been promoted at the hospital to head surgeon—if I want it, that is."

Lively beamed at her brother. "Of course you want it! That's wonderful news, Increase. Why would you think we have to discuss it first?"

"It means more time at the hospital … away from you and David. It will require me to be on call and to direct students. There really are many more responsibilities." The magnitude of the offer was just sinking in as Increase watched his son looking through a picture book.

"We'll be fine. It isn't as if you're home all that much as it is," Lively said. "I get lonely, though, and I hope you won't mind if I visit with Mariette. David will be starting school next term too."

Increase looked at his sister, as if waking from a dream. "How can it be?" he asked. "David is just a baby. … These six years have passed so quickly. Lively, you've been a godsend for certain. I don't know what I would've done without you. Of course you must be friendly with Mariette. You need to have more friends."

"Thank you. It's been my pleasure to help. David is a sweet child and all I will ever likely know as a son of my own. I only hope Annie would approve of how I've treated the child."

The mention of Annie's name darkened the moment, and Increase turned to the nearly empty glass in his hand. "You're right, Lively. It's time I start living and not just existing. Call the Shevenells and invite them for dinner tomorrow. We'll celebrate the good news together."

He stood up and strode to the decanter. After one last swig he pounded the glass down on the table and walked out.

*Go up to Gilead and get balm, Virgin Daughter Egypt.*
*But you try many medicines in vain; there is no healing for you.*
*~Jeremiah 46:11~*

# CHAPTER 4

*"*MEDICINE IS MORE THAN SOMETHING *you take,"* Jehan had told me as he showed me to a patch of mint. *"Medicine is also something you do."*

Now alone in his herb garden, I dug in the earth to loosen the roots of the mint that had already taken hold. The patch was getting out of control and needed culling, according to Jehan. At least it smelled better than sick patients.

I threw the new shoots and stringy pieces of roots into a pot, letting my mind return to thoughts of home. Pater had slept well last night, or maybe I was finally getting used to the coughing. He had gone out to the courtyard to sit in the sun as I'd left in the morning. How many times had he walked out of the house and looked back one last time at me? Now the tables were turned. I had walked away, a dark cloud casting its shadow over me.

*I'll go to Asclepius and offer a sacrifice.* The rake in my hand rattled against a rock. I dug it out and threw it near the wall just as a woman walked through the gate.

"Watch out," she called and jumped aside. "Be careful who you're stoning, young man."

I stood quickly to apologize, but saw her eyes sparkle and her mouth turn up at the corner.

"Syngnōmēn ékhe—Sorry. I didn't see you coming." I walked toward her. "I didn't hit you, did I?"

"No, no," she said. "I was teasing you. All is well. I'm Ludia, and you are…?"

"Loukas, son of Aegeus. I'm assisting Jehan."

"Good. The old fellow could use some assisting—getting slow in the foot." She laughed and looked past me.

"Still spry enough to keep up with you," Jehan said from behind me. "How are you, Ludia?"

I moved aside to let Jehan through. He shook hands with the woman and kissed her cheek. She returned the kiss.

"Healthy as a Roman horse," she said. "And you? I never thought you'd take on help." She looked at me and smiled.

"Loukas is a doctor. Studied in Athens and Rome. He came back to care for his father, but I thought a little work might be good medicine for him." He winked at me. "Today he's learning about the healing power of soil."

"Have you taught him about woad yet?"

"Woad?" I asked.

Jehan grinned. "She's a dyer from Thyatira."

"Red is my specialty, though," Ludia said.

I nodded. The red dyes of Thyatira were famous, draping even the emperor's palace.

"But she makes a tidy profit on blues and purples. Woad is popular in Gaul. Not many around here know about it." Jehan smiled and turned toward another part of the garden. "It's still a little early, Ludia, but you can look in on it."

The two walked toward a plot of ground with small clumps of shiny green leaves. I could still hear them talking.

"When did you get back?" Jehan asked.

"Just yesterday. The winds finally changed and sailing was fair. How was winter here?"

"Cold." He laughed. "More soldiers were sent in from Rome. My plate is full, but I think Loukas will work out very well."

I smiled to myself.

"He's still just a seedling," Jehan went on, "but he seems to be the right sort of plant."

"Hmm," she said. "More soldiers mean more business for me. I may even have to find a little seedling to follow me around."

"Not many could keep up with you." Jehan's voice lowered: "And how is the crop in Thyatira growing?"

"Quite well. The Lord blesses us daily."

They stooped to inspect the woad leaves and their conversation planted itself in the soil at their feet. I wondered what Ludia was growing and why she had come from Thyatira. Jehan might prove to be an interesting individual after all.

They stayed in the plot of woad turning leaves, counting plants, and surveying the surrounding herbs. Finally they came back as I finished loosening the soil around the mint plants.

"Will you stay, Ludia?" Jehan asked.

"No. I need to catch up with my clients. And find some new ones, it sounds like. The store needs to be cleaned too. The servants let things go while I was gone. Will you be at the prayer meeting?" She pushed a strand of gray hair under her head covering.

"Yes. You know I will."

"Loukas, will you be joining us?" Ludia asked.

I looked from Ludia to Jehan and back again. "Prayer meeting?"

"There's a synagogue by the Strymon, outside the gates," Ludia said. "Jews are few in this area, but those living nearby meet to pray in the evenings. Will you come?"

"I'm not a Jew." I was taken aback. I had heard of the Jews, of course, but not many had crossed my path. I felt surprised that Ludia was one.

She shook her head. "I wasn't either. I'm from Thyatira." Her laughter sweetened the air. "But the Lord convinced me I should be. Come and see."

I eyed her, then said, "I'm committed to Dionysus and Asclepius."

Ludia nodded. "I understand. Still, you might find a reason to join us. The Lord has cured many diseases and bound up many a wound."

"Really? I hadn't heard that he was a healing god."

"He's the Great Physician," Jehan said. "He heals the sick and opens the eyes of the blind."

"You go to the prayer meeting regularly, then?" I asked Jehan. I honestly hadn't noticed any of the strange customs I had heard about the Jews.

"I do."

I looked at Ludia. "I'll think about it," I said.

Ludia nodded and turned out of the gate.

Midmorning, when the sun bore down on my back in the garden, Jehan said it was time to visit the sick.

"Today we will tend to some of my local patients," he said, as he lifted the pot of roots and dying leaves. "There are some other phthisis patients, and I'll look in on Aegeus."

I rose and stretched my back. "I dealt with phthisis when I was training. It's such a long, consuming disease."

Jehan nodded. "Then you should be able to help. I gathered up some bourse de pasteur. I'll show you how to mix the tea's ingredients."

I followed him into the little cottage. The dimness blinded me at first, but I saw the herbs laid out on the table as my eyes adjusted.

"We'll have a bite to eat before we begin. Gardening improves the appetite."

"Yes, it does." I rubbed my stomach and grinned.

"It's good medicine. See?" The old man's eyes lit up as he reached for a bowl. "And your head is clearer too, I suspect."

I was surprised to realize the dark gloom that followed me from home had lifted.

"Have a seat."

Jehan motioned toward a bench and I sat down at the table. He cleared a space for us and we ate some olives and crackers.

"What's woad?" I asked.

"Mostly a dye, but it's good for healing bleeding wounds and curing a few sicknesses too."

"Is it rare? I haven't heard of it."

"Mm. No, not rare, just not used around here. I brought it with me." He bit into a cracker.

"You brought a lot of things with you." I smiled and sucked on an olive. "How did you know what to bring?"

"Every doctor has his favorite medicines. You'll find yours in time."

"Asclepius has been helpful to me many times. I'm thinking of taking Pater to Pergamum. Maybe Ludia will know the best way to do that."

"Ludia would not suggest loyalty to Asclepius or going to Pergamum. She follows the Lord, the only true God and the only true Healer." He took a drink of water and set the cup down. "Are you ready?"

He showed me how to trim the leaves and which ones to crush before storing them together. The larger mint leaves were bundled together and hanged from the rafters. Jehan gathered his medicines together in a knapsack on his back and pulled the door closed as we headed out the gate.

Thick smoke hung over the stone hut snuggled in a hollow near the east wall. An ancient man knelt in front of an altar where a cock burned. The man coughed and wheezed so badly I could hear him from the road.

"You shouldn't be breathing all of that smoke," Jehan called out to him as we left the road. "You'll just make it worse."

The man bowed to the altar and then slowly stood. He turned and walked toward us. I saw beads of sweat tracing the sharp angles of his bony face. There wasn't much time left for this one, I was sure.

"I brought you some more tea and some leaves to plaster for your chest." Jehan pulled the sack off his back.

"No, no." The man shook his head and held up his hands. "The gods will send the cure."

"There's no cure, but there is help. The tea and the plaster will help. You'll be more comfortable." Jehan took the man's arm to lead him to the house.

"No." The man shook himself away from Jehan. "The gods … they will heal me. … I … I …" A coughing fit grabbed hold of him and he bent over trying to catch his breath. Blood dribbled onto his beard and sweat poured off him.

"Then let the gods heal you while you rest inside. Surely they can find you in your bed."

Jehan stood on one side of the man and wrapped an arm around his waist. I braced myself under his other arm, and the two of us fairly carried him into the house and laid him down in the bed.

"Some hot water, Loukas," Jehan said as he opened his bag.

The sick man feebly shook his head and looked away.

"No medicine from me," Jehan said, "but you won't say no to some hot water to ease your lungs, will you?"

He didn't answer. I brought a cup and handed it to Jehan. The man watched carefully, but Jehan didn't put anything in it. Instead he sat on the bed and offered the cup to the man's lips. He sipped and then put his head back.

"I promised the gods I wouldn't touch your antidotes … if they would only heal me. It's not you. … You've been kind, kind to my Claudia, you were … but I promised." He patted Jehan's hand and took a ragged breath.

"Promises are important," Jehan said. "I understand."

Jehan held the cup to the man's lips until he finally slept fitfully.

"Why would he refuse help?" I asked as we walked out of the smoky hollow.

"He made a promise."

"But the gods give us power to help, so isn't that the same? Why would he want the suffering to be worse?"

"He believes the suffering shows his commitment to his gods." Jehan took a deep breath as a breeze blew away the thick haze of wood smoke.

"I made a promise to Asclepius."

Jehan glanced at me. "Oh?"

"I promised to serve him if he would teach me the healing arts." I looked down at the road as we headed toward the city gates. "I want Pater to live."

"That's a choice Aegeus has to make for himself," Jehan said.

We left the city gates behind and started the climb toward Mount Pangaion.

*There's no point in seeking a remedy for a thunderbolt.*
~Syrus~

# CHAPTER 5

DAVID HAD BEEN FED EARLY, but was allowed to help Rebecca in the kitchen while the company ate dinner. He enjoyed stirring the cream into the pot and dipping out ladles of hot steaming soup into the fine china dishes. The first course was placed on the tray and Rebecca carried it out. David peeked from the swinging kitchen door.

"So what is the wonderful news?" Mariette was bursting with curiosity. Her father had intimated that he knew, but stoically refused to share any information.

"Just wait, Mariette." Dr. Shevenell looked at Increase. "My daughter has always been bold and impatient." He laughed. "I'm afraid I was too indulgent raising her. But what is a man to do when bringing up a daughter on his own? You would've been better served, Mariette, if I'd had a sister like Increase has." The older man smiled at Lively.

"I've been lucky to have Lively," Increase said. "And the luck continues. I've agreed to take the position of head surgeon at the hospital." His smile was contagious.

"Merveilleux! How exciting," Mariette exclaimed. "You must be a very talented doctor."

"Don't let his behavior fool you, dear girl," Dr. Shevenell said. "Increase is an excellent surgeon and physician. The administration would have been mad not to offer the position to him."

"It's an honor to hear you say that, sir," said Increase. "I'm certain the position must have first been offered to you, however."

"Orphans are my concern. There's no one better for head surgeon than yourself," Dr. Shevenell said.

"When will you begin the new position?" inquired Mariette.

"Administrator Boyles said I will begin right away. ... Excuse me a moment, please. I see something that needs attending to in the kitchen."

Increase rose from the table and strode to the kitchen door. His long arm shot through and pulled out the eavesdropping David. The boy's cheeks burned red.

"I believe it is time to put the butler to bed," Increase said. "Say good night to our guests, son."

Lively started to rise, but Increase stopped her. "I'll put David to bed tonight. Please, continue eating. I'll be right back."

David tucked his small hand into his father's and they ambled out together.

"He's a good father," Mariette said. "I remember you tucking me in at night, Papa."

"As do I." Her father smirked. "It was 'One more story, Papa, please' and three stories later you would still be wide awake," he said, laughing.

"Those memories are so precious," Lively said quietly, tracing the china pattern with her finger. "I do cherish the times I've had with David. He's the only son I'll likely ever know."

The streetlights were lit, casting shadows on the dark stairs. Increase pushed the house door open and clicked it back in place behind him. He walked into the house like a cat on the prowl, silent and alert. The lights were out except for a low lamp on the study table.

"Lively, are you still up?" Increase whispered, staring through the darkening gloom.

A hunched form sat up in the parson's chair near the table. "Increase, you're home. I tried to call the hospital, but they said you were in surgery and couldn't be reached." Lively's voice cracked with pain.

"What is it, Lively?" Increase crossed the room. "Is David alright?"

"Yes, yes, David's fine. It's Mother, Increase. I had a call this evening from Concord. She's had a spell. She needs me to come home. Increase, I have to leave. It's Mother." Her voice trailed off into a hazy mist of memory broken by the present needs. "Mariette has agreed to come get David in the morning. Rebecca will have to go with me. I can't believe it. Mother has always been strong. David will be fine. He likes Mariette. But ... Mother, Increase." She fell with bitter tears into Increase's arms.

"I'll come with you," Increase said. "I have two surgeries tomorrow, but then I can leave. Dr. Shevenell will cover for me."

"No, you have too much to do, and David can't come. He'd be under-foot. It's all taken care of." Lively drew a deep breath and pressed her hair back into place. "I better go to bed now. Tomorrow will be a long day. I'm glad you're home now, Increase. Good night."

She kissed his cheek and wandered off into the dark hallway, a ghost of benevolent care and thoughtfulness.

*How will I manage without her?*

True to her word, Mariette was on the doorstep just after the breakfast dishes were cleared. She promised David a fine time of carousel rides at the park and trolley trips around town. David was excited to begin the adventure and waved gaily to his aunt and father. Increase left Lively in a heap of baggage and reminders.

"I'll call as soon as I know something," Lively repeated again. "Mariette will come by to get more of David's things if they are needed. Rebecca has put some food aside for you in the icebox. Oh, and don't forget to pick up your shoes from the repair shop. They'll be finished Tuesday."

"Everything will be fine, Lively. Just take care of yourself and Mother. Don't worry about things here," Increase said and shut the door to the bustling house.

The trolley was pulling near the corner. Increase hastened down the stairs and jumped aboard.

Weeks went by, with brief calls from Concord. Mother was convalesc-ing, but her heart was weak. Lively was unsure when, if ever, she would be able to return. Increase was needed at home now more than ever, but he threw himself into his work instead. Head Surgeon Increase Graves was a focused, though fatigued, man.

*The darkness of death is like the evening twilight; it makes*
*all objects appear more lovely to the dying.*
~Jean Paul~

# CHAPTER 6

IT WAS TO BE A marriage of convenience—whose convenience was a topic never addressed. The boy needed a mother, and the only mother he had ever known was gone to care for a convalescing old woman known only as "your grandmother." David had met his paternal grandmother only once in his memory. The loss of Aunt Lively to that stranger had caused his mouth to clamp closed and his sparkling eyes to dim. The only one who brought a glimmer of light to him was the vivacious Mariette.

Increase wandered down the hospital hallway, a stethoscope around his neck. He had just released another young boy who had suffered a factory accident. He was doing better than expected thanks to the new surgical clamps the hospital had purchased. They were the miracle that so many needed.

It had been difficult to arrange time off for the wedding. As the new head surgeon, Increase was in demand spending long hours at the hospital. That was what precipitated the wedding. Lively would not be able to return to Boston now that their mother needed so much attention, and the boy couldn't be sent so far from his father. David was only six, and though Increase would never admit it, he was too attached to the boy to let him go away as so many had suggested.

Mariette had been kind to care for David in Lively's absence. He could scarcely believe the daughter of his mentor would take over the duties of caregiver to his son, but the months since Lively's departure had shown she was to be trusted.

"God bless you, Dr. Graves," a nurse said in passing. "Have a beautiful wedding and we'll see you when you return."

"Thank you." Increase absentmindedly acknowledged her.

There really was no romance to speak of. Mariette cared for David all day while Increase was at the hospital. At first David stayed at the Shevenells' home, but as time passed, it became clearer that Lively would not be returning anytime soon. David needed to sleep in his own bed, so Mariette began waiting at the house until Increase would arrive home.

Sometimes she stayed to visit, the listening ear that he so badly needed. A few times Increase arrived home so late that Mariette was already asleep in the guest room next to David's. A twenty-two-year old, beautiful French caregiver alone in the house all night with a single, widower doctor meant tongues began to wag. She was spotted leaving the house late at night by those returning from the theater and their eager imaginations stopped to visit in the gutters. When Mariette was seen leaving the house disheveled before morning coffee, the women of the neighborhood couldn't pass up the opportunity to share the news. Though neither Increase nor Mariette had passed the boundaries of modesty or propriety, their reputations were tarnished. A marriage seemed the only possible solution.

A short man in a gray overcoat and yellow scarf approached. "Excuse me. Dr. Graves?"

Increase stopped. "Yes?"

"Dr. Graves, I'm Mr. Neal." The gentleman extended his hand. "I'm the administrator for the hospital in Dunstable Plains."

"Dunstable Plains?"

"Yes," the man said. "It's a small town outside of Lowell. We're looking for a doctor to head up our new hospital, and your name was mentioned by several town residents who come to Boston for their health needs. I'd like to talk to you about the position, Dr. Graves."

"That's very kind, Mr. Neal, but I've just taken the position of chief surgeon here, and I couldn't possibly think of leaving. I'm sorry you came all this way for naught. I really can't even offer to visit with you. I'm on my way to my wedding," Increase said.

"Your wedding! Right now?" Mr. Neal's round face grew larger. "Then you must be on your way, of course. If you should reconsider the position, though, I'd like to talk with you."

He produced a card with his name and address. Increase glanced at it politely and then slipped it into his coat pocket.

"Certainly." Increase walked toward the front door, then turned back to wave at Mr. Neal. He chuckled to think anyone would give up chief surgeon at St. Patrick's Memorial Hospital in Boston for a position in Podunk.

"You better hurry, sir," the doorman said to Increase. "St. Leonard's is a far drive. You don't want to keep your bride waiting."

The doorman opened the door to the hired car Increase had reserved. Increase threw his overcoat on tightly around him as the brisk December wind tried to snatch it from him.

The driver pulled out while Increase mulled over the doorman's warning—*"You don't want to keep your bride waiting."* A wedding, a bride ... It should have been a happy day, but the bride that waited in Increase's mind was not named Mariette. He didn't consider her long black tresses or the thin, curving shape of her youth. Nor did her name roll off his tongue with the ease he knew it should.

Annie was his bride. She was the only one he had ever loved. They were married two years when the consummation of their love tore her from him. She died in childbirth while he, Dr. Increase Graves, watched helplessly, her lifeblood draining away. His resolve began to fade.

"So you're getting married? I'd have thought a handsome doctor like you would've been caught by some young filly by now," the driver said. "Best thing that'll ever happen to you, though. Been married eighteen years myself. Got five youngsters to my name. Yes, sir, you're going to like being married. Just you wait till those babies come along." The driver smiled.

Increase hadn't thought about babies, not with Mariette leastwise. It was a baby that had taken away his sweet Annie. No, that wasn't right. It was Increase who sent Annie away. He should have been able to save her, but instead he only stood by and watched her die.

The red brick cathedral came into view. Dr. Shevenell waited outside the church. He waved as Increase jumped from the car and paid the driver.

"I was becoming concerned," the older man said.

"I needed to release a patient before I could leave."

"Come this way," Dr. Shevenell said. "There's a room to wait in before the music begins."

A priest led the way through the magnificent arched church and showed Increase into a small chamber. "Wait here until the bishop returns."

Increase had not been to church since Annie's funeral. It wasn't a deliberate absence at first. He just didn't have time to take care of spiritual matters while raising a child and helping the sick and injured. He was doing good work and that was what mattered. But as time went by, his bitterness toward God held him hostage outside the church walls.

Mariette and her father had insisted on their marrying in St. Leonard's. Increase didn't see the need. A wedding at the Shevenells' house would have been pleasant enough. They had a beautiful home. But it was Mariette's wedding too, and it didn't seem right to take away the ceremony of it just because Increase was a widower.

"I want a church wedding," Mariette had said at dinner. "It doesn't have to be very fancy, but I want it to be at the church."

"Your father has one of the finest houses in Boston," Increase said. "A quiet wedding here should be sufficient."

"A church wedding is more proper," Dr. Shevenell said. "People are already talking about the marriage as it is. We don't want to give them more reasons to gossip. Besides, St. Leonard is the saint of laboring women. Perhaps he'll help Mariette when the time comes." His voice trailed off as he recalled the loss of his own wife twenty-two years before.

"The saints didn't help Annie nor your own wife, why should they intercede now?" Increase said, unable to keep the anger from his voice. "What is needed are competent doctors, not saints and superstitions."

The argument had been set aside in favor of maintaining good relations in the family. Now Increase was regretting the decision. Actually he was regretting the marriage completely. *I still love Annie.*

He enjoyed Mariette's company. She was charming and attractive. Most importantly she got on well with David. She would be the mother that he needed. The marriage would solve many problems for Increase, but the memory of Annie was always before his eyes.

The bishop called Increase to the front of the cathedral. Guests sat in the pews waiting for the wedding march to begin. The groom's side of the cathedral was noticeably empty; not even Lively had been able to make it. The organ blared and everyone stood.

Mariette and her father entered the rear of the sanctuary. The simple wedding gown elegantly accentuated Mariette's graceful march down the aisle. A sheathe of lace veiled her face, though a glow of smiling innocence could still be seen. It was her wedding day, and even if it was precipitated by evil gossip and slander, Mariette was excited and in love.

The many evenings spent listening to Increase talk about his patients revealed his compassion. The times that he mentioned his wife, Annie, assured Mariette that he was a man of tenderness and great love. She had seen him with his son and knew that David was the reason he continued to live. Mariette had no false assumptions about Increase's feelings for her. She knew she was not the love of his life, but she felt certain one day she would be.

Her own father had mourned for his lost wife as long as Mariette had been alive. She knew the pain of an abandoned man and also that of a child. She was confident that she could improve the lives of Increase and David. Already she had seen Increase stop drinking so often. Winter's strength might be just around the corner, but young love's sunshine warmed her heart and gave her hope of conquering the cold.

"You may kiss the bride."

Increase lifted the translucent veil to the back of her head. It was the closest he had ever come to hugging her. His lips brushed her cheek, and he took her hand.

"May I be the first to introduce Dr. and Mrs. Increase Graves," the bishop announced.

Everyone stood as the couple marched back down the aisle into the soft light of a December evening. A carriage with white horses waited at the curb to carry them to the harbor, where a vessel would sail through the night to Martha's Vineyard.

"Take good care of my baby girl," Dr. Shevenell said with tears in his eyes.

"I'll do my best, Doctor," Increase said.

"You must call me 'Maurice' now," the older gentleman said. "We are both family and friends now. I'll see you when you return."

Mariette stayed in the cabin of the small sailing ship while Increase went out to smoke a pipe. They barely spoke on the drive to the harbor, and Mariette was unsure what to do with herself. The four years in a Parisian art school had educated her about more than just art, and she knew that the honeymoon had high expectations. The thought of the thin silk gown tucked carefully away in her trunk made her cheeks burn.

It was well after midnight when the coach pulled up to Maurice's summer cottage. Increase helped the driver carry the trunks to the porch. The groundskeeper was waiting near the door with a lit lantern.

"Good evening, Miss Mariette. Evelyn cleaned everything fresh today and put some bread and food in the cupboard for you. She said to tell you she'll be up midmorning to help with the lunch and whatever else you might need. She didn't think you'd want her before that." He winked.

"I'm most grateful, Walter. This is my husband, Dr. Increase Graves. Increase, this is Walter Briggins. He takes care of Papa's cottage, as well as other cottages on the island."

Walter and Increase shook hands.

"I've known Miss Mariette and her papa for many years now. You're a lucky man to marry this little lady," Walter said, smiling at Mariette, then eyeing Increase. "Well, I'll leave you be now. There's a lit lantern on the kitchen table too," he said as he handed off the hurricane lamp he was holding. "Have a good night."

Mariette changed in her old room while Increase settled into the master bedroom. The many strings and buttons of the wedding gown and corset stubbornly refused to budge under Mariette's trembling fingers. When she finally entered the bedroom, Increase was heavily breathing the sleep of exhaustion. She nervously climbed in beside him and whispered his name.

The silence of the dark night was broken only by Increase's steady breathing. It was not what Mariette had expected, but she was pleased to have this time to look uninterrupted at her new husband. Gently she raised a delicate finger to his face, tracing the weary lines etched deeply around his eyes.

The corners of Increase's mouth twitched with a smile as Annie caressed his hair. It was so familiar: the bed, the fire, the pain of labor.

"Hold my hand," she said as he finished checking her vitals. "It will still be awhile, I expect. What do you think it'll be, a boy or a girl?"

"There's only one way to know for sure." Increase frowned. "You're nearly ready for the hard part."

"No," she replied. "The hard part comes later. The hard part is life." She relaxed her head against the pillows and softly smiled as light from the fireplace flickered on her cheeks.

Her face twitched with the pain of a contraction. "Increase, I need you." Annie doubled over, bracing herself against the ripping torment of separating mother and child for the first time. "It hurts," she gasped. "Send for the dressmaker." Sweat broke out on her forehead and her hand trembled in his grasp.

"The dressmaker?" Increase laughed. "The child doesn't need clothing now."

"Not for the child—for my coffin, you murderer!" Annie reached toward Increase and then fell lifeless onto the bed. As quickly as it began, it was over.

Increase looked at his wife lying in the bed, two babies at her side. He fell on his knees sobbing and clutching at her body, holding her face, begging her to speak, but Annie never moved. Instead there was a soft cooing from her side.

Increase pulled aside the blanket from the first child. His tiny fist waved and a whimper caught in its throat, but the second child was insistent. It would be heard.

Increase reluctantly pulled aside the second blanket, already sure of what lay beneath. "You did this!" it accused. "You killed his mother and your wife!"

Annie stood at the bedroom door clothed in her black funeral dress. "I'm gone forever," she said. "A new wife waits for your death curse." With that she floated through the door and out of his life.

"No, wait!" Increase shouted. "I'm sorry! I didn't want to. You're my love, Annie! Come back!"

Increase sat up in bed. Mariette lay by his side curled in a tight ball of white silk and black hair framing a peaceful face. Increase knew it was unfair to her, but his love seemed forever twined like ivy on the house of his first love, to his Annie.

Mariette would wake in another hour, but now before the rising sun softened the room with the pink glow of morning, Increase lay alone and mourned again the loss of his wife. He rose quietly and stole to the decanter on the small corner table. The brandy shook in his hand as he tried to ease the pain of memory.

The wedding week passed with walks along the shore and evenings reading or talking. He never spoke of his nightmares, though Mariette often heard him cry out in the night. She didn't know what kept him from her, and he didn't try to explain. They returned to Boston no more married than when they left.

*Suffering is permanent, obscure and dark,*
*And shares the nature of infinity.*
~William Wordsworth~

# CHAPTER 7

"WILL YOU STAY AT OUR house now?" David begged.

"Yes." Mariette laughed. "Forever and ever. Will that be acceptable?"

His answer was a full-body hug that nearly knocked her off her feet. Increase was astonished to see how quickly David accepted Mariette as his mother.

"Je suis si heureux—I am so happy," David said.

Increase and Mariette looked at each other over the child's head.

David smiled. "Pepè Maurice said I should learn a little French … to talk to you." He looked up at his new stepmother, never letting go of her.

"Pepè?" Increase asked.

"Dr. Shevenell said I should call him 'Pepè Maurice' since he's my grandfather now," the boy said with a front-gapped smile.

"Help us with the baggage, David," was all Increase could manage. It was kind of Maurice to try drawing the child into a family, but Increase was far from ready to say good-bye to the old way of life.

The first day back at the hospital, the staff tried to congratulate Increase and ask after his new wife, but the doctor was all business. He made every attempt to segregate personal and professional duties, and the doctors and nurses soon took their cue from him.

On his first set of rounds Increase discovered the young boy with the shattered arm had returned; infection had set in after all.

"I see you're back."

"Yes, sir," the boy answered, sounding fragile and weak. "My arm was doing right fine, but the stitching-up you did turned all heated and angry. That doctor with the funny accent said I have to stay here for a while longer, but I just can't. … I have to get back to work."

"Dr. Shevenell," Increase reminded the child. "You should be able to go in a week or so. We just have to keep our eye on it for a while to clear up the infection."

"But I can't stay in here that long." The boy's lips quivered. "My brothers and sisters need me to work. They'll starve without me." Tears glistened in the child's eyes.

"I'll make sure someone checks on them," Increase said. "Dr. Shevenell helps orphans. He'll find a way to help your family too."

Increase finished his rounds and left the hospital early. He needed to see David. *I can't let him be alone.*

The hallway was shining brightly when Increase entered to piano music and a man's voice singing. A scraping sound in the parlor drew him. There stood Mariette atop the sitting chair that once belonged to Annie. She was teetering on the edge, placing books on top of the shelf.

"What are you doing?" Increase called loudly above the din of phonograph music.

"Oh, hello! I'm rearranging this room," Mariette said. "I ordered some new chairs to put near the window and some lighter drapes to bring in more sunshine. This room is so dark. We'll be entertaining more now that you're married."

"You did what?" Increase said. "And what is that racket?"

Mariette climbed down from her perch and took the needle from the record. "I was just trying to brighten the dreariness of this place. It always seems so dark and gloomy."

"Where is David?"

"He's reading in his room. We stopped at the bookstore while we were out and got him a couple new books. Is something the matter, Increase? You're home early."

"Nothing's the matter. I just want to see my son." Increase turned and strode from the room.

David was quietly reading in his room just as Mariette had said. Increase paused to check on his day and the new books, and then went into his own bedroom. He poured a glass of brandy and stood by the window.

*She ordered new chairs? What for? Why do we need new chairs—and drapes?* There had always been plenty of light in that room before when they sat talking into the late evening. He threw back the last of the brandy and shook his head. He couldn't help thinking that Annie would have talked to him first.

Mariette walked into the bedroom, taking in the empty glass by the decanter. "I'm sorry if I upset you, Increase. Papa said that you and Annie used to have guests for dinner and visit with friends. I was hoping you might feel up to it again." She smiled and motioned toward the chair.

Increase slumped into the seat and reached for her hand. "I'm sorry, Mariette. I shouldn't have been so brusque. It surprised me; that's all. Of course we should have guests over. We need to invite your father to dinner first to thank him for keeping David while we were gone."

"Of course we'll have Papa over for dinner, but I was thinking we should invite some of the doctors and their wives," Mariette said. "The hospital administration would be a good idea too."

"Slow down." Increase sighed. "Let's start with your father."

Increase knew it wasn't fair to Mariette, but he hated the changes she was making. New bedclothes were ordered and curtains changed out. The things that reminded Increase of sweet Annie were tossed aside. David's bedroom was painted and the papering changed. Mariette was right that David was no longer a baby and a nursery was no longer appropriate, but Annie had chosen the décor and placed everything just so to prepare for the baby's arrival. It felt like he was reliving her death every time he came home from work.

It didn't help that each night Mariette curled up beside him holding his hand, stroking his hair. He knew it wasn't right, but Annie visited his dreams each night and condemned him as the murderer that he was. He couldn't bear to do more than kiss Mariette's forehead and wish her a good night's sleep. Each morning he sat alone, a victim of the nightmare that never let him sleep in peace.

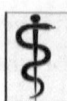

The nurse looked at him. Increase realized that she had asked a question. "I'm sorry," he said. "What did you say?" He stared at the empty hospital bed.

"He passed at two in the morning according to the night staff," she repeated. "Will you be filling out the paperwork or would you like the resident on duty to take charge of the affair?"

The fever had been too high; the boy's body too weak. Increase had failed again, another patient sent to the grave by Dr. Graves. "I should have stayed longer," Increase murmured. "I should have looked to the wound cleaning myself."

"The paperwork?" the nurse reminded him.

"I'll take care of it. He was my patient," Increase replied.

Maurice sat near the fire enjoying an after-dinner coffee. "I had a meeting yesterday with a Mr. Neal from Dunstable Plains. He said he met you on your wedding day."

Increase tipped his head and thought. "A short man?"

"Yes, that's him. He said he offered you the position of head of the hospital there."

Mariette's eyebrows popped up. "Well, that's something," she said. "You should be honored."

"I suppose so." Increase shrugged. "But why would I want to leave St. Patrick's?"

"Oh, not that you should," Mariette said. "But it still is an honor that your name has made it so far. Where is Dunstable Plains, Papa?"

"Across the border in New Hampshire," Maurice answered. "It isn't far from Lowell. I believe you can take the train there. Mr. Neal was trying to get me to take the position, but I really feel the need to stay here and help with the orphanage."

They talked late into the night. Increase relayed the news of the orphan boy's death, and Maurice started making plans to contact the child's siblings the next day. David fell asleep on Maurice's lap, and Increase carried him to bed when Pepè left. Mariette waited in bed for Increase to come into the room.

After he walked in, she said, "I've been thinking that perhaps we need a new house."

"What?"

"For the children that will come." She blushed. "David will be too old to share a nursery and we'll need an extra room for a nursemaid. This house won't be big enough."

Mariette had hoped Increase would take this opportunity to explain his behavior, but instead he stood by the window and poured a shot of whiskey. He stared down at the street.

"I need to take care of some business before bed. You go on to sleep. I'll go down to the study. I don't want to disturb you," he said, placing the glass on the bedside table. "Good night, Mariette."

"Good night, Increase."

Her tears flowed as the door closed behind him.

Increase paced the floor, wondering if it was the right thing to do. His signature to the letter had made it feel final, but until it was in the mail, there was still time to turn around. He had written Mr. Neal to ask if the position was still available.

Death seemed to have a stranglehold on Increase, and the hospital was sure to recognize it soon. He was a cursed man; his name was Increase Graves, wasn't it? Leaving Boston, leaving the home that he and Annie had shared, it had to be the right thing to do. *If there's no home, no memory, then there's no death,* he reasoned. He would drop the envelope in the post at the hospital tomorrow.

Climbing the stairs to bed, Increase wondered what Mariette would say. He should discuss it with her, he thought, but she had said it was an honor to be considered. She wanted a new house, and he needed a place that didn't condemn him for living without Annie. There was no discussion needed. If the position was still offered, they would go to Dunstable Plains. He crawled into bed and listened to the slow breathing of the woman he wished he could love.

The late-January snow was piling high, and darkness was settling in when the phone rang. Mariette and David looked at each other. No one ever called if Increase was at the hospital. Mariette left the warm kitchen and braced herself for the cooler hallway where the phone was attached to the wall.

"Hello?"

"Hello, Mrs. Graves?" a voice asked. Static jumped across the line.

"Yes."

"This is Mr. Neal in Dunstable Plains. May I speak to your husband, please?"

"I'm sorry. He isn't at home. May I take a message?"

"Yes, thank you. Please tell Dr. Graves that I received his letter and the position is still available. We would love to have him take the position. If he'll call me, we can establish a start date. Thank you."

"I'm sorry, Mr. Neal. The line is crackling. … Did you say a start date?"

"Yes. That's right."

"Thank you. I'll let him know. Good-bye."

Mariette stared at the phone, unable to comprehend what it could mean. Surely Increase wouldn't have spoken to someone about a job without consulting her. Their marriage was not perfect; she knew he didn't love her, but surely he respected her.

David was long ago in bed by the time Increase arrived home. It had been a tiring day of surgery with two appendectomies and an amputation of a gangrenous foot. The trolley didn't run so late at night and Increase had decided to walk home instead of hiring a car. He was surprised to find a light shining in the parlor window.

Opening the front door, Increase softly stepped into the hallway and hung his hat and coat. He peeked into the parlor and found Mariette sitting stiff in the chair by the fire.

"Why are you still up? I thought you'd be asleep by now."

"I thought I should wait for you. It is the sort of thing a wife does for a husband, isn't it?"

"Yes, I suppose." Memories of Annie waiting late in the night passed like ghosts. "Is anything the matter, Mariette? You look pale."

"Nothing is the matter. I have a telephone message for you," she said, pointing toward the table by the window.

Increase walked to the table and read the note. He didn't say anything, but poured a glass of brandy, biding time to consider his words. Mariette was obviously upset.

"This is the hospital director and doctor position that you said was an honor," he said, trying to make it as positive as possible.

Mariette looked at him sideways.

"I wrote Mr. Neal a couple of weeks ago after we had dinner with Maurice. I thought you were right."

"I didn't say you should take the job. I said you should be honored. Good heavens, Increase. Don't you think this is the type of decision we should make together? What about David? And my father, is he to be left here without anyone? I thought you were more compassionate than that." Her voice raised with emotion.

"Quiet," Increase growled. "You'll wake David. I made the decision that I think is best for us. You're my wife and you will do as you're told. I'll call Mr. Neal tomorrow and settle a date. I'm going to bed now." He stormed from the room as Mariette's muffled sobs followed him up the stairs.

*Above all things let us never forget that mankind constitutes one great broth-
erhood; all born to encounter suffering and sorrow, and therefore bound to
sympathize with each other.*
~Albert Pike~

# CHAPTER 8

A LIGHT GREEN BLANKET DRAPED OVER the trees as we climbed the mountain. Tiny leaves uncurled their bodies toward the spring sun. Shadows dappled the pathway, and the citrus smell of juniper renewed my energy.

"Where are we headed now?" I asked.

"The mines," Jehan replied.

"Asyla? Why there?"

The gold mines were why Philippi had been colonized. Some tried to say the city was important for shipping or because of the mountain where Dionysus lived. No one could deny, though, that the gold pouring out of Asyla had increased Philippi's importance to the empire.

"I check on the workers there once a week."

"Is there something contagious?" I wondered what could be so necessary to check so regularly.

"Cruelty."

"Syngnōthí moi—Excuse me? What did you say?"

"Cruelty," he repeated. "It's quite contagious." He paused and looked me up and down. "Though some are immune." He walked on.

*What a strange man.* My arms swung beside me as I matched Jehan's pace. I couldn't gauge how old he was for sure, but I knew captives were taken from Gaul long before I was ever born. He was definitely older than Pater.

We passed through the gates and stopped in front of a guard.

"How are you today, Octavian?" Jehan smiled at the officer.

"Doctor Jehan." The man smiled and motioned toward me. "Who's this?"

"This is Loukas, son of Aegeus. He's here from Rome to help me."

I wasn't sure about the explanation, but it was the truth.

"Salve." He greeted me in Latin, then returned to the local Greek. "I know your father. A good man. Is he improving?"

"No, but Doctor Jehan …" I smiled toward the older man. "… is easing his discomfort."

"Hmm. I've never know Jehan to put anyone at ease." The officer laughed at his own joke and motioned us to go in.

Dust was heavy in the air. *If this is spring, what must the summer and autumn be like?* Men pulled heavy wagons of dirt out of the tunnels burrowed into the hillside. They positioned the carts near a stream that had been manipulated to flow through the center of the camp. Others unloaded the wagons and sifted the dirt through the flowing water.

Jehan walked toward a long, low stone building. Another guard stood at the door.

"How are the officers today?" Jehan asked as he stopped outside the lodge. "Have Albanus and Cornelius improved?"

"Yes, they seem to be doing much better. Go on in and have a look."

We passed into the cool darkness of a roomful of beds. Two men lay on their backs at the far end of the room.

"Cornelius, how are you today?" Jehan stopped in front of the first soldier's bed.

The man raised himself on his elbow and grinned. "You're a miracle worker, Jehan. It's all cleared up." He stuck a finger in his ear. "Better than new."

Jehan pulled out a small funnel and looked into the man's ear. "You're right. The infection is gone. You can head back to work after lunch."

Jehan turned toward the other soldier. "And how are you doing, Albanus?"

The man rolled over under the light linen cover to face us.

"Still sore?" Jehan asked.

The soldier nodded and looked at Jehan. "Little better. The broth helped." He struggled to speak, sounding like the frogs in the swampy marsh south of town.

Jehan nodded and felt the man's head. "A little fevered. Loukas, get out the vial of willow oil." He continued talking to the man. "Have you been sweating?"

The interview lasted a few minutes. Jehan prescribed a fever reducer and a pain reliever for the man's throat.

"It's nearly run its course. I'll come back in a few days to be certain," Jehan said before we headed back into the bright sunlight.

As we passed by the guard and turned toward a ramshackle group of wooden and stone huts, Jehan muttered under his breath, "Now for the real patients."

The first hut had a dirt floor. A small grate along the back wall was filled with ashes from a long-dead fire. Pallets were lined along the wall head to foot and several men were curled under filthy rags. Jehan tended to their ailments with deftness and precision.

"You'll be good as new before you know it," he said as he washed their bodies. "I've left some medicine for you...."

Each hut contained one or two sick men, each needing nourishment as much as medicine.

"Who are they?" I asked as we entered the fourth building.

"Prisoners, slaves, captives." Jehan opened the wooden door. "They work for the empire, mining gold, hoping for a reprieve."

I smelled it as soon as I walked in. The stomach-wrenching odor of infection.

"This is the house for hard cases." Jehan took the medical bag from me. "You start at that end washing wounds. I'll come behind you and apply the plasters." He went to the grate and kindled a fire, then started pulling out bandages for plasters.

I went to the well many times, always breathing deeply of the dusty outdoors; anything was better than the putrid smell of pus. Some men never even flinched as I removed the crusty bandages and washed the wounds; others cried out in pain and fear. I mimicked Jehan's soft tone and gentle words.

"Ti prátteis—How are you? Is there pain anywhere else?"

The infected bandages piled in the middle of the room spoke of the pain and neglect these men suffered. The morning was past and the afternoon well into the heat of the day before we left the makeshift sanatorium.

"What happened to them?" I asked as we headed down the mountain toward town. Fresh air had never seemed so precious.

"Many things." Jehan shrugged. "Some have cut their feet on rocks and tools. Infection sets in, but until they can no longer walk, they must continue to work. Others, well, I'm sure you've seen floggings before."

I had witnessed floggings and whippings in Rome. My friend Theophilus and I had been on duty once after a public flogging. The criminal was a well-known politician, so the beating had been mild and we were ordered to clean him up before the final sentencing.

"But why are they beaten? If they're already slaves, why…?" My question hung in the air like an ostrich, heavy, unable to fly.

"Because cruelty is contagious, Loukas. Cruelty is contagious."

"I'll go in with you, if that's alright?" Jehan stopped in front of the house.

"Yes … yes … of course," I said, still deeply affected by the senseless suffering I had encountered today.

Casper met us at the door and smiled at Jehan.

"Good afternoon, Doctor Jehan. Aegeus is resting in his room."

We walked down the hallway, our sandals whispering on the tile floor. I inhaled the cinnamon and cloves that would be a part of dinner. *How blessed I am.*

"Pater, Jehan has come to check on you."

"Jehan." Pater coughed and wheezed. "Aspádzomai—Welcome. Come in. Loukas is good for you, yes?"

He grabbed Jehan's hand and smiled ear to ear. I went to the other side of the bed and stood looking at the two men. I couldn't help noticing that the much older Jehan was also much stronger.

"Yes, Loukas is a good man … and will someday be a great doctor." He held Pater's hand but smiled at me. "You are blessed to have such a fine son, Aegeus."

Pater coughed into a cloth and then rested his head on the pillows. He nodded and sighed.

"I'm proud of Loukas, studying in Athens and Rome." He stopped to catch his breath. "And now working under you. … You're a fine doctor, Jehan. All the soldiers say so."

"Thank you, Aegeus. Now let me listen to those lungs."

I watched as Jehan pounded on Pater's back and chest, then listened to his breathing, the deep crackling plain even without his doctor's tools.

Finally Jehan stepped back and looked Pater in the eyes. "The tumors are larger. They're filling your lungs."

My father nodded. He knew the prognosis.

"The bleeding is increasing. I'll leave more tea; drink it as often as you like. I'll also leave some opium. You understand…?"

"Thank you for taking on Loukas. He'll be a great doctor under you."

Pater wouldn't speak of the end. Jehan left for home.

I stayed to offer relief, distraction: "The spring festival will be soon. I'll make a special offering. Perhaps Dionysus will return you to me."

A tear escaped as Pater patted my hand.

*Suffering is but another name for the teaching of experience, which is
the parent of instruction and the schoolmaster of life.*
~Horace~

# CHAPTER 9

MARIETTE STIFLED HER SOBS AS she waved good-bye to her father. This was very unlike the trip to Paris four years before. No doting grandparents waited at the other end to welcome and comfort her. The train stop in Lowell falsely buoyed Mariette's spirits. There was an electric trolley, and streetlights like in Boston. Churches and stores lined the brick roads. Advertisements for traveling shows were pasted to the train station wall. Perhaps Dunstable Plains would not be so bad after all, she imagined, looking at an advertisement for ladies' shoes from Paris.

That hope soon became mired in the rural mud of New Hampshire. Farms and unpaved roads met Mariette's eyes as Lowell was left behind. The barrenness of winter trees and the grayness of overcast skies quickly snuffed the flame that had started to burn in her heart. The only shoes here would be sturdy and practical, not Parisian.

Increase had arranged for a house to be rented until they could settle in. Mr. Neal was at the station in his automobile to drive the family to their home. Mariette graciously shook hands with the administrator as Increase paid the cabby driver to load their trunks and follow Mr. Neal. The oyster-shell roads crackled and popped under the dusting of snow that had recently fallen.

The first week passed easily. David and Mariette unpacked trunks and cases, finding new homes for all of their articles. The larger things would arrive in the spring once they found a house to buy. Mariette tried cooking dinners for Increase, but her skills were so lacking and his schedule so unpredictable that they often ended up with hot soup and store-bought bread.

"I must find a helper," Mariette said during Sunday dinner. "We always had a cook, and I'm afraid you and David will starve without one." She tried smiling to keep back the tears as Increase cut a dry and burned pork chop.

"I heard there are cooks in the row houses," Increase said. "Perhaps you could find someone for hire there."

"Is it safe there? It seems so dark and run-down. The slums are not a place for ladies."

"I haven't heard anything bad," Increase said as he tried to spoon up runny cranberry sauce. "The town seems safe enough, just not well-kept. The mill owners should keep up the houses but they don't seem to put any care into them."

"Alright then," Mariette said. "I'll go tomorrow and find us a cook."

The early-morning bell clanged, time for work. Doors flew open as men, women, and children hurried to the mills. The fifteen-minute walk to the factories by the canals was punctuated by the hushed calls of good morning. It was just another day ruled by bells in Dunstable Plains.

The bells sounded their sentence. All were ruled by something. Some were slave to the superintendent checking the length of cloth on the loom. Others were mastered by the incongruities of life: two children born at the same time but to different parents—one lived in squalor, the other was a prince. And others still were slaves to their choices: an alcoholic who couldn't stop drinking, a husband who couldn't stop cheating, or a father who couldn't stop grieving. And all persons, every last one, was a slave to the continual passage of time. The sun and moon marked its path like the bells of Dunstable Plains. Get up, work, eat, sleep. Clang, clang, clang.

*Death bells have tolled for too long in my life.* Increase watched from the window. *I've tried to escape their clamorous dirge, but now, here I hide behind a dark window from the curse of my name, Increase Graves.* He pushed the curtain back in place and headed down to breakfast.

The second morning bell rang. Breakfast in the slums was over and the people were headed back for the longer morning shift. The workers had to be inside the mill gate by seven or they would lose a day's wage. *Promptness seems crucial in this industrial town*, thought Mariette over her toast and coffee. Increase had eaten early and headed to the hospital while she had taken her time rising. He was trying to put things right in the chemist's closet. The inventory system was ancient, and he had spent the entire first week arranging medicines and instruments appropriately.

Mariette and David struck out at nine o'clock. They wandered along the main street looking in windows at the displays and people inside. Dunstable Plains wasn't Boston for certain, and even little Lowell made it look frightfully primitive, but there was a certain je ne sais quoi that encouraged Mariette. *With time this little town could be something … especially with a new hospital and an excellent physician like Increase.*

"Come along, David," she said to the dawdling boy. "Let's get there and find someone who can cook. Then you and I can stop at the store for a horehound stick."

The brick row houses had seen better days. Paint peeled from shutters and doors that appeared to do little more than slow the winds blowing through the filthy streets. Latrines were stationed at each end of the buildings, but Mariette's nose was certain they were not being properly maintained.

A little boy about David's age sat outside one of the stoops forming dirty snowballs in his bare hands. He looked up as they neared and waved at David, who grabbed hold of Mariette's hand and slid behind her skirts.

"Good morning," Mariette began. "We're looking for a woman who can cook. Is there someone at home we could talk to?"

"Mamere is a good cook. She's sleeping inside."

A young woman with a tear-stained face walked up from behind. "Clement, why are you outside? You should be in with Mamere," she scolded. "Can I help you?" she asked Mariette as she passed on the stairs.

"We're in need of a cook," Mariette said. "Your son said his grandmother is a good cook."

"My son?" The young lady looked confused. "Oh … no. Clement is my brother. Mamere takes care of him while I work at the mill … but today I was late because she has a fever. I tried to convince them to let me in. I have to take care of Clement too." Her voice softened and then trailed off as her eyes swam in gray pools of distress.

"I'm sorry your grandmother's ill," Mariette said. "My husband is the new doctor at the hospital. Perhaps she should go see him."

The girl smiled sadly. "We take care of our own. The fever will leave soon. It's just that Clement needs someone to look after him." She paused. "But you said you need a cook. I don't know anyone looking for work right now. The mills are hiring and people are moving in all of the time. The mills pay well if you can do the work." She sighed.

"Well ... can you cook?" Mariette smiled hopefully. "I really am a pathetic cook, and my husband is beginning to look sickly himself. I'm sure we can pay whatever the mill pays you."

"Me, ma'am? I've never been a cook. I've only worked in the mill."

Mariette turned to the little boy. "Clement, can your sister cook? Do you like what she makes to eat when Mamere is ill?"

"Rachelle does alright, but her bread isn't as good as Mamere's. She does make better pumpkin mush, but don't tell I said that." The little boy grinned and looked toward the door to make sure he wasn't overheard.

"Then that settles it," Mariette said with finality. "You will come today for lunch and show us how well you cook. Clement can come too so your grandmother has time to rest."

Rachelle's morning despair was quickly overcome in the kitchen. She outdid herself with chicken and noodles swimming in a delicious broth. Everything was on the table by the time the lunch bell rang through the town. Clement and David played easily together outside after lunch while the women made final arrangements. Rachelle would arrive at six o'clock each morning and stay until six in the evening. She would prepare the meals and teach Mariette some culinary skills. Rachelle would also tidy the house, wash the laundry, and do the shopping. Mariette felt more than relieved.

"Here are the new beds ... straight from New York," Mr. Neal said. "They arrived on the late-night train." The short man seemed pleased by his town's efforts to provide a modern hospital. Bringing Dr. Increase Graves from Boston was the final brick in the foundation of this growing town's entrance into the modern world. Perhaps they were coming to it late, but now they had arrived and Mr. Neal was bursting with excitement.

"I hope you and your wife have found the town to your liking," he continued. "There's a new library on the hill near Prospect Street. Perhaps you and Mrs. Graves will enjoy some of the lectures scheduled in the evenings."

"Mariette and I are happy to be here," Increase managed to say, but not before a sigh escaped.

"Good, good," Mr. Neal said as he walked on. "And how are you finding your nursing staff? Nurse Hall was trained in New York, and the night nurse, Nurse Lindelof, has been in the area for years."

"They're doing a fine job." Increase nodded approval.

Nurse Hall, the lanky day-shift nurse, nodded hello from behind the desk near the front door. The hospital used to be the home of Mrs. Fred North. A widow without children, she had become a generous benefactress to the town. The house was her last gift. *A hospital from a dead woman.* Increase had sneered at the irony. *How appropriate.*

"It's been a quiet week. Is there another doctor in the area?" Increase asked the director.

"There's a doctor this side of Lowell who will drive up and check on people. Then there's the wealthy mill owners who go to Boston for their health needs. That's how we heard about you, Dr. Graves." Mr. Neal's caterpillar brows wiggled above his eyes.

"Dunstable Plains is big enough for several doctors with all the mill workers," Increase said.

"Well," Mr. Neal drawled, "Nurse Hall and Nurse Lindelof take care of them a good bit. The workers look after themselves mostly, though."

"You've done well so far, and I've had no patients all week. Why did you bring me here if all is running so smoothly?"

"The hospital needs a doctor on staff. The town's seen a lot of growth in the last few years, and it just seemed time to take the next step. Mrs. North's donation was a true blessing."

A gentle tap on the front door interrupted their conversation. Nurse Hall glided to the door and greeted three young mill workers. Two females about twenty years old were holding up a younger girl between them. The younger one was doubled in pain and sweat dripped from her face.

"Bring her in," Nurse Hall commanded.

The girl was laid on a new bed. Her fevered face contorted in pain as she curled into a fetal position.

"What's her name?" Increase said as he started taking vital signs and Nurse Hall placed a thermometer in the girl's mouth.

"Rose. Rose Janelle," one of the girl's stammered in a thick accent. "She's my cousin."

"How long has she been sick?" Increase asked.

The girls looked at each other. "Her stomach hurt. We gave her baking soda. Please help."

"How long?" Increase nearly shouted at the girl. "How long has she been this way?"

"Three days." Tears spilled down her cheeks.

"Temperature's 103, Dr. Graves," Nurse Hall said as she shook down the thermometer.

The swollen belly and high fever were telling enough. He would have to do surgery and soon.

"Bring my bag into the surgery. Take these girls away, Mr. Neal. I'll wash up and be right there, Nurse."

Adrenaline raced through Increase's veins and strong acid poured into his stomach. He had performed appendectomies before, but not under such primitive conditions. The surgery room was nothing more than Mrs. North's private bedroom. A tray of scalpels, probes, and clamps was assembled on the bureau top. An oil lamp was positioned on a high table near the bed to provide better lighting.

The sick girl was now unconscious. Increase carried her into the operating room and removed her frock. "Have you used chloroform before, Nurse Hall?"

"No, Doctor."

*So I'm to be doctor and anesthetist.* It was likely the girl wouldn't awake at this point anyway, but the chloroform would keep her sedated while the organ was removed.

The swollen, angry appendix was easily apprehended. A couple hours more and it would have burst, killing the girl with its poison. In an hour's time she was stitched up and placed in a bed, the hospital's first patient. Increase sprawled on the empty bed beside her. *I would pray, but it wouldn't do any good.* Instead he closed his eyes and listened to the erratic beating of his heart.

The rest of the day passed without incident. Rose awoke for a few minutes and then drifted back to the safety of unconsciousness. The fever was slowly abating. Mr. Neal brought in lunch for Dr. Graves and Nurse Hall. They ate in silence at the front desk. Nurse Hall sent a message to the night nurse that she was needed. When Nurse Lindelof finally arrived, Increase gave her orders and threw on his topcoat. The cold walk through the dark winter streets constricted the ache in his chest. If the girl should live, it would be a miracle. Most likely infection would invade the incision and death would clamor at the door.

The last work bell of the day sounded. The shuffling of tired feet echoed down the cobbled streets of Dunstable Plains, the walk of the living dead heading to their dinner and beds. The final metal clang echoed as Increase stepped onto the porch of his temporary home. The windows were dark.

The smell of roasting meat and vegetables greeted Increase at the front door. *Maybe she's finally learning to cook.* "Good evening," he called. "Something smells delicious."

A young lady was placing dinner on the dining room table when Increase walked in and came to a sudden stop. "Good … evening," he said. "Is Mariette in the kitchen?" he asked, looking past the girl, wondering who she was.

"No, sir," she said, glancing out the dining room window. "She should be back soon. She rode the train in to Lowell, sir."

"Excuse me?" Increase was incredulous. "Who are you?"

"Rachelle Michaud. Your wife asked me to come cook and clean for you. She said you would be pleased." The girl spoke hastily and blushed. "I expect them on the next train."

"Thank you," Increase said. "I'll start without them." He poured a glass of brandy and sat at the table. "It's very good," he said, dipping into the hot stew.

"I need to go, sir. Mrs. Graves said I would leave at six. Mamere hasn't been well. Do you need anything else?"

"No," Increase sighed as he pulled apart another roll to dunk in the steaming stew. "Go on home. It's been a long day for everyone."

"Je vous remercie—Thank you."

The front door opened, allowing a cold draft to race through the house. "Hello," called Mariette's young voice. "Are you here yet, Increase?"

"At the table."

"Good evening," she said as she bounced into the room. "David, hang your coat before you come in. How was your day, dear?"

"How was yours?" He turned on her. "Why did you need to go to

Lowell? And who is this girl in our kitchen?"

"Rachelle. Isn't she charming? She made chicken soup for lunch. C'etait delicieux—That was delicious. So she had everything under control and it was such a dreadful day here, so cold and dreary." She smiled. "I thought a shopping trip in Lowell would make us feel better. It's such an easy train ride; I could go every day. Right, David?"

"Mariette bought me a new book," David said, holding it up for his father's inspection.

"There's a library in town. You don't need to buy more books."

"This is a new one. They wouldn't have it yet," Mariette said with pronounced patience. "I see you're having brandy with your dinner. Is Rachelle still here?"

"She's just leaving," he grumbled. "Sit down and eat. David, come to the table."

"I found a beautiful rug for the front room," Mariette said as she placed a napkin in her lap.

"What's wrong with the way it is?" Increase tried holding back his temper, but it simmered so close to the top that the lid started to quake.

"It'll make the room more comfortable in the cold," she said. "We'll be having guests soon. Everyone will want to meet the new doctor. How was your day? Did you find everything to your liking?"

"I did not. The hospital is not nearly suitable. I had to perform emergency surgery in a bedroom of all places."

"What?" Mariette choked on her dinner. "What kind of surgery? Whose bedroom?"

"The hospital is the former home of Mrs. Fred North. She passed away and left it to the city. Appropriate that I should be the head of a hospital in a dead woman's house." He snorted and tore into the bread like a wild animal.

"Increase, that's enough. You're a wonderful doctor; Papa always said so. Tell me what happened."

"A young lady was brought in, one of the mill girls. She needed an appendectomy and the operating room is Mrs. North's bedroom. Her bureau was the table for the instruments. The nurse didn't even know how to administer the chloroform, so I had to take care of the anesthesia as well."

"How dreadful." Mariette shuddered. "I still don't understand why you dragged us out here in the first place, but I can see this town needs you, and very badly. Aucun doute la dessus—There is no doubt about it."

"Maybe you don't have doubts … but I do."

"Will the lady be alright?" David asked.

"Hopefully. Time is the real doctor. If she doesn't get an infection, the possibilities are good. At least we can try to keep her clean in the hospital. The slums these mill workers live in are atrocious."

"Clement lives with the mill people," David whispered. "Is he going to get sick?"

"Who?"

"Rachelle's brother," Mariette said.

"We met him today when we found Rachelle. He lives with his grand-mother and Rachelle in the mill houses," David went on, his dark eyes pleading. "He won't get sick, will he, Daddy?"

"Little boys don't usually get sick, David. Clement will be fine. And this girl will be fine because she's in the hospital." He smiled and placed his large hand over David's.

"Finish your dinner, then I'll read to you in bed," Mariette said, changing the subject. "I want to read about the newest adventure too."

Increase began to relax under the spell of warm food and the domestic scene at his table. *Annie would've been an excellent mother, but Mariette's trying her best. It isn't her fault she was raised by a doting father.* Mariette's natural mothering skills surprised him, considering she was motherless all her life as well. Perhaps the loss of her own mother at birth made her more sympathetic to David.

Mariette and David bounded up the stairs to the bathroom. The sounds of running water, laughter, and rounds of "Frere Jacques" echoed down the stairwell. He poured another brandy and relaxed in the parlor arm-chair. The nightly routine was not yet established, but it was safe to expect them to be occupied for another hour.

The night chill had settled into the house, and the fireplace blaze was dying when Mariette appeared in the doorway.

"I need to clear the table," she said. "Would you like a cup of chamo-mile before we go to bed?"

"No, thank you. I had another brandy."

She glanced at the empty glass on the side table and frowned. "I wish you wouldn't drink so much, Increase. You didn't drink like this when we first met."

"Some days require a few drinks, Mariette. I'm worried about Rose."

"Rose?"

"The appendectomy." *How could she forget so easily? Annie was always conscious of my fears and insecurities. But then, we were friends for so long, our whole lives.*

"The nurse is on duty, isn't she?"

"Yes, but I'm not certain about the nurses' skills. They took care of the people while there was no doctor, but that doesn't mean they're trained properly. I better go check on her before I turn in. You go on to bed, Mariette." Increase rose and brushed her cheek with his mouth.

"If anything is wrong, the nurse will send for you," Mariette said. "Come to bed with me. Rachelle can clear the table when she gets in tomorrow."

"No. I wouldn't sleep. I'll go check on Rose and be back before you know it."

He threw his coat on and hurried down the front stairs. Standing on the brick walkway, he watched Mariette through the window. The filmy drapes softened her image and light glowed behind her in the kitchen as she slowly cleared the dishes from the table. *She's a good woman*, he thought. *She takes great care of David and she does what she can with the house. I shouldn't be so hard on her because she grew up having servants to cook and clean. She'll never be Annie, but then who could be?* Stuffing his hands deeper in the pockets, he braced his chin against his chest and headed into the wind.

*The more sand that has escaped from the hourglass of our life,*
*the clearer we should see through it.*
~Jean Paul~

# CHAPTER 10

MORNING BELLS AND THE SMELL of frying bacon pulled Mariette from her slumber. She had stayed up until midnight hoping Increase would return, but finally sleep covered her worries with the wooly blanket of exhaustion. She couldn't be sure, but she thought she had spent the night alone. Throwing on her work dress, she scrambled downstairs to be a part of the morning rituals.

"David?" she called. "Are you up yet?"

"Yes, Mariette." His voice mixed with the banging of pots and running water.

She entered the kitchen to find Rachelle filling a pot at the sink and David flipping bacon.

"Careful, David," Mariette gasped, rushing over to help him. "You aren't big enough to do this alone."

"Rachelle says Clement can cook already and I'm a year older than he is." David blustered and puffed out his chest.

Mariette glanced at Rachelle and then back at her new son. She was lost. Servants had taken care of her needs as a young child. Without a mother to teach her the fine art of cooking, she had never learned. But she also never learned how to mother. She knew she was a pathetic disappointment to Increase in the kitchen; she just couldn't fail him with David.

"Well, be careful, then," she said, standing nearby to keep watch. "Did Dr. Graves leave without breakfast?" she asked Rachelle.

The girl looked up, clearly confused. "I didn't hear him," she answered. "Perhaps he left before I arrived."

"Daddy had to perform surgery yesterday. She was a girl from the mill slums," David said.

Mariette turned bright red. "You mean the mill houses, David."

"Maybe you know the girl, Rachelle," David said, oblivious to the hurtful remark he had made. "What's her name, Mariette? Some flower name."

"Rose. Rose Janelle, I believe," Mariette said, looking at the floor.

"Yes. She's a neighbor. She's been sick for nearly a week," Rachelle said.

A draft pushed through the kitchen as the front door opened. "That must be Increase," Mariette said. "He probably left early to check on his patient. I'll go see, if David can stay with you?" she asked. Child care had not been a part of their agreement.

"Of course." Rachelle smiled. "David's not a problem."

The cold morning air piercing Increase's lungs was nothing compared to the icy glare that Mariette threw him.

"You didn't come home last night, did you?"

"No. I stayed at the hospital all night. Nurse Lindelof was needed at one of the mill houses. I sent her on and stayed to watch over my patient."

"Is she going to be alright?" Mariette asked.

"She's young and strong. The odds are in her favor. If we can keep infection at bay, she should be fine."

"Were you able to sleep?" Mariette asked. "Rachelle is making breakfast. I can bring some up to the room if you want to go on to bed."

"You're very kind. That would be wonderful."

"It is not kindness that causes a wife to care for her husband, Increase. I love you, and I'm concerned about you." Mariette's cheeks burned at the mention of her love, but she said it all the same.

He shouldn't have stayed all night, Increase knew. Nurse Lindelof came back soon after he sent her out. He had known Mariette would stay up waiting for him, but the thought of facing her again glued him to the patient's bedside. Others thought him a devoted doctor, but the truth was that he couldn't face his wife. He embraced Mariette with one arm and then headed for the stairs.

The bells rang throughout Dunstable Plains, dismissing the workers for lunch. Increase opened his eyes as sunlight streamed into the room, lighting up particles of dust dancing heavenward. He swatted at the specks, scattering them across the beams of light. Annie's heavenward dance had come too quickly—*If only I had been able to scatter the path.* Guilt darkened the afternoon as he realized he was thinking of Annie while lying in Mariette's bed. He rose like a sentenced man and prepared for the day.

A strange voice was talking as Increase descended the stairs. A man and Mariette were in the vestibule near the front door. They looked up as Increase planted himself on the last step.

"What are you doing?" Increase asked, trying to hold back his anger.

"A telephone will allow you to stay home at night," Mariette said. A large telephone was now attached to the wall where previously only bare wall had been.

"I told you in Boston I didn't want a telephone. We're no better than anyone else and a telephone is a sign of arrogance." He managed to restrain his voice, but the telephone installer glanced sideways at Mariette.

"Well, what if something happens to David while you're at the hospital? How will I send word to you when the only help we have is Rachelle?"

Mariette had obviously thought this through. She knew his protective tendencies toward David ran strong.

"It's only to be used for emergencies," he grumbled, then turned to the parlor, dismissing the whole affair.

Fifteen minutes later Mariette bounced into the room. "This will be for the best, Increase. You'll see. The hospital can call you when there's an emergency, and if something happens here at home, I can quickly …" Her voice trailed off as she spied the shot glass in his hand. "You haven't had lunch yet."

"Don't start. Where's David?"

"He's in his room playing. We tried to be quiet so you could rest," Mariette said as she settled into the chair across from him.

Silence and alcohol were his only refuge. Mariette and David were growing accustomed to the quietness too. A boy of six shouldn't always be so docile and quiet, but it eased Increase's spirit to sit by a fire and think. Friends had told him in the beginning not to spend so much time thinking, but after a while the friends disappeared; then he enjoyed the quiet all he wanted.

Lively had been the only lifeline he had to the world. She would chat with him after work, and she helped David learn to deal with his father's moods. Now Mariette was the go-between for Increase, both in his relationship with the world and with his son.

"Lunch is ready," Rachelle called from the hallway.

"Did your patient die?" David asked as he passed the plate of bread.

Increase startled to hear it put so bluntly. "No. No, she's doing well actually."

"That's good. Rachelle knows her," David went on. "They're neighbors. Rachelle said her grandmother tried to help. She gave her wine to clean out her body. I told her that was a good idea."

"Yes, if it had been a simple case of stomachache, that would have been a good idea," he said. "But it was a very serious issue and she should have come to the hospital sooner."

"She doesn't have the money for the hospital," Rachelle said as she brought out a plate of steaming potatoes.

"So you know Rose?"

Rachelle eyed her employer. "Yes. She's my neighbor. She's older than I am. She's worked in the mill for four years. Her father sent her from Canada. Her cousin lives in the same house."

"Two young women brought her in. Their accent was heavy; one did say she was her cousin."

"Yes. I took dinner to them last evening when I got home. It was better in the days when each house had a keeper. Now there's little time for the daily chores. Many times the girls skip dinner and just go to bed."

With that she turned back into the kitchen. Mariette blew on her spoon of chicken stew. The warm aroma of gravy and roasted vegetables lulled Increase into a mellow mood.

"Have you made any friends yet?" he asked David.

"Only Clement, Rachelle's brother."

"We should join a church," Mariette spoke up.

"What?"

"Yes. … If we join a church, David will meet some families and other children. You're an important person in this community, or you will be, and you should be a part of a church."

"I don't think that's the reason God made churches," Increase said, pursing his lips.

"Rachelle!" Mariette called into the other room. "Come here, please."

"Yes?" Rachelle asked as she came in wiping her hands on a dish towel.

"Where do you go to church? We need a good church, a place for David to make some friends and practice his French."

"I go to St. Anne's, but we don't speak French there. The Canadians who speak French keep it in their homes."

"Well, at least there will be French speakers. Surely there are cultured people at St. Anne's?" Mariette looked expectantly at the young woman.

Rachelle blushed. "It's a Catholic church, ma'am. There are some people of standing in the community there, but most go to the Protestant church."

"Well, Dr. Graves and I are Catholic, and we will go to St. Anne's. Then the community will know that it's a reputable church," Mariette huffed.

"*You* are Catholic," Increase said.

"What does that mean?" Mariette stared at her husband in disbelief. "We were married at St. Leonard's in Boston. David was baptized there and his mother buried there. Lively told me. Of course you're Catholic."

"I just mean that being Catholic hasn't done anything for me. God doesn't seem to give me any preference for it. I don't think I am Catholic or Protestant. I'm …" He paused trying to gather his thoughts.

He believed in God. He knew that much. But he didn't trust God. God had let him down too many times. Patients who had done nothing wrong died under his care. Prayers often went unacknowledged. Like a game of roulette, he never knew which prayer would be answered.

Then there was Annie. Neither God nor any of his patron saints had paid attention as sweet Annie bled to death. No. There might be a God, but he and his saints were fickle and uncaring, and Increase didn't see any reason to be a part of a church.

"You're a doctor in this community and it will be expected that you go to church," Mariette said as invisible sparks flew from her eyes. Seldom had she spoken so. "I'll go to the church tomorrow and meet the priest. It's important that we join quickly so David can have friends."

The afternoon at the hospital did little to improve the doctor's mood. Nurse Hall met him at the door.

"Dr. Graves, the patient is getting dressed. Her cousin is here and they say they're leaving. I tried to stop them, but I was afraid of tearing her stitches."

Increase stomped into the room of empty beds. "What are you doing?" he said. "You can't go anywhere. You need to stay here until you are recovered."

The young ladies, barely women, backed against the wall. Rose was bent over in pain, but still she tried pulling on her overcoat.

"She cannot stay here." The words were halting and thick with accent. "We cannot afford the hospital. The medic will come to the house tonight."

"What's your name?" Increase said.

"Marie," the girl said, her bravado beginning to fade as Rose moaned beside her.

"Marie, the nurse can't visit all of the sick and Rose needs to be here. She risks infection at home."

"The medic will take care of her. She'll be fine."

The young woman wrapped her arm around Rose's waist. Rose leaned her weight against her cousin and the two hobbled down the line of beds. Nurse Hall looked at her boss for direction.

"Wait," Increase said. "I'll drive you to your house. Rose shouldn't walk so soon." Increase ordered a carriage from the community stable.

The carriage arrived with a strong north wind. Nurse Hall padded the seat with blankets, then Increase lifted Rose onto the bench. Marie wrapped more blankets around her as Rose settled uncomfortably into the corner of the seat. The oyster-shell roadway jostled the passengers with every turn of the wheels, but thankfully the ride was short.

The smell of boiling cabbage and potatoes drifted into the street from every rundown house along Maple and Walnut Streets. Any trace of trees had long since been removed, replaced with brick sidewalks, cement stairs, and smoky chimneys lifting solitary branches of soot toward the darkening sky.

Marie pointed out which house to stop at and Increase pulled on the reins. The horse stood still while he lifted Rose as gently as he could. He carried her up the stairs and into the dusky hallway of the home. The structure had formerly housed young women who left their rural homes to find work in the industrial northeast. Now it was a labyrinth of hallways and tiny rooms, each holding one or more families. The encroaching darkness hid the rodents whose tiny scratchings along the floorboards assured Increase that Rose would not be safe from infection.

He followed Marie into a small room and placed Rose on the lumpy tick that served as their bed. It was obvious that several girls shared the room and bed. Three dresses hung on wall hooks. A wash stand in the corner was draped with a towel drying over the limited air space.

The afternoon work bell was ringing when he covered Rose with the light blanket that served as the only bed covering. "I'll come back this evening and check on her," he said. "I'll come at seven o'clock. Only give her broth for dinner."

"No," Marie answered. "The medic will look at Rose. We cannot pay you."

"The nurses aren't trained to help Rose if something is wrong. I'll come at seven. You don't need to pay me." He let himself out the way he had come in and took a deep breath of cold air. He would need to bring antiseptic, he thought. Rat traps would be too offensive.

Workers straggled back to the mills for a couple hours more of labor. It was a dreary life marked by heavy bells, poor food, and little sleep. *Not much different than my own life,* Increase mused. *But at least the food is improving.*

The rich smell of roasting meat and fresh bread welcomed him home. David's childish lisp sang along with Mariette's soprano. Electric lamps glowed in the parlor and oil lights burned in the dining room. The atmosphere was so different from Rose's small apartment that he put her out of mind.

"Hello," Increase called as he hung his heavy coat on the coat tree. "I'm home."

David tore through the kitchen doorway. Mariette came laughing behind him.

"What are you two up to?" he asked as David wrapped himself around his legs and Mariette kissed his cheek.

"We have a surprise," David said, but Mariette hushed him.

"David," she said, "go change your shirt for dinner. You have gravy splattered all over your front."

"It will just get more on it at dinner."

"Obey Mariette," Increase commanded good-naturedly, wondering when it would feel natural to call her his mother.

"You forgot to remove your hat, sir," Mariette teased as she stood on tiptoes to remove his felt hat. Her head came only to his chest even then.

Increase unexpectedly grabbed her round the waist and lifted her up, surprising the both of them.

Rachelle walked in to announce dinner, clearing her throat and glancing at the floor. Mariette's cheeks blushed a fresh, pale pink and her blue eyes sparkled. Increase put her down and held her hand as they walked into the dining room. David came barreling down the stairs at top speed as always.

Hot bowls of soup waited on the table as they took their places. "Now?" David asked as he beamed at Mariette.

Mariette gave a gentle nod and bowed her head.

"Bénissez nous, Seigneur, et bénissez le repas que nous allons prendre. Au nom du Père, du Fils, et du Saint Esprit. Amen.— Bless us, O Lord, and bless the meal we are about to take. In the name of the Father, the Son, and the Holy Spirit. Amen."

It was a short prayer, but the boy was obviously pleased with himself. He wiggled in his seat as he looked from his father to Mariette and back again.

"Mariette taught me." He giggled.

"I went to the church today and met the priest. He said we'll be most welcome to attend at St. Anne's." Her voice trailed off as his face darkened.

Rachelle brought in sliced bread and butter. "Do you need anything else with your soup?" she asked, hesitating in the uncomfortable silence.

"Yes, Rachelle," Increase answered. "Didn't you say you live near my patient, Rose Janelle?"

"Yes, sir."

"I went to her apartment today. I'll be checking on her at seven o'clock. Since I'm going that way, you should wait to go home. I'll give you a ride in the carriage, and pay you for the extra hour. Perhaps you would like to accompany us, Mariette?"

Mariette's face drew tight and pinched. "I need to help David prepare for bed. Why has the patient gone home so soon? Shouldn't she still be in hospital?"

"Rose can't afford the hospital," Rachelle spoke up.

"That's right," Increase agreed. "David can come along with us this one time. Mariette, shouldn't he learn Christian works along with his prayers?"

Mariette knew when she was being coerced. She would not rise to the bait. "I'll clean up the kitchen tonight; that way you can leave earlier and get Rachelle home," Mariette said. "David should stay home in this weather, anyway. A hot bath and an early bedtime will drive away that coming cold." She nodded toward the sniffling child wiping his nose on his sleeve.

"David, use your handkerchief," Increase said. He hated being outdone, but Mariette had him in a corner when it came to David's health. He would never jeopardize his son.

Increase knew they had arrived, though dark night enveloped him. The smell of rotting latrines pervaded the blackness even in the freezing cold of winter. A rat charged over a snowbank just as Increase opened the door for Rachelle. Her cheeks burned brightly as they entered the dim hallway. She looked at the floor.

"Thank you for bringing me home, Dr. Graves. It was kind of you to give me a ride. Would you like to meet Mamere and Clement?" she asked with hesitation.

"You're welcome for the ride, Rachelle, but I better see to my patient. I'll visit your grandmother another time."

Rachelle nodded with obvious relief and entered the stairwell to the second floor. Increase turned down the hallway to the small apartment of Rose Janelle. Marie opened the door before he could finish knocking.

"You said seven o'clock." Her eyes narrowed.

"Yes, I know I'm early, but I was giving your neighbor a ride home. I hope it is a favorable time to call," Increase said, hoping to lighten Marie's dark glare.

"Of course," Marie answered widening the doorway. "The medic is here now."

Increase walked into the small room. An older gentleman stood over the bed, palpitating Rose's abdomen.

"Where's Nurse Lindelof?" Increase asked.

All heads turned toward him in questioning confusion.

"Nurse Lindelof. The night nurse. Who is this?" Increase nodded toward the man standing over Rose.

"This is Jean, the medic," Marie said as she walked to the bedside.

"The medic?" Increase asked.

The older man held out a hand in greeting. "Jean Giatros. You must be Dr. Graves. I heard you have come to work at the hospital. It's good for Rose that you were here. You did an excellent job."

Increase crossed the room in three strides. He took the gentleman's hand and shook it. Why hadn't anyone told him about this doctor?

"Thank you," Increase said, relaxing a bit. "Marie mentioned a medic this morning. I thought she meant the visiting nurse. You must be the doctor that comes from Lowell." He was trying to get his bearings.

"Oh, no." Jean laughed, shaking his head. "I live here in Dunstable Plains."

"Oh …" Increase fumbled. "Mr. Neal told me there were no other doctors here."

"Well, I work at the mill too," Jean said. "I just look after the people who live here. Some of the higher-ups might say I use old wives' tales, but my doctoring is time tested and proven. I don't get paid to be a doctor, though, except for some occasional gifts."

Jean Giatros was clearly a gentle man, concerned for others' welfare. He reminded Increase of Maurice Shevenell, a doctor who used his gifts to make life better for his fellow man. Increase took to Jean like a spring breeze in winter.

"So, Rose, you are doing well?" Increase asked taking her wrist in his large hand.

"Oui," she replied, but her hands were trembling.

"You need to keep the bandages clean," Increase said. "It's imperative that the incision not become infected."

"I'll come twice daily to clean it," Jean said. "The environs may seem filthy to you, but the people's habits are not."

"The Public Health Department should enforce the sanitation codes," Increase said. "Conditions like this shouldn't be tolerated. Boston is very clean compared to here."

"Perhaps that is the part of Boston you are aware of," Jean said with a kind smile.

A vision of the dying young boy who couldn't care for his family came to Increase's mind. "You're right, of course," Increase said. "However, it doesn't mean it has to be that way. You're in good hands," Increase said as he looked down at Rose, "but I'll still come to check on you tomorrow. Good evening."

He let himself out and walked down the darkened hallway toward the crack of dim light that outlined the door. How unfair that the door opening to his freedom was the same that locked its occupants into a life of slavery. The church bells marked the hour as Increase climbed into the carriage.

"Dr. Graves, here to see the director of Public Health," Increase said to the matron at the front desk. The city building was located in the Masonic Lodge, a large stone structure looming at the edge of lavish and opulent.

"Good morning, Dr. Graves. Everyone has heard of your arrival. We're so excited to have you in Dunstable Plains. I'll let Mr. Taylor know you are here." The roll of her double chin quivered as she spoke.

The long skirt and high-necked shirtwaist blouse did nothing to hide the expansiveness of the woman. Increase watched her walk away. Though she must be in some financial need to be working in the office, she obviously was not hurting like the tenants of the slums she was hired to protect.

The clicking of her shoes returning down the hallway drew Increase back to the reason for his visit. Rats and vermin were roaming the corridors of the homes of the good citizens of Dunstable Plains. Something had to be done or disease would become epidemic.

"Mr. Taylor will be happy to see you now," the woman said as she motioned down the hall. "Third door on the right."

The office was finely furnished with dark walnut cabinetry and a large desk. Two stuffed chairs faced the desk of Mr. Taylor, a rotund man with red cheeks and a balding pate. He stood to greet Increase.

"Come in, come in," Mr. Taylor said. "I've been looking forward to making your acquaintance." He beamed, a genial host. "The city officials were very impressed with your resume and credentials. Please sit down. Can I offer you some tea or coffee?"

"No, thank you," Increase said, wanting to get straight to the matter. "Sir, I have a patient on Maple Avenue. I attended her there yesterday, and I was appalled at the conditions of the building ... and the entire neighborhood."

"Yes, that area needs a good paint job," Mr. Taylor said as he pulled his chair closer to the desk.

"Paint job? It needs sanitation. It needs fumigated. The vermin are running rampant in the hallways." Increase blustered, gesticulating with his hands for effect. "The Public Health Department should have done something about this a long time ago. It's a veritable epidemic in the making."

"Maple Avenue and all of the houses in that area are owned by the various mill owners," Mr. Taylor said. "It's up to the owners to attend to their needs."

"I see. But it is the mandate of Public Health to ensure that those needs are being met."

"The mills employ a lot of people. They're providing good jobs for those people. You can't expect the owners to pay out money for housing and for wages, Dr. Graves. They would go broke, and then where would we be?" Mr. Taylor kept his head lowered, looking at his clasped hands. "It is the tax money from the mills that keeps our city alive. Those taxes pay for Public Health and Sewage, the library … *and* the hospital," Mr. Taylor said.

"But if the workers become too ill to work, the mills will have to close." Increase wouldn't back down. He knew how to turn an argument. "And if that happens, where will this town be? I'll be welcomed back to St. Patrick's Memorial, but where will the head of Public Health be—the one who allowed a cholera outbreak?"

"I don't think that will be an issue." Mr. Taylor grunted and narrowed his eyes. "These French Canadians are a dime a dozen. The work force will be replaced. The mills won't close. The machines will keep running."

A tentative knock at the door made both men look up. "Dr. Graves, there was a call that you're needed at the hospital. There was an accident at one of the cotton mills."

"Excuse me," Increase said as he stood. "I'm sure we will meet again soon, Mr. Taylor. Good day."

"Yes, good day," the red-cheeked man replied.

Increase jumped over the last two steps and bounded through the front door of the hospital. "What happened?" he asked as soon as he saw Nurse Hall.

Two men in wool overcoats were standing over one of the hospital beds. They looked over a man writhing in pain, holding his face.

"A pulley broke on the line in the spinning room," the older man said over top the injured man. "It flew through the air and hit Earnest here in the face. Looks like he'll lose his eye."

A wail came from the bed and the two men looked down at the man lying there. They shifted their weight and sighed.

Increase managed to hold his temper and focus on the matter at hand. "I'll be the judge of that. I'm the doctor. Step aside to the waiting area, please."

Unfortunately the exam proved the men right. The eye was surgically removed and the vessels cauterized. A large bandage covered half the man's face when he was finally placed in the hospital recovery room to rest. Luckily the other eye was uninjured. Increase always dreaded breaking bad news; trying to find something positive in these painful processes had always been Annie's forte.

He left the patient in a drug-induced stupor. Blindly he wandered home and poured a shot of whiskey. *Three of us have lost our sight*, Increase thought: *the health department, the worker, and myself.* "What should I do, Annie?" he asked the darkened room.

A small choke sounded at the door. "It's Mariette, Increase." She was calm. Her long skirts rustled as she rushed to him. She wrapped her arms around his waist from behind and rested her head against his back. They stood that way for an eternity, the whiskey shaking in his hand.

*When healthy, we all have wonderful advice for the sick.*
~Terence~

# CHAPTER II

A SALTY BREEZE WAFTED THROUGH THE open windows. The cool evening air released Pater's lungs like a house being freshened. I floated out of the house on the briny zephyr and into the streets of town.

Most everyone was inside their homes finishing dinner, visiting with family about their day. A gaggle of children hurried past, kicking a ball. A few old women sat outside in the fading light preparing fawn skins for the maenads as the sun slid toward the horizon of the plain.

I passed through the city gate toward the Strymon River. I could hear some people singing near the bank. A small alcove in the trees had formed an arbor among the poplars and oaks. The leaves weren't in full abundance yet, but I could see why benches had been set up underneath. It would be an oasis of peace and shade in the hot summer months to come.

I walked to the water's edge and looked down the river. The last of the day's light reflected in orange and pink rivulets as they flowed toward the sea.

"Loukas? Is that you?"

I turned to see Ludia approaching. I raised my hand in greeting and she smiled.

"Have you come for the prayer meeting? Jehan is here already." She half-turned toward the arbor, drawing me in with her.

"Oh … no. I mean … I was just taking a walk … to clear my head." I tried to talk low, avoiding her eyes.

She took my arm. "There's no better way to clear your head than to ask God. Come on."

I spotted Jehan. He moved aside on the bench, making room for me. I joined him, my face burning with embarrassment. I hated interrupting and causing a fuss.

The song ended and Jehan stood up. "This evening I want to tell you a story of Moses after the Exodus. The children of Israel had been wandering many years in the wilderness. They'd had some successes, but they forgot about the times their God helped them.

"They hoped to go through the land of Edom, but the king of Edom would not allow it. Moses told the king that they would stay on the main road and neither eat nor drink from the Edomites' land, but the king refused.

"Moses tried again, sending a message that if anyone ate or drank anything of the Edomites, then the Israelites would gladly pay for it, but the king of Edom had resolved that the Israelites should not go through his country."

I looked around at the faces listening to the story. I had heard of Moses, the man who led the Israelites out of Egypt. The god that had performed so powerfully in the past seemed to have forgotten his people these days. The ragtag group of followers looked pitiful, and the only ones I knew, Jehan and Ludia, were still wandering far from their homes.

"So they had no choice but to head south toward the Red Sea," Jehan continued. "The people stopped to mourn the death of Moses's brother Aaron. Then, fresh from their grief, they moved on. The king of Arad heard that the Israelites were approaching. He attacked and took many of them captive.

"So the Israelites prayed to God. They asked for victory over the Canaanites, and God blessed them. They recovered the hostages and completely destroyed the Canaanite cities in that area. They devoted the cities to God, and he was pleased."

Heads nodded and Ludia looked over at me. She reminded me of my grandmother. I smiled briefly and turned my attention back to Jehan.

"But it didn't take long for the Israelites to forget their victory and their promise. The desert around Edom is rough and rocky. The people were tired and worn down. They wanted fresh food and fresh water.

"'We're dying out here,' they complained to Moses. 'The food is rotten and the water is foul. Why did God bring us out here to die?'

"God became very angry. His anger burned against them like a scorpion's sting. He sent the poisonous serpents of the land to attack the Israelites. The rasping sound of snake skins rubbing against each other warned the children of Israel that they were in danger. The hissing and swishing filled their ears as the cobras left their hiding places and surrounded the ungrateful complainers."

I shuddered as the tree branches rubbed together in the evening breeze. *I hate snakes.*

"The snakes began to bite, releasing their poison into the people. The death was horrendous—painful and slow. The people became frightened. They went to Moses and apologized. 'We're sorry we insulted you and the Lord. Please save us from these vipers.'

"So Moses prayed to the Lord and the Lord told Moses to make a bronze snake and put it on top of a pole. Whenever a person was bitten by a snake, all they had to do was look at it and they would be healed.

"Many of the people looked at the snake and the painful spasms and bleeding stopped. Their bodies healed, and they were saved.

"But some … some did not look to the bronze snake. They chose to die rather than give God their attention."

Jehan sat down and the group bowed their heads. A man stood and led them in a prayer, then they sang another song and began drifting off toward the city gates, back to their homes of exile but with good food and fresh water.

"I'm glad you came," Jehan said as we wandered out of the dark alcove into the dusky twilight.

"I enjoyed the story. I'm not sure I understand, though."

"What concerns you?" Jehan slowed his pace and we let the last of the townspeople pass us. The houses began to glow in the lamp lights.

"Well, the people of Israel were like that ridiculous man who refused medicine yesterday. But they should have known better. Their god told them what the medicine was; they didn't make some silly promise."

Jehan tilted his head and walked beside me. "Explain."

"Well, the Israelites asked their god what they should do to be healed. He told them what the cure was … and it was so simple. Why wouldn't they look at the snake, Jehan? That doesn't make any sense." I lifted my hands in exasperation.

"Some people would rather die on their own terms than admit that they're wrong or that they aren't in control. The God of the Israelites isn't a god who can be manipulated. He knows your intentions and he heals accordingly." We stopped in front of the gate to Jehan's garden. The Nehushtan was still warm from the day's sunshine. "What about you, Loukas? Will you look at the snake?"

I stared at the serpent twisted on the gatepost. It seemed so simple in the story, but would I have been stubborn? Would I have looked?

"See you tomorrow, Jehan." I turned to leave.

"Good night, Loukas."

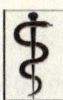

I wandered on through town, the stars appearing as tiny lights to lead me home. Stopping at the public baths, I threw a coin into the fountain of Asclepius. *Don't forget Pater,* I prayed.

I could hear men in the tavern. They were drinking to Dionysus, asking him for a fruitful grape season. They asked for fair weather, sunshine, and rain to make the grapes sweet.

It wasn't fair. Pater hadn't insulted Dionysus or Asclepius. He hadn't refused to come to them for health. I had done everything for him that I knew to do, and Jehan had also offered his expertise. So why did the gods make him suffer?

I walked home, anger fueling my legs and increasing my stride. *What good are gods who refuse to help when you ask?*

Pater was asleep on the bed, his breathing rasping like snake skins rubbing together, just as Jehan had suggested in his story. Pater's face looked pale, and dewy drops of sweat wetted his thinning hair.

*I don't want him to die, but this suffering … What am I willing to do to make Pater better?*

*You pray for good health and a body that will be strong in old age. Good—but*
*your rich foods block the gods' answer and tie Jupiter's hands.*
~Aulus Persius Flaccus ~

# CHAPTER 12

COLD WIND BLEW THROUGH THE small alleys with hurricane force. Increase stood at the entrance gate of the Hoop Mills compound. They were the largest employer in Dunstable Plains, and as Increase discovered, they had the best reputation for benevolence in the community. He had decided meeting with Mr. Hoop and his sons at the mills would be the best way to get something done.

The bell sounded, calling the workers to the first morning shift, but Increase was already there, waiting and watching. Doors opened and quickly slammed closed as the residents vainly attempted to keep what little heat there was inside their hovels. The flicker of lighted and then darkened doorsteps framed the small town's citizens heading to work in the twilight of dawn. Threadbare coats were pulled around the coarse cloth that mill workers wore. The thicker, softer fabrics were for those of nobler callings.

The iron gates swung open as workers filed in, offering their salutations to neighbors and friends and looking curiously at Increase in his heavy Woolrich coat and thick red-and-white lamb's wool scarf. He pulled the scarf around his ears as a gust of wind swooped down his neck. The gatekeeper's eyes flitted to him from across the square, but he never took his focus off the crowd that filed past.

As the last straggler entered the gate, the bell rang again to signal the start of the workday. A woman ran on the slippery walkway, trying to reach the gate before it completely closed.

"No admittance," the guard muttered.

"Please, George," the woman said. "Henri is sick. I came as fast as I could. Please, I can't miss work." Her eyes searched George's face for some sign of compassion.

"Mr. Hoop, sir," George exclaimed as he opened the gate wide.

The woman took advantage of the distraction and bolted inside.

"You are to close the gate at the bell, George," Mr. Hoop said. "No one is to be paid a full day's work if they won't work a full day." Then he snapped his head toward Increase. "And who are you?" he asked.

"Dr. Increase Graves, sir," Increase said, extending a hand. "I've heard about your fine mill and thought I would pay a visit." He smiled his most congenial smile. Flattery did not come naturally to Increase, and he hoped his intentions weren't too transparent.

The gray-haired gentleman shook hands with the doctor and motioned for him to follow. The iron gate clanged shut as the chain was put back in place to bar any other late arrivals. The two men walked silently toward the disappearing crowd that flowed into the warm cotton mill. *At least the people are warm when they're at work.* It was to be the only positive thought Increase would have that morning.

Large wooden doors closed behind Increase, shutting him in the factory with finality. A spiral staircase to the right of the door twisted to the seventh floor of the massive structure. Following Mr. Hoop, Increase began the ascent, twenty-two steps between each floor. Step after step swelling his resolve to help these people, step after step making him more certain of his mission. By the time Increase reached the top, he knew there was no turning back.

Each floor of the mill had a different purpose. Raw cotton went in the top floor and came out the bottom a finished piece of fabric. Spinners, weavers, oilers, cleaners … All worked alike, rushing to be sure each piece of machinery was working properly.

"So you want to see my fine mill, do you?" said Mr. Hoop finally. "I'm not sure of your intentions. I saw Mr. Taylor at the library social last evening," he said. "I'll show you my factory, but don't try to talk me into renovating the row houses. They were built for utility, just like this mill, and they are fulfilling that role just fine."

"But, sir …" Increase started, but the elderly man turned away and ignored him.

They stood at the entrance of a large room. The floor was dusted with bleached, wooly whiteness.

"This is where the cotton comes in. The men carry it up the outside of the building on the wooden stairs. Here it is cleaned and prepared. Ah, good morning, John," Mr. Hoop said to a worker. "Dr. Graves here would like to know how you fare."

The young man stopped at the mention of his name and obediently gave the expected answer. He was happy working at Hoop Mills; the work was pleasant, the conditions safe, and the pay generous. And so it went as they descended each curve of the spiraling stairs to another floor of labor. Men, women, and children sang the praises of their beneficent employer, an angel in disguise.

The ground floor of clanging, vibrating looms was both deafening and deadening. Increase's ears filled with the pressure of noise, dust, and humidity from the steam-driven machines. The workers, the floors, and the machinery were all covered in the dust and lint of cotton fabric. Young boys, Increase gauged to be about eight or nine, rushed between looms watching over the state of the threads. They were all part of the massive, monstrous machine at Hoop Mills.

Finally Increase and Mr. Hoop exited the building. The thundering vibration of the looms pounded into the wooden bridge over the canal. "So you see, Dr. Graves, all is well in Dunstable Plains. I hope to see you at the next library lecture. Good day."

Five hours of kowtowing and pulsating thunder had worn Increase down. "Good day," he said and turned to the gatekeeper. "At least you can hear yourself think out here."

"I'd rather be warm." The guard coughed and shrugged deeper into his oversized coat as he opened the gate. "Have a good day." The creaking of the gate was drowned out by the bell signaling the half-hour lunch break.

Increase stepped to the side of the walkway and let the weary workers trudge past him. They had half an hour to walk home, eat, and return to work. No time for good food, no time for rest—it was yet another stone in his shoe.

"Hello, Dr. Graves," an older man said, breaking into Increase's thoughts.

Increase focused his gaze on the small, gray-haired gentleman. "Good afternoon, Dr. Giatros," he said in pleasant recognition. "You work at Hoop Mills?" he asked, noticing Jean's lint-covered coat and hair.

"Call me 'Jean,' please. And, yes, it helps me pass the time."

"But why do you work at the mill if you could doctor instead?"

"The people can't go to the doctor in the daytime. They have to work," Jean said. "Even if they could go to a doctor in the daytime, they couldn't afford to keep me fed. So I work for my supper and care for my fellow man at night."

"You must be heading to lunch," Increase said, suddenly realizing he was wasting Jean's precious time. "I'll let you go. Perhaps we'll meet again soon."

"Soon. Yes," Jean said as he waved and walked away.

Increase stopped by the hospital to check on Earnest's eye. His eye socket seemed to be recovering, but he was suffering deep depression. His wife had spent the last two evenings visiting, but she also worked at one of the mills and her income was desperately needed now. The short evening visits were all she could manage.

"You'll be able to go home in a few days," Increase said as he took the patient's pulse. "You're recovering nicely."

"There is no recovery." Earnest frowned and turned his head on the pillow. "My eye will never be recovered."

"True," Increase said. "You still have your other eye, though, and good sight in it. Once all the vessels heal, you can go back to work and return to normal."

Earnest just grimaced. "You don't get it. … There will never be a normal."

"You have a new normal," came Jean's voice as it echoed down the short row of beds.

Increase turned and looked at the gentleman removing his coat.

"I decided a visit with Earnest might taste better than the boiled cabbage waiting at home." He grinned at Increase, then looked at Earnest. "Your wife says you're bitter about the accident," Jean said, focusing on the bandaged man tensed under the blankets.

"As I should be," Earnest answered. "The pulleys were neglected, and now I'm blind. What good will I be to Hettie if I can't see?"

"But you *can* see," Increase said. "Your other eye is perfectly fine, and soon we can cover the damaged socket with a glass eye."

"Yes, and once I return to the mill? What then? Another accident that takes what little I have left?" Earnest sounded more agitated. His hand trembled as he pointed at Increase. "I don't have the luxury of doctoring those who are injured. I live with and become those who are injured," he spat.

"Earnest," Jean said in a soft voice, "God directs each of us down different paths. Our mission is to walk that road to the end and help others along the way. Dr. Graves may appear to have an easy life, but he too must struggle. You have to decide if you'll let your struggle make you better or continue to make you bitter."

Earnest looked away from the gentleman sitting on the side of his bed. He didn't seem convinced that anything could make it better.

Increase walked away, leaving the two men in quiet emptiness.

That afternoon Increase visited two more mills. Sheppard Mills mostly produced flannels, while Lytle Mills focused on ticking fabrics for bedding. Each owner greeted Increase and started immediately into a tour of the factory, extolling the fine workers and their products. Everyone had a story to tell about how well everything was going.

Increase talked with the owners about safety precautions in the mills as well as cleaning up the mill house district. His warnings of disease and epidemics were swept under the rug of profits and progress. By the time the supper bell rang, Increase's head throbbed like a wooden hammer nailing the shuttlecock from one side of the loom to the other. He longed to sit in his armchair by the fire and rest.

The short walk up Spring Street helped clear his head. Dusk had fallen and the brilliant glare of snow cast an iridescent glow across the walkway. There was no wind and the quiet hush of the town preparing for evening meals felt comforting. He stopped outside the front stoop to breathe deeply and exhale.

"Daddy!" David called, swinging the front door wide. "I've waited all day for you. Come see what I made."

The boy's excitement at the sight of his father lifted Increase's weary shoulders.

Mariette stood behind David, framed in the light of the doorway. Her black hair was loose and curled; her lips twitched with an easy smile. "Good evening, Increase," she said. "We've missed you today."

Increase skipped up the front stairs two at a time. "Then I better hurry and come in," he said. "And what is it that you have made?" he asked his son.

David grabbed him by the hand and pulled him toward the front parlor. "It's a surprise!"

"Let me take off my coat." Increase laughed as he shook his hand from David's.

"I'll get your coat." Mariette smiled as Increase shrugged from its heavy clutches. She whisked the hat from his head and uncoiled his scarf. "Now go see this great architectural feat," she said with a twinkle in her eye that made Increase's stomach turn topsy-turvy.

David pulled Increase into the parlor where a large fire cast out every chill and draft. In the bright light of the flames and electric lamps, a large structure of blocks stood. Tall towers and window-pocked buildings were encompassed by a gated wall.

"What do you think?" David smiled from ear to ear, clearly proud of his creation. "It's Hoop Mills. Here's where everyone goes in to work, and here's the tall tower where the bell ringer goes. I'm going to build a mill someday and be the boss." He dropped to the floor and showed his father all the details.

"You did a good job," Increase said as he squeezed the boy's shoulder. "And if you own a mill someday, I'm sure you'll take good care of your workers."

"Yeah." David beamed as he straightened a wooden block here and there. "I'll be a great owner … like Mr. Hoop."

"Better than Mr. Hoop, and Mr. Lytle and Mr. Sheppard," Increase said through gritted teeth.

David glanced up at his father.

"Of course he will be better. He's a Graves and no finer man could there be," Mariette said as she reached for Increase's hand.

He accepted her remarks and her hand with a smile and a nod.

"Graves Mills!" David exclaimed. "I wonder what I should make at the mill? Clement says cotton is king still, but I think I'll make tanned leathers. Maybe I'll make baseballs for the Boston Beaneaters. Then I could go to all of their games."

"That sounds like a wonderful idea," Increase said, relaxing into his reading chair. "Will dinner be ready soon? It's been a long day."

"Dinner is ready whenever you are. I sent Rachelle home to be with her mamere," Mariette said. "She's been sick for so long, and Rachelle is very worried. I hope a hot bowl of bean soup will satisfy you."

"Of course. If David is going to go to all of the Beaneater ballgames, then I suppose we ought to get used to eating beans." Increase smiled at Mariette. "It was good of you to let Rachelle go early. Maybe I better go over and check on her grandmother."

"I thought you might say that. I told Rachelle you would visit tomorrow after church."

The family meal reminded Increase of his boyhood home. His parents sat at each end of the table talking over the day's events. The children were allowed to ask questions if there was a lull in the conversation, and then his father would read aloud from the paper or a new book and ask the children questions. Lively had enjoyed those conversations more than he had, but now they visited him as pleasant memories.

"You're smiling," Mariette said. Her cheeks were a soft pink and wisps of black curls floated around her forehead and neck. She brushed a stray hair out of her eyes.

"I was thinking of family meals when I was a child. Father used to read to us and ask us questions."

"Papa and I often ate in the kitchen. It was always warmer there, and it was just the two of us. You were blessed to have your parents and Lively."

"I miss Aunt Lively," David said, his bottom lip protruding. "She and I ate in the kitchen with Rebecca when Daddy would work late at the hospital."

"But now you have Mariette to watch over you. Maybe Rachelle will let you eat in the kitchen with her sometimes."

"No," David said. "Rachelle says the French-Canadians are not to eat with Americans, but Clement came over one day and we ate together then. Was that alright?" David looked at his father, his big, brown eyes pleading.

"Yes. In our family we eat with everyone who invites us, and we invite everyone to eat with us. Right, Mariette?"

"Assurement, especially the French. Now why don't you two relax in the parlor, and I'll clear the dishes. Then, Increase, you should read to us like your father used to read to you."

The quiet evening set Increase's mind at ease. The long day of politicking the mill owners had worn him down, but warm food and time with David had lightened the dark cloud of doom. Even Mariette added a warm glow to the horizon's setting sun. There were problems in the

world, problems here in Dunstable Plains, but they were not insurmount-
able. He would find a way to make things better.

*If we would only become when well,*
*the men we promised to become when we were sick.*
~Pliny the Younger~

# CHAPTER 13

MARIETTE WAS UP BEFORE INCREASE for a change. Her soft humming at the vanity mirror pulled him from sleep. She was dressed in a green woolen skirt and waistcoat of the newer fashions Increase had seen the women in Boston wear. Over it all she had attached a muslin apron. She was removing the rag curlers that wrapped around the ends of her long black hair.

"Going somewhere?" he asked.

Her reflection smiled at him in the mirror. "It's Sunday."

That seemed to be all the answer she was going to give. She was scooping her hair into pins at the back of her head when she called for David to rise and shine.

"David may go to church with you as long as he wishes," Increase said, "but I won't have your beliefs forced upon him."

"There's no force needed to help a person see the Lord. In fact forcing it would do no good." She shrugged her shoulders and stuck another pin in the cascading fall of curls. "Neither will I try to force you to attend a church in which you feel uncomfortable. I'll be sure to give Mr. Sheppard your best."

"Mr. Sheppard?"

"Yes, the mill owner. I believe you met him yesterday. I saw Mrs. Sheppard at the church when I went to meet the priest. She was relieved to see the doctor's family is Catholic."

"Mr. Sheppard seems like a nice enough man. He just doesn't seem to be aware of the conditions his tenants are living in. He doesn't see how their living conditions affect him, either economically or physically."

"I believe their children are about David's age," Mariette went on, ignoring the rabbit trail Increase tried scenting her to. "Perhaps they'll make friends."

Increase stretched and swung his feet out of the bed. He stood and nonchalantly scratched his back. "I think I'll go with you, just to show my face. It might be good for the hospital."

St. Anne's was a tan brick-and-stone structure that rose to a crescendo in the center ridgeway topped off on both ends with soaring steeples that directed the eyes heavenward. The front steeple housed three bells. The crisp morning air reverberated with the tolling that called the community to worship instead of work.

Unintelligible conversations were whispered in French and English. Heavy accents greeted friendly faces. Increase recognized Rose's cousin, Marie, and nodded a good morning from across the aisle. Father Cartier offered the message, the choir sang some hymns, an offering was given, a prayer said, but Increase only noticed Jean in the row directly across and one in front of the Graves family.

Jean watched each person in the sanctuary, his focus intense. He appeared to be praying, mumbling quietly, adding to the murmur that floated around the hushed room. When the service was over, the congregants gathered in small groups to greet one another and share news. Mr. Sheppard and Jean reached Increase at the same moment.

"Good morning," Mr. Sheppard said. "It's good to see you in church. This must be your wife."

"Yes," Increase said as he grasped the man's extended hand. "Mariette, this is Mr. Sheppard. Mr. Sheppard, my wife, Mariette."

"Nice to meet you, ma'am," Mr. Sheppard said. He bowed from the neck, a show of manners but not deference.

"And this is Dr. Giatros," Increase continued, holding Mariette's elbow and directing her attention to the diminutive gentleman.

"Doctor? I didn't know there was another doctor in town. I'm happy to know Increase will have someone to offer him some relief." Her contagious smile lit up the faces of those around.

"Oh, he isn't a real doctor," Mr. Sheppard said. "He works at Hoop Mills." His voice dripped with disdain. "His medicine is wives' tales, broths, and oils."

"He's done well with my patient, Rose," Increase said.

"Many people don't appreciate the ancient wisdom," Jean said. "But Christ has called all of us to be physicians. He asks us to heal the sick, give sight to the blind and hearing to the deaf. He asks us to touch each other, even the lepers. Ancient wisdom should not be lightly dismissed. It was pleasant to meet you, Mrs. Graves. Good day, gentlemen."

"Can you believe that bay frog? Who does he think he is preaching to us?" Mr. Sheppard said.

"Il est un homme gentil—He is a nice man. Papa would like him," Mariette said as she watched the retreating back of the old doctor. "You should invite him to dinner, Increase," she said, turning back to the men. "Perhaps Mr. and Mrs. Sheppard could come as well."

The rich aroma of beef and carrot stew penetrated the walls of the house and welcomed Increase on the porch stairs. Mariette wiped snow from David's shoulders. The light flurry had dusted all of them with damp snowflakes that clung to their hair and lashes.

"This is good snowball weather," David said. "The boys at church said they'll be meeting on Spring Street after lunch for a big snowball fight. May I join them? Isaac Sheppard asked me to come."

Increase's gloved hand paused on the brass doorknob. "I'm not sure you should play with Isaac Sheppard. He might not be a good influence."

"We don't even know the boy," Mariette said to Increase. "He shouldn't be judged for the sins of the father. Perhaps David can even teach Isaac a little French." She giggled.

"Je ne parle un peu français—I speak a little bit of French," David answered with horrible pronunciation.

"Oui. We will have to continue your studies soon, so when Pepè Maurice visits, you can impress him."

"Yes, Mama. But may I go to the snowball fight?" David asked.

The slip of tongue was not lost on Mariette nor on Increase. The term "Mama" fell so easily from the child's lips that he didn't even notice. Mariette's eyes glistened as she raised her face to Increase. His own face turned gray and his eyes were unreadable.

"You may go to the snowball fight after lunch, but I suggest you find other friends than the Sheppard boy," Increase said, choosing to ignore the joy he saw on Mariette's face.

David threw his arms around Increase's legs. "Thank you, Daddy," he said. "I'll find lots of boys to play with, not just Isaac." Then he raced indoors, leaving Increase and Mariette alone.

"Oh, Increase, did you hear? You heard, right? He called me 'Mama,'" Mariette said.

"I heard," Increase said through tight lips.

"What's the matter?" Mariette asked.

"Nothing is the matter." Increase shrugged. "All is as it should be. It's time he claimed a mother."

"And it is time you claimed a wife," Mariette added.

"I already have," Increase muttered and walked in the house. Shaking snow from his overcoat, he hung it on the coat tree while Mariette stared at him from the cold outdoors.

"Do you mean me or Annie?" she asked just above a whisper from the porch.

"You're my wife. Now … I would like something hot to eat." Increase sighed, resigned to the fact that he could do nothing about the current situation.

*Wherever the art of medicine is loved, there is also a love of humanity.*
~Hippocrates~

# CHAPTER 14

DARKNESS LINGERED AFTER THE DAWN. Thick clouds hung heavy in the sky and snowflakes created by the steaming mills floated in the air like cold death. Workers sullenly greeted the doctor as he stood on the hospital steps watching the march of mill workers trudging to another day of tedium and torment. From the throng Marie raised a hand in salute and then trudged along with the rest, a thin sapling wrapped in tatters.

Increase turned away from the sad scene and opened the hospital door. The strong smell of vinegar and lye wakened him from the reverie that the quiet march had instilled.

"Nurse Hall, what on earth are you doing?"

The angular brunette was on her knees, rag in hand, bucket by her feet. "Rats are getting brave," she said. Her face was red and her breath came in short huffs. "Saw two in the back closet when I took out clean linens for the empty bed."

"Well, they won't live long in here. They'll be asphyxiated by the smell."

"I should hope so. I suppose that's what we get for bringing in those bay frogs."

"Excuse me?" Increase stopped in his tracks, his hand on the doorknob to his office. *Surely she didn't mean Rose?*

"Oh, don't get me wrong. It were a blessing from heaven that you saved that girl, but now she'll likely fill up with infection and die anyway. That kind don't try to live like normal folk. They're filthy." She dipped the rag back in the bucket and went back to scrubbing.

"I don't think they are filthy by intention, Nurse Hall. They don't have adequate housing. I stopped by Rose's home. The mill owners should be held accountable for what they're doing. They wouldn't let their own kin live in a place like that."

Increase stepped into his office and firmly shut the door. The smell of vinegar and lye still clung to the inside of his nostrils. He shook his head and sat down in the black wooden chair. There was more than doctoring to take care of in Dunstable Plains.

The brisk winter air and crisp blue sky did little to encourage Increase. He was headed toward Maple Street to check on Rose. Marie had gone to work, he had seen that himself, and he knew Rose would be left to fend for herself. The stitches were still so new and fragile. She shouldn't be left alone for long.

The long rows of dingy brick houses stood in stark contrast to the tree-lined streets of his own rented home. Two toddlers played king of the hill on a snowbank while an old woman swept snow off the icy walkway in front of her stoop. Her long skirt whipped in the wind and shouted the obvious. The woman was dying. Maybe not today, maybe not tomorrow, but Death was dancing up the path to the door.

Increase tipped his hat at the matron, turned left, and stopped at the door of Rose's house. The darkness of the narrow hallway blinded him at first and he stood with the door cracked open.

"Were you raised in a barn?" an irritated voice greeted him from one of the door frames. "Shut the door behind you."

Increase apologized and pushed the door closed behind him. Cold air wafted in from the unsealed cracks. He followed the passage to Rose's apartment and gently knocked on the door.

"Come," a man's voice called.

Opening the door, Increase peeked into the room. Rose lay in bed, an extra coverlet thrown over top her spare form. She was little more than a bump in the sagging bed. Jean was sitting beside her, holding some papers.

"Ah, Dr. Graves, come again to check on his patient. Good." Jean stood up and put out a hand in greeting. "I was just reading Rose a letter from her mother."

Increase closed the door behind him and entered the room. He shook the older man's hand. "I thought you'd be at the mill."

"Not when Rose needs me. There are others who can take my place at the mill."

Increase nodded once to Jean, then looked at Rose. "How are you today, young lady?"

"Bien—Good. My side is still sore, but I've gotten up a few times."

"You mustn't push yourself," Increase said. "You should stay in bed. I saw Marie heading to work this morning, so I thought you must be alone. I wanted to check in and make sure you're behaving yourself." He smiled at the girl and then nodded toward Jean. "The medic is taking good care of you?"

"Oui," she said. "Medic Giatros is wonderful." Her cheeks pinked and she looked at her toes curling under the covers. "He brought me wonderful medicine and this coverlet too."

"Medicine?" Increase asked. He pulled back the covers and inspected Rose's incision.

"A little ointment to ease the pain," Jean explained. "Poplar buds infused in oil."

"I can give you some laudanum for the pain. Home remedies are not always effective." His patronizing smile spoke volumes as he placed clean bandages on the wound.

Rose's eyes explored Jean's face and then darted back to Increase. "The medic's medicine is good. Thank you for coming by." She turned toward the wall and rearranged her clothing.

"Laudanum is not bad, Rose," Jean said. "You just have to be careful not to use too much of it. Dr. Graves only wants to help." Jean patted her shoulder and pulled the covers up higher.

"I'm fine. Thank you." Her voice was small, her breath coming in short pants after the exam. "Mama would have made the ointment too, if she were here."

"Is your mother a doctor?" Increase couldn't stop himself. This sort of backwoods thinking was unacceptable. *I'm a doctor from Boston, for the love of God.*

"I'll walk Dr. Graves out," Jean said. "The peony root tea should be ready when I get back."

Increase gathered his bag and crossed to the door Jean held open. The two men walked through the narrow passageway and into the cold light.

"Where did you practice medicine before?" Increase asked, disdain dripping like the melting icicles on the eaves.

"I have offered healing wherever I have gone."

"Advancements have been made, sir, and teas and tree oils are no longer the best medicines."

"Ancient wisdom should not be lightly dismissed," Jean said. "Some medicines never lose their efficacy."

"Pphhtt." Increase snorted. "The new medicines are better. And surely our surgeries and equipment have far surpassed that of the ancients."

"Perhaps, but there are stronger medicines than even you have discovered."

"And how do you know about these medicines?" Increase felt himself growing perturbed by the man's searching gaze that bored through his coat and left a chill in his soul.

"There are ancient medicines: plants, broths, herbs, and oils. But," he said, then paused, "there is spiritual medicine as well, to heal the spirit."

"I suppose next you're going to tell me that prayers are as strong as morphine."

"At times." Jean nodded. He stood with his feet apart and his arms crossed lightly over his chest. His head cocked to one side. "Do you not trust that type of medicine?"

"I doctor with experience," Increase answered. "And my experience says that real medicine and real doctors provide real results. Prayer is not medicine, and God is not a doctor."

"So you haven't given up on God; you just don't trust him."

"Trust is earned. I need to get back to the hospital. I'll check on Rose again tomorrow." Increase stomped past Jean, who moved gently aside.

"See you then," he called.

The two young women were a contrast to the snowy scene. Rachelle wore a yellow coat flecked with tiny wildflowers, one of Mariette's castoff robes from last season. Mariette's own royal blue coat was a warm summer lake in the midst of a snow-covered street. Their laughter and happy conversation glowed like sunshine on the passersby.

Clement and David raced down the sidewalk searching for patches of ice to slide on. They stopped to watch a horseless carriage sputter and turn left onto Spring Street. Large icicles popped out of a snowbank like a picket fence. The boys unsheathed the long ice-swords and began a fencing bout.

"En garde!" Clement began the calls, striking a pose.

"Allez—Go!" David answered and the fighting began.

The thick ice lasted three whacks, and they were on to the next set of sabers.

"I'm happy that David has Clement," Mariette said. "He needs a boy his age to play with. I think he's been lonely a long time, but never knew what to call it." Mariette waved to David as he caught her eye. He brandished an icicle and started another assault.

"Clement is happy to have a playmate too. Mamere's not such a good playmate." Rachelle chuckled.

"He'll go to school soon, just like David. Then there will be lots of playmates. Of course, David will have a private tutor. Where will Clement go to school?"

"There's a school at the end of Washington Street for the mill children, but not many can go," Rachelle said.

"Why not?"

Rachelle jerked her head and looked at Mariette. "They have to work, of course."

"But they can't work so young. It's illegal." Mariette stopped walking to stare at Rachelle.

"Food is more important than books." Rachelle shrugged. "The mill owners are willing to look the other way, and the parents remember too well the farming days in Canada. Work without books is better than no work."

"Did you go to school?" Mariette asked.

"Oui, I finished two grades. Then Mama had Clement, and I had to stay home to help. We lost Mama that spring. The land was blooming while Mama faded. We buried her on Fête de la Saint-Jean-Baptiste."

"I don't know the day my mama was buried. She died when I was born. I suppose it was a few days later."

The women walked with their memories for a while.

"So you didn't get to finish school. You can read, though?" Mariette returned to the present.

"Très peu—A little," Rachelle said. "I can sign my name." Her head hung and her pace slowed. She crossed her arms against the wind. "I don't need to read to work at the mills … or for you."

"I suppose not," Mariette said, "but wouldn't you like to read for other reasons? There're wonderful stories to read, places to learn about, just … so much." She raised her hands and spread them wide as if that was reason enough.

"I don't have time for that sort of thing." Rachelle snorted. "Mamere would tan my hide if she caught me sitting to read a book."

"What about letters?" Mariette said. "Wouldn't you like to write letters to your papa? I write to my papa every week."

"Yes … that would be nice," she said. "Sometimes Beatrice, the girl down the hall from us, writes a letter for me. When Papa sends a letter, Beatrice reads it to me."

"Then we shall start lessons immediately." Mariette smiled, her head bobbing with emphasis. "You and I will spend an hour every afternoon working on your reading and writing."

"Oh, no, thank you. I have work to finish. I can't possibly learn to read and write."

"It will become your work," Mariette said. "We have time for an afternoon walk, so we have time for reading and writing. Besides, you'll need to learn so you can help Clement with his studies next year."

The electric lights did little to dispel the darkness that filled the room. Increase had brought a dark, billowing cloud of rage home with him. Rachelle hurried to get the last of the dishes on the table so that she could go home. Mariette and David stared at their empty plates.

"Would you say the blessing, please?" Mariette asked Increase when the last serving bowl was presented and Rachelle had exited the dining room.

Increase bowed his head. "This food smells great. I'm happy to have good food." He lifted his head. "Pass the pork roast."

Mariette looked up in surprise, passed the roast, and handed a roll to David. "Did something happen at the hospital, Increase?"

"Nurse Hall cleaned with vinegar and lye," he grumbled.

The darkness that invaded the room settled over the table, a suffocating heaviness that engulfed its inhabitants.

"Clement and I had a sword fight today." David tried to pull his father toward the light.

"Good."

"Mama is going to teach Rachelle how to read and write. Then next year Clement and I can go to school together."

"I don't think you'll go to school together, David," Mariette said. "But you will be able to study together. You'll have a tutor. Right, Increase?"

"You're going to teach Rachelle to read and write?" Increase asked, surprise and pleasure beginning to roll up the darkness around them.

Mariette smiled. "Yes. Rachelle said she had to quit school when her mother died. That was when Clement was a baby. She only finished the second grade."

"That's an excellent idea. You could teach the other French-Canadian mill workers. Some barely speak English."

"No ... no," Mariette said. "I'm just going to help Rachelle; that's all. An hour in the afternoon, between her chores."

"That's a good start, but you should do more. You could go in the evenings to the church and work for a while with the young women, maybe the men."

"What? No! I will not," Mariette said. "I am not a-a-a ... teacher!"

"Then how will you teach Rachelle?" Increase smirked. "It would be good for you to get off your high horse and help others. I didn't know you were such a snob when I married you."

The words were out before he could stop them. Mariette winced and bit her lip. David stopped chewing and put his hands in his lap.

"I need a drink." Increase stood, causing the chair to tip over on the heavy wool carpet. He strode from the room into the parlor across the hall.

"Finish your dinner, David," Mariette mumbled as she shuffled the food around on her own plate.

Mariette settled David into a warm tub of water and then cleared the dinner table. The parlor was still dark when she entered.

"Increase?" Mariette turned on an electric lamp.

"Not now."

She struggled up the stairs, helped David dry off and change into his bedclothes, then tucked him in. She managed to read him one chapter of *The Jungle Book* before a growing headache forced her to her own bed.

*Some, through fear of death, prayed to die.*
*~Pliny the Younger~*

# CHAPTER 15

"HOW IS PATER TODAY?" I looked over my cinnamon tea at Casper.

"The same."

Casper was always a man of few words. He was cautious, thoughtful, and restrained. That was why I knew Pater was in a desperate state when I was sent for in Rome. Casper wouldn't call me lightly.

"Is he awake yet?"

"Yes."

I rose from the table by the eastern window and looked out across the valley below. The blue of the Aegean glittered in the distance. It would be another fair day.

"Pater," I called as I headed toward his room. "Pater, I'm going to Jehan's."

Pater turned his head toward the arch where I stood. He smiled and lifted a hand from the covers.

"That's good. You'll be a great doctor soon. My son …"

A tear slipped down his cheek and he licked his dry lips.

"What's wrong?" I walked to the bedside and held his hand.

"I dreamed last night that snakes came into my bedchamber. They came through the windows and doors."

"That's wonderful, Pater. A sign from Asclepius." *My prayer worked.*

"No." He shook his head slowly. "The snakes circled my bed and looked on me. Then, as one, they turned and left. They offered no healing. … I will die."

"No, Pater."

*He must be mistaken. Asclepius sent a vision—a vision after my prayer. Pater will be healed. We followed the plan, gave the sacrifice, offered the prayers.*

"Loukas, we all die. I evaded Thanatos in so many battles. I came home to you and your mother every time, but now he will come for me. It's decided. It's alright; he isn't coming today, not yet. You go to Jehan. I'll wait here."

I hugged him and kissed his onion-skin cheek. The whites of his eyes were beginning to yellow. The liver was affected. I kissed him again and left.

The sun shone bright and clear, the air fresh with the scent of spring. How did the world not feel my anguish and join in? Dark clouds of grief threatened to flood my heart, and hailstones of anger and fury pounded inside my head.

"Loukas!"

I turned around to see Jehan waving from the herb garden. I had stormed past his place without noticing. I shook my head like a wet dog and headed for the garden.

"I called you several times. You looked like a charging bull." The old man grinned and handed me a rake. "What's upset you?"

"The gods are evil." There, I had said it; it was too late to take it back now. "Evil," I repeated for good measure.

Jehan set his lips in a fine line and gave a firm nod. "Start weeding here by me."

We stooped to the ground and loosened the dark soil, pulling out the weeds that would choke the tender shoots. It was good medicine; Jehan was right. The anger loosened its hold as the soil turned over, then the pain and fear watered the plants.

"When you're ready," Jehan said, and he left.

I finished the row of verbena and then stood to stretch. A pail of water sat in the shade of the garden wall and I splashed my face. I carried the hand rake to the house and set it on the shelf with all of the tools. I could hear Jehan inside.

"Khaíre—Hello! Can I come in?" I stood at the door, looking into the welcoming hut.

Jehan turned from the table to look at me. "Yes, of course. I'm getting the bags ready for our visits." He turned back to the table of herbs and oils. "Are you feeling better?"

"Yes."

"Good. An angry doctor is seldom a helpful doctor. You must be peaceful around your patients to soothe and comfort them." He pulled the top of the bag tight. "Ready?"

I took the extra bag from Jehan and slung it over my back. Bees hummed over the flowers and bushes that were beginning to bloom. White clouds chased a hawk across the sky. The storm had passed.

"Why are we going back to Asyla?" I asked as we headed toward the mountain. "I thought you would wait a week."

"Would you wait a week?" Jehan raised his eyebrows.

"Well, no." The inflamed whip marks came to mind. "But you told—"

"The guard doesn't like me to fuss over the workers. If I tell him I will come back tomorrow, he'll deny me access, but if I tell him I thought of another remedy through the night for poor Albanus, well, then … He won't mind so much if I look in on the others as well."

"You're a crafty old man." I smiled.

"Gentle as a dove and wise as a serpent." Jehan chuckled.

The mention of serpents brought Pater's dream to mind. I slowed unconsciously and focused on the stone pavement.

"Sometimes, though, it is best to come right out with it." Jehan had stopped and was looking at me.

"Pater had a dream last night."

Jehan nodded and moved to the side of the road, setting his bag at his feet. We leaned against a poplar tree and looked at distant Pangaion. A cuckoo called from the bushes nearby.

"He dreamed that many snakes came to him in his bedchamber. I thought that was a good sign. After I left you last night, I stopped at the baths; I asked Asclepius to heal him. I gave him some money."

Jehan nodded to go on.

"But Pater …" I cleared my throat. "Pater says the snakes turned away without slipping into the bed. He won't be healed."

"Let me ask you something, Loukas. When you studied medicine in Rome …"

He paused and I looked over at him.

"Did the doctors suggest snakes as a remedy for phthisis?"

"No, of course not. But—"

"So would it not make sense that the serpents left your father alone last night?"

"But it was a vision from Asclepius. He … He …" I raised my hands to the sky, aghast. What could Jehan be thinking?

Jehan held both his hands up to stop me. "Could it be that another god, a stronger more powerful god, will offer healing?"

I began to understand. "I'm not a Jew, Jehan, and I don't plan to convert. Dionysus and Asclepius are my gods."

"So you won't look to the serpent." Jehan shook his head, and then lifted his bag and started for the road. "Come along."

"Back again?" It was the same guard.

"I'm going to try something different for Albanus. Thought about it last night."

"You're a good doctor, Jehan. So thorough and trustworthy."

He waved us on in and we passed without any trouble. The weather was the same as yesterday in the compound, dry and dusty. The sounds of the workers struggling with their heavy loads replaced the songbirds' chorus.

"I'll look in on Albanus; you go ahead and start on the real patients." Jehan waved to the guard of the workers' low huts.

The officer let me by and I checked on the sick patients first. They were faring well under the circumstances. I stayed in the last hut longer. The weeping wounds were still inflamed, but the plasters were doing their job. The oozing pus was noticeably decreased.

Jehan had evidently planned out our agenda and devised his scheme. My bag was filled with aloe, comfrey, and woad. Bandages were rolled tightly into the bottom of the pouch. Teas for fever and pain, as well as some opium, were nestled in between.

As I rewrapped a man's foot, he started hacking. Phthisis. *Will it never leave me alone?*

"How long have you been coughing like that?" I asked as I tied up the end of the bandages.

"Just since I've been here. The air in the tunnels is poisoned and foul."

I brought him some fresh water and felt for his temperature. There was fever, but that could be the infected foot. His skin, though, was sallow like phthisis.

"Sit up here. Let me listen to your lungs."

I cupped his chest and his back. The lungs were full, but it wasn't liquid. No signs of tumors either.

"When you cough, is there blood?"

"No, thick phlegm."

"I'll make you an expectorant. That should help." I pulled open the bag and started cutting and mixing a strong tea blend.

"How's it going?" Jehan walked in, stopping to inspect the first man's dressing. "Looks good."

"The plasters are working well. Think we can make it back tomorrow?" I asked as I shook down the tiny leaves into the linen pouch.

"Doubtful. I did too good a job with Albanus." He smirked. "What are you doing?"

"This man needs an expectorant. Actually …" I paused as several men joined in the wheezing and choking cough. "They all probably need it."

"Mm, yes." Jehan nodded. "It's miner's cough. Have you checked for kyanós?"

"Kyanós?" That was new to me. "Blue what?"

"Extremities. The less air they breathe, the bluer they get." He pulled the covers off one of the whipping victims. "Here. See his feet and hands?"

The wrinkled skin was bluish and cool to the touch.

"What can be done?" I asked.

"They need fresh air, but won't get it in the tunnels, plain and simple."

We finished instructing the men on using the expectorant and packed up the medical bags. I remembered the oath I had taken as a medical student, to do no harm. Didn't that mean helping these men?

Several officers were standing in the unloading area as we passed. I stopped to talk with them.

"Khaírete—Hello! I'm Loukas, one of the doctors. You have some very sick men here."

"Not plague, is it?" The tall officer's eyes grew big with fear. "I've seen enough of that."

"No, no. They're suffocating from the dust. They need fresh air. They need to have shorter shifts in the mines."

I noticed a small group of Roman officers joining us.

"We can't do that. Next thing you know, they'll be wanting days off and larger rations. They're criminals, slaves. They work for the empire." The officer speaking pulled himself up straight. "Aren't you Aegeus's son? … How do you think he got paid? Gold, boy. That's what's important."

"But if you keep mining at this rate, soon there won't be any workers able to do the mining. Then what will the emperor say?"

"Oh, go on. We never had any problems from Jehan. He's a good doctor."

"He's from Gaul." A woman's voice rose above the gathering crowd.

I looked around to see Ludia break out of the smaller group.

"Jehan's from Gaul," she repeated. "Loukas here, he studied in Rome. He should know what's best."

I picked up on Ludia's scheme. "In Rome we would—"

"I don't care where you studied. They're here to work, and work they will. Now get on with you." He stepped forward.

Jehan and I walked on toward the gate with Ludia close on our heels. I knew you could only push a Roman soldier so far, and I had teetered close to the edge.

"Sorry, Jehan," Ludia said. "I know you're a wonderful doctor. Just thought it might help some of the slaves. It makes me sick to go in there." She stomped down the hill beside us.

"I know," Jehan said. "It was worth a try." He looked sideways at me. "Remember, Loukas, an angry doctor is seldom a helpful doctor. You alright?"

I was breathing hard and my hands were shaking. I didn't want to get Pater into trouble. I hadn't thought it would be such a problem.

"Why are they so cruel to them? Romans shouldn't act that way. It isn't like that in Rome."

"Hmph." Jehan snorted. "You just weren't aware. There are people suffering all over the empire."

"So if your god is so powerful, why doesn't he do something about it?"

"He did." Jehan smiled and Ludia laughed. "He made you."

*Because in the school of the Spirit man learns wisdom through humility,*
*knowledge by forgetting, how to speak by silence, how to live by dying.*
~Johannes Tauler~

# CHAPTER 16

PANDEMONIUM RACED DOWN THE STAIRS and greeted Increase in the pale dawn. A few stray snowflakes landed on his shoulder, oblivious to the warmth of the hospital that would soon be their demise. The smell of disease reached his nostrils at the front desk, and he looked around.

"What's going on?" he asked Nurse Lindelof. "Where did all these people come from?"

"Train derailment over near Nashua," she said. "They phoned the hospital an hour ago and said they were on the way. There were too many people for Dr. Manning to take care of."

"Why didn't you call me? The phone is there for you to use! Who needs attention first?"

"Oh, there aren't any serious, not like that."

"Don't you smell that?" He nodded toward a family sitting beside the desk. "Bread. Don't you smell it?"

"I suppose." Nurse Lindelof shrugged.

"Typhoid. They have typhoid." Increase marched to the first chair on the wall and called with gusto. "Everyone be quiet. Is anyone hurt? A broken bone, a wound, or injury?"

A young mother raised her hand. "My son. He was knocked aside in the car. My trunk fell on him. His arm is hurt bad."

The boy slept in her lap, resting his head on her chest. His brow furrowed in pain.

Increase crossed the room, scooped the boy into his arms, and told the mother to follow him. As he headed to the surgery, he hissed, "Take their temperatures, Nurse. Quarantine the fevered. Anyone who smells of bread put in one room together. Don't let anyone leave."

The boy was four years old, a scrawny thing who lacked good nutrition. His clothes were thin and worn, but he appeared to be clean and healthy. There was no yeasty odor clinging to him.

The arm was only dislocated. Thankfully the boy was asleep; it was always easier that way. Increase grabbed the dislocated bone and deftly popped it back into place. The child wasn't asleep now. His mother consoled him as Increase set a sling to let the arm rest and the swelling go down.

"He'll be fine. Where were you headed before the derailment?"

The woman never looked at Increase, just held the boy close to her, rocking and swaying to keep him calm. Over the boy's head the woman replied, "We were headed to New Bedford. We left Manchester last evening and hoped to get to New Bedford today. I have a job there."

"But what about the boy? Where is his father?"

"He was killed last year in an accident. He worked in the mills in Manchester. They were going to take Richard away and put him in the Manchester Children's Home. I heard the housing in New Bedford is clean and safe. I thought we'd be better off there."

The child slept again, now whimpering in a bad dream.

"Who will keep Richard while you work?" Increase thought of David and how much he had relied on Lively, and now Mariette, to care for his son.

"He's a good boy. He can take care of himself while I'm at work. It will be alright, but if I don't get there soon, they'll give away my spot." Now she looked at the doctor, fear glistening in her wide eyes.

"No worry. He can travel. The arm will heal in a few weeks. Keep it in the sling for two weeks, then wean him off it a little at a time. Good luck."

"God bless you, Doctor."

"Yes, well, thank you."

Increase walked the woman out. She struggled under the dead weight of the boy in her arms. Increase opened the front door for her and took a deep breath of the cold air before turning.

"Nurse Lindelof, has Nurse Hall come in yet?"

"No, sir. She went to the mill houses. There was an outbreak of diphtheria at one of Hoop's houses on Beech Street."

"Have you managed to separate the patients yet?" Increase growled as he tripped over a carpet bag.

"Mostly, Dr. Graves. There were five with fevers and a yeasty odor. I put them in the extra patient room. There weren't seats for them all, though." She pulled a thermometer out of an old man's mouth, appraised it, and then shook it down. "This one's clear. There's one with an infected ulcer on his leg. I put him in bed. I'll get him cleaned up soon."

"Good. I'll start on the others." Increase squared his shoulders and turned to the sick room. At the door he paused. This was the part of doctoring he disliked. He had to help these people, perhaps stop an epidemic. But it meant that he might infect himself. Then what would happen to David?

The unused room was chilly. Yesterday's fire hadn't been stoked, and the smell of ash and smoke mixed with the stench of unwashed flesh. Increase pulled the window shade and a flood of light streamed across the wooden floor. The fevered patients never moved.

A young man's coughing fit propelled Increase to his side. Nurse Lindelof had written the patient's temperature on a paper and attached it to his shirt—103. Increase had seen worse; perhaps this wouldn't be a bad case.

Increase treated all five with quinine and then returned to the main room. Nurse Hall was back; she and Nurse Lindelof had cleared the area. Only the leg ulcer remained.

"I cleaned the ulcer with iodine, Dr. Graves, and put a clean bandage on it. He says a ram took him down last year and he's had the ulcer since."

"Thank you, Nurse. I'll take a look."

There would be no lunch at home with David today. It looked like business was picking up at the small hospital. Increase wasn't sure if that was good or bad.

A foretaste of spring wind licked at the edge of winter. The stress of treating typhoid patients and the knowledge that a woman would be required to neglect her injured son fluttered in the breeze and lifted from Increase's shoulders. *Fresh air and sunshine are the best medicine.* Increase breathed deeply as he picked up the pace to Beech Street.

A group of little girls skipped rope in the wet road. Their laughter brightened the muddy dullness of the gray row houses. A crippled man cleaned the high windows at the south end of the row house. The rickety ladder he used looked no more whole than the man, but he seemed satisfied to swipe at the dirty panes with a tattered rag. A bucket of water balanced precariously over the side of the ladder.

Increase waved to the man as he pushed open the side door to the house. Stale, stagnant air struck him. The carefree walk was over; reality took its place.

This house was different than Rose's. It opened to a large room of chairs and tables. Increase could see the bottom of the ladder outside through the large windows that flooded the common room with light. A woman snored at one of the tables.

Increase cleared his throat and the woman startled awake. She brushed her hair back and stood in one movement. The chair fell behind her.

She jumped, turned, and righted the chair, then said, "I'm sorry, sir. I weren't 'specting no one. They's all left back to the mills."

"I'm Dr. Graves." Increase thought it best to get straight to the point. "The nurse said there's diphtheria in the house. I'd like to see the patients."

"Sure, of course. It's the little ones what's spreadin' it t'each other'n. Down the hall here … Doctor? Graves, did you say?"

"Thank you. Yes."

"Hmm. That don't sound good for a doctor, now does it?" The woman chortled and showed a mouth of crooked, rotten teeth.

Increase didn't respond, and she stopped laughing. She took him to the kitchen and opened the cellar door. "They's all down there. I 'spect you'll find 'em just fine. Six children with the diphtheria and their mama."

The stair was lit with oil lamps at each end. Black soot marred the wall above each glass globe. Increase descended, holding the rail in his left hand and his medical bag in his right. The stairs creaked and groaned under his weight.

At the bottom of the stairs, the cellar storehouse kept preserved foods cool on wooden shelves attached to the wall. An electric light hung on his left from a wire in the ceiling. The smell of damp earth mixed with the odor of moldering potatoes and turnips; the last of fall's harvest lay in the wooden stalls on his right. He knocked over a tin bucket as he walked toward the back of the dank room.

Four small rooms had been fashioned out of the rest of the cellar. A door stood ajar to the first room and Increase peeked in. An old rope bed stood in the center draped with a grimy quilt. Two hooks on the wall held an old work shirt and a long nightgown. Increase stepped back and knocked on the next door.

It opened a crack and a small woman peered out.

"I'm Dr. Graves. I came to look at the children."

She opened the door wider to let him in and stepped aside. Two beds took up the room. Four children slept together crosswise on one of the beds. They snuggled together like a litter of forsaken kittens, their necks so swollen that their breathing came in quick gasps. The smallest one was wheezing.

Increase walked around the bed to set his bag on the other feather tick. An unhappy mewling came from under the bed. Increase looked down to see a makeshift pallet on the floor. Two tiny children clung to each other, their bodies wrapped in a woolen shawl.

"What do you use for heat?" Increase asked the mother. "The children need to be kept warm and dry."

"The keeper of the house warms bricks for us at night. We put 'em in the beds under the covers. They's warm enough. They snuggle together and keeps warm. But I'm scared, Doctor. Jeannie don't sound right. She been whistling like a teapot for two days now."

"Jeannie is the little one?"

The mother nodded as she stared at the shivering child. "I gave 'em all some broth from up the kitchen, but Jeannie choked and sputtered till I couldn't bear to give 'er no more."

Increase took the child's pulse. It was as faint as her breathing. "She needs to be in the hospital," Increase said. "She's close to needing a tracheostomy tube."

The woman shook her head. "We can't 'ford the hospital. My husband's got to pay the rent here and the food bill is comin' up."

"Where is your husband?"

"He works at Lytle Mills. He'll be home for dinner soon."

"Ma'am, Jeannie needs to go to the hospital or she's …" Increase looked at the mother, unwilling to finish in the presence of all the children. "You can pay the bill as you get the money. We can work something out with the mill."

Tears slid down her face as she just shook her head. "Jeannie's goin' to be fine. We just got to pray harder, that's all."

Increase blew out his lungs and rubbed the back of his neck. "Prayer isn't enough. Jeannie needs real help right now."

"Can't you do it here?" The mother looked from the bony bundle on the bed to the doctor. "Please? We can't 'ford the hospital," she repeated.

"Let me get the nurse. I'll be right back."

Increase hurried into the dark cellar and took the stairs two at a time.

The creaky door bumped into the mistress at the top of the stairs.

"Watch out, now!" she scolded. "Oh, Doctor, it's you. Well, how're the babies?"

"Freezing and wretched. How can you let them live down there?"

She stepped back and wiped her hands on the front of her dress.

"Never mind," Increase said. "I have to get the nurse. I'll be back in a few minutes."

He let himself out the side door and nearly crashed into the crippled man on the ladder. Increase grabbed the side and steadied it as the bucket sloshed water over the edge. "Sorry," he called as he hurried off.

"Dr. Graves!" Jean Giatros's voice rang out. "Wait."

Increase looked across the street to see Jean standing near an old woman. He handed off a covered basket and patted her shoulder, then trotted over to meet Increase.

"You look like a rabbit on the run. What's going on?" Jean asked as he paced himself with Increase's long gait.

"Diphtheria. A whole family of little ones has it. One needs to be in the hospital, but the mother won't allow it. The girl nearly needs a tracheostomy." Increase kept his focus straight ahead, talking and quick-walking like he used to do at St. Patrick's Memorial. "I'll have to get Nurse Hall to come help. The hospital is full, but she'll just have to come."

"I can help if you like." Jean's unassuming voice took a moment to register in Increase's mind.

"Can you? I mean, have you done that before?" Increase stopped walking to study the man at his side.

"I have given breath to many people over the years." Jean stopped walking and smiled.

"Come on, then." He turned on his heel and started the fast pace back to the house. "They're staying in the basement of that … that … home."

Increase turned the knob on the door and threw it open in his haste. The housekeeper was setting large pots of soup on the tables in the main room.

"Well, you're back awfully fast. He ain't your nurse, though." She motioned toward Jean with her head while she set the heavy pot down. The smell of cabbage-and-onion stew turned Increase's stomach.

"Doctor Giatros is going to assist me," Increase replied. "I'll find the stairs on my own," he added as the two men crossed the large common room toward the back of the house.

The lamps threw black shadows on the wall as the men hurried down the creaky wooden stairs. Increase felt like he was descending the last steps into utter darkness. Surely death was already taking up residence.

"This way," he said, trying to sound in control of the situation.

Jean followed him to the end of the room where the small apartments stood like prison cells in a dungeon. The door to the woman's hovel opened and she stood there, silent and resigned. She stood aside for Increase, but stepped forward when she recognized Jean.

"Where's the nurse?" she asked, looking straight at Increase.

"I met Dr. Giatros on the street. He'll help me with the procedure. We need to move Jeannie to the other bed."

"No."

"It will be better if the other children aren't in bed with her—" Increase started to explain.

"No. That man can't touch my Jeannie. He's one of those bay pigs."

Increase's mouth fell open as he looked from the mother to Jean and then back again.

"I can help Dr. Graves," Jean said gently. "Jeannie needs to breathe. Her neck has swollen with the diphtheria and air can't get in her lungs. You can hear how difficult it is."

The little girl's wheezing sounded like accordion bellows.

"No," the mother insisted. "Bay pigs is filthy. You'll infect m' little girl."

Increase couldn't believe the woman would accuse Jean of improper hygiene standing in a room that smelled of dirt and mildew. The children were covered in phlegm and snot. They certainly had lice, and fleas were probable. Jean was a blanket of fresh snow in this pit of a home.

"Then I won't touch her," Jean said. He remained calm. "Would it be okay if I hand things to Dr. Graves?" His smile was tender and patient.

The woman nodded slightly, almost imperceptibly, as she looked into the gentleman's face. "That'd be okay."

"Good," Increase said as he picked up the child and moved her to the other bed.

Jean moved between the two beds to block the other children's view while Increase opened his medical bag.

The entire procedure took less than five minutes, but Increase had broken a sweat by the end of it. The two tiny children on the floor continued their mewling cries while their mother sat on the bed with the rest of the litter and sang. Increase's stomach was churning from the smell of antiseptic, mixing with the filth, the dampness and decay, and the hint of cabbage-and-onion stew that drifted down the stairs.

*Why did I ever leave Boston?*

Increase walked the streets in a daze, not caring where he was headed. Jean was at his side, quiet and attentive.

"How can they live like that? How does the city get away with it? There are rules … laws. People shouldn't live that way in today's world. And you. You were so calm. I would have stormed out of there. She shouldn't have called you that."

Jean shrugged. "People see what they want to see. But in the end love won; she couldn't let little Jeannie go on like that. That's what matters. Sometimes, though, people are too stubborn to give in to love." He looked at Increase, watchful and intent.

"I need more help. The town is growing. Two nurses won't be enough. If I can't get the Public Health Department to do anything, maybe I can get the hospital board to approve something."

"What're you thinking?"

Increase stopped walking to stare at a tree. Tiny, fuzzy buds had popped out at the edges of each branch, a promise of something better to come. "I don't know. I don't have time to train another nurse, but if things don't change soon, diphtheria outbreaks are going to be the least of our problems."

"What about a school?" Jean asked.

"A school?"

"To train nurses. Instead of just training one nurse, you could train several at a time. Then the hospital would be staffed as well as having nurses for traveling to the homes."

"A nursing school. Hmm … Do you think the board will go for it?"

"A cord of three strands is not easily broken," Jean replied. "Having help is always a good idea." He smiled at Increase. "Is it not true at home? Are you not better off now with your new wife to help you and David?"

Increase turned from the tree, glanced at Jean, then started walking toward the hospital. He needed to call Mr. Neal about the possibility of a nursing school. He would think about Mariette later. Jean trotted at his side.

"I'm stopping here." Jean pulled up short, interrupting Increase's thoughts. "Have a good day."

Increase tipped his hat as Jean walked up to another of the long row houses. "Thanks for the help. I'll see you around."

"You're welcome," Jean said as he walked up the slab stairs and opened the door.

*The art of living well and the art of dying well are one.*
~Epicurus~

# CHAPTER 17

MARIETTE HAD LEARNED IN FRANCE that keeping busy would lessen the feelings of homesickness and loneliness. Now in Dunstable Plains she decided to do the same. A meeting at the public library had been advertised in the grocer's window, and she decided to attend. Now she was fearing it had been a mistake.

"Mrs. Graves, I want you to meet Mrs. Hoop," Mrs. Sheppard said, an older woman clinging to her arm. Both greeted Mariette with plastered smiles. "Mrs. Graves is the new doctor's wife." She spoke to Mrs. Hoop, but continued looking at Mariette with hawkish eyes.

"Nice to meet you," Mariette said, offering her hand to Mrs. Hoop. The hand that touched hers was limp and cold. Mariette had been acquainted with better fish. "I'm excited to be a part of planning for the library."

"Mrs. Graves," Mrs. Hoop said and nodded. It sounded like an insult. "Yes, it's a shame your husband couldn't be here," she said in a nasal voice drenched with disdain.

She let go of Mariette and wiped her hands against each other, apparently removing some disgusting filth that only she could see. Mariette had met that kind at school. It was best to say the niceties and move on. But Mrs. Hoop moved closer to Mariette, blocking her hole of escape. The rabbit was trapped.

"I hear your husband has ideas … plans, you may say … for our community," Mrs. Hoop said.

"We both look forward to helping make Dunstable Plains a thriving, pleasant place to live," Mariette said, smiling but guarding herself against the hawk's sharp beak that surely was searching for a spot to tear into.

"Yes, Dunstable Plains is a thriving community, and I dare say, a very pleasant place to live," Mrs. Hoop said. "But we have traditions here, ways that things are done. We take good care of our workers and they don't complain. Everyone is happy here."

"I'm glad to hear it," Mariette said.

She looked over Mrs. Hoop's shoulder and waved as if she saw a friend. The older woman's talons dug deeper.

"Mrs. Sheppard tells me you were at St. Anne's on Sunday. I'm so happy to hear that she won't have to sit alone at the Catholic church anymore. It must be so dreadful to be the only people of society in a church of … foreigners."

"Not as dreadful as one might think," Mariette said. "Remember our Lord was a foreigner while here on earth. S'il vous plaît excusez-moi."

Mariette darted around the two women before they knew what was happening. The captor's sharp grip was lost.

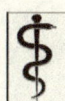

The smell of coffee shook Mariette awake. The place next to her was empty and cold. *Increase must have left early for the hospital.* She rose and slid her feet into house shoes. Her robe was warming over a chair near the fireplace. Mariette wrapped it around her as she walked into the hallway. David's bedroom door was ajar. He still slept under the heavy quilt. *Leave him for now. I need some coffee.*

Rachelle's soprano sang a familiar tune, humming part of the words. Mariette pushed open the kitchen door and greeted the young woman. "Good morning, Rachelle. The coffee smells wonderful." She walked over to the stove and inhaled.

"Oh, good morning. You startled me." Rachelle giggled and went back to the pot she was stirring on the stove. "The oatmeal will be ready soon. Would you like me to pour you a cup of coffee?"

"No, thanks. I can get it myself. How is your mamere this morning?"

"About the same. She got up for a few hours yesterday, but Clement said she coughed the entire time. He's learning to take care of her."

"It's good that you have each other. Life is better when you share it with someone." Mariette picked up the hot coffeepot and poured from it into a cup on the counter. She added cream and sugar and then sat at the kitchen table. "You don't mind if I drink it in here, do you? Dr. Graves is already gone and I don't feel like being alone."

"Of course. You don't bother me any. And you're right: it is better to have someone. Some people are far away from their loved ones." Rachelle kept stirring the oats.

Mariette sipped her coffee and let the cup warm her hands. "I know. When I was in France, I had my grandparents, but I missed Papa so very, very much. At least here I get letters more often."

Rachelle opened the oven and slid in a loaf of bread that had risen overnight. "Would you like an egg with your oatmeal, Mrs. Graves?"

Mariette smiled. How different "Mrs. Graves" sounded from Rachelle's lips than from Mrs. Hoop's. "Rachelle, I think we are going to need to be friends. Please, call me Mariette."

"I'm glad to hear you say that … Mariette." Rachelle walked to the icebox. "Now, do you want your egg fried or scrambled?"

"I don't want an egg, thank you. Oatmeal will be enough." She sipped some more of the coffee. "If your mamere sleeps in the afternoon, Clement should come here to play with David. That will keep David occupied while we work on your reading lessons."

"He'd like that," Rachelle said. "There aren't many boys for him to play with. A few go to school, but so many are already at work. Most of the kids left in the neighborhood are girls. Clement doesn't want to play with them." Rachelle smiled. "I'll stop and ask him to come over when I go out to the store."

A gentle rapping on the front door pulled Mariette from her needle-work. Rachelle wasn't back yet from the store. Mariette went to the door.

"Yes?" she asked as she opened to a middle-aged man in a worn coat and trousers.

"Are you Mrs. Graves?" the man asked, his voice deep and booming.

"Yes."

"Rachelle said I should come talk to you." His loud voice echoed off the porch floor and wall.

"I'm sorry. About what?" Mariette had no idea why this man was at her front door.

"Rachelle said if I come over on my lunch hour, you might write me a letter."

The man wrung his hands and then slipped them deep into his pockets. He looked harmless, but his voice!

"What kind of a letter?" Mariette opened the door a little wider.

The man blushed deep red. He looked out at the street and then back at Mariette. "I want to write to a lady friend back home."

"Well, what do you need me for?"

The man looked at his feet and then back out to the street.

"Can you not write?" Mariette guessed at his discomfort. "Do you need someone to write it for you?"

"Oui." The man looked relieved. "Could you do that? I can pay you, ma'am."

"Can't someone else write it for you? Someone from the mill, per-haps?"

"Well, I suppose someone could, but … you see, well, it's a lady friend. See?"

"You don't want the mill workers to know. Is that it?" Mariette smiled.

The man nodded and smiled back. "Rachelle said maybe you could write for me. I can pay you," he said again.

"I couldn't take your money. It would burnish the love. Come in, Mr. …?"

"Mr. Viollette. Frank Viollette. Thank you, ma'am." He stepped across the threshold and wiped his feet on the rug. "I'm sorry, ma'am." His deep baritone reverberated in the small foyer.

"Come in here," Mariette said as she led the way to the parlor.

Mr. Viollette stayed planted in the foyer. Mariette looked over her shoulder to see him still standing there. She smiled and motioned for him to follow.

"Come on."

He blushed and followed her into the parlor. She crossed the room to the writing desk that sat near the front window. "Have a seat," she said, motioning toward a cushioned chair.

"Oh, no, ma'am. I'd get it dirty for sure. I'll just stand if you don't mind."

"Suit yourself," she said as she riffled through the desk for paper and a pen.

"What's that?" The man bent down a little and tried looking at Mari-ette's face. "I don't hear so good. The mills took my hearing."

"I said, suit yourself. But maybe you'd better sit." Mariette looked around and eyed a hard chair in the corner. "Why don't you bring that chair over to the desk?"

Mariette soon learned that Frank Viollette was a kind man. He and Ethel had been courting back in Quebec. He came to Dunstable Plains looking for work in the mills, hoping he could get enough money to bring Ethel one day as his wife. The letter he dictated to Mariette was sincere and heartfelt. He spoke of his work and the people he met at the mill. He told her he was saving some money, but that rent took a fair amount of his pay. He was being careful, though, and soon he might get a promotion. He was watching the mechanics; maybe someday he could fix some of the machinery. He ended the letter with words of endearment that brought tears to Mariette's eyes.

"I hope that's okay to say, ma'am." Frank looked at Mariette, a twinkle in his eye. He twisted the edge of his collar. "You see why I can't ask no one at the mill to write for me. Plus not many can write in French."

Rachelle walked into the room. "Lunch is ready, Mariette. Oh ... Frank, I didn't get to talk to Mrs. Graves yet."

"It's alright, Rachelle," Mariette said. "Mr. Viollette and I worked everything out. You better fix a sandwich for him or he'll be late back to work, though." She folded the paper and handed it to the man. "Please come again whenever you want another letter written."

"What'd you do today?" Increase asked David at the dinner table. "Did you build anymore mills or are you planning to build baseball stadiums now?"

"Clement came to play while Mama taught Rachelle her words. Clement likes to play stickball." David wiped his mouth with the back of his hand. "I like it too."

"Use your napkin, David," Mariette said. "How was your day, Increase? You were gone early this morning." She lifted a fork to her mouth, never taking her eyes off her plate.

"Earnest came in early for a checkup. His eye socket has healed and I can place a glass eye in it soon. He's back at work at the mill."

"That's good."

"I suppose. ... He's worried that something else will happen and he'll lose the good eye. There's danger in everything, but I think he has a point. I'd be nervous about going back."

Mariette took a long sip of water, peering at Increase over her glass. "I didn't get to tell you about my evening at the library last night," she said, placing the glass back in its spot.

"How was it?" Increase asked before spearing a forkful of carrots. "Did you meet anyone?"

He chewed and reached for another roll. The conversation bored him. He knew Mariette was lonely, but hobnobbing with the elite of Dunstable Plains didn't interest him.

"Mrs. Sheppard was there. You remember, from church?"

"Yes." Increase buttered his roll.

"She wanted to introduce me to Mrs. Hoop. Her husband owns Hoop Mills." Mariette paused for effect. "She wanted to welcome me to town."

"That was nice of her," Increase said through a bite of bread.

"Yes. But I think she was more interested in meeting you." Mariette watched her husband for a sign that he knew what was going on.

Increase looked up at his wife. "Me? Then she should come over to the hospital. Did she seem ill?"

"Ill? Perhaps." Mariette glanced at David.

Increase looked at his little boy licking jelly off the side of his hand. Increase nodded and went on eating.

A knock at the front door made everyone look up.

"I wonder who that could be?" Increase said as he scraped his chair back on the carpet.

Mariette wiped her mouth on the cloth napkin and started to stand.

"Stay. I'll get it," Increase said.

Mariette heard Increase open the door and then step out on the porch. A minute later he came back in with a small parcel.

"Who was it, Daddy?" David had jelly on his mouth and nose now.

"Wipe your face, David," Mariette said. "Well, who was it and what did they bring?"

"It was a Mr. Viollette," Increase said, looking directly at Mariette. "He said you helped him today and he wanted to bring you a gift."

Mariette turned pink and bit her lower lip. "He needed someone to write a letter back home. Rachelle knows him and told him to ask me. I … I thought it would be okay."

Increase smiled. "He seemed very appreciative. He wanted to give you something for your trouble." He walked to her at the end of the table and kissed her cheek. "Your apples, m'lady."

Mariette looked up at Increase, her eyes crinkled in pleasure. "So you don't mind that I had a man in the house? I was afraid you would get upset, but he seemed genuine. The letter was to a lady friend."

Increase laughed. "No, I don't mind. I'm glad you were able to help him." He sat back at his place and picked up his bread. "Pass the jelly, please, David. It looks too good to pass up."

David was nestled in bed and the upstairs lights turned out. The low fire glowed in the parlor. Increase was reading the Boston paper from last week, an unfinished glass of brandy on the table next to him.

"I see you're relaxed tonight," Mariette said as she entered the room. "I'm sorry I missed you last evening." She sat in the chair opposite him.

Increase put the paper in his lap. "So what got to you at the meeting last night?"

Mariette grimaced and looked into the fire. "It was like being back in school with the girls letting you know who has the upper hand." She sighed. "Mrs. Hoop seems to think you're causing trouble for the mills." Mariette looked across at Increase. "Have you done something?"

"I suppose my actions could be upsetting, but if the owners would look at the big picture, they would see that taking care of their workers will make their businesses stronger." Increase folded the paper and placed it on the table.

"What do you mean?"

"The problems I see—the health problems, I mean—are accidents that are senseless and diseases that could be prevented. Take Earnest for instance," Increase said as he shifted in his chair. "The belt that broke and took out his eye hadn't been replaced. It was weak and overworked. It was a senseless accident that cost a man dearly. The most important thing is keeping your workers safe. Safe workers are good workers. They stay longer, understand their work, enjoy their jobs. How could that be bad for the mill?"

"But why would Mrs. Hoop be upset with you?"

"I visited the mills … Hoop, Sheppard, and Lytle … in order to talk with the owners. They didn't seem too receptive." Increase snorted and picked up his glass. "The working conditions are dreadful. It's a wonder anyone comes here for a job. I met a woman from the train derailment that was headed to New Bedford. She was leaving Manchester because of the working conditions. She had no plans to come here either." He sipped the brandy, feeling the warmth spread into his chest. A small log popped in the fire and a spray of sparks floated up the chimney.

"What changes did you suggest? Mrs. Hoop seemed quite upset." Mariette leaned forward, waiting. She had combed her hair out while David changed for bed, and now the long, black waves framed her pale face.

Increase took another sip, then placed the glass on top of the paper. "Well, I didn't get to suggest anything to the owners. They were very intent on showing me how happy their workers are. Probably what she meant is that I spoke to the Public Health Department. The workers' living conditions are deplorable. I suggested that Public Health intervene and make the owners fix the housing issues."

Mariette nodded. "That's probably it. She made a comment about the 'foreigners,'" Mariette said, wrinkling her nose. She shrugged her shoulders and looked back at the fire.

"And what did you say?" Increase tipped his head and looked at his wife. A smile played at the edge of his lips.

"I just reminded her that our Lord was a foreigner at one time. I might have thrown in a little French." She clasped her hands in her lap.

Increase burst out laughing. "Good for you! I like it when you fight back."

"It's good to hear you laugh. I've missed it," Mariette said. She looked down at her hands and twisted the ring on her left hand. "It's been a long time since we sat and talked into the night."

"Yes, it has," Increase said.

*Character cannot be developed in ease and quiet. Only through*
*experience of trial and suffering can the soul be strengthened,*
*ambition inspired, and success achieved.*
~Helen Keller~

# CHAPTER 18

JEHAN AND I FINISHED HOUSE visits and headed home. The swallows were chasing insects above the busy town. We walked down the road into the labyrinth of houses. *Philippi has really grown since I was a little boy.*

I shaded my eyes as we approached the house. A Roman officer was coming out the door in a hurry. He looked both ways and headed down the street away from us.

"Look. That must be one of Pater's friends come for a visit. That'll cheer him up."

"Yes," Jehan said. "So often patients become weaker when they lose contact with the world. The suffering becomes even more severe. It takes tremendous fortitude to stay in touch."

I opened the door and invited Jehan in.

"Would you like to come in, stay in touch?" I chuckled.

"I'll come by tomorrow and check on him. The day is getting late." Jehan looked to the sky. "Get some rest. You did well today."

I waved as Jehan went on down the street, then turned up the hill to his house. The medicine bags swung side to side on his back, crumpled and nearly empty.

I grabbed a handful of raisins from the kitchen and walked back to Pater's room.

"How're you doing? Have a good day?" I popped the raisins in my mouth and chewed.

Pater stared at me, glowering like a minotaur. "I had a visitor."

I nodded. "I saw him leaving as I came up the street. Is he an old friend?"

"No. He was sent by the centurion at Asyla. Said you were causing trouble today."

I drew back. "You're kidding. I helped heal their workers, and tried to keep more from getting sick." My voice raised. "What did he say?"

"Just that I should warn you to keep out of official business. You probably shouldn't go there with Jehan anymore." He sighed deeply and a coughing fit took his breath.

I sat on the bed and rubbed his legs. He had so little energy now; he wasn't getting up enough to keep the blood moving. The muscles were beginning to atrophy.

"I'm sorry, Pater," I said. "I didn't mean to get you in trouble. I'll be more careful. Jehan has plenty of patients I can see without going to Asyla. Soon I'll have my own patients."

Pater smiled. "My son, the doctor."

His eyes closed and his breathing mixed with the evening breeze coming in the window. I curled up at his feet and stayed there all night.

"Doctor Jehan is waiting for you," Casper said as I finished my morning meal.

"Me? Where is he?" *I thought he was coming to see Pater.*

"He checked on Aegeus while you were washing. He said he'd wait for you in the courtyard."

I downed the last of the kefir with a handful of almonds and headed to the little walled garden we shared with the neighbors. A fog had crept in overnight and was just lifting, the sunbeams casting a glow over the little quince tree.

"Hypíaine—Good morning!" I said. "How are you today?"

Jehan was seated on the stone bench by the wall. He stood and walked toward me.

"Your father said there was some trouble yesterday."

"A little. Not much. I don't think I better go with you to Asyla anymore, though. You'll have to complete your subterfuge without me." I winked.

"I'll stay away for a while myself. Just in case." He handed me a full medical bag. "Today we go to the marsh."

We walked out the garden gate together.

"The marsh?"

The marsh was a swampy area on the way to Neapolis near the sea. We used to play there as kids, hiding in the tall grasses and hunting frogs. Maybe we were collecting some plants there today.

"Mm-hm. There's a group of farmers, moved in a couple years ago. They drained part of it and are trying to grow barley."

"So why are we visiting them? Is something wrong?"

"They should be starting to have some trouble. Worms."

Jehan was such a talker.

"Using tansy and pomegranate?"

"Wrong worms. Last year, after they had been in the marsh nearly a year, they suffered from dracunculiasis. I treated them, but now it's time to check back." Jehan hitched up the bag on his back and kept walking.

"I haven't worked with that." I tried to imagine what this dragon worm might be.

"You'll need an iron resolve," he said. "It's a painful process. Can take up to a week for just one worm."

"How do you pass it … that long?" I tried to imagine.

Jehan chortled, then explained. "The old folks call it 'the fiery serpent.' The worm forms a blister on the skin, usually the feet and legs, and then eats its way out of the skin when it's ready to lay eggs. You have to pull it out, but carefully. You don't want to break it."

"You put camphor on it?" I tried to imagine what I was heading into.

Jehan nodded. "Camphor is good once it's out. The main thing is to keep the patients from putting it back in the water."

"They put it … back?" I was stunned.

Jehan threw his head back and laughed. "No, Loukas." He wiped his eyes and snorted. "It burns like fire. They put the affected limb in the water … to cool it down. When it hits the water, the worm lays its eggs and keeps on coming out." He chuckled again and said to himself, "They put it back."

I was quiet the rest of the way to the marsh.

"Doctor Jehan is here."

The cry went out as soon as we entered the clearing. Cypress trees had been cleared for the gardens and a large barley field stood where I remembered the marsh reaching when I was younger. A small village stood on an elevated area to the east.

"You came." An old man, likely the head of the village, kissed Jehan.

"Of course I came." Jehan returned the kiss and clasped his hand. "How are you?"

"I'm fine. It's the children who suffer. Come."

I followed behind, not sure what I would find. We went into a low stone hut chinked with marsh grasses. A blackbird called from the thatched roof.

The room was filled with sniffling and moaning children. Mothers wiped their faces and whispered soothing words, but worry lined their faces.

"It's Doctor Jehan," I heard them whisper.

The children wiped their eyes and noses and tried to sit up.

"So you've felt the dragon's fire." Jehan sat on one of the infirmary beds. "Let's have a look."

He lifted the child's foot and I saw a three-inch long, slender worm wiggling as if checking the soil for safe escape. Jehan pulled the knapsack from his back and dug through it. He pulled out a small twig, polished smooth and soft as willow.

"You've put it in the water already?" Jehan asked.

The mother nodded firmly and lifted a nearby pail.

"Good. You didn't dump it near the drinking well?" Jehan looked intently at the woman.

She shook her head. "No, Doctor Jehan. We poured it out on the road like you said."

"Good." He turned back to the child. "Now let's catch that fiery dragon."

He wrapped the worm around the twig and turned it slowly, pulling gently as the worm wiggled and wriggled out of the child's foot. Tears poured down his cheeks, but he didn't make a sound.

"You're very brave," Jehan said. "You would put a Roman soldier to shame." Then he turned to me. "Loukas, when the worm appears, put it in a bucket of cool water. Then slowly wrap the worm around the twig. I put a bundle of them in your bag." He paused while I shuffled through the bag. "If you can get it all of the way out, apply the camphor. There's some catnip in your bag too if the child needs it."

I nodded and moved to the far end of the room. Some children had already begun rolling up the worm, while others only displayed the tell-tale blister. A few needed a chew on the catnip, but most were stalwart and brave.

When we finished, Jehan led us out of the hut to the village center.

"Are there others?" Jehan asked.

The old man we had first met nodded, sadness swimming in his eyes. We followed him to a few huts that had older men and women in various stages of expelling the worms. It was painful to watch. I was ready to leave before we were finished.

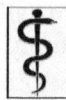

"How did you know it was time to visit the village?" I asked on our way back up the road to Philippi.

"It has been nearly a year since the last infestation," Jehan replied. "The worms lay their eggs in the water and then unsuspecting people drink the water. It takes nearly a year for the eggs to hatch and grow. Then, when they're ready, they burrow out of the skin looking for water to lay more eggs."

"That's why you told them to pour the buckets in the road." Sometimes light dawns in the evening.

"I taught them last year to cover the water, filter it, before they drink. … But the children … well, they play in the marsh water as children will do. They won't be so careless after this week, I dare say." Jehan sighed.

"Why were some of the adults suffering? Surely they knew better."

"Mmm. Consequences. Even when you change your ways, sometimes you still have to suffer the consequences. Perhaps they drank contaminated water before I taught them to filter; perhaps they chose to ignore me." Jehan shrugged. "Whatever it was, the fiery serpent will teach them a lesson."

"Like a Nehushtan." I considered the likeness of the dracunculiasis wrapped around a twig.

"Yes." Jehan nodded. "Look to the snake."

*... They sell the innocent for silver, and the needy for a pair of sandals.*
*They trample on the heads of the poor as on the dust of the ground and*
*deny justice to the oppressed....*
~Amos 2:6b–7a~

# CHAPTER 19

MARIETTE WELCOMED THE WINDY SPRING days. She enjoyed walks through town now that the muddy snowmelt was nearly gone. She would need some new shoes, and David had grown so that he needed new outfits as well. A mist of green and pink veiled the rolling hills as the train sped toward Lowell. *Maybe I'll find something for Increase.* David curled up in the seat next to her, holding her hand and watching the scenery pass. *I wish Increase felt this comfortable with me.*

She had left Rachelle outside, busy throwing rugs over the makeshift poles in back of the house. The girl banged the carpets so hard that dirt and dust covered the back wall of the garden. It was good the wind was blowing or she wouldn't have been able to breathe. There were still the walls to wash down, the grates to clean, the stoves to be polished, but that didn't bother Mariette. She trusted Rachelle could take care of it all.

Nurse Lindelof greeted Increase at the hospital door. "Good morning, Dr. Graves. I thought you'd be in sooner. All was quiet here last night, but a call came in from over near Hollis. George Hartman's wife went into labor; she's having a terrible time."

"I was enjoying my coffee this morning. You should have called me. I'll head over there now. You're sure everyone here is fine?"

"Yes, Doctor. Nurse Hall was going to check on some people over Beech Street before she comes in. I'll wait for her."

Increase called the stable and got a horse and carriage. *Maybe Mariette would like to go for a ride; it's such a pleasant day.* He walked to the stable and took charge of the rental. The black mare's hooves echoed on the quiet morning streets.

Increase set the carriage brake in front of the house and skipped up the stairs. "Mariette," he called as he swung open the door. "Want to go for a ride? Mariette?"

He searched the house, then found Rachelle outside hitting rugs with gusto. "Rachelle, where is Mrs. Graves?"

"She went to Lowell, sir. She and David left just a bit ago on the train. Is something the matter?"

"No, no, I just thought she might want to ride over to Hollis with me. Thanks." Increase waved good-bye and walked back through the quiet house. *Now why would she go to Lowell?* He jumped up on the carriage seat, released the brake, and clucked to the horse all in one smooth motion. It was a long drive to Hollis.

The memory of Annie came flooding back the closer Increase got to the Hartman farm. The familiar knot in his stomach tightened and his tongue was dry and thick. *I should have brought someone with me. I should have called the doctor from Lowell to drive up in his horseless carriage.* The fears piled up like logs in a river jam.

The wind blew in Increase's face, making his eyes water, but the sun was warm. A flock of geese flew over, migrating north. Green haze covered the trees, and carpets of emerald fern were poking their heads up from the forest floor.

The sun was high in the sky when Increase pulled up to the Hartman house. Two children playing in the front yard ran inside as he hitched up the horse.

"Good mornin'," called a young man from the top step. "You must be the new doctor over Dunstable Plains."

"Yes, Dr. Graves. Increase Graves."

"Nice to meet you, Doc, but I'm afraid you've made the trip all for nothing. Mary had the baby 'bout two hours ago. I sent Fred over the store to call you, but they says you already left. Sorry 'bout that." He shook Increase's hand before they entered the house. Mr. Hartman was young, but his face and hands were leathery, a man familiar with work.

"That's alright. I'm just glad to hear your wife is fine. Maybe I'll just have a look at her and the baby since I'm here."

"Sure, they're in the back room by the fire."

The house was small. Each room was sparsely furnished, but warm and friendly. The back room had a coal stove with a pipe that vented out the wall. The mother and child were seated in a rocker wrapped in a light quilt.

"Mary, this is Doc Graves. He says he'll go ahead and take a look at you and the babe since he's here." Mr. Hartman looked at Increase. "You want I should have Alice fix some tea?"

"No, I'm fine, thank you. So, Mrs. Hartman, who do we have here?"

The mother couldn't have been more than twenty. "This here's David," she said and pulled back the coverlet. "He didn't want to come visit, but I guess he finally got tired of waiting. I know I was right tired."

"David. That's my son's name," Increase said as he took the infant.

"Really? How old is your boy?" Mr. Hartman asked.

"He's six, nearly seven." Increase looked the child over; everything seemed fine. He took out his stethoscope.

"Ain't you planning no more babies? Seven years is a long time between young 'uns," Mary said.

Increase sat on the edge of the bed and put the stethoscope in his ears. He listened to the baby's heart. All sounded well. "David's mother died. He never knew her."

"Oh, I'm sorry, Doctor. I shouldn't to of said nothin'." Mary looked at the baby. "How terrible sad."

"You're still wearing your ring, though," Mr. Hartman pointed at the hand cupped around Baby David's neck.

Increase finished listening to the lungs and wrapped up the babe. "I remarried. Last fall." He handed the baby back to Mary. "Your David seems perfectly healthy, no worries." He gave a thin smile.

"I bet there'll be another baby for you real soon, Doc," Mr. Hartman said. "Thanks for coming all this way for naught." He turned toward the door.

"Good-bye, Mrs. Hartman. I'm sure you and David'll be just fine."

Increase turned and followed out the door. He heard the creaking of the rocker start back up as Mary hummed an unknown tune. George Hartman pulled the door shut and motioned Increase to go out ahead of him.

The bright sun glared down on Increase as he climbed back in the carriage. "Call again if you need me," he said as he tipped his hat. The horse trotted off around an elm tree and back out on the main road. *There won't be any more babies if I can help it,* he thought.

The front door to the hospital was wide open when Increase returned. He looked up and down the street, then climbed the few stairs to the entrance. No one was at the front desk. He closed the door behind him and checked in the ward. Every bed was filled and both nurses were hard at work.

"What's going on?"

Nurse Hall looked up from her patient. "Typhus, Doctor. I was checking on some mill workers this morning on Beech Street. There's a house full of bachelor Frenchmen and near to all of them have it."

"Figures. Well, are there reports in any other houses?"

"Not yet." Nurse Hall shook her head and put another wet cloth on the patient. "This one has a fever of 105. He must be well into it. His brother says he's been feeling miserable a week now. The fevers started yesterday."

"Did he keep on working all that time?"

Nurse Hall looked up in surprise. "Of course. They all work, unless they're on their deathbeds." She swooshed past Increase at the end of the bed and moved on to the next, where another young man lay hacking and moaning.

"Who still needs attention?" Increase asked.

"I think we've about got it covered," Nurse Hall said as Nurse Lindelof walked by with a pan of vomit. The odor followed her out of the room.

"Nurse, you were here all night. Why don't you go on home after you clean that up?" Increase called after her.

She turned on her heel. "You'll be needing me to stay all day at this rate. One house won't keep to itself for long. I already sent word back home not to expect me." She turned and walked out the rear door.

It was late when Increase dragged himself into the house. A glimmer of light shone from the dining room. Mariette sat in the large chair at the head of the table, her head hanging to one side and her mouth open in gentle breathing. She looked like a sleeping angel in her white nightgown and robe.

"Mariette?" Increase stole into the room. "You should have gone to bed. Come on. It's late."

She stirred at his voice and sat up, rubbing the crick in her neck. "Where were you? Is everything okay?"

Increase reached for her hand and pulled her out of the chair. "Typhus. It's going to be a long spring." He headed toward the staircase.

"Don't you want some dinner? I kept a plate for you on the back of the stove."

*Annie and Lively both used to do that. Maybe I'm too hard on her.* "No, thanks. I'm too tired to eat now. I just want to sleep."

They climbed the stairs together and fell into bed; Increase never even bothered to take off his shoes.

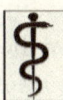

The sound of a bird chirping in the room woke Increase. He rolled on his back and looked around. He was covered by the heavy quilt and his shoes were off his feet. *Mariette must have done some tucking in.*

The bird kept chirping, but he couldn't see it. The sound seemed to be coming from Mariette's vanity drawer. He swung his feet over the bed and sat up, then rubbed his face with both hands and slowly stood.

"Good morning, dear," Mariette said as she cracked the door open. "I thought you might sleep a little longer. I was just going to peek in and check on you." She walked over and gave him a peck on the cheek. "Feeling better?"

"Yes, but there's a bird somewhere in the room. That's what woke me up." He walked toward the vanity. "I'd swear it's in one of these drawers."

Mariette giggled. "That's a present for you. I didn't realize it was set." She crossed to the table and pulled out the second drawer. A square gift-wrapped box lay inside. She pulled it out and handed it to him. She was warm sunshine and clear skies.

"What is it?"

"Open it. I saw it yesterday in Lowell and knew you'd love it."

Storm clouds darkened his face and his eyes shot lightning at the memory of yesterday. "Why did you go to Lowell? I came back to the house to take you on a house call with me and Rachelle said you were already gone."

Mariette took a step back. "It was such a pretty day, the beginning of spring really, and David needed some new things. He's grown so much, Increase. And I needed some new shoes after walking in this mud all winter; I thought it was a good day to go. ... I'm sorry I missed you. You've never asked me to go out with you before."

The bird inside the box kept chirping. "And this?" Increase spat. "This was also a necessity?"

"No. I ... I just saw it in the window and thought of you. I thought you would enjoy it. ... Unwrap it." The sunshine had faded and clouds were covering her smile.

Increase slid the ribbon off the box and tore back the silver paper. A wooden box stamped with a clockmaker's trademark lay inside. He opened the lid. The chirping bird was somehow captured inside a small clock.

"It's an alarm clock." Her slender fingers wrapped around the box and took it from Increase. "I know how the work bells bother you. I thought the bird would be a happier way to awaken." She lifted the clock from the box and switched off the alarm. "I didn't mean to upset you." She looked up at his face. Uncertainty bit her lower lip and fear hid at the corner of her eyes.

"It was thoughtful of you. You're right; I do dislike those bells." He sighed deeply and held her in his arms. "It was a pretty day, like you said, and I was disappointed that you weren't here to go with me." Surprise made his heart race as he realized the truth of his words. He had been disappointed that she was gone. "Show me how it works."

The house phone rang while the family sat at a late breakfast. Mariette and David looked at Increase. "That'll be the hospital." He rose and walked to the hallway telephone. A minute later he was back.

"I have to go," he said, lifting his coffee cup. He took a long sip of the strong, hot liquid. "There are two more houses with typhus. The hospital can't handle them all. I'll be making house calls all day. Don't plan on me for dinner."

"I'll bring some food by ... for you and the nurses," Mariette said.

Increase smiled. "That would be great. Thanks. Bye, David." He stopped by the boy and tousled his hair. "Be a good boy and listen to Mariette."

"Yes, sir."

Mariette stood and met Increase behind David's chair. "I'll pray no one else catches it," she said as she lifted her chin to give him a kiss.

"Thanks, but it'll take more than prayer. I'm going to have to go over to Public Health again; I can tell you that." He tipped his face and let her kiss his cheek. "Don't wait up tonight. I'll be late again."

The smell of human waste slapped Increase as he crossed the street to the next mill house. The latrines at the corner of each row house were in desperate need of cleaning. A dead rat lay at the bottom of the stairs to the next house.

Already he had seen five men and three children with typhus, and the morning was young. He knocked on the door. "Dr. Graves," he announced himself as he pushed open the door. This was no time for social propriety. "Is there—"

Increase stopped when he saw Jean standing in the middle of the common room, talking with the keeper.

"Good morning," Increase said. "I didn't expect to see you."

Jean lifted a hand in greeting. "I noticed several workers out yesterday and thought I better check on everyone today. How are you?"

"Fine. Busy, though."

"There are three families with typhus upstairs and the keeper's daughter is starting to have symptoms. I've started them on hot baths and dousing them with turpentine."

"Turpentine?"

Jean nodded. "To kill the lice."

Increase nodded. "I'll just go check on them too if you don't mind."

"Of course," Jean said, "but there're many more houses to check. It'll go faster if you trust me."

"I don't know what they'll say at Public Health, my being the doctor and all," Increase said. "Though they don't seem to care too much about what goes on in the mill houses anyway," he added as an afterthought. "Okay, you take the west end and I'll head east from here. That'll give me time to go over to the Public Health Department and see what can be done about those latrines. Spring is just around the corner."

The lunch bells were ringing as Increase finished the rounds. He had passed Jean on the way to the hospital and the news was not good. Every house had at least one person infected. It was the same on the east end,

Increase informed the Frenchman. An epidemic was beginning.

Increase stood outside the large Masonic building, contemplating the best approach. Mr. Taylor was not much help last time. His priorities were less health related and more wealth inspired. He was concerned with the economy of Dunstable Plains and its businessmen.

*That's where I'll begin. The economy is dependent on public health. If the workers aren't healthy, production suffers.* He walked up the front stairs and into the wooden cathedral of offices and city business.

"Good afternoon, Dr. Graves," the matron said, smiling like the cat who swallowed a canary. "Spring is in the air."

"So is typhus. I need to see Mr. Taylor."

The receptionist's color drained. "Typhus? Oh dear. Where?"

"Over in the mill house quarters," he said, jerking his head toward Beech Street.

"Oh," she said, the color returning. "I thought you meant in our part of town. I'll let Mr. Taylor know you're here."

She walked down the wooden hallway, her shoes echoing her disdain like an empty barrel of apples. The barrel didn't matter so much as long as the trees were safe.

"Every house has someone affected," Increase said and then blew on the cup of coffee. He'd agreed to join Mr. Taylor in a cup to smooth over his veiled threats at their last meeting. It didn't appear to be helping.

"Typhus is common," Mr. Taylor said, adding another spoonful of sugar to his cup. "It makes the rounds every year about this time." He sat down behind his desk.

"And likely it always will," Increase said, "but it doesn't have to be an epidemic, and honestly we are headed that way this minute." He sipped and looked at the balding man in front of him. Mr. Taylor held the white cup in his pudgy hands and stared back. "The workers' quarters need to be cleaned up. The latrines are full and need immediate attention. There isn't time now to get sewer lines over there, but that would solve a lot of our problems for next year."

"*Their* problems. And sewer lines are not on the city's agenda."

"Well, they should be, because it isn't *their* problem; it's ours." Increase took another sip to soften the blow of his words.

"I don't see how it's ours." Mr. Taylor put his cup back on the saucer and poured in a drizzle of milk. "You don't see typhus epidemics over here. There's no accounting for ignorance."

"Ignorance didn't fill the latrines. Ignorance didn't invite rats into their homes. Ignorance didn't make them sick. It's neglect on the part of the landlords." Increase kept his eyes down and shifted in his chair.

"The housing is adequate. Compared to what they lived in back in Canada, they should be grateful. They live in palaces here."

"Typhus rates have gone down significantly in the large cities where public sewage is regulated. Joining the mill houses to the existing city lines would be inexpensive compared to the loss of productivity from sick workers."

"Dr. Graves, the houses you are referring to are privately owned. We can't force the landlords to install sewage lines. Why, we would have to start requiring all houses to be a part of the system." Mr. Taylor leaned back in his chair and looked Increase over. "You surely can't expect that. Either taxes would be too high or landlords would lose too much money." He smiled and lifted the cup to his lips. "Either way, your patients would have to pay higher rents. I'm sure they would not be happy to find out it was the fault of their good doctor." He slurped the hot coffee and swallowed hard. "Is there anything else I can do for you?" He put the cup back on the saucer and placed it on top of a stack of papers. "I have a lot to do today."

"I can't take care of all these people by myself. If this turns into an epidemic, which I am sure it will in the next week, I must have help."

"You have two nurses. Pay them overtime if you must." He shrugged in dismissal.

"That still isn't enough. I need trained workers who can administer drugs, check vitals, teach proper hygiene ..." Increase raised his free hand in the air. "I just can't do it alone."

"Mr. Neal said you were interested in starting a nurses' training school," Mr. Taylor said, squinting his eyes in calculation. "But there aren't enough funds in the hospital coffers. If Public Health threw in some money for the school, perhaps ... A nurses' school would bring some notoriety to our little town. Could be the thing we need." He was talking to himself. "What do you say? You could train the nurses to be just what you want."

He smiled at Increase, his neck red from the tight, buttoned collar.

"A nurses' school would be helpful," Increase said, "but it doesn't solve the immediate problem."

Mr. Taylor stood up and extended his hand. "I'll talk to Mr. Neal and the rest of the hospital board right away," he said, dismissing the topic of concern. "Thanks for coming by."

Increase stood and shook his hand. *Wars are won one battle at a time.*

*A wise man should consider that health is the greatest of human blessings, and learn how by his own thoughts to derive benefit from his illnesses.*
~Hippocrates~

# CHAPTER 20

"HERE IT IS," INCREASE SAID as he shook the newspaper open wider. "Our advertisement for the new nursing school."

"That was quick," Mariette said. "When do they think they can start?"

"Mr. Neal is planning for this summer. Doesn't help me out now, but I suppose summer is better than never."

"Is it really so difficult?"

Increase put down the paper and looked at his young bride. "I only have two nurses to help with several thousand people. Typhus is spreading more every day. Jean helps too, but I can't keep up even with his help."

"Then why don't you train the girls already here. Surely some of them want to be nurses instead of mill workers."

"They can't read." It was a simple fact. The locals could learn to run a machine, learn a routine, but if they couldn't read, they couldn't take orders and provide appropriate care. "I'm not sure how good an idea it is to bring in girls from Lowell and Boston, though. They may not want to serve in such a … well, in such a different place." Increase folded the paper and stood. "I better start my rounds."

Mariette tipped her cheek up for his good-bye kiss. It was mechanic and routine. She felt she had learned the ins and outs of being Increase's wife. She could read him now, and he was a different book than she had expected.

"I'm taking David into Lowell today," she said. "He needs—"

"Yay!" David interrupted. "Can Clement come too this time? He says he hasn't been on a train since he came here from Canada."

Increase smiled at his little boy. "Yes, Clement may go with you," he said before Mariette had a chance. "It will be good for him to get out of the mill houses for a day."

"We'll have to ask Rachelle," Mariette said. "We can't make decisions about Clement without her, no matter how much he is becoming a brother." Her lips smiled at David, but not her eyes. *Friends might be the only siblings you ever have.*

The boys sat opposite each other staring out the window at the passing countryside. A few hardened snowbanks remained along the tracks where they had piled up over the winter. Coal soot made them look like the black lava rocks Mariette had seen in a picture book of New Zealand. *I can't wait for this winter to be over.* The green blanket of baby leaves was a blur as they sped by wooded areas.

"What language will they speak in Lowell?" Clement asked.

Mariette turned her gaze from the window. "English, of course."

"Oh. I thought maybe French."

"Oui, some French speakers live there," Mariette said. "But it's still America. In America they speak English."

"Pas tout le monde," Clement said and giggled at Mariette.

"No, not everyone, gentil garcon," Mariette said.

"Hey," David said, puffing out his chest. "That's not fair. I can't understand you when you start speaking French."

"Then you better learn," Clement said. "I understand when you speak English." He poked David in the stomach and the two of them started wrestling.

"Settle down and watch out the window, boys." Mariette was glad David had found a friend. She wished she had someone to joke around and recreate with. *Loneliness seems to be my lifelong friend.*

The train came to a slow stop in front of the small brick station. Mariette gathered her handbag and took David by the hand. Clement grabbed hold of her skirt and followed behind.

"What shall we do first?" she asked as they walked to the end of the platform.

"The bookstore!" David answered.

"Clement?"

Clement nodded his approval and the three headed down the lamp-lined sidewalk. A few store owners had flower boxes in the windows, and purple crocuses had popped up to welcome shoppers. They walked slowly, looking in windows and watching the busy streets. Horses and carriages clopped by. A few automobiles honked their horns like the mean ganders that chased Mariette in Champ de Mars on her solitary walks through Paris. An electric trolley crossed the intersection and rang its bells.

"Can we ride the trolley—please?" David said.

"Later." Mariette laughed. "We have all day, David. And what we don't get to, we will do another day. Clement can come as often as he wishes."

Clement smiled and came from behind Mariette's skirts. "Merci," he whispered. He took her other hand and walked beside her. His hand was wider than David's, but the simple gesture confirmed his apprehension. He was a little boy in a big world.

"Here's the bookstore. We'll go in and browse. You may look at the book covers, but do not pick them up." She opened the door and scooted the children in before her. "Stay with David and you'll be fine," she whispered as Clement passed her.

The boys looked at the children's books with their three-color covers and illustrations. Clement stood with his hands behind his back, and David kept his in his pockets. When the boys found a book that interested them, Mariette would pick it up and look through the pages. Finally she gave her approval to two books and walked to the front of the store.

The store clerk wrapped the books in newsprint and put them in a bag with handles. Clement watched bug-eyed as the bag was handed over the counter to Mariette. "Thank you. Come along, boys," she said and ushered them out the door.

Standing in the bright sunshine, she asked, "What now, Clement? What would you like to see?"

"The books were enough, thank you. I've never seen so many books."

Mariette looked at David and he laughed out loud. "The library!" David shouted.

"Manners, David," Mariette said, looking around at the passersby. "This way."

They strolled down the walk under the store awnings. Some windows had paintings on them, others had posters tacked to the glass. Mariette stopped outside the chemist's shop. An advertisement for a nursing school in Dunstable Plains, New Hampshire, was taped to the window.

"This is for Daddy's nursing school at the hospital." Mariette showed David.

"There's Daddy's name." David pointed. "See, I can read."

"Very good," Mariette said.

"I can't, but Rachelle says she'll teach me when you finish her lessons," Clement said.

"Do you want to read?" Mariette asked.

"Oh yes. Books are amazing."

"Just you wait," Mariette said.

They stopped at the corner of Merrimack and Shattuck Streets. The large building looked like a palace with its turrets and tall clock tower. They climbed the front stairs and Mariette held open the door.

"You may touch these books, Clement."

They spent the rest of the morning wandering the aisles of books. Sun streamed through the lead windows and warmed the golden wood archways. The boys slid books out of the rows of paper and leather-bound volumes and carefully turned the pages. Mariette sat at a table and looked through the latest fashion magazines from Paris.

Finally David tugged at her arm. "We're hungry, Mama."

"Then let's find some lunch."

The three sat at the counter of the department store soda fountain, sharing toasted club sandwiches. Mariette sipped a strong cup of coffee, but she splurged for the boys and ordered them ginger ales. They watched the customers in the large mirrors over the cook's station.

Some young ladies in last season's hats sat at the table behind Mariette. She watched them with interest as they waited for their food to arrive.

"Did you hear about the new nursing school starting in Dunstable Plains? There was a sign on the chemist's window," said the girl facing the mirror.

"What about it?"

"I'm thinking about applying," she replied.

Mariette studied the girl. She didn't look like a working girl.

"You can't do that," said the girl with her back to Mariette. "Your father would have a fit."

"I have my own money, and I can do as I wish. I want to help people, and nursing is a respectable profession." She smiled at the boy serving their bowls of bean soup and cornbread. "Father knows I want to strike out on my own. Lots of girls are doing it these days."

"What should we do next?" David interrupted Mariette's eavesdropping.

The boys had finished their meal and were swinging their legs on the high stools.

Mariette wiped her mouth and placed the napkin next to her plate. "Whatever you like," she said, taking a few coins out of her handbag to pay for lunch.

Two very tired boys leaned against Mariette as the train clattered north toward Dunstable Plains. It had been a long day for all of them. The boys had walked through the department store looking at all of the items, even the seed packets and farm equipment in the back of the store. Then they explored the candy store, watched the water wheels on the mill canals, and rode the trolley from Boots Mills to the other end of town.

Mariette enjoyed the day with David and Clement, but it was the girl at the lunch counter she couldn't get out of her mind. When Increase had mentioned nurses, she had expected ruddy country girls who wanted to bypass the loud, steamy mills. But the girls at lunch had been attractive, fashionable. Jealousy nibbled at her self-assurance.

She was young and attractive, but she had only studied art. Perhaps Increase would like a wife who was more academic, more medically minded. What if the girls who applied for the school, the girls from Boston and Lowell, were more interesting to Increase? *Maybe that's why he hasn't been a real husband. He wants a woman who can share his interests as a physician.*

The train pulled into the wooden train stop as the sun was setting. Mariette shook the boys awake and pulled them down the train steps. "Rachelle will be waiting dinner on us," she said, but her mind was still consuming lunch.

"We're back," Mariette called as the boys ran into the house. "Hang your coat, David. Clement, go on to the kitchen. Your sister's probably in there."

The house was unusually dim. Rachelle always lit the dining room and parlor in the evening. Mariette wanted Increase to see light and warmth through the front windows when he walked home late from work. She placed her dress coat on the hanger in the foyer closet.

"Rachelle!" the boys yelled as they ran out the kitchen door and sped up the stairs. "She's not in the kitchen, Mama," David called over his shoulder as he charged up the staircase.

Mariette headed to the pantry when a knock came on the front door. She turned back toward it. The knock came again before she could reach the knob.

"Patience, Rachelle," she said as she opened the door.

Jean in his black coat and muffler stood on the front porch.

"Oh, Dr. Giatros. I'm sorry; I thought it was going to be Rachelle. Won't you come in?"

"Thank you," he said as he walked in, looking around the entryway and then around the corner into the parlor. "I came as soon as I heard the train come in. I've come for Clement. Rachelle was called home this afternoon and asked me to give you her apology. She said she appreciated you taking Clement to Lowell."

"But why did she leave before we got back? The lamps aren't lit and dinner isn't on the table."

"No." Jean cleared his throat. "Rachelle's mamere went home this afternoon."

"Went home?" Mariette waved her hand toward the parlor. "Come sit down, please."

"She's not upstairs anywhere," David said from the landing. "Oh, hello, Dr. Giatros."

"Hello, David, Clement," he said to the boys.

"Why don't you and Clement go play with your blocks until Rachelle … returns," Mariette said. "Please, Doctor."

Jean waved to Clement and David as they raced back to the playroom. He walked into the parlor and sat near the fireplace of glowing coals and embers. "She had been very sick. I suppose you know that," Jean said as he looked up at Mariette. She moved to the chair across from his and nodded. "Pneumonia is the old man's friend. She left late this morning, just before lunch. The work bells tolled the news."

"And Rachelle? How is she?"

"I called for her before it was too late. She told her mamere she loved her and that everything would be alright. She's fine, but weary and worn. I should get Clement."

"I should go to Rachelle. She shouldn't be alone," Mariette said, wringing her hands in her lap. "I can leave a note for Increase. He'll understand."

"No, David can't go. There's typhus in the house."

Mariette drew in her breath. "Then Clement should stay here as well. We'll tell him that Rachelle gave permission for him to stay. She can come tomorrow to get him and tell him the news then. Let her know she should take her time tomorrow. Arrangements will need to be made."

Mariette was stirring a pot of oatmeal when Increase stuck his head into the kitchen. He smiled briefly and walked into the room.

"Where's Rachelle?"

"Oh, Increase. I wish you didn't have to work alone. Sometimes I need to talk to you."

"What's the matter? What happened?" Increase moved toward her and stopped her stirring.

She turned and looked into his eyes. Tears glistened at the edge of her lashes. "Clement is upstairs in bed with David. Rachelle's grandmother passed away yesterday." A sob choked her and she took a breath. "Now they're all alone."

Increase took her in his arms and let her cry on his chest. He stroked her hair and wondered at the kindness of her heart. Her weakness might be material things, but her strength was a love for her friends and family. He shouldn't dismiss her so often. *There was a reason I spent all of those nights in Boston talking late with her.*

*Wisdom comes alone through suffering.*
~Aeschylus~

# CHAPTER 21

THE AFTERNOON BELLS HAD LONG since called the workers back, and Rachelle had still not returned for Clement. Mariette assembled a luncheon basket and gathered the boys for the walk to Rachelle's house.

"Why are we taking food to Rachelle?" David asked. "She's a better cook than you are."

"Well, thank you for your honesty," Mariette muttered. "I just thought it would be a nice gesture to take her something."

"But why didn't she come to our house this morning?" David asked.

"Does Rachelle have typhus?" Clement asked from behind Mariette.

She stopped and turned to look at the little boy. Stooping down, she tucked his hair behind his ear. "No, Rachelle is fine," she said. "But she is sad and needs some love and attention."

"Why is she sad?" Clement took her hand.

"That … is for Rachelle to tell you. Come on," she said and took his hand as they walked toward the row houses.

A house sparrow perched in a tree welcoming them with its lonely "Cheep, cheep, cheep." The latrines were overly ripe in the afternoon sun. Mariette could only imagine what it must be like in summer's heat. A group of girls sat in a grassy spot playing a hand game. Their singsong seemed so out of place in this hovel of hell.

Clement walked faster toward the house, pulling on Mariette's hand.

"Mariette!" a voice called. "Wait!"

Mariette stopped and looked up the walkway. Increase was coming out one of the houses. Clement dropped Mariette's hand and ran ahead into the house. David paused beside her.

"What are you doing?" Increase asked as he walked closer. "You shouldn't be here." He reached them and placed both hands on David's shoulders.

"Rachelle never came for Clement," she said. "I thought we better check on her. I brought some food." She pulled the cover back on the basket to show him.

"The priest is with her now, and all of the neighbors have been checking on her. I just finished rounds there. David can't go in there."

"Why?" David asked. "Is Rachelle okay?"

"Rachelle is fine," Mariette said. She knelt close to David and looked him in the eye. "But, Amoureux, Clement and Rachelle's mamere has gone to heaven. That's why Rachelle didn't stay yesterday to get Clement. She had to go home to take care of things."

"Is she crying?" David asked looking up at his father. "Is that why I can't see her?"

"No, David. There's typhus in the house. It isn't safe for you to be there. You might get sick."

"But what about Rachelle and Clement? What if they get sick? I don't want them to go to heaven too." David's eyes burned red and his nose twitched. "They're my friends."

"Can David stay here with you a few minutes while I check on Rachelle?" Mariette asked as she straightened. "I won't be long."

Increase nodded and took David's hand. Mariette hurried up the sidewalk and pulled open the creaky wooden door. Leaving the bright spring sunshine blinded her. She stopped inside the door as her eyes adjusted. Funereal voices echoed like ghosts down the hallway.

Mariette blinked and walked up the stairs toward the sound. She pulled her skirts high to avoid the rat traps along the baseboard. Someone stepped back into a room and shut their door. Mariette kept walking, lifting her hand to her face to temper the overwhelming smells.

She stopped in front of a door and tapped on it. Glancing side to side, she knocked again with more force. Father Cartier opened the door.

"Mrs. Graves," he said and smiled. "Come in. Rachelle will be glad to see you. She's just given Clement the news."

Mariette walked into the small apartment. It was clean and tidy, though furniture was sparse and bare. An older woman took the basket from Mariette and offered to take her coat. "No, I can't stay long. My son is outside," she murmured.

Rachelle heard her voice and looked up. Her eyes were puffy, but she smiled at Mariette. Mariette rushed to her and hugged her long and hard. The two women swayed and rocked as grief and comfort flowed between them. Clement joined the two and rested his head on Rachelle's hip.

"How are you?" Mariette asked, ending the embrace. "I've been so worried."

"Thank you for allowing Clement to stay last night. Did you have a good time in Lowell?" Rachelle asked, turning her attention to the boy. "How was the train ride?"

Clement stared at Rachelle as big tears squeezed out the corners of his eyes and rolled down pudgy cheeks. "I want Mamere."

Rachelle picked up Clement and held him close. "I know, Amoureux."

Mariette drew in her breath, realizing that Rachelle was now in the same position as herself. Rachelle must become mother to this little boy. Mariette rubbed his bony back and placed another hand on Rachelle's shoulder.

"Let Clement come stay with us. You do what needs to be done here. Father Cartier will keep us informed about the arrangements." She smiled and nodded her head, encouraging Rachelle to accept the offer.

"Merci. That is very, very kind, but no. Clement and I need to be together." She held him close to her breast and his legs wrapped tightly around her waist.

"Then both of you should come to the house. It isn't safe for you to be here. Dr. Graves says there's typhus in the house."

"We'll be fine. This is our home," Rachelle said. "I'll come back to work in two days, after the funeral. The ground is soft now and Mamere can be buried quickly. Dorothy has offered to watch Clement now that …" She paused and nodded toward the closed bedroom door.

"No. That won't do." Mariette's voice was hard. "You'll bring Clement to work with you. He and David will be good playmates. It'll be safer." She hugged the two again and then turned to leave.

The world wore a green mask of happiness. The day was warm and inviting, and a familiar refrain echoed along the water.

"Alouette, gentille alouette, Alouette, je te plumerai." Clement's voice rose above David's as he taught the nursery song to his best friend. The two had become inseparable since the death of Mamere. Mornings were spent building intricate towers and playing indoors, then lessons after lunch, with Rachelle making great progress and the boys fidgeting to be finished. The afternoon sunshine beckoned to them, and picnics along the canal were constant requests.

"It's good to have an afternoon in the fresh air," Mariette said as she flung her arms wide and inhaled deeply. "I remember many days in Paris wishing I could walk through the Jardin des Tuileries, but my teachers would have told Grand-père that I was missing."

"Did you not like school?" Rachelle asked. She sat down on the bank and watched as the boys threw pebbles into the water.

"I did. Oui." Mariette sat down next to the girl. "But I was lonely. It was difficult to make friends and my grandparents are old. They don't entertain anymore." She shrugged her shoulders. "I was happy to come home." She looked at the boys teasing each other with shoves and pushes. "I'm glad that David has a friend now. It's hard to be so lonely and so young."

"But now you aren't lonely." Rachelle looked at Mariette and smiled. "You have David, and Dr. Graves, and Clement and me."

Mariette smiled back and held the girl's hand.

*Gird your hearts with silent fortitude, suffering, yet hoping all things.*
~Felicia Hemans~

# CHAPTER 22

"I'M SENDING YOU TO TROAS." Jehan was packing a bag with medicines. "I have a friend there in need of some things."

"In Troas?"

Jehan looked up at me. "It won't be long, a couple weeks perhaps."

"Pater ..." I couldn't bring myself to say it.

"Aegeus is better than you suppose. Casper will take care of him, and I will check daily. I still have some remedies on my shelf." He smiled, the gentle smile of comfort and familiarity.

*No wonder Pater trusts him.*

"How will I—"

"It's all taken care of," Jehan interrupted. "Go over to Neapolis and catch the merchant ship leaving this afternoon. The winds will change soon, so you need to leave today."

Jehan explained the details and sent me home to pack a bag and say good-bye to Pater. On the way there, I stopped in the market to get one of Pater's favorite fish.

"Jehan says he'll check on you each day, even has some remedies to add to your prescription." I tried to smile. "He says it won't take long, maybe a couple weeks. If I find this man quickly, then I could be back within the week."

Pater patted the bed and I sat next to him.

"I'll be fine. I know you're worried that Thanatos is coming any moment, but I can feel his distance. He's on the way ..." Pater nodded, coughed, and then paused for air. "But there are others to gather first."

I bit my lip and inner cheek to keep the tears from breaking the dam.

"Now you go to Troas and make me proud. Serving Jehan is a worthy calling."

I kissed my father's cheek. *Will the cheek still be warm the next time I kiss it?*

The journey to Troas was common for merchants, not so much for doctors prone to seasickness. I sat in a corner of the deck breathing deeply of the fresh salt air and watching the horizon for the Mysian coast. It couldn't come soon enough.

The Etesian winds were late this year. We passed across the Aegean in two days and landed at the port in Troas. I was the first to debark, not caring that the sailors didn't even try to hide their mirth.

I jumped over the boarding plank and landed on the wooden dock. The bag of medicines flopped on my back. I made arrangements to pick up the other bags after I found Ignatius. My new sandals barely kept my feet from blistering in the heat radiating from the thick wooden beams of the dock. I headed toward the stone street beyond the sea wall at a brisk trot.

Jehan had instructed me the way to his friend's house, but had warned he might not be there. "You'll be welcome to stay until he arrives. Aegeus will be fine. Wait and don't leave until you have made the delivery in person."

*Doesn't he trust his servants? You could leave anything with Casper and know it would be safe.*

"Yes, Jehan," I'd said.

The house was a three-story mammoth of unknown heritage. It probably dated to Antigonus. Sections were added with each new generation, the stone and mortar conveying periods of want and plenty, currently in want.

I knocked on the door and a young girl answered.

"Ignatius lives here?"

The girl's eyes widened and she closed the door without a word. *Now what?*

I could hear children running inside the house, calling to each other in their play. I knocked again and waited. Passersby looked my way but kept going.

I knocked louder. Slow, heavy steps lumbered inside. *Finally.* The door opened a crack and an old woman peered out.

"Yes?"

"I'm looking for Ignatius. I was told this is his house?"

"Who told you that?" Her eyes searched me.

"Jehan. He's a doctor in—"

The door opened, and with surprising agility the old woman reached out and grabbed me by the robes.

"Get in." She pulled me inside and closed the door with hurricane swiftness. "Well, where is he?"

"Where is who?"

"Jehan, of course."

"In Philippi. He asked me to bring—"

She turned and lumbered down the stone corridor to a set of stairs. I followed her, wondering where we were going. The girl who first answered the door sat on the bottom step. The old woman nodded to her, pushed me in front of herself, and then turned down the dim hall.

"Follow me," the little girl whispered.

I watched the old woman disappear, pulled the bag higher on my shoulder, and followed up the stairs.

"In here," the little girl said, her eyes on the floor. "Ignatius will return soon."

I walked in the room. Several chairs and a bench lined the walls. I set my bag on a chair. A large table was in the center of the room; a patch of sunlight from an open window made the wood gleam. The door closed behind me, and I was alone.

I looked out the window at the busy street below. The house sat on a hillside overlooking the city. To the west the port glittered in the sunlight. I squinted, looking for the ship I had arrived on. *Maybe I can get a ride back with them.*

Three men stopped on the street below and looked up. I stepped back inside. *What am I doing here?* I paced, peered out to see the men entering the house, then stepped back again.

I slung the medical bag over my shoulder and walked to the door. *I'll wait outside. Perhaps someone on the street can tell me about Ignatius.*

The door opened and the little girl showed in the three men from the street.

"Khaírete!" one said. He sounded Syrian. "I'm Paolo. This is Silvanus." He turned to the man on his right. "And this is Timotheos." The young man extended his hand in greeting.

I looked them over, considering how safe they may be. Paolo was not a handsome man, but he stood like a mountain bear, dignified and assured. His garments were well spun and his beard trimmed. Silvanus was tall and thin like a Mediterranean cypress. *Looks like his name.* I shook hands with Timotheos. *Gentle. Friendly.*

"Khaírete! I'm Loukas, son of Aegeus. Are you friends of Ignatius?"

Paolo laughed. "Not yet, though we are brothers."

I closed an eye and pursed my lips. "How's that?"

"We're followers of the Way; some call us Christians … after Jesus the Christ."

"Anyone who is a Christian is part of the family of God. We're all brothers," Silvanus said. "We haven't met Ignatius yet, but we heard this was a safe place for Christians to stop."

"So you are a brother as well, Loukas?" Paolo asked.

"No. I've heard of the Jesus followers, though. Mostly Jews, I thought." I looked at Timotheos. "You don't sound like Jews."

The men laughed.

"What brings you to see Ignatius?" Paolo asked.

"I'm a doctor in Philippi. Jehan, my mentor, asked me to bring some supplies to Ignatius. I just arrived this afternoon, and I haven't seen him yet." I glanced at the three. *Seems safe.* "I was wondering if I should leave and ask people on the street about him. The reception here was … suspect."

The three nodded. Silvanus walked to the window and looked down on the street. Timotheos followed, but Paolo sat down on a chair. A heavy sigh made him slump and he rubbed his eyes.

"You should have your eyes checked," I said.

He looked up, still scratching his beard.

"Someone has arrived." Silvanus bent out the window for a better look. "Definitely a man, and he didn't wait out front."

We all gathered near the door. A few minutes later a broad man with a personality to match opened the door.

"Welcome to my home." His voice was powerful, echoing like thunder through the valleys of Pangaion. "I'm Ignatius. May you find peace and shelter here."

He shook our arms and kissed our cheeks. Motioning toward the chairs along the wall, he invited us to sit. He sat on the bench and waited while the little girl who had first met me came into the room to wash our feet. She was quiet, working in fluid movements that caressed our feet and legs. I felt refreshed and at ease when she left the room.

"Now," said Ignatius, "what brings all of you here today?"

"We come to share the good news of Jesus," Paolo said. He introduced them and then continued. "We've most recently been in Galatia and Phrygia. I had hoped to go on to Bithynia, but the Spirit stopped me. Now we have come here to spread the word of Jesus."

"Wonderful! I've heard a little about you, Paolo. We look forward to hearing from you. This evening, perhaps?"

Paolo nodded. "I would be happy to share. Is there a meeting?"

I cleared my throat. The men all looked at me.

"I … I'm not with them." I wasn't sure how this had happened. "I'm Loukas, son of Aegeus from Philippi. Jehan—"

"Jehan! You know Jehan?" Ignatius stood and grabbed me from my chair. "Welcome, Loukas. You are an honored guest." He embraced me so hard I lost my breath. "Why did Jehan send you?" He stood back, holding me by the shoulders.

His grin was infectious, but the truth was I didn't really know why Jehan had sent me. Troas was a large enough city, on an important shipping route. There didn't seem to be any particular reason to send medical supplies here.

"He wanted me to bring you supplies. I left them at the dock."

Ignatius nodded as if that was explanation enough. "Jehan is kind and thoughtful. Always providing." He kissed my cheeks again. "You must be a good man to be sent by Jehan."

"I'm a doctor too. Jehan and I have been working together."

"Then you are welcome to stay as long as Jehan has allowed."

"The supplies … I left them at the dock until I should find you."

"Of course, of course. I'll send for them."

The evening meal was a jovial affair. It seemed many families lived in the house. Children were everywhere. They were good children, helping where they could, bringing plates piled with bread, fish, olives, and fruit. They kept our glasses filled, always smiling, always bowing. The old woman who first offered me admittance directed the children.

"You have so many children. How many wives do you have?" I asked during a lull in the conversation.

Ignatius roared with laughter, his head thrown back and his wide smile showing rows of strong, white teeth. The old lady huffed and left the room.

"I don't have any wives. The children find me."

"Oh." I turned red at the implication.

"No, no." He laughed again. "They aren't my children; they're just children who need a home. That's why Jehan sent the supplies. Many come from homes of sickness. The parents die; the children aren't wanted." He took a drink and set the glass back down. A young boy filled it immediately. "Jesus said the kingdom of God is filled with children." He placed his oversized paw on the boy's head. "I'm just giving them a home until they make it back to God."

"I couldn't have said it better." Paolo smiled at the boy next to Ignatius.

"Are there sick children here?" I asked. "Should I look in on anyone?"

Ignatius sobered. "That would be a blessing. The doctors here think the house is cursed. They don't want to come."

After dinner my little servant girl guided me through the maze of rooms to the sick ward. The children there were easily cared for; thank goodness there was no dracunculiasis. I treated fevers and some cuts and abrasions.

The house was quiet and dark when my hostess showed me to my sleeping quarters.

The shrill yells of children playing in the hallway awoke me. I turned my head, taking in the surroundings. *Ignatius. Troas.* I stretched and yawned as yesterday's events replayed. I sat up and scratched.

A tap at the door made me look up. It opened and a little head peeked in.

"Papa Ignatius says to come for breakfast."

"I'll be right there." The smells of morning drifted in through the open door.

"So you see, we can't stay any longer," Paolo said as I walked in.

"Loukas, Loukas. Come, sit." Ignatius invited me in, moving down on the bench.

"Hypiaínete—Good morning." I sat at the long wooden table and took a sip of hot tea. "You're leaving?" I looked at the three men across from me.

"He had a vision," Timotheos said.

Paolo looked at me and nodded, his face clouded. "I'm being sent to Macedonia. No one has taken Jesus there yet."

"And you think you should?" I took another sip and held the bowl to warm my chilly hands.

"In my dream a man stood on the shore and begged me, 'Come to Macedonia. We need help.' I … I thought I should go to Asia, but I guess I was wrong. Would you … I mean … Would you be willing to lead us, Loukas? You could introduce us to Ignatius's friend, Jehan."

I set down the bowl of tea and exhaled. "Jehan's a good man, but I have to tell you … He's a Jew. I don't know if he will want to hear what you have to say."

"An introduction is all we ask. God will take care of the rest," Silvanus said.

Paolo nodded. "A good Jew will not deny strangers a place of rest," he said.

"Ah. Well, he is a good Jew. … Yes, I'll take you to Jehan."

*Suffering is part of the divine idea.*
~Henry Ward Beecher~

# CHAPTER 23

"THE TYPHUS OUTBREAK HAS ABOUT run its course," Increase said over breakfast. "I only have two patients at the hospital and a few in the mill houses."

"That's a relief," Mariette said, holding her coffee close.

"Good. Clement won't get sick now." David clapped his hands. "He says there are lots of kids like him."

Mariette looked at David and raised her brows. "What do you mean … like him?"

"With no mama or papa," David said and shrugged his shoulders. He stuffed a spoonful of oatmeal in his mouth. "I used to be like that."

"Don't talk with your mouth full, David." Increase reached for some bacon. "There's been some talk about raising money for an orphanage. Mr. Sheppard thinks the church can have a fundraiser to help out."

"What a marvelous idea," Mariette said. "We could have a cake walk and a raffle. I'm sure Papa would donate something for it. He always supports orphanages. Independence Day is coming up. That would be a great time for a carnival." Her face shone from the inside out. "What can we help with, David? A book perhaps?"

Increase was surprised to see Mariette's interest in the idea. "So you'll help arrange it? I didn't know what to tell Mr. Sheppard when he asked for your participation."

"Of course I'll help. I'll talk to Father Cartier this afternoon. We can walk over there and take him some of Rachelle's pastries. I don't think his cook gives him treats."

"So many of the children have been left without one or both of their parents," Mariette said over a plate of cherry turnovers. "A children's home would be a wonderful way to reach out to the community. The children could be assured of an education instead of working in the mills. And the health of the children, well …" Mariette sipped her coffee and shuddered to show her disapproval of living conditions in the mill houses.

"It's a wonderful idea, but I just don't think it will be received well," Father Cartier said, folding his hands in his lap.

"Why ever not?" Mariette placed the cup back on the table. "There's no one to take care of the children with their families so far away in Canada. They need a home like this."

"Have you seen any children left alone?"

Mariette nodded. "Dr. Graves has told me about all of the children left without parents and—"

"Yes, but not left alone," Father Cartier interrupted. "The community takes care of them."

Mariette thought about Dorothy, who would have watched Clement while Rachelle was at work. "How about we talk to the people? You could say something at Sunday's service," Mariette said.

"Why wait? Let's go over and talk to them now." The priest smiled as Mariette squirmed in her seat.

"We don't want to interrupt their day. They may be busy. Wouldn't it be better when everyone is together at church?"

"More convenient, perhaps, but why wait so long? The children must be helped." Father Cartier dusted his hands off and rose from his chair. He reached for Mariette's arm.

"Of course," Mariette said and stood. "The children."

A summer shower had washed the dusty streets, but the humid air clung to the smell of poverty. Mariette breathed deeply of the honeysuckle vine on a picket fence. Father Cartier pressed her on to the end of the street.

"Now, in this house there have been four children left without a father," he was saying. "All in one family, so the mother must work as well as the older son. He's fourteen, so work isn't anything new."

Mariette held her skirts as she climbed the few steps to the front land-ing. "How old are the other children?"

"Ten, seven, and three." He pushed the door open and called out, "Good afternoon, Mrs. Kittle. We've come to check on the Fortier children."

A smiling woman hurried to the door. "That's so kind, Father. They're all working in the kitchen. We're baking today."

To Mariette's surprise the kitchen was large and clean. The children were covered to their elbows in flour and dough. The second youngest was rolling out pie crusts and singing David's favorite tune, "Alouette." They visited for a while and Mariette was pleased to discover that the children seemed well cared for.

The next stop involved two families that had lost parents. Both the father and the mother of the Gaspard children had passed in the recent typhus epidemic, and the mother of the La Rue family had been lost to pneumonia. Mr. La Rue was working at the mill as a mechanic and made good money. He took in the Gaspard children and paid the keeper's daughter to watch them.

Father Cartier was leading Mariette to a third house when Jean passed them on the street. "Good morning, Mrs. Graves," he said and stopped to visit. "I see the priest has invited you on his rounds." Jean smiled and nodded to Father Cartier. "I was just visiting the Pérette house. Baby Anne is doing well."

"Thank you for finding her a home," Father Cartier said, placing his hand on Jean's arm. "You're so kind to the children."

"Baby Anne?" Mariette asked. She raised her eyebrows and studied Jean.

"Yes," Jean answered. "Her mother was too weak from typhus to deliver. The baby was taken last Monday as her mother died. I found a nurse for her."

"But what about her father?" Mariette asked.

Jean shook his head slowly. "That's probably what made the mother so weak. Now Anne is an orphan." Jean looked toward a small house at the end of the street and sighed.

"This is why we need an orphanage," Mariette said, grabbing Father Cartier by the elbow. "All of these children need to be cared for."

"An orphanage?" Jean asked, turning his attention back to Mariette.

"Yes. There are so many children left alone after the typhus. The par-ents who survived need to work. It would be such a blessing to have a children's home to care for the little ones here in town." Mariette was getting louder.

"But there aren't any children alone," Jean said. "Dunstable Plains is filled with good Christians who have taken them in." He lifted his arms and motioned toward all of the rundown houses.

"Yes," Mariette said, "but—"

"Just what I have been trying to explain to Mrs. Graves," Father Cartier said. "A children's home is a good idea at times, but not here, not now."

"Hmph," Mariette snorted.

"They haven't a clue what those children need," Mariette said, passing the roast to Increase. "Men have no idea what it takes to raise a child."

Increase grinned. "Really? How have you managed to live this long, son?" He looked at David, then back to his wife. "And I believe you were raised by a … What was it? Oh, yes. A man."

Mariette glared at him across the table while David giggled. "I believe your Aunt Lively had a lot to do with raising you before I came along," she said, hushing the giggling boy. "And whether you realize it or not, I am a woman." She directed her words forcefully at Increase.

"You're right," Increase said. "I'm sorry." He speared a piece of meat and put it on his plate. "But I think that only proves the point."

"How so?" Mariette wasn't ready to back down.

"Lively and you both rescued me and David. When you were little, your father found nursemaids to help. The children you met today, didn't they have someone looking after them?"

"Yes. So? A children's home could do so much good. Just look at the house where Papa helps." Mariette stared at Increase, pointing her fork down the table at him.

"And in Boston that seems to be needed. But here … well, it just doesn't. It seems that the need is being met in another way." He shrugged his shoulders and took a bite of the juicy meat.

Mariette paused and looked at her plate. "Perhaps," she said and turned her fork. "I suppose God meets needs in many ways."

"Hmm," Increase muttered. "Or people do."

*If suffering brings wisdom, I would wish to be less wise.*
~William Butler Yeats~

# CHAPTER 24

THE DINNER TABLE WAS CLEARED and the little family retreated to the parlor. A small package from Concord had arrived earlier in the mail.

"Yes! How wonderful," Mariette exclaimed. Letters had arrived from Lively, and the family was poring over them in the parlor. The glowing lamplight was no comparison to Mariette's beaming face.

"What?" David looked up from the sketches Aunt Lively had sent him.

"What is it?" Increase asked, putting his own letter on his knee.

"She's coming for a visit!" Mariette squealed. "She'll be here next week. 'Mother is doing very well, and I miss you all so much. I simply must squeeze my little apple and drink him all up. I need to see Increase and you too, sister.'" Mariette let the letter fall in her lap. "Oh, it will be wonderful to see her again. I hated that she missed the wedding. It was awful that you didn't have family there."

"I was there," David blustered as he stood up and stomped to Increase. "I'm family. Aren't I, Daddy?"

Increase wrapped his arms around the boy and drew him in his lap. "Yes, you're all the family a man could ask for, but if a guy's going to get extra family, don't you think Aunt Lively is the best thing?"

The rest of the week was spent tearing the house apart and putting it back together so that everything would be fresh as roses for Lively's arrival. Increase visited patients at home and released the last of the typhus victims from the hospital. Rachelle baked lemon squares and strawberry shortcakes and dainty croissants filled with cheeses and jams. Mariette arranged flowers in vases in every room and sprinkled rose petals on the guest bed the day Lively was to arrive.

David and Mariette stood on the platform watching for the train to appear. The bells had called the workers back for the long afternoon shift, and the town was quiet and drowsy. Mariette fanned herself and stared down the tracks.

"When will she get here?" David asked again.

"Soon," Mariette said standing on her toes to see a little farther. She longed for a friend.

A distant throbbing vibrated through the tracks and into the wooden stage like the ticking of an ancient clock.

"It's coming. She's coming," David exclaimed and ran to the edge of the platform.

"Stand back, David," Mariette said, placing her hands on his shoulders. But she didn't pull him back, instead her neck craned past the boy to be the first to see the train.

Lively's trunks were filled with treasures for the little family. There was a new silk shawl for Mariette and a pipe for Increase. And a special treat for David: a new ball glove, and one for a friend to play as well. "Whoa! Now Clement and I can play catch. Thank you, Aunt Lively! Can I go show Clement?"

Lively laughed. "Of course you may."

David ran off to find Clement helping Rachelle in the kitchen. The back door slammed as the boys raced outside.

"I'm so glad he has a friend," Lively said. "He missed that in Boston, being an only child and all." Lively smiled at Increase. "But not much longer, I'll wager. Mariette was simply glowing at the train station."

"We're all glad you're here," Increase said. "It's been too long. Tell us about Mother."

Summer's haze mellowed the green leaves and grasses. The hospital beds were empty again as the townspeople spent more time outdoors, eating fresh foods and breathing clean air. Swimming in the canals was a popular Saturday evening recreation, and Sunday was spent in worship and rest.

Increase lay in bed listening to the bells call the morning shift after breakfast. The hustle of the typhus epidemic was over. Being the only doctor in town kept him well-paid, but also well-worked. He was exhausted.

"Are you sleeping all day?" Mariette opened the bedroom door and walked to the window shade. "David and I are planning a picnic today with Lively and Clement." She pulled up the shade and sunlight filled the room. "We're taking a carriage and riding out to the pond. Will a late dinner be alright? I suppose you have rounds to make until evening anyway." She turned to look at him.

Increase stretched and rubbed his face. "Well, actually I do not." He plopped his arms down on the coverlet and smiled at her. "How would it be if I picnicked with you?" He smiled.

"Really?" Mariette's skirts rustled as she skittered to the bed. "Can you really go with us?" she asked as she sat on the side of the bed next to him. "You haven't done anything with us in so long."

He took her hand and put it to his face. "The price of the job, I'm afraid. But things are going along fine now that summer's here. Let me call over to Nurse Hall and make sure everything is in order."

Increase lay snoozing on the blanket at the edge of the wood. Mariette and Lively stood in the shade and watched the boys playing with sticks in the creek that fed the pond. "Increase needs rest," Lively said, glancing at him on the quilt.

"Yes," Mariette said. "The typhus epidemic wore him out. Maybe now he can get some rest."

The laughter of the boys caught their attention and the women strolled toward them.

"And how are you? Are you getting the rest you need?" Lively asked.

"Yes," Mariette said, stopping at the top of the pond bank. "Rachelle is a big help. She's really becoming a friend. I'm teaching her to read."

"Oh? And what else fills your time?"

"Well, I write letters for a man in town." Mariette giggled and looked away. "He's in love with a woman in Quebec. He needed someone to write in French," she said. "They're very romantic letters. He's sincere and kind."

"Like Increase?" Lively grinned broadly, showing perfect teeth like her brother's, but Mariette only returned a thin-lipped smile.

"What's wrong?" Lively asked. "Isn't Increase sincere and kind?"

"Yes."

"Then … what?"

"David will not be getting a brother or sister," Mariette said. She turned her face away from Lively and looked across the water. Clement was wading at the edge grabbing minnows.

"Sit down," Lively said and gently pulled Mariette to the ground with her. "Have you been to a doctor? Is something the matter?"

"No." Mariette shrugged. "It just isn't happening."

"Oh, sweetheart, these things take time. You haven't been married a year yet."

"You're right about that," Mariette said, anger tinting her words like black paint on a palette.

"You mustn't get angry," Lively said. "God will send a child when the time is right."

"I think there was only one child to be sent that way," Mariette spat.

Lively looked at her sister-in-law. "What do you mean?" she asked, smoothing Mariette's hair behind her ear and reaching for Mariette's hand.

"Watch, Mama!" David called and then skipped a stone across the smooth surface of the water. "Three skips! Beat that, Clement."

Mariette cheered the boys and then said, "David is the only one who will call me 'Mama.' Increase refuses to … you know, 'fulfill his duty.'"

"What?"

Mariette turned red and tears trickled down her cheeks. Her lower lip trembled as she confessed, "He doesn't want me. He still yearns for Annie. I hear him call her name at night."

Lively gasped.

"Oh, he's kind to me and I believe sincere in his friendship," Mariette said. "But we aren't married any more than we were before the wedding."

"Do you want … I mean, should I say…" Lively stumbled to help.

"No," Mariette said and shook her head. "He just doesn't want me. Perhaps God only gives us one true love, and Annie was his."

"That isn't so," Lively said, stroking Mariette's arm. "Maybe he just needs time."

The smell of smoke greeted them along the road home. "What's burning?" Clement was the first to ask wiggling his nose in the air. The women sat up taller in their seats and peered into the retreating forest.

"Smoke ahead," Increase said and urged the horses on. The town was a flurry of movement, water trucks pumping water on Lytle Mills, people passing buckets to the canal and back, and others helping injured workers to the hospital. Increase pulled into the stable.

"Go on, Increase," Mariette told him as he helped the ladies out of the carriage. "I'll take care of this." Increase nodded and took off for Spring Street. He would be gone all night, Mariette was sure.

Smoke filled his nostrils and choked his lungs as Increase charged up the hospital steps. Nurse Lindelof and Nurse Hall were both inside directing the injured to beds and chairs. Two young girls were washing wounds and applying bandages haphazardly.

"Dr. Graves, thank God," Nurse Hall exclaimed. "We called the doctor over in Nashua to come and help. He should be here soon."

"What happened?" Increase asked as he pulled back covers and helped a young man whose leg was turned at an awful angle.

"They're saying it was a belt. Friction caused it to overheat, and all the cotton lint and dust caught a spark. It didn't take long to go up, that's for sure." Nurse Hall shook her head as she scanned the men and women crowding into the small ward. "I've put the worst burns in the surgery," she said, indicating with her head the open door.

"I'll start there."

Increase headed to the new burn unit. Five women from the mill were sitting on the bed and chairs in the room.

"Who's the worst?" Increase asked as he entered.

"Sasha got the worst of it," one of them said. "She's on the bed. Got her shoulder pretty bad. The pipe knocked her out."

"Pipe?" Increase walked to the bed and looked at the young woman.

"Oui. Knocked her upside the noggin when it fell."

Sasha was dazed but compliant. Increase checked her pupils and vital signs. She had some difficulty answering questions, but was starting to come around. The nerve endings along her back and shoulders were still dead. That was good for her. The pain coming her way was going to be immense.

Increase removed her clothing and placed salve on the burns, then loosely covered the area and left her on her stomach. An injection of morphine would help her through the next few hours.

The other women had burns on their hands and arms. "These aren't fire burns," Increase commented. "What happened?"

"The iron steam pipe let loose and fell on Sasha. We had to get it off her. By the time we got her freed, the place was in an uproar. The fire was upstairs in the spinning room." The older woman held her hands gingerly in her lap. "Carrying her out was the hardest part. Everyone pushing and screaming. Smoke choking us and things starting to fall from the ceiling. It was a blessing we work on the bottom floor. God save their souls." She crossed herself.

"Help!" a deep voice echoed.

Increase raced to the front desk. The large man who had brought Mariette apples—Frank—was standing in the doorway carrying a full-grown man whose clothes were burned to his skin. His hair was singed and his face nearly gone.

"In here," Increase said, motioning toward the surgery. He ran to the bed and helped Sasha stand. "Take her to the nurse," he said, passing her arm over to one of the other burned women. "Here, set him down. Gently," Increase said, helping to settle the poor man on the bed.

"I found him stumbling on the stairs," Frank said, his voice one moment strong, the next breaking. "It's Howard Locke. He was fixing some gears up in the looms. They was all screaming and running. He must've got trampled. He's got no family." The man shoved his hands in his pockets. "I hurried fast as I could, Doc, but his breathing's not so good."

Increase was listening to the patient's lungs and heart while Frank told what he knew. Increase was afraid to say what he himself knew. The best he could do was make the man comfortable until he passed. It wouldn't be long. Several ribs were broken and probably pierced his lung. His breathing was very shallow, and that didn't take into account the extent of his burns. *"Sometimes a doctor hopes for death."* He remembered Maurice saying that once. How true.

Increase pumped Mr. Locke full of morphine and then ushered Frank back out to the main room. "Thank you," Increase said as he took Frank by the arm. "You did good today."

"Will he be alright, then?" Frank tried to whisper, but his voice carried through the room.

All eyes turned to Increase as he struggled to find the right answer. Given the extent of the burns and injuries, it would be best if the man died. The life he might possibly live wouldn't be anything Increase would wish on an enemy. Frank saw all those thoughts in Increase's face.

Frank nodded. "He'll be alright. He was a good man."

Time passed in a vacuum. No hunger pangs crossed the line of patients to remind Increase of the hour. After every couple of new patients, Increase would return to the surgery to check on Mr. Locke.

A familiar form sat on the edge of the bed praying over the burned shell of a man. Jean held the victim's hand and whispered unintelligible words.

"He'll be gone soon," Increase said, moving Jean's overcoat and sitting down for a second. "A mercy it is, too."

"Yes, to leave this world and its pain is always a mercy," Jean said. "Death is the first step toward life."

"Hmph," Increase snorted, then stood back up. "Death is only death. At least the pain will be gone. For him anyway."

Jean looked over at Increase. "You're not talking about Howard."

Increase stared at the disfigured face and charred body. "I have patients." He turned and strode out of the room.

Increase worked late into the night setting breaks and sprains. When Jean pulled the surgery door closed and walked out of the hospital with bowed head, Increase knew Howard had left as well. There was no time to mourn; others were waiting for help and comfort.

Several patients needed gashes stitched up. The nurses held their own with the less severe cuts and scrapes. "Who are they?" Increase asked Nurse Lindelof, jerking his head over his left shoulder.

The two young ladies who had been helping when Increase arrived were now checking on patients, bringing them drinks, and making them comfortable. "Those are your new student nurses," Nurse Lindelof said.

"Came this morning on the ten o'clock train from Lowell. Mr. Neal brought them over just before all hell broke loose."

"Baptized by fire, I guess you'd say," Increase said and tried to laugh. He couldn't quite make it, though. "I'm heading home. Tell the girls to report tomorrow at nine o'clock. Send them on home now."

"Yes, Doctor."

The smell of smoke still lingered in the air. Ashes floated carelessly like snowflakes in summer. *Snowflakes in summer.* Increase walked across the street and headed toward home. *I could use a snowy night by the fire. Perhaps Mariette will still be up with Lively. I need a night of talking.*

A lamp had been left on in the hallway upstairs. A hush pervaded the house. *They must be worn out from the day. I know I am.* Increase stopped in the parlor for a nightcap. The glass clinked against the silver tray.

"You're home," Lively said, stirring and stretching on the couch. "I didn't know when you might get back."

"Did Mariette go on to bed?" Increase asked, throwing back the whiskey.

"No. She's gone to Lowell on the last train."

"Lowell?" Increase slammed the glass down. "What in the world has got into her now?" His eyes burned and his nostrils flared.

"Something bad's happened …" Lively started.

"David?" Increase gasped.

"David is fine. It's Clement. We took him home after you left for the hospital. His sister came by a few hours later. He was burning with fever and delirious. Mariette looked in on him and stayed awhile, but came back distraught. Said she's seen kids like this in the orphan homes her father helps with."

"Well, why didn't she come to the hospital?" *Even my wife thinks I'm cursed.* "Why take him all the way to Lowell?"

"She stopped by the hospital before she came home. She said the lines were so long, there wouldn't be anything you could do to help. She bundled him up and took off with Rachelle on the train. She said you could call her at the hospital there tomorrow after you sleep. … Mariette's a good woman, Increase."

"I'm going to bed." Increase climbed the stairs into the depths of exhaustion.

*The* LORD *is close to the brokenhearted....*
~Psalm 34:18~

# CHAPTER 25

WE SET OUT RIGHT AFTER breakfast. *Good. I'll get back to Pater quickly.* We found a ship headed to Samothrace and then to Neapolis. *Two days and I'll be home.*

The winds were fair, the currents to our advantage. We spent some time on land in Samothrace, but slept on the ship. Neapolis couldn't come soon enough.

"There." I pointed out the small coastal port to Timotheos. "We'll go ashore there and walk to Philippi. It's less than half a day's walk. The road is paved and easy. Philippi is a Roman colony, you know."

I turned back to look over the marshy hollow as we passed, remembering the children who set their faces in strong determination. Like Pater they accepted the pain that was theirs to bear—only, Pater's suffering would lead to death. It seemed so unbalanced, the result of suffering. *If you are going to suffer without relief, then why don't the gods just let you die?* I bit my lip and focused on the road. *Will Pater still be there when I get home?*

The land was rising and we stopped to catch our breath. From the stone pavements I looked back to see the sparkling harbor beyond Neapolis. Two distant figures walked up the Via Egnatia, headed toward Philippi and carrying their loads for market.

"Probably fishermen headed for the market in Philippi." I pointed to the men gaining ground on us.

"Maybe they'll sell us some." Paolo's stomach rumbled. "I'm ready to eat." He grinned and rubbed his stomach.

"There's a large cypress up ahead with some rocks. We can stop there and wait for them," I said.

We continued the climb, the tree ahead growing on the horizon. I shaded my eyes with my hand.

"Looks like someone already beat us there." I pointed to the large rocks under the tree. "Mm. Maybe ... I think that's Jehan." I laughed. "He must've been back to the marsh to check on our patients."

Jehan watched us trek up the hill.

"Loukas, I thought you might be coming today." He waved to the rock beside him. "Who are your companions?"

I flopped down and wiped the sweat from my eyes. "This is Paolo, Silvanus, and Timotheos."

They all waved in greeting.

"I met them at Ignatius's house."

"Welcome. Welcome. Are you hungry?"

"Yes, indeed," Paolo said.

"I don't have much, but what I have I'll share. Open the bag, Loukas."

I reached into the medicine bag. At the very bottom Jehan had packed a small basket. I slid it out of the bag and opened the lid. The briny smell of anchovies woke my hunger.

"Lay it out here," Jehan said as he brushed aside leaf litter on the rock.

I set down my outer cloak and laid out the lunch between us: anchovies, barley bread, radishes and onions, and a small mound of goat's cheese. Jehan poured a flask of water over his hands and prayed.

Then Jehan waved to the ground in front of us and the men sat. He trickled water over their hands, and they dripped dry before taking any food.

"You come from far?" Jehan asked, sucking the salt from the fish.

"Not so terribly far in such a large empire." Paolo was every bit the politician. "We come from Jerusalem, but we've stopped many places. We hope to stay in Philippi for a while. ... Is it a fair city?"

"You'll stay with me," Jehan said. "It isn't much, but the beds are clean and the food nutritious. You look like you could use a good rest." He looked at Paolo and touched his own eyes.

Paolo's eyes were red and inflamed, swollen like a bad bee sting. He touched them gingerly.

"Yes. I've tried aloes and ointments, but no luck. Some days are worse than others." He shrugged and tore off a chunk of bread. "We would be honored to stay with you. Thank you very much."

"I have some Phrygian powder at home. I can try that if you like."

I felt pleased Jehan had taken to Paolo. I liked him too.

Paolo smiled and nodded. "I'd like that very much. Praise God for sending us lunch and good doctors, brothers."

"He always provides," Silvanus said.

Paolo sat in the courtyard enjoying the shade of the quince tree. The afternoon sun was strong, burning the light, winter-bleached skin.

"Did you get in some poison?" I asked Paolo, applying the salve I had purchased from a Laodicean dealer in Rome.

"No, I was struck by the God of the Israelites."

I stood back and stared. "What did you do to him?" My mouth hung open.

"I tried to stop his Son."

He looked toward me, unseeing, his eyes covered with the thick salve.

"Why would you stop a god's son? I worship Dionysus, son of Zeus, and Asclepius, son of Apollo. You must be mad."

He chuckled. "I certainly see the error of my ways now." He tipped his blind face toward the sky. "I didn't know who he was."

"So now you suffer." I massaged his temples. "No different than the rest of the world, I suppose. Everyone suffers."

"Hmm. What do you suffer from?"

"Nothing right now; my time hasn't come. But Pater, he suffers with pthisis." I looked over Paolo's head to the house. "It's almost over, though."

"Can I see him when you're done with my treatment?"

"Yes, of course." I smiled. "Pater enjoys visitors."

"Pater ... Pater."

I knocked gently on the wall and walked into the room. Pater was sleeping, his breathing shallow and rasping. I touched his shoulder and gave a gentle nudge.

"Pater, I've come back ... and brought a visitor."

"Loukas." Pater's voice cracked.

He opened his eyes slowly and blinked to focus. A half smile raced across his face and then was gone like sunshine behind an autumn cloud. He tried to hold my hand, but couldn't get his out of the cover.

"Lie still, Pater. It's okay. This is Paolo."

Paolo joined us at the bed.

"He's traveling through Philippi," I said, "staying at Jehan's house."

Pater turned his head toward Paolo. "Khaírete! Welcome to Philippi. Jehan … will take good care of you."

"Loukas has taken good care of me too. He's treating my eyes."

Pater smiled and nodded. "He will be a great doctor one day."

I stroked his arm and was concerned to feel the heat radiating from him. I took a rag from the water basin and smoothed it across his forehead.

"I used to worry about Loukas." Pater paused to catch his breath. "Now he worries about me."

"I would like to thank Loukas … for helping me," Paolo said. "Would it be alright if I give you something?"

I looked at Paolo. He was watching Pater, and he took his hand. *What does he have to give? He barely had anything in his bag when we stopped at Jehan's.*

Pater nodded and Paolo began to speak. "There is a God of healing. He has been kind and generous to me, healing my heart and soul. Now I ask him to grant healing to your body, to your lungs, to your life."

Pater closed his eyes. I was sure Paolo meant well, and this was likely all he had to give: a prayer, a blessing, a wish. My eyes filled as I realized that this was all we had left: wishes.

Pater breathed deeply, filling his chest with air. His eyes opened, bright like the noonday sun. His skin turned pink, the blood flowing through his veins with renewed life.

"I can breathe," Pater said, his voice growing stronger with each word. "Loukas! I can breathe."

He sat up in bed so quickly that I grabbed him by the arm to prevent a fall, but he pushed my hand aside and jumped out of bed.

"I can breathe!"

He stood there, half naked, taking deep breaths and blowing them out again like a breaching whale. He laughed and grabbed hold of me, spinning me around as if I were ten again. I laughed with him, the room spinning not just from Pater's antics.

Pater let me go and looked at Paolo. "You … You did this." Pater fell to his knees and pulled me down with him. "It's Asclepius."

*How can fear and joy flow from the same river?* Tears of gratitude and great awe washed me. Pater bowed and I followed, my face touching the floor.

"No, no." Paolo pulled us up by the arms. "I'm no god. Don't bow to me."

We lifted our heads and struggled to our feet, unsure how to behave in front of a god.

"It was your dream, Pater. You were right: Asclepius wouldn't heal you. It was this … this … Paolo."

"No." Paolo shook his head and grinned. "It was the God of the Israelites and his Son, Jesus, the Christ."

"But you said he struck you. Your eyes …" I felt dumbfounded.

"Yes." He touched his face and a shadow passed over him. "You should feed your father, Loukas. He's weak after such a long sickness." Paolo shook Pater's hand. "I better head back to Jehan's before dinner. Hypíaine, Aegeus. Hypíaine, Loukas."

We watched Paolo leave the room, then I raced to catch up.

"Paolo, wait."

He stopped and turned.

"Thank you," I said. "Thank you for healing Pater. I don't understand … I … I don't …"

Paolo grasped my arm and smiled like a mother over an infant. "You are welcome, Loukas. You and your father. Good-bye."

Pater and I carried large baskets on our shoulders as neighbors and old friends stared, some waving, some stopping to speak. We climbed the hill to Jehan's. Pater never stopped once to catch his breath.

Silvanus was in the garden, watering some new sprouts. "Good evening, Loukas." He put the pail down and walked to us. "Is this your father?"

"Yes. Pater, this is Silvanus. He's traveling with Paolo." I turned back to the tall, slender man. "Silvanus, this is my very strong and healthy father, Aegeus."

"It's good to meet you. Paolo told me about you." He took the basket from Pater. "Please come in. Jehan and Timotheos are getting dinner ready."

"We brought you dinner … and more besides." I lifted the lid on the basket to let Silvanus peek inside.

It was a celebration like no other. I never expected that I would eat with my father again, and here he was talking and laughing with the men while we feasted on Casper's fresh fish, leeks, olives, cheeses, breads, pastries, almonds, and walnuts. There was plenty of wine and shepherd's tea as well. I didn't want it to end.

But night falls even on the flames fanned by happiness and gratitude. The moon shone on the aromatic herb garden as the men walked us to the gate.

"Will you join us at the prayer meeting tomorrow evening, Aegeus?" Jehan asked.

"Yes," Paolo said. He stepped forward. "Please come. I'll tell you more about the God who healed you." Paolo looked at me. "You too, Loukas."

"We'll be there," Pater said.

Jehan put his hand on my shoulder. "Stay with your father tomorrow. I can handle the rounds on my own."

I nodded, feeling his breath on my cheek, an Etesian wind, warm and unsettling.

Pater walked into the cove like a deer entering a meadow. A god that could heal without first requiring payment or sacrifice was a god to fear. The leaves were daily growing fuller now, and the cove was shady, mysterious. Pater sat on the edge of a bench.

I followed behind and sat next to him. Ludia came in and squeezed my shoulders like an old aunt or grandmother.

"I'm glad you're back," she said. "Who's this?"

"Ludia, this is my father, Aegeus. Pater, this is Ludia. She knows Jehan."

"Ah, a friend of Jehan is a friend of mine. You already know my Loukas, huh?"

"We've met a couple of times. He has a … gift …" She looked at me and back at Pater. "For saying the hard things."

"A good trait for a doctor." Pater nodded his approval.

"Aegeus. Loukas. I'm glad to see you here." Jehan came in with Paolo. "Our guests have offered to speak to us this evening."

Pater's eyes shone. "I'm anxious to hear what they have to say."

After singing and prayers, Paolo stood in the middle of the small group. "Friends and followers of the Holy God of Israel. Thank you for inviting me and my friends, Silvanus and Timotheos, to your prayer meeting. We have traveled far across the Roman Empire, and everywhere we go, we look for followers like you, people who will welcome us, as you have done so abundantly.

"I was born in Tarsus across the sea, but I belonged to the tribe of Benjamin. My parents were concerned that I should know the Holy Scriptures, so we moved to Jerusalem where I could study under the best scholars. I was a Pharisee, most well versed in Jewish law."

I saw Ludia lean forward, her gaze never straying from Paolo. I wondered what she would say if she knew about Pater and the miraculous healing.

"I finished my formal education and was gaining ground in the ranks of the Pharisees, when a man named Jesus began preaching a new way. Some said he performed miracles, healings, and signs. But it seemed that he was defying the Jewish laws and traditions. In my great fervor to defend the Lord of Israel, I joined other Pharisees in condemning the man.

"He was sentenced to hang on a cross, and he died as any blasphemer should." Paolo's voice cracked and his eyes filled with tears. "After he was crucified, rumors started that he had been raised from the dead. I believed it was his disciples making up stories, perverting the great history of God's people."

Paolo smiled as if in apology, then wiped his eyes with the back of his hand and finally went on. "I was given permission to hunt down the followers of this man, Jesus. I tore into their homes and secret assemblies. I threw them in jail and even had them killed."

He shook his head and took a deep breath. "I was doing what I thought was right. I was defending my Lord, protecting his sacred truths."

Silvanus stood and placed his hand on Paolo's shoulder. "Your heart was in the right place. Remember he says, 'I am God, and there is no other; I am God, and there is none like me.' You did your best."

"Yes." The Jews in the arbor agreed with him.

Paolo put his arm around Silvanus's waist. "Silvanus is my shelter when I attack myself. It's true that I was doing my best to honor God, but I was wrong."

The audience looked at each other. How could it be wrong to honor God? Even I knew all gods should be honored. *Maybe Paolo really is crazy.*

Paolo raised his hands to quiet the group and continued. "It wasn't wrong for me to honor God. No, not at all. ... But ..."

We watched him like owls studying the night ground.

"It was wrong, because I was wrong. ... But I'm getting ahead of myself. I was given permission to travel to Damascus to root out and unearth followers of the Way. My companions and I had traveled over a week and were getting close to Damascus. I remember the sky was dark, and we were headed down a slope. The river was high and I was wondering about crossing. Then ..." Paolo looked up at the trees overhead. "A bright light shone on us, and a voice spoke.

"I was terrified, a lamb caught in a lion's mouth. 'Why are you persecuting me?' the voice asked."

I knew what was coming, sort of, so I watched the others. Ludia's eyes were large, unblinking. Pater listened like a child around a winter fire.

Paolo dropped to the ground as he said, "I fell to my knees. 'Who are you?' I asked. 'I am Jesus,' was the answer."

The crowd gasped.

"That was my reaction," Paolo said and smiled. "I was told to go to Damascus and stay on Straight Street, fitting I suppose, since I needed straightened out." He chuckled as he stood back up. "But the light ... it blinded me." Paolo looked at me, his lips thin. "I was blind for three days until a man named Ananias, a follower of this Jesus, came to the house where I was staying and opened my eyes so I could see again."

*I wonder what medicine he used?*

"I was horrified to find out that Jesus was the Son of God. All of that time I had been trying to serve God, but I was actually fighting him. I was baptized immediately, giving myself up to the one I had tried to destroy. I stayed in Damascus learning about Jesus, then I went into the synagogues and gave testimony that Jesus is the Son of God."

The small group under the boughs began to whisper and titter.

*He's lost his mind. He blasphemes.*

I stood up. "I don't know much about your god, but this I do know."

The group quieted.

"My father was sick ... with phthisis. He ..." I hesitated to say it in front of Pater. "He was nearly dead. I'm a doctor, trained in Athens and Rome, and I can tell you that folks don't recover, not at that stage."

Pater looked around and nodded to the people.

"Paolo came to our house yesterday and prayed over Pater, in the name of this Jesus, and Pater sits among you now, breathing ... healthy ... strong."

Pater stood up and took a deep breath, pounding his chest like a glad-iator. "It's true," he said.

"Asclepius and Dionysus, neither one, could heal Pater ... but Jesus did." I sat down, my legs shaking.

Pater took another deep breath, pounded once more for good measure, and then sat on the seat next to me.

Paolo smiled and looked at me. "You may not know the Holy One of Israel, but you have encountered his Son, Jesus the Christ. If you are will-ing to turn your life over to him ..." Paolo turned to look at each person. "Anyone who is willing to turn to Jesus ... he will accept you. Join me in the greatest healing you'll ever experience: the healing of your soul."

Ludia stood up. "What do we need to do? Offer a sacrifice? I have a calf at home."

Paolo shook his head. "Jesus was the sacrifice when he hung on the cross. Now the sacrifice he asks is that you offer your life to him."

We all gasped again. Ludia tilted her head and raised her brows.

"No, no," Paolo said. "Nothing like that. Jesus asks for your life in ser-vice, to help others, show others the way to a whole life."

"There's wisdom in that. How do I start?" Ludia asked.

"The same as I did: be baptized, here, now, in the river. Then live for Christ, teach others, share the good news." Paolo lifted his arms to the trees above. "God beckons all of you to come to his Son, come for life and healing."

Ludia walked toward the riverbank, Paolo and Silvanus by her side. They helped her down the steep incline into the icy waters from Mount Pangaion. They plunged her into the flowing water, and when she came up, it was as a woman giving birth. The waters separated and something new, something I didn't understand, was born.

Pater and I walked home in silence.

*It is not death, it is dying that alarms me.*
~Michel de Montaigne~

# CHAPTER 26

THE FINAL WORK BELL ECHOED through the empty streets as Increase entered the hospital. Morning light was just breaking the horizon and a chill lingered in the smoke-tainted air.

"Good morning, Doctor," Nurse Lindelof greeted him.

Increase nodded and walked to the front desk.

"Sasha is sleeping fitfully," she continued in whispers of compassion and dread. "I gave her another shot of morphine an hour ago."

"Good," Increase said and turned to enter the surgery. "All we can do is try to keep her comfortable."

A shaft of light fell across the room as Increase opened the door. The curtains were pulled tight, but a small lamp glowed in the corner, keeping vigil. The body of Howard Locke still lay in the bed, draped with sheets. Increase pulled the cover back and saw that the body had been cleaned. A familiar overcoat was wrapped tightly around the peaceful body.

"Jean," Increase whispered.

"It's Mrs. Graves, Doctor," Nurse Hall said standing next to the phone. "She wants to speak to you."

Increase walked to the phone and took the earpiece from her. "Hello?"

"Oh, Increase," Mariette sobbed on the other end. Her breath caught in little choking gasps that tore at Increase.

"What is it?" he asked as the vision of dead Mr. Locke in the next room floated before his eyes. *Not Clement, please.*

Mariette took a deep breath, calming herself. "It's terrible, Increase. I can't bear to see him this way, and poor Rachelle is beside herself with fear."

Increase relaxed his shoulders; at least it wasn't the worst.

"He has a terrible fever and cries in pain whenever he's awake. He says his whole body aches, and now he's vomiting uncontrollably. The doctors say it will get worse before it gets better. I just don't think I can take anymore." Her voice trailed off, leaving the line quiet.

"What are the doctors saying?" he asked.

"Polio." The word slithered across the line like a poisonous serpent.

"God help us," Increase said. An outbreak in Vermont about five or six years ago had taken well over a hundred people. *Why, God? Can't we recover from one calamity before you send another to tear us down?*

"I need to stay with Rachelle at least the rest of the week. I suppose Lively can stay with David?" She was pragmatic, businesslike, and sensible. Of course David would need watching while Increase attended to things at the hospital.

"I'll call Lively, but I'm sure she'll be happy to help," Increase said. "Be very careful, Mariette. Polio is very contagious." His voice was husky. He cleared his throat. "Give Rachelle and Clement our best."

"Good-bye, Increase."

"Good-bye." *Lively is right. Mariette is a good woman.*

Mariette and Rachelle returned on the Saturday evening train. Increase, David, and Lively waited on the platform for the passengers to disembark.

"There she is! Mama! Mama! Over here," David called as Mariette looked over the crowd from the top step. Her smile reawakened the sun and lit the dusky train station when she spotted the jumping boy. Mariette waved and descended the last few steps.

David ran to the train, barreling into Mariette with arms wide and ready for a hug. Mariette's laughter and David's chatter made all those around her smile.

"I missed you so much," David said. "Aunt Lively and I read *The Jungle Book* twice. And she taught me how to make fried tomatoes. Daddy was grumpy the whole time you were gone too. Aunt Lively says that shows how much he missed you."

Mariette bent to kiss the boy's head and cheeks, and squeezed him hard. "I missed you too. And I dare say I was grumpy myself." She raised herself up and hugged Lively. "Thank you for taking care of David."

"Anything for my sister," Lively said, brushing Mariette's cheek with her lips. "And who is this?"

Rachelle stepped forward and dipped her chin. "Good evening, ma'am."

"This is Rachelle, Clement's sister. You met the night after our picnic."

"Of course." Lively looked at the sunken cheeks and dull eyes, scarcely recognizing the girl.

Increase stood behind Lively like a sailor without his sea legs. "We're glad you're back. How's Clement faring?"

Mariette and Lively let go of each other. "He's holding his own now. Rachelle could barely tear herself from him, but we can't do anything more at this point. Time, you know," Mariette answered, looking into his eyes.

"Can we give you a ride home?" Increase asked Rachelle.

"No, thank you, Dr. Graves. The walk is short and will do me good. I'll see you Monday. Thank you, Mariette." She curtsied and tried to turn, but Mariette caught hold of her and hugged the girl long and hard. Tears coursed down Rachelle's cheeks as she gave a last embrace.

Mariette let go and watched her leave. She took a deep breath and turned back to Increase. "How are you holding up? How is the burn patient?"

"No talk about work tonight, please. Let's go home." He took her arm and headed toward the carriage. "You look like you could use a long bath and a good night's rest."

"Yes." She sighed and leaned her head onto his arm. "I missed you," she murmured. He let go of her arm and circled her shoulders instead, drawing her close beside him. David trotted next to them, holding her skirt.

The morning light was beginning to infiltrate the lonely room. Rachelle held vigil the entire night in the wooden chair by the window. The kitchen was where she felt the ghosts of family and familiarity. It was here that Mamere taught her to cook and sew. Here, too, was where she had said good-bye to the woman who had been a mother to her. *What will I do, Mamere?* Wet, salty cheeks were her only reply.

A light tapping on the door startled her. Rachelle crossed the room in a trance and turned the doorknob. The medic stood in the dark hallway.

"Come in," Rachelle managed to say. The words choked in her dry throat.

Jean crossed the threshold and swung the door closed behind him. "You haven't slept," he said, noticing the wrinkled dress she had worn all week.

"No." She shook her head and looked at the floor. "Come, sit," she invited as she turned back to the kitchen.

Jean followed the girl into the small room. He pulled the curtain aside to let in the growing light and then sat on the bench between the stove and the table. "How is Clement?"

"Improving, the doctors say at least. The worst seems to be over. I was so afraid, Medic." Her eyes swam in pools of despair. "It was good of Mariette … Mrs. Graves … to take us to the hospital. Clement wouldn't have made it otherwise." She stood to look out the grimy window. She took a deep breath and sighed staccato breaths. "But how will I ever pay it all? Papa can't send me any money, and there isn't any way to pay it back with my job." She turned, looking straight into Jean's face. "And how will I ever go back to work with a paralyzed brother to care for?" The wracking sobs shook her body.

Jean moved to her in one motion. "The Great Physician heals more than bodies." He held her close and rubbed her back. She buried her face in his chest and cried freely.

Increase left Mariette sleeping in bed and headed to the hospital for the morning rounds. He wanted to be back before the bells called everyone to church.

"I didn't expect to see you, Doctor," Nurse Lindelof said from the side of Sasha's bed. "I guess you heard about the fevers over on Elm Street."

"Fevers?" Increase stopped.

"Vomiting, fever, aches …"

"No," Increase said, shaking his head in disbelief. "I thought we avoided the polio when nothing came earlier." He hurried to the surgery to get his medical bag. "I'll head over there now," he called as he rushed across the front room and out the door.

The early September morning was just warming as Increase knocked on the first door on Elm. "Thank goodness you're here," the keeper said as she ushered him in. "I've been worrying all night. It seems to be spreading across the whole building."

Increase flew from one person to the next. There was no rhyme or reason to the sickness; every family seemed to have someone affected. Thankfully only a few had the severe form of the disease that often led to paralysis. Increase prescribed fever reducers and analgesics. There was little more he could do.

He pinned the last "Quarantined" sign on a door and turned down the walk.

"Good morning," a voice rang out. "I hear your lovely wife made it back to town last night." Jean walked up to Increase and clapped him on the back. "You must be so relieved."

"Yes," Increase said. He tried to smile but it just wouldn't come.

"You've been checking on the sick, I see," Jean said, glancing at the sign on the door. "So much sickness can wear on the soul. Are you and Mariette heading to church?"

"Church? For what?" Increase couldn't hide the bitterness he felt.

"Increase, no physician enjoys suffering. The point of the physician is of course to heal—"

"And yet healing is arbitrary," Increase cut in with the vehemence of a spirit-weary man. "Sometimes the methods work; sometimes they don't. And how do I live with the knowledge that my life's work is arbitrary, random at best?"

"Your work is not arbitrary, good man. Your work is necessary and vital." Jean searched Increase's face and stepped closer. "Your methods, your prescriptions, perhaps your diagnoses may be wrong, even at times arbitrary, but your mission is still to heal."

"If my mission is to heal, then why can't I be successful? There's too much loss," Increase said and looked at the ground. The weight of the past week felt heavy on his shoulders.

"Do you know the story of Job?" Jean asked.

Increase looked at Jean. "Of course, and that right there's an example of God's arbitrary dictates," he said, reloading his guns for the fight. "Job had done everything right, said the right things, offered the right things, even tried to protect others with his sacrifices. But God failed him, let them all die." His face was red and his chest heaved. "Maybe he got it all back at the end, but it wasn't fair to let him lose it in the first place, not the ones he loved."

"To you loss looks like the wrong solution, but loss often fits into a greater scheme than your own life. Job had a choice in his loss. He didn't understand the losses … the pain and suffering … but he chose to honor God. The choice of how he responded to suffering affected the very heavens. God and the angels sang his praises, and Job showed Satan that good is always better than evil." Jean placed his hand over Increase's heart. "You so often let the evil win, my friend."

"But what did those people ever do to deserve the evil of polio? What did they ever do to deserve a poor excuse of a doctor like me?" Increase towered over Jean. He could never understand why this peaceful man produced such anger in himself, but here he was ready to knock him down on the street.

"You aren't talking about polio anymore, are you?" Jean stood his ground. "You left your wife, Mariette, in bed this morning, warm and safe, but now it's your first wife that calls your name."

"What do you know about Annie? You're not even married."

"Perhaps not, but I know about love." Jean looked away and started walking again.

Increase matched his pace, watching his face from the side. "I know I'm not a great doctor. I know I fail so many times, but why couldn't I help Annie? Why did I have to lose her? Why me?"

"Your successes and failures as a doctor have nothing to do with losing Annie. And why not you? What did you ever do to deserve Annie in the first place?" Jean's voice remained calm and his stride rhythmic.

Increase shook his head. "So … So you're saying God shouldn't have given me Annie in the first place? That I never deserved her to start with?"

Jean smiled. "Well, did you?"

The two walked through the warm morning sunshine deep in thought. Jean pulled up short at the corner. "I'm headed to the church. Perhaps I will see you there. Good day, Increase." He tipped his hat and turned.

Mariette was pinning a hat in her hair when Increase walked in the bedroom. "Good morning," she said and smiled at him in the mirror. "Is everything alright at the hospital? I thought you would be back sooner." She swiveled around on her stool and looked up at him. "It sure is good to be home."

"I'm glad you came back safely. We'll have to keep an eye on you, and Lively and David too. I spent the morning making house calls. The polio is starting after all. I guess Clement was just the first unlucky victim." Increase took a deep breath and plopped down on the bed.

"Oh no." Mariette moved to the bed and stroked Increase's temple. "Are you up to coming to church or are you too worn out?" Her worried frown made him smile.

"I'll go for you. I'll be okay soon," he said, tucking a curl behind her ear. "Are the others ready?"

Mariette smiled and leaned down to kiss his cheek. "David wanted to see Father Cartier before service, so Lively offered to walk with him. I was waiting to see if you might get home soon."

"I would have been home sooner, but I met Jean Giatros along the way."

"And how is Jean? He's such a sweet man." Mariette stood up and pulled Increase from the bed.

"Mm. Sweet? I don't know. He has a good heart, though. Come on."

The murmuring of voices rustled through the church like a breeze through summer trees. Mariette and Increase spotted David and Lively and sat down next to them. The choir sang as the mass began: "All glory, laud, and honor to you, Redeemer, King, to whom the lips of children made sweet hosannas ring."

Increase looked over at David, his lips mouthing the words. *Why should his lips or any lips bring praise to a healer who chooses not to heal?* The thought came unbidden and nestled down, preparing for a long stay. Mariette brushed the back of his hand with her fingers. It was something Annie used to do when his mind was laboring over a difficult patient. He thrust his hand into his jacket pocket. He couldn't focus the rest of the service.

"Before the Concluding Rites, I would like to say a few words," the priest's voice broke into Increase's thoughts. "Some folks in our community have introduced me to the idea of a children's home, like the ones in Boston. The typhus epidemic this past spring excited those who were unaware of our community's commitment to each other. So many of you stepped in and offered the hand of charity and love to your neighbors." Father Cartier nodded and smiled at Mr. LaRue, who bobbled a child on his knee while three others lined the pew beside him. "But now we have another difficulty. ... As many of you know, little Clement Michaud has been hospitalized in Lowell for polio."

A hushed tittering could be heard throughout the chapel. The priest held up his hands to silence them.

"Medic Jean Giatros tells me that Rachelle is worried about paying the bills. I assured him that we, her family, will handle the matter."

After the final blessing the congregation stood as one and filed past the offering box. Every hand deposited a gift; even the tiny fist of the littlest LaRue.

"I can pack a sandwich for the train ride back to Concord," Lively said as she dropped her coins in the box.

"Can I have the money you would use for my next book?" David whispered as he pulled on Mariette's sleeve.

Mariette opened her velvet handbag and pulled out twenty dollars. "How about enough for a library?" She smiled down at David. He hugged her waist and then deposited the entire amount with one exultant plunge into the slot in the wooden chest.

*There are four questions of value in life, Don Octavio. What is sacred? Of what is the spirit made? What is worth living for and what is worth dying for? The answer to each is the same. Only love.*
~Lord Byron~

# CHAPTER 27

*SHE LOOKS LIKE A BOUQUET of flowers wilting in a tight grasp.* Increase entered the bedroom and surveyed the ring of children around their mother. One wiped her brow with a damp cloth, another held her hand, and a third sat near her feet caressing her legs as if they were precious gold.

"Scoot on out while I look your mother over," he said, taking the one at the foot of the bed by the shoulders. "It'll just take a few minutes," he said as they turned aside and gazed toward the bed while walking out the door. The oldest pulled it shut behind him.

"They're worried," the sick woman croaked through dry lips.

"Everyone is these days. Open." Increase placed a glass thermometer in her mouth and started counting her pulse.

"Iss jus' a little something," she tried to say.

"Shh. I'll be the judge of that. Any headache?"

She nodded. She would be the seventh polio patient in the last two days. Increase had been to the Health Department already, but Mr. Taylor was reluctant to call an epidemic yet. *It hasn't spread to his side of town, that's why.*

"I'll be back tomorrow. I'll have Nona bring in some chamomile tea; it'll help you rest." He pulled the coverlet up, though the Indian summer day was warm. She nodded and shifted her weight. *At least she's still moving,* he thought.

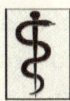

The hospital was hushed and dim when Increase entered. Nurse Hall was at the front desk, wiping her eyes. "Afternoon, Doctor," she said. "Harvey just passed."

Increase turned into the larger room of beds and saw Jean seated on the bed where Harvey, a stoic boy only four years old, had spent the last two weeks. Jean pulled the sheet over Harvey's face as he finished praying.

"Why does he take them so young? What did this little one ever do to him?" Increase muttered as he lifted the boy to carry him from the room.

Jean picked up the wooden rabbit Harvey had clung to and followed behind Increase to the surgery. The family would be there soon to gather the body.

"I don't understand how you can keep praying to a god that steals children from their families." Increase straightened the limbs of the boy as he laid him on the bed. "What kind of god would do that?"

"Are you asking me or yourself?" Jean tucked the little rabbit into the boy's hand.

"I don't know," Increase answered. He sighed and his shoulders drooped. He looked into Jean's eyes, like a fawn staring at his first human, curious but fearful.

"The child, like all children, already belongs to God," Jean said. "He doesn't steal them; he welcomes them."

"But why so young? Why when they have so much life left to live?"

"Perhaps Harvey could have lived longer. His life may even have brought great goodness to those he loved. But surely his life would've also included suffering. If he didn't die today, he would die another." Jean's tender gaze moved from the boy's face to Increase's. "Everyone on earth dies sometime."

"Well, why can't we live forever?" Increase huffed his lips and stared at the other man. "Tell me that."

"You can. Everyone can … if they choose to, anyway."

"I'm not talking about your heaven and hell. I just don't understand why." Increase stepped back to look fully at Jean.

"You don't understand where polio comes from either, but instead of avoiding people with polio, you try to help them. Why?"

"Because I don't want them to suffer."

"And God doesn't want them to suffer either."

"Then why won't he let me heal them?"

"No!" Harvey's mother screamed from the front room.

"It's time to ease more suffering." Jean turned to meet the mourning parents who fell into the room.

"I told her he could stay with us. There's the room off the kitchen where we can put two small beds. That way she can be here to watch over him." Mariette pulled apart another biscuit and spread apple jelly on it. "Would that be alright with you?"

Increase chewed on the thick bacon, wondering how many mothers like Harvey's he would have to comfort before the Health Department would do anything.

"Increase?"

Increase looked up. "I'm sorry. What were you saying?"

"Rachelle brings Clement back from the hospital this week. I told her they should stay here. They can have the room off the kitchen and we can put two beds in there. Does that sound good?"

Increase noticed a tenderness in her voice, like Annie's when she talked about growing their family, but also like Maurice's when he spoke of the orphans on the streets. "Yes. Of course." He cleared his throat. "It would be good for all of us, I think. Rachelle would be here for you while I'm so busy with the community, and David will be thrilled to have Clement nearby."

Mariette smiled. "Thank you. I'll let Rachelle know."

Rachelle was expected on the ten o'clock train, but she hadn't arrived. Mariette paced. *I'll wander over to the hospital and check on Increase. He'll know what to do.*

The morning air was faint with the last of summer's harvest. Somewhere a farmer had cut hay and the sweet breeze mellowed Mariette. The front door of the hospital stood wide open to the morning sun.

Mariette knocked gently on the door and called out, "Good morning."

Voices echoed in the small surgery. Mariette crossed the front room and waved to Nurse Hall in the ward room. The door to the surgery was slightly ajar, and Mariette could make out Increase's deep bass. She tapped on the door and pushed it open.

Four young girls were gathered around Increase as he explained the surgical tools. All eyes were fastened on him. No one noticed Mariette's quiet entrance. She stood just inside and listened.

"I was reading a paper last night about new research in Germany on the influenza virus. It seems so very hopeful," a petite brunette was saying. "The needles they're using are so much smaller that the children aren't as fearful."

Increase nodded. "I'm glad to hear you're adding to your reading list, Helen. The influenza research will be beneficial this winter, but right now we need help with the polio epidemic."

"Of course, Doctor." She smiled.

Mariette cleared her throat and Increase glanced up.

"Is something the matter?" he asked. "Is it David?"

Mariette shook her head. *Why does he always assume something is wrong when I show up?* He so seldom seemed pleased to see her. "David is fine. I left him at home while I went to the train station, but Rachelle wasn't on the ten o'clock."

"Probably took longer to get Clement checked out of the hospital. If she isn't on the next train, I'll call the Lowell hospital." He nodded to dismiss her.

She backed out of the room and pulled the door closed behind her to the tittering of the petite brunette.

"Mrs. Graves?" Nurse Hall was back at the front desk.

Mariette glanced up and forced a smile. "Yes?"

"Mr. Viollette is here. He saw you pass by and asked if you could read him a letter. I can tell him you don't have time ..." She paused and smoothed a few hairs under her white nurse's cap.

"Mr. Viollette? Yes ... of course I can read to him. He's a friend of mine." She smiled at Nurse Hall's surprise and turned into the ward.

Frank Viollette seemed to spill from the bed. His broad shoulders spanned the width of the cot and his long legs dangled off the end. His toes peeked out from the too short covers. "Bonne madame du matin— Good morning, madame." His deep voice echoed in friendly ripples across the room.

"Bon jour. I didn't know you were in hospital." Mariette sat in the chair beside the bed and reached for Frank's hand. "You seem well enough to me."

"Oui. I am nearly better, so the good doctor says. Took three of the mill men to carry me in here. The fever 'bout to killed me. But listen." He pulled a paper from under the sheets and looked around conspiratorially. "I have another letter from Ethel. Would you?" He held the paper toward her.

Mariette smiled. Ethel's letters were always a pleasure to read. "'Dearest Frank, I received your letter today and right away knew I must answer it.'" Mariette peered over the paper at Frank. Light danced in his eyes and color pranced across his cheeks. "'All is well here, though you are always missed. The days are growing shorter already and I feel certain a long winter is ahead. I watched a flock of geese heading south today and longed to fly with them to your New Hampshire. They would continue on, of course, but I would be content to stop. I missed our long evening visits last winter. The other men here never want to talk, and no one plays Up Jenkins as well as you. Watch for the geese tomorrow. I may be riding on the back of one. Would you catch me if I fell? With much love, Ethel.'" Mariette folded the thin paper and slid it back in the envelope. "I'd like to meet Ethel someday," she said as she handed back the letter.

"Perhaps you will, but life will have to be different here first. I can't take her away from her family without a hope of something better." Frank tucked the letter back under the covers and rested his hands over it. "Her family may have nothing, but at least they have each other. What could I give Ethel here but only nothing?"

"One person can be more than enough … if there is love," Mariette said, looking toward the surgery.

*Life is short, but troubles make it longer.*
~Syrus~

# CHAPTER 28

DAVID JUMPED UP AND DOWN as the train's coach attendants lifted Clement down and into the waiting wheelchair. Mariette tried to hold him back. "Attention, mon amour. Clement is still very ill. You must be patient and calm."

"Je vous ai manqué—I missed you," Clement cried as he spied David and threw his arms wide.

David squirmed from under Mariette's grasp and ran to his best friend. The boys embraced and started talking all at once.

Rachelle gathered the last of the bags from the porter and turned to Mariette. "Je suis désolée—I'm sorry. The doctor wouldn't let us go until he was certain we knew how to handle everything. He's still worried about Clement's breathing." She glanced down at the boys, then back to Mariette. "I assured him that Dr. Graves will be very nearby, and we will have everything we need. Thank you again for allowing us to stay with you. It puts me at ease." Grateful tears glistened at the corners of her eyes.

"We would have it no other way. The whole family insists." She took the small bags from Rachelle and turned toward a carriage. "I ordered a carriage for us, but I wasn't thinking of a wheelchair. Perhaps it will be okay to walk home?"

"Oh, oui, yes!" Clement interrupted. "I haven't been outside for so very long."

Rachelle smiled and agreed. "I can push if you can carry the bags."

"I can help too," David said as he grabbed one of the cases. "I'll take good care of Clement."

The Graves' home discovered a new routine. Rachelle rose early to prepare breakfast for Increase and Mariette. After the adults' breakfast, the boys ate together in the small room off the kitchen where Clement and Rachelle now lived. Then followed chores and therapy.

David enjoyed having Clement so close and became a second set of legs to the invalid boy. School lessons continued in the afternoon for Rachelle, and the boys didn't mind them as much now either. Then Clement had to rest, and David built tall towers and large cities for the boys to play with later in the front room. Clement could not attempt the stairs.

"The air is cooler this morning," Mariette said over her tea and toast.

Increase continued to read the paper, but said, "Yes, October is under way. Thanksgiving will be here before you know it."

"Something else will come before Thanksgiving." Mariette set down her cup and looked expectantly at her husband. She twisted the wedding band on her finger.

Increase looked up from his paper. "Something else?"

"Our anniversary." Mariette felt disappointed that he didn't remember. She frowned and furrowed her brow. "I thought we might have a special meal together."

Increase smiled. "I've already spoken to Rachelle about the menu. I'm not as heartless as you may think."

Mariette brightened. "I know you're busy, but I was hoping we could—"

"I have a Board of Health meeting Friday, but Rachelle has assured me that she can manage the menu fine. The boys will go to bed early and we can have a quiet dinner and then sit in front of the fire like we used to."

"It was those talks that got us in trouble." Mariette giggled as she buttered her toast. "Mrs. Brown could never mind her own business."

"I'm glad she couldn't," Increase said.

Mariette jerked her head up. She looked across the table into his face. Her own turned pink all over.

The week was punctuated by two deaths, like exclamation points proclaiming Increase's inadequacy. Sara Cloutier had recovered from polio, but she was still weak. The baby she carried came early. Increase was too late for both of them.

The late-afternoon sun penetrated his coat, but so did the brisk wind that flew down from the north. *At least tonight will be warm by the fire.* He waved to Mr. Neal who was walking into the Masonic Lodge ahead of him.

"Good afternoon, Dr. Graves." He held the door open, waiting for Increase to come in. "It's a brisk wind blowing. How are things at the hospital today?"

"The hospital's good. It's the house calls that are so hard. Mrs. Cloutier and her baby died this morning."

"Cloutier? I don't believe I know her."

"Another mill worker."

"Of course." Mr. Neal nodded as if that explained everything. *No need to know mill workers.*

The conference hall table was long enough for all eight board members, as well as Mr. Taylor and the mayor. Several chairs were lined around the wall. Mr. Neal gestured toward a seat and Increase took his place. The large woman who always stood sentry at the front desk now sat at a small table across the room, taking notes.

The door opened and Jean Giatros slid into the room. He scanned the table and chairs along the wall, spotted Increase, and crossed the room. He sat next to the doctor and waved briefly at Mr. Neal. "Good afternoon," he whispered.

The roll was called and all were present, so Mr. Taylor began. "The summer season went well. There are no major difficulties to report." He sat back in his chair and smiled. "Dunstable Plains is right on track to do well in the twentieth century."

"Have all of the new sewer lines been installed? I saw Spring Street has been re-bricked," one of the board members said.

"Yes, yes, all of that's been taken care of," Mr. Taylor said. "We're set up to add new lines as new houses are built. We expect quite a number of new homes now that Lytle Mills is rebuilding. More investors will be heading our way."

Increase stood up. "Why aren't we extending the lines to the mill houses? If everything is already set up in that direction, wouldn't it be easy to implement?"

All heads turned.

Increase cleared his throat and went on, "The typhus epidemic was so bad this past spring that the mills had to cut shifts. Now polio has decimated the workers' numbers."

Voices murmured in the room as heads nodded agreement and looked back at the mayor and Mr. Taylor.

"More immigrants come in daily on the trains," Mr. Taylor said. "There's no need to worry about shifts getting cut again. There are lots of laborers to get the work done."

"Diseases spread." Increase wasn't willing to let it go so easily. "It won't matter how many workers you bring in here. If you don't have sanitary living conditions, they will get sick. And we've all seen with the polio virus, it doesn't isolate itself to the poor."

"So if it isn't isolated to the poor, how will sewer lines to the mill houses help?" one of the members asked. "If we extend the lines to all the houses, the town will be broke."

"If you don't do it, the town will still be broke," Increase answered. "Having to care for all of the sick workers costs money. More nurses and doctors both will have to be added. We'll get a bad reputation and future workers will pass us by. Already I've met people who are going on to New Bedford because their housing is so much better."

"Indoor plumbing is a luxury … for those who can afford such things," Mr. Taylor said. "It isn't necessary. Just look how long we managed without it." He looked around the table to see who was on his side. "There's no evidence that it decreases disease."

"But there is," Jean said and stood. "Boston has seen a decline in public disease rates since they installed sewage lines; even little Nashua is installing lines."

More murmuring broke out.

"It's true," Mayor Thomlinson said. "I sat in on some of their meetings last year. If we want to keep up with the rest of the country, we need to add those lines."

"We don't want to keep up," Mr. Neal said. "We want to lead. Isn't that why we added the hospital and brought Dr. Graves here? Only the best— you all said so yourselves."

"Who's going to pay for it? That's what I'd like to know," Mr. Hoop broke in.

"The city can cover the lines to the houses," Mr. Sheppard said, "and the mills can put in large bathhouses at the end of the rows." Mr. Sheppard stared at Mr. Hoop, daring him to disagree. "I'll even give my workers a week to build the bathhouses. Paid."

Mr. Hoop's eyes bulged and his nostrils flared. Heads turned from one mill owner to the other, waiting to see what would happen. A chair creaked, breaking the silence.

"Can you have the lines to the houses before Thanksgiving?" Mr. Sheppard asked, looking at the mayor. "Any later and the ground will freeze."

"I'm sure we can handle that," Mayor Thomlinson answered.

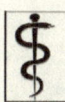

"What are you doing here?" Increase asked Jean as they headed down the front steps.

"It was a public meeting. I thought they might need a little coaxing, but you had it all under control." Jean clapped him on the back. The wind whipped them in the face as they left the building. "Whew, good night for a fire." Jean rubbed his hands together.

"Yes, it is … Mariette and I are celebrating our anniversary this evening." He didn't know why he shared that or why he suddenly felt the blood rush up his neck. "David and Clement are going to bed early, and Rachelle is making a special dinner for us. Then we'll enjoy a warm fire."

"Congratulations. It sounds like the perfect evening for a husband and wife. Good night."

Jean headed toward the mill houses and Increase turned for home.

"I'm glad Mariette is my mama now," David said as Increase tucked him into bed. "She takes good care of us."

"Didn't Aunt Lively take good care of us?" Increase asked as he turned the quilt under David's chin.

David smiled. "Yes, she's a good aunt, but Mariette is my mama."

"What's the difference?"

David shrugged and turned his head, thinking. "Aunt Lively always knew me and loved me." David looked back at his father. "But Mariette chose to love me."

Increase kissed his son on the nose.

The dining room glowed in the light of kerosene lamps. Mariette had taken special care with her hair and there was a faint scent of rose water. She stood at the end of the table by her chair.

Increase crossed the room and helped her with her seat. He kissed her cheek as he gave the chair a final scoot. *David is right. It's better to be chosen.*

*Suffering becomes beautiful when anyone bears great calamities with cheerful-*
*ness, not through insensibility but through greatness of mind.*
~Aristotle~

# CHAPTER 29

"WHAT DO YOU THINK?" I asked.

The night was deep, the stars in the sky brilliant. The white clustered flowers of the manna tree glowed in the courtyard candlelight.

Pater shook his head. "I've heard about the Jesus followers. They only claim one god, though that hardly makes sense because they say Jesus is his Son. … They cause trouble, or trouble follows them anyway."

"Mm. They were showing up in Athens too. Some say good things; others bad." I leaned my head back against the wall and looked at the night sky. "But, Pater, you know the gods didn't heal you—not our gods."

"Yes, but … I wouldn't want to anger them."

"A god that can heal like this … I don't know. Don't you think he could protect us from the others' anger?"

I kept thinking about Pater's pale skin, his erratic breathing, his immi-nent death. Asclepius had refused to help; even the vision said he wouldn't help. And Dionysus … well, it was spring—too early to count on him.

"One thing is certain. Jesus is a healer … a very powerful healer." I stood, stretched and scratched, and leaned down to kiss Pater. "I'm very glad you're better, Pater. Hypíaine."

"Good night, Loukas." Pater patted my hand. "Good night."

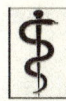

Casper filled our cups with hot tea. I hadn't eaten with Pater for so long, breakfast at the table was a treat. I picked up the mug and let the steam rise in my face.

"How did you sleep?" I asked.

"Like a baby," Pater said. "I had forgotten how good it can be to sleep."

"I'm going to Jehan's this morning. He has some patients he wants me to see."

"Good. Good. ... I'm going to the baths. I'll leave something for Asclepius—don't want any jealous rivalries forming after last night." He winked at me. "I'll leave a little something for you too."

I nodded and finished my tea.

Small grasshoppers scattered as I walked through the high grass. Jehan and I were headed to a farm beyond the walls, where barley and wheat were grown.

"Pater is doing well. Said he slept like a baby last night." I kept my eyes to the ground, avoiding the sharp rocks. "Is Paolo staying long? We'd like to thank him again somehow."

"I don't know how long he will stay. I told him to stay as long as he felt it beneficial. His eyes are still bothering him; I gave him some fennel oil to try."

"Good choice." I nodded. "Jehan ... What do you think of this Jesus business?"

As soon as I asked, I wished I hadn't. There was so much I was still pondering. I didn't want Jehan to think I was ready to convert or anything.

"I mean," I said, "do you think Paolo and Silvanus are right? Do they really heal in Jesus's name?"

"What did you experience?" Jehan seemed calm, trudging up the path to the terraces above.

"Pater was very ill, most certainly near death. But all Paolo did was ask Jesus to heal him, no sacrifice, no payment, no ... nothing."

"And can a god heal without sacrifice and payment?"

"Well, why would a god want to if nothing was offered? But I asked Asclepius and Dionysus both to heal Pater. I left sacrifices, I gave money, I prayed and prayed, but they never helped. Pater even had a vision from Asclepius that he would not help."

"You studied the practices of the great Hippocrates." Jehan stood still and looked at me. "What was his prescription for phthisis?"

"He would have left Pater to die, knowing there was to be no recovery." I played with the edge of my sleeve.

"So the great Hippocrates, a descendant of Asclepius, would have left your father to suffer and die."

Jehan started walking up the path again. I followed, uncertain if a response was expected. At the ridge of the hill, we stopped by a large rock and Jehan sat down. I sat beside him and looked out over the city beneath.

"I still don't know what you think about Jesus." I sounded like a child asking for bread.

"It doesn't matter what I think. What do you think?" Jehan gazed toward the sea.

"I don't understand him, but I want to know more. When other gods would look away from Pater's suffering, why would Jesus turn his face to him?"

"Perhaps you should ask Paolo, but Loukas …" He paused and put his hand on mine. "No matter what he says, you have to make a decision for yourself."

Paolo was transplanting some herbs for Jehan. His stooped shoulders curved over the hand tools as he dug and loosened the soil. I opened the gate and walked in.

"Good evening, Loukas," Paolo said, stopping to look up. "How's your father?"

I walked to him. "Very well. Thank you, again. We want to do something for you, to show you how much we are grateful."

Paolo stood and shook his head. "It has nothing to do with me. Jesus healed Aegeus; I was only the messenger." He smiled and dusted his hands on his robes. "Ludia is having a meeting at her house. Would you like to come with me?"

"A meeting for what?"

"She wants to hear more about Jesus."

"I'd like that too."

The house was large, decorated with tiled mosaics and tapestries made with the red threads of Thyatira. Paolo and Silvanus knocked on the door.

I stood behind Timotheos, shuffling like a frightened chicken.

"Come this way."

A servant led us through the house to the inner courtyard. It was much large than our shared garden. Ludia stood in a group of people talking and laughing. She spotted us and came straight over.

"Paolo. Silvanus. And Timotheos." She kissed each of them on the cheek. "Welcome." She stepped back and looked over their shoulders. "You brought Loukas. How wonderful." She moved through them and kissed me as well. "Welcome, Loukas. I'm glad you came."

I returned the welcome, then moved as quickly as I could to the outer edges of the group. Ludia welcomed everyone and asked them to sit. Various benches and chairs were provided, and soft cushions were scattered around the paving stones. We all sat and turned our attention to Paolo.

He spoke for several hours, sharing his background, his zeal for the Israelites' god. He talked about the way he had gone after the followers of Jesus and tried to stop them, to destroy them. He wept over the story of a young family he had separated and executed, the child left alone to fend for himself.

Then he told us about his encounter on the road to Damascus, the light, the voice, the blindness. And then he shared the miraculous healing. His face shone like a freshly scrubbed boy, and he wiggled in excitement. I felt certain he was sincere.

The rest of the evening was spent asking questions of Paolo and his friends. They were patient, knowledgeable, and, as far as I could tell, honest, introducing us to Jesus and the life he lived. They didn't ask for money or housing or anything other than the opportunity to speak. I stayed on my cushion next to a large potted tree and listened.

Finally I spoke. "I thank you for healing my father. He had phthisis." I looked around at the people. "Paolo healed him with just a prayer. But …" I turned my attention back to Paolo. "How is it that you can heal something so deadly, and yet you are unable to heal yourself?"

"I didn't heal your father, Loukas. The Son of God … Jesus, he healed him."

"But if you are working so hard serving this Jesus, why doesn't he heal you?" It was the most baffling part for me. "Why doesn't he care enough about you to heal you?"

"I'm not going to say I haven't struggled with that question myself, Loukas. When God can do such mighty miracles through me, why doesn't he perform a miracle on me?" Paolo took a deep breath and slowly exhaled.

"Sometimes I think it is the consequence."

Paolo sat on a bench and looked at all of us. "I hurt a lot of people in the name of God. I told you; I destroyed families—men and women who loved the Lord. Honestly I deserve death. But Jesus Christ has forgiven me for my dreadful past, and he doesn't require a physical death. Instead I die to myself: my desires, my wants, my concerns. I live for someone else, with a new purpose.

"I suffer with my weakness; it's true. My eyes hurt, light bothers them, especially at sea. Yet my Lord has asked me to go far and wide telling others about his Son. Only through my suffering can I fully rely on Jesus. The suffering actually leads me closer to the one I want to be with, so sometimes I think my suffering is a gift.

"I know my tendencies, Loukas. If I were to be healed, pride would pick me up and carry me off. My suffering reminds me that there is someone greater than myself. Sometimes it's the suffering that saves me.

"I guess the answer is … that I don't have an answer. But this I know: the Son of God was willing to suffer for me, and I can do no less for him."

I nodded. "Then neither can I. Take me to the river."

*Justice turns the scale, bringing to some learning through suffering.*
*~Aeschylus~*

# CHAPTER 30

CLEMENT'S WHEELCHAIR WAS SURROUNDED BY a large wall of snow and ice. The boys had worked on it for two days. Now they plastered each other with snowballs. Other boys joined in the war, and Mariette could hear their squeals and laughter from the front room.

Rachelle was helping Mariette hang garlands of holly around the room. This would be their first Christmas in Dunstable Plains and she wanted to make it extra special. Cranberries were packed away in the cellar, waiting for the sauce. Dried dates and oranges had been baked into a cake that was soaking in brandy. Mariette had even ordered a turkey from the local butcher to be delivered Christmas Eve.

"Watch it, buddy, or I'll nail you in the kisser!" David yelled.

Clement's hearty guffaw let them know who had thrown the offending snowball.

"I hope he doesn't hurt David," Rachelle said as she bit her lip.

"It's fine if he does. Clement's getting stronger and that's a good thing." Mariette smiled and clipped another holly strand to the curtain rod. "To think we didn't know if he would be here this Christmas and now he's out there having a snowball fight with the neighborhood boys. God is good."

"Yes, He is very—" A knock sounded on the front door. "I'll get it."

Rachelle opened the door to a fine gentleman who put a finger to his smiling lips. Two carpetbags sat on the porch near his feet. He walked in past Rachelle and mouthed "Mariette." Rachelle pointed toward the front room.

"Who is it, Rachelle?" Mariette called from her perch.

"Il est Père Noël—It's Santa Claus," came a familiar male voice.

Mariette grabbed her skirts and bounded from the chair. "Papa, Papa! You came? Why didn't you tell me you were coming? How long can you stay? Oh, Increase and David will be so thrilled." She flung her arms around her father and smothered him with kisses.

Maurice laughed and returned the hug. "Ma chère fille que je vous manqué—My dear girl, I missed you. Now … where is my grandson? And who is this sweet little lady who let me in?"

"Papa, this is Rachelle. She and her brother Clement live with us now. I wrote you about them. Rachelle, this is my papa, Docteur Shevenell."

Rachelle curtsied and Maurice kissed her hand. "It's a pleasure to meet you. Mariette has told me what a friend you've been to her. Je vous remercie—Thank you."

"You must be cold. I'll make some tea. Excuse me." Rachelle turned and ran for the kitchen.

Mariette and Maurice hugged again and laughed at the clattering of the teakettle on the stove.

"I think you frightened her," Mariette said. "The children are playing outside. I'm surprised you didn't see them."

"Ah. I believe I just missed one of their snowballs. David is well?"

"You won't even know him. He's grown so much. He really ought to have a tutor by now, but Increase and I aren't ready. I give him lessons in the afternoon with Clement. We're very happy." Her eyes crinkled and her pink cheeks glowed. "Sit down, here by the fire. Let me take your coat."

He shrugged out of the heavy coat and unwrapped his muffler.

"Should I call David in?" she asked as she headed for the coat tree in the hallway. "He'll be so excited to see you."

"No, not yet. I want to visit with you alone first." He sat in the chair in front of the fire and warmed his hands.

Mariette came back in and sat across from him. "I just can't believe you're here. Why didn't you tell me you were coming? I could've gotten a room ready and had things prepared."

"I called Increase at the hospital last week and asked him not to tell you. I wanted to surprise you." Maurice smiled at his daughter. "How is Increase?"

"He's well liked here. The mill workers trust him, but it took a long time." Mariette looked at the fire blazing strong.

"Good. It's helpful for a doctor to be liked. But how is he, really?" Maurice stared at his daughter. "Is he kind to you? Does he love you?"

"Papa." Mariette blushed and looked at her hands. "You've known Increase a long time. Of course he is kind to me. He's a good husband; just look at our home." She glanced around the room. The Christmas greenery added an extra flamboyance to the comfortable room.

"Yes," Maurice said and nodded. "But your letters seem so … sad."

Rachelle came in carrying a silver tray of tea things and cookies.

"Thank you, Rachelle," Mariette said. "Perhaps you better call the boys in; we don't want Clement getting too chilled." She rose to pour the tea and Rachelle backed out of the room.

"Increase is a good doctor, Papa. He never thinks he is, but he is. He works very hard. Perhaps what you read as sadness was only a touch of loneliness." She brought the cup of tea to him on a saucer and placed the china plate of cookies on the side table. "Rachelle is a good friend and helper. And David and Clement keep me busy. I've helped at the library too. So you see, I'm getting used to it here. Just like France, it will take awhile to make new friends."

There had been no warning of Maurice's visit, so the fare was plain. Rachelle and Clement were invited to join the family in the dining room, where the boys regaled Maurice with their day's adventures attacking the neighborhood children and their snow forts. Increase didn't make it home from the hospital in time for dinner, though.

Pépé and David were nestled upstairs reading a chapter of *Treasure Island* when Increase finally blew in the front door.

"Sorry I'm so late," he called as he unwound the long scarf from his neck.

Mariette turned the corner from the front parlor. "It's okay. We had a special visitor for dinner—but that's no surprise to you, is it?" Her eyes twinkled bright blue. "Why didn't you tell me Papa was coming?" She flung her arms around Increase before he could get his arms out of his coat. He fell against the wall and Mariette planted a kiss on his mouth.

"Hey! Where's the mistletoe?" Maurice laughed on the landing.

"Daddy!" David shouted from the top of the stairs. "Pépé came to visit. He's staying until after Christmas." David tore down the stairs ahead of Maurice. "This is going to be the best Christmas ever!" He jumped into the middle of Mariette and Increase and bear-hugged them both.

Increase grabbed David and swung him across his back. "The best ever, huh? Well, not if you don't get to bed. Santa Claus is watching, you know." Increase trotted up the stairs and handed David off to Maurice. "It's good to see you again, Dr. Shevenell."

Maurice raised his brows.

"I mean … Maurice," Increase said. "Would you mind putting David to bed while I get settled? Then we can have a drink in the parlor and catch up."

"I would be honored," Maurice said, taking David off his father's back and swinging him by his pajama bottoms up the last few steps. "We just finished reading. I'll be down after prayers. Come on, mon petit."

Mariette met Increase at the bottom step and grabbed his coat as he shrugged out of it. He turned to hand her his hat, but instead he grabbed her by the waist and picked her up. "It's good to be home," he said and buried his face in her neck. "It was a long, long day."

Mariette wrapped her arms around her husband and returned the embrace. "I'm glad you're home now. What was happening at the hospital?"

"A woman came in with appendicitis and needed surgery. Old man Muncett is down with pneumonia and the LaRue children have scarlet fever. Looks like measles is going to make an appearance for Christmas as well." He took a deep breath and then set her down. "You're like a little china doll, but soft as a teddy bear."

Mariette blushed. "I saved some dinner for you. Rachelle and Clement have gone on to bed. Would you like it in the parlor by the fire?"

Increase sighed. "That sounds wonderful." He walked into the front room and poured a drink for himself and one for Maurice. The glowing fire crackled and popped. Increase exhaled as he sank into the chair.

"Here you are," Mariette said as she carried in a tray of food. She placed it on the small table by the chair. "A thick slice of pork roast and onions and potatoes will fix you up right quick. I brought coffee too." She took the glass of whiskey from his hand and gave him the plate of food.

"Don't go too far with that," Increase said as he stabbed the roast with his fork.

Maurice walked in and Mariette offered to get him a drink, but Increase raised a hand. "I already poured one for him," he said through a mouthful of potato. "It's on the table."

"I'll wait until you're finished with your dinner," Maurice said and settled himself in the chair across from Increase.

Mariette put the glass down and joined the men. "Increase has had a busy day, Papa." She settled her skirts around her on the divan.

"No rest for the wicked, they say." Increase wiped grease from his winter beard. "How are things in Boston?"

Maurice told them about the new doctor who had replaced Increase, about the influenza outbreak that included most of the nursing staff, and the newest residents at the orphans' home. "We're adding a work program for the older children." Maurice sat up taller in his chair. "The community has really rallied around them."

"We tried talking about getting an orphans' home here," Mariette said, "but the community would have nothing of it."

"It's a different place, Mariette." Increase put his plate back on the tray. "They take care of each other." He sipped the hot coffee.

"Yes, you're right. Like we take care of Rachelle and Clement."

Maurice looked at Increase. "How is the boy, Increase? Mariette's last letter said he was walking a bit, but he was still in a chair when I came today."

"Mariette may have been too optimistic," Increase said. He placed his feet on the stool. "One day he may walk, but for now it's a step here and a step there. The chair is best for him still."

"He's getting stronger," Mariette said. "The crutches are heavy for him, but he's getting there. He'll walk by spring."

The talk went long into the night. Morning found Mariette burrowing farther into the mattress and pulling the covers over her head. *Why are the bells ringing so long?* Increase had left over an hour ago, but she wasn't ready to get up yet.

Clang, clang, clang …

"Mama, there's a fire!" David burst into the room. "Don't you hear the bells?" He pulled the covers back and pulled on her sleeve. "It's Sheppard Mills. I can see the smoke."

Mariette jumped from the bed and wrapped her robe around her. "Let me get my slippers on." She shuffled her feet into the small white shoes Increase had given her for a birthday present.

David pulled her from the room and toward the stairs. "Pépé said he would go to the hospital to help Daddy. Can we watch the fire trucks, Mama? Please?"

"No, David. It wouldn't be safe and we would just be in the way.

Where're Rachelle and Clement?"

"They already had breakfast. Rachelle's washing dishes. Can we watch from the porch?"

They were downstairs now and the smell of smoke penetrated the foyer. "Yes, if you stay on the porch. Don't get down in the street, David. Promise?"

"I promise! Come on, Clement." David raced out the door while Clement rolled after him.

Rachelle came behind, carrying the dish towel. "It can't be good with all that commotion," she said and shook her head.

"Papa and Increase will be late at the hospital today. Perhaps you could make something for me to take to them for lunch? I'm sure they'll need—"

"I can see the pumper truck, Mama! Come watch."

Mariette stepped out on the porch. Her nose burned in the cold air and acrid smoke. "I hope they all made it out." She took David's hand into her own.

Mariette delivered the basket of lunch to the hospital. Rachelle packed enough for the nurses and their students as well. One of the girls took it from her and shoved it under the front desk. People lined the walls and all of the beds were full. The door to the surgery was closed. Mariette backed out of the room, a stray kitten afraid of the big dogs.

Wood smoke floated through the dark street like a winter fog. "'When smoke is low, you know it will snow,'" Maurice recited. "I've ruined another pair of shoes." He watched his feet walk along the brick sidewalk. It had been a long day removing shrapnel from the victims.

"Thanks for all of your help, Maurice. I don't know what we would've done without you." Increase was shuffling along, his hands jammed in his coat pockets, his head hunkered between his shoulders. "It's frightfully cold."

Maurice breathed deeply. "I wasn't sure if we would ever get out of there. Dunstable Plains needs a larger hospital. And definitely newer equipment. I thought we were in a navy hospital in Santiago." He blew out his lungs and shuddered. "You're a good man to stay here, Increase. These people need you."

"Mmm. I wasn't much help to those poor souls on the bottom floor." He sighed, thinking about the smashed bodies that had been pulled from the collapsed building.

"You can't save them all, Increase. You did what you could."

"But my job is to save them, not to let them die."

"No, son. Your job is to comfort and help, and that you did magnificently."

Soft snowflakes floated gently down, covering the smoky fog with a clean blanket.

*A man who fears suffering is already suffering from what he fears.*
~Michel de Montaigne~

# CHAPTER 31

"**D**ID YOU HEAR?" DAVID'S CHEEKS were bright red with cold and excitement.

"What?" Mariette asked as she poured hot ginger tea into a mug for him.

"There's going to be a New Year's Eve party. It'll be at the Masonic Lodge and the whole town is invited. They're even going to have fireworks. Man! I've got to tell Clement." David pushed past Mariette into the darkened room off the kitchen. "Clement, wake up," he said in a false whisper.

*A party. I haven't been to a party since I left France.* Mariette sat down to drink the tea herself. She wouldn't have time for a new dress, but she could spruce up her hat, and Increase had given her a new brooch for Christmas that would look perfect on her green silk.

David couldn't contain his excitement. "Have you ever seen fireworks, Pépé? I haven't, but neither has Clement."

Maurice smiled across his plate at the little boy who had stolen his heart. "The first time I saw fireworks was on the Champs de Mars when I was a boy. The cherry trees were just blooming and my parents took me to the emperor's birthday celebration. I remember being frightened by so many people and so much noise."

"I won't be scared," David said as he shoved a large potato in his mouth.

"Use your knife to cut your food, David," Increase said. "And what about you, Mariette? Have you seen fireworks?"

"Yes." Mariette looked across at her husband. *There's so much you don't know about me.* "It was only a few years ago, when I was in Paris. I was also on the Champs de Mars, Papa. It was Bastille Day. There were no cherry trees in bloom, though. The weather was hot and humid. But you …" Mariette looked at David, who was attempting to stab a piece of pork roast with his knife. "You will have to dress warmly for your first fireworks."

"What about you, Daddy? When did you see your first fireworks?" David's large eyes were round with wonder and excitement.

Increase looked at his son. So much time had passed, so much fear, so much worry, so much sadness and despair. "It was just over eight years ago. Your mother and I saw them together in the harbor for Independence Day. The noise must have frightened you then, because your mother said you jumped and kicked inside her like a wild donkey." Increase chuckled at the memory.

"Well, this time I'll see them with my new mother and I won't jump at all." David stuck out his jaw and looked over at Mariette. "I promise. I won't kick you."

Laughter rang out. *It's the first time I've thought of Annie and not wanted a drink,* Increase realized. He smiled at Mariette and winked. It felt good.

WELCOME 1900 was printed on the banner draped across the Masonic Lodge. Several men had formed a band and were playing lively music in the front reception hall. Increase and David found Mariette behind the library table. She had been drafted to hand out candy and books to the children.

"Look what that lady gave me," a little girl said to her mother as Increase and David passed by. "Isn't she beautiful?" The girl's gaze lingered on Mariette as Mariette smiled and waved to her.

"She's my mama," David said, stopping. "She likes books. You should go to the library and check one out. Mama helps them pick out really good books." His chest puffed out.

The little girl grabbed her mother's skirts and hid. Increase steered David by the shoulder to the library table.

"Isn't she darling?" Mariette watched the shy child peek back as her mother maneuvered the crowded hallway. "Are you just getting here, Increase? Where's Papa?" She stood on tiptoe and looked around. A sea of black coats and plaid shawls tossed from one side of the room to the other.

"He stopped to talk to Jean and Father Cartier." Increase noticed the brooch Mariette had pinned to her dress. It matched the blue of her eyes. "You wore your new brooch."

"Yes." Mariette slid her slender fingers across the sapphire pendant. "I thought it would brighten up my dress."

"You brighten up this whole room," Increase said. The pulse in his neck throbbed.

Mariette blushed. "I have to help here for another hour. Should we plan to meet somewhere?"

"Bon jour, Mademoiselle Graves," a booming voice interrupted. "I got another letter this week. I didn't want to disturb your holidays, though." Frank Viollette held out his hand to Increase. "Your wife is very kind to me, sir. Thank you for letting me come by sometimes."

Increase shook Frank's hand and glanced down at his wife. "She's very kind to a lot of people ... including me. Please come by tomorrow and bring your letter. I believe Mariette enjoys reading your letters as much as you enjoy hearing them."

"Yes," Mariette said. "Come by tomorrow for tea at 4:00. I want you to meet my papa."

David stood by Clement's chair on the edge of the lodge's front porch. The colorful bursts of light exploded over the river near the canal entrance. The other children had raced to the waterfront to get a clear view, but David had stayed with his best friend.

Maurice watched as the two boys "oohed" and "aahed" over the red and white flowers blooming brightly in the sky. The loud bombs echoing off the brick mills only excited them more. Finally the band broke into "Auld Lang Syne" and the party broke up. The little family headed down the walkway to home as the church bells tolled.

"I spoke to the priests about raising money for the hospital," Maurice said. "They're as concerned for the orphans of Dunstable Plains as I am for Boston's waifs, Mariette. They're good men, and I think they serve good people. Maybe they will be able to help you get what you need, Increase."

"That would be great, Maurice, but there's precious little money in the workers' coffers. It's the mill owners who will have to see the need."

"But Maurice is right to start with the spiritual leaders," Jean spoke from behind.

The little troop turned around.

Mariette said, "Good evening, Dr. Giatros. I hear you already met my papa." She waited for Jean to catch the group. "I'm sorry I didn't get to speak to you this evening. There was so much excitement; it was exhilarating," she said.

"Yes, I had the pleasure of working with your father earlier this week. Increase. Maurice." Jean nodded to the men. "In fact your papa and I were speaking tonight. Maurice knows it will take more than money to heal the town. The church should be a part of the process."

Increase snorted and said, "The church doesn't know the first thing about medicine."

"Perhaps not," Jean said, "but it knows a lot about healing. Those with money often need healing in the worst way, and it's the church that can offer that type of medicine." Jean peered up at Increase. "Self-absorption is a terrible disease."

"Daddy." David pulled on Increase's sleeve.

Increase looked down at his son.

"Clement is shaking. He's cold." David pointed toward the small boy in the wheelchair.

"You need to take care of the child," Jean said. "I hope to speak with you again, Maurice. Good night, Increase. Mariette." Jean turned toward the mill houses and walked into the darkness.

Rachelle gathered Clement up as soon as they arrived home and wrapped him in warm blankets with hot bricks at his feet. A steaming cup of cocoa was poured for each boy while the men enjoyed a nightcap. Mariette turned down the beds, prayed with David, and stoked the bedroom fireplace. Warmth invaded every corner by the time Increase retired and found Mariette was sitting up in bed.

"Did you have a good time at the party?" Increase asked.

"Yes, I haven't been to a party since I left France. I loved watching the children see the fireworks for the first time. It's such a special time in life to enjoy every opportunity, every event." She leaned over to kiss his cheek as he climbed in beside her. "Did you enjoy the party?"

"Yes …" Increase paused and looked at his feet sticking up under the heavy quilts. "What did you think of Jean's comment? That self-absorption is a terrible disease?"

She gave a small nod. "I believe he's right. It's funny how the people who can afford to take care of more than their own needs usually don't even notice what's going on around them—while those who can little afford to help others, do just that."

"I suppose. … But do you think he was talking about the mill owners?"

"Who else would he be talking about?" Mariette took Increase's hand. "You looked very pretty tonight."

"Thank you." Mariette smiled and looked down at the covers.

"I wonder … Perhaps … Perhaps Jean was talking about me." Increase stumbled over his words. His eyes never moved from his feet. "My work has always been my passion. At first, with Annie … She spent a lot of nights waiting in the chair by the fire, just like you did back in Boston. Other doctors went home before I did. I could have gone too, but I needed to make sure everyone was taken care of, doing their best." He paused, remembering the many nights that nurses assured him it was safe to leave, that even Maurice had insisted he go home.

"Then when Annie, well, when Annie was gone, I threw myself into the work even more. Poor Lively, all alone in that big house, taking care of David. It wasn't right."

Increase looked over at Mariette. Her lips curved into an embrace of encouragement.

"It wasn't even that I was so worried about the patients. No." He looked back at his feet and sighed. "If I'm honest, it was because I wanted … I needed … to heal. They were bodies, illnesses, and diseases, not patients, not people." His voice trembled.

Mariette squeezed his hand.

"Then, bless your sweet self," he said, "you came along at just the time I needed you. I needed someone to care for David, it's true, but even more I needed someone who could bring me home again."

"Oh, Increase," Mariette whispered. She stroked his hair.

"But I wrapped myself up in blankets of self-loathing. The kinder you were, the heavier the blanket became." Increase shifted under the quilts and looked into Mariette's eyes. "I've been self-absorbed, like Jean said, and I haven't paid attention to you. I haven't seen you for the wonderful woman you are. You care for David as if he were your own; Annie would love you. You moved here at my insistence, barely making a fuss, and you've put up with the long days and many nights alone."

"It hasn't been so bad," Mariette said. "David is very dear to me, and I've made friends. I've found a place for myself. But I—"

"No," Increase interrupted. "I haven't been fair to you. I haven't been a husband to you."

Mariette looked down as the color in her face rose. Increase lifted her chin with a crooked finger. Her eyes glistened and her lower lip quivered.

"I'm sorry, Mariette. I'm sorry if in any way I made you feel like you weren't good enough, that I regretted marrying you. It wasn't that way at all." He held her face in both his hands. "I've been afraid. Afraid that something will happen to you, and I won't be able to help, to heal." Tears streamed over his cheeks.

"Increase, your fear has caused more pain than you know." Mariette drew in a deep breath to steady the wracking sobs that threatened to spill out. "But that pain can be healed. Love me, darling. Love me while I'm here and don't worry about whether something bad will happen. It will; it always does."

She wrapped her hands around his face and leaned in to kiss his mouth. Pulling back, she looked into his eyes. "I've tried to be patient, but I can't wait much longer."

"I'm sorry, my Love."

Mariette gasped at the endearment as Increase pulled her onto his chest. "Forgive me."

The ringing phone pulled him from sleep like a groundhog whiffing at the first scent of spring blowing down his burrow. Finally Increase flung the covers off himself and slid out from under Mariette's head and arm resting across his chest. Over the past few months, he had grown to like the feel of her warm body nestled next to his own. After sliding his feet into slippers, he threw the robe around himself and headed for the phone downstairs.

"Hello." His gruff voice cracked with dryness and irritation. "Dr. Graves."

"I'm sorry to wake you, Doctor," Nurse Lindelof's voice said across the line. "Mr. Vanderhese called. His wife is in awful pain; sounds like she's having seizures. Can you get there soon?"

He had visited Mrs. Vanderhese a few weeks ago. This was her first pregnancy, and she had developed diabetes. The young couple lived in a large farmhouse with several generations of Vanderheses. Increase had stressed the need for dietary restrictions, but it was always difficult to convince the older women that it wouldn't hurt the baby.

"I'll be there as soon as I get dressed. Can you call the stable and have a coach sent here to the house?"

"Of course, Doctor."

As Increase hung up the receiver, he heard Nurse Lindelof ask the operator to connect her to the stables.

Starlight reflecting off the fields of snow scattered the darkness into a dusky blue. The pounding of horse hooves echoed in the silence. Increase urged the horse on, only slowing when he approached the lane. Lights shone in the windows of the two-storied farmhouse.

Old Mr. Vanderhese met him on the porch. "I'll get the horse in the stable, Doc. She's up the stairs. You remember."

"Very well."

Increase hurried inside and up the walnut staircase that shone in the lamplight. The smell of fear and worry invaded the upstairs hall.

"She's having tremors still, Doctor, but I think the worst is over." The matron of the house crossed herself and moved aside for Increase to pass.

Increase nodded to the room's occupants. The grandmother, stooped and bent, was still in her white flannel nightgown. She stroked the young woman's hair and wiped her face with a damp cloth. The young husband stood at the foot of the bed, tears of fear clinging to his eyelashes.

"Is she going to be alright, Doc?"

"Let me check her out. You and Mrs. Vanderhese go down and get some coffee. I won't be long." Increase opened his medical bag and took out the stethoscope.

The dusky light turned to bright glaring day and back to darkening twilight. The hours passed slowly with family coming in to check on the young woman and leaving again in silence. Someone brought tea, a bowl of soup, a slice of leftover pie. Finally, amid the tears of tearing flesh and the sugar-induced seizures, a child was born.

The blue-tinged wrinkled skin fell loosely around the slack chest. Increase held the baby in one hand and swiped fluid from its mouth with his other. He rubbed the baby briskly with a towel, jostled it upside down, and hoped for the best. His best was not good enough.

Riding back toward home, Increase could still see the young husband trembling, the babe wrapped in a blanket in his arms. *She has suffered a lot. … It's too soon to say. … May never be the same again.* The younger Mr. Vanderhese had stood silent while the elder stood at his back, a hand on his son's shoulder. The two older women rocked silently in their chairs by the fire staring into the flames.

"Whoa." Increase pulled the horse to a halt.

A man in a familiar black overcoat was walking along the side of the road.

"Jean? Is that you?"

Jean turned and lifted a hand. "Increase, how good to meet you. Are you headed back to town?"

"Get in, old man," Increase said. "What are you doing out here?"

Jean climbed into the carriage and sat with a sigh. "Thanks. I was helping a friend with a calf. These heifers always seem to pick the coldest nights to have their babies."

"You were helping a cow to calve?" Increase's eyes grew large and his mouth fell open. "Are you a horse doctor too?"

Jean laughed. "It's all about the same when it comes to giving birth. Were you making a house call this late at night?"

"Mmm. Been out all day in fact." Increase shook the reins and clicked his tongue. The snow muffled the sounds as the horse started up again. "Vanderhese house. You know them?"

"Oui. How'd it go?"

"I couldn't do much. Not much at all. She had sugar and went into seizures. The baby was lost. Mrs. Vanderhese might still be for all I can do." He looked straight ahead and sighed from within.

"You do what you can and leave the rest to God."

"To God?" Increase's nostrils flared. "Why bother to do anything if it's all up to God?"

"Because God has gifted you to help others, Increase."

"It didn't seem like much of a gift today. I watched helplessly as the tremors came and went. There was nothing I could do for the baby. At least it never knew."

"You were there. You offered comfort; you offered help. That is all that's required."

"Well, this much I know: I'll never be the reason another woman goes through that."

"What do you mean?" Jean looked over at his friend. The reins were taut in Increase's white-knuckled hands.

"I won't be responsible for another child coming into the world. I couldn't save Annie … and I … I won't put Mariette in that position."

"There is something worse than death, Increase, and you stand at the edge of its great chasm."

Increase scoffed. "I don't know. Death seems pretty bad, a chasm of its own that I can barely escape. What could be worse?"

"Living in fear is worse than death, because it is no life at all. You're unable to enjoy the great gifts you've been given because you've stayed in the shadow of death for so long. Bleeding is only one kind of death, Increase. Out of fear you have denied yourself the gift of love and life that Mariette offers."

"And I will continue to do so," Increase said. "I won't be the reason another wife dies."

The lamps made the front room glow like amber. Mariette peered out into the dark street for the hundredth time that evening. She had called the night nurse when Increase wasn't back after supper. Nurse Lindelof assured her Increase would be late and very tired. A shadow moving on the icy walkway caught her eye. She was at the door before he reached the top step.

"Is everything okay?" Mariette held the door open and shivered. "I was so worried, but Nurse Lindelof said you might be awhile."

Increase kissed the offered cheek and hurried inside. "It was a long day, Mariette. Get me a drink, would you?" He slid out of his coat and pulled the scarf from his neck.

Mariette walked quietly into the parlor and poured a shot of whiskey. "How are the mother and child?" she asked when Increase entered behind her.

He took the glass from her hand, threw it back, let out a long breath, and poured another. Then he stood by the fire and stared at his feet. Mariette sat in the chair in front of him and looked up at her husband.

Gray hairs marched across his sideburns and temple. Deep lines were being etched in the corners of his eyes. *He's aging before his time. Perhaps we should have stayed in Boston where he would have other doctors to help.*

"Would you like me to get you some supper? Rachelle made baked pumpkin tonight. David thought it was magnificent." She smiled at him.

"Mariette, I need to talk to you."

"Of course."

Increase drank the last of the whiskey and then put the shot glass on the mantle. He turned his back to Mariette and stared into the fire.

"Mrs. Vanderhese had a terrible time. She suffered from diabetes during the pregnancy. Seizures wracked her body all night and day before the baby came. I couldn't do anything to help. … The baby died."

"Oh, Increase. How sad. Is the mother going to be alright?"

"I don't know. You see, she might have brain damage. It will be awhile before we can tell how bad it is." He paused and turned to face his wife. "You know I love you."

"I'm glad of it too." Mariette blushed when she thought about the months of passion that had finally consummated their marriage.

"I can't anymore." He took her hands in his. "It isn't fair to you, and I wouldn't be able to bear it if I lost another wife. And think what poor David would go through if he lost another mother."

"But, Increase … we're married. It's God's design, His gift. …" Tears trickled down her cheeks. "Do I make you unhappy?"

Increase pulled her close. "No, Love. Just the opposite. You are very kind and patient with me and with David both. I just can't lose another wife. That's it. I'm sorry." Increase stood and dropped her hands. "I need to go to bed. Good night."

She looked up at him. "But, Increase … I could die of typhus or pneumonia. I could be in a fire and be smashed by a building. You can't protect me from everything." Mariette stood and grabbed his arms. "Don't you see, Increase?"

"I see that you must be very careful. And I will be as careful as I can. You'll not die by something I can control." He strode from the room.

Mariette fell back into the chair. She sat there, stunned, until the first work bell rang in the morning.

*Although the world is full of suffering, it is full also of the overcoming of it.*
~Helen Keller~

# CHAPTER 32

THE SPRING DAYS WERE GROWING longer. A warmth rose from the ground, swelling with the smell of rain and dirt, promising the harvest ahead. Several of us were walking to the river for the prayer meeting. Paolo and Silvanus led the way, pouring stories into our ears like wine into a tall glass.

"Here she comes again," I whispered, pointing to a small slave girl on the wall.

"These men," she shouted as we neared, "are servants of the Most High God. They are here to lead you to truth and salvation." She jumped from the wall and began following us. "This is it. This is the way to heaven. Live with the gods. These men will tell you how."

The louder Paolo spoke, the louder the girl shouted. We had met her all week on our way to the river, always with the shouting.

"Enough!" Paolo turned around and looked at the girl. "Out! In the name of Jesus Christ, I command you to get out of this little girl."

The little girl shrieked and fell to the ground.

"Pick her up," Paolo said.

Silvanus lifted the girl in his arms and held her against his chest. "She's breathing."

He blew lightly on her face. Strands of curly black hair floated in the air and her eyelids fluttered. She looked up at the tall Silvanus and gasped.

"It's alright. The spirit is gone," Silvanus said as he placed her on the ground.

She stood in the middle of us, confused and scared, a rabbit in a snare. Suddenly she broke free and ran. Paolo and Silvanus chuckled, then went on teaching and preaching.

"Stop. You there, stop." Two men came hurrying toward us at the city gate. They dragged the little girl between them, her legs barely touching the ground. "Did you do something to our little prophet?"

Paolo was the first to speak: "We freed her from the evil spirit, if that is what you are asking."

"She's not worth her salt, now." The bigger man's nostrils flared. "How dare you take our profit."

"We didn't hurt the girl," Silvanus said. "She can still serve you."

"She earned her living by telling fortunes and futures. That's gone now. She can't serve us."

"She's better off now that the demon is gone," Paolo said.

Paolo tried to appease the men, but they grabbed him along with Silvanus and pulled them toward town. They created such a ruckus that a crowd gathered and joined in the march to the center of town. No one would listen to reason.

At the marketplace the slave owners threw Paolo and Silvanus at the feet of two magistrates. "These men stole from us. They are Jews, perverting the ways of the emperor and all of Rome."

I watched as the crowd turned violent. I pulled Ludia and her servant aside and took them home. "This is no place for women."

When I returned to the market, Paolo and Silvanus had been stripped and were being flogged. The long, heavy rods knocked them to the ground. I was certain ribs were broken.

After the beating, they were handed over to the local jailer and thrown in prison. I went home for my medical bag.

I returned to the jail and begged entrance, but the jailer was afraid of the townspeople. They were sure that Paolo and Silvanus were turning people against the local gods. In their opinion death would have been too good for my friends. I returned home without seeing them.

A gentle knocking at the door made me look up from the steaming cup of tea. A boiled egg and some onions sat untouched on my plate. Casper went to the door and returned with Jehan.

"Are you ready? They're expecting us at the marsh today."

"I'm sorry, Jehan. I don't think—"

"Come along. It will do you good. I have a story to tell you on the way."

I squinted my eyes at the old man. "A story?"

"Come on. The children are waiting."

I took a long drink of the hot tea and picked up the egg to eat along the way. Jehan handed me one of the medical packs to strap on my back and we left.

"What's the story?" I asked as I pulled the door closed.

"Not yet." Jehan shook his head and headed for the Via Egnatia.

The sky was pink and orange, a certainty of rain. Swallows flitted above us, dark flashes in the morning brightness. I turned my head as we walked past the marketplace. I hated to think what would happen to Paolo and Silvanus today. I kicked a stone in the roadway.

Jehan turned and I started to question him, but he raised his hand for silence. We crossed several street intersections, backtracking our steps, and ended up at Ludia's house.

"What's going on?" I asked.

Jehan smiled. "The story is inside."

The smell of roasting meat greeted me. A large table in the inner courtyard was laid out with food. There were figs and dates marinated in wine, all kind of olives, several different cheeses, and breads covered in syrups and honey. People milled about talking and laughing, and in the middle of it all, I could see Silvanus's head above the rest.

I pushed my way through the crowd, twisting and turning past elbows and stepping on toes. In the center I stopped. *How?* There stood Paolo and Silvanus, no chains, no stocks, just a few bruises to confess yesterday's terror.

"Loukas." Paolo pulled me to him and kissed my cheeks. "I'm glad you came."

"But?"

"It's quite a story." Silvanus laughed and kissed me as well.

"Please."

"You're the last one, so …" Paolo raised his hands for quiet. "Thank you everyone for coming to say good-bye to us. After yesterday Silvanus and

I believe it is best to move on, but we want to tell you how we came to be free men."

The roar of voices hushed, their echoes bouncing off the walls one last time. Everyone found seats on the benches we had used so many times in the last week or so. Ludia was a conscientious hostess, always anticipating our needs. I knelt on a cushion near the two men.

"We were taken into custody; our feet locked into stocks in an inner cell. There was no way to turn over, so we lay with our backs on the floor and let the cool stone sooth our bruises. Silvanus and I were praying and singing to calm our spirits; in fact a calm seemed to fall like refreshing dew on all of the prisoners.

"The night was dark—I'd guess it was about midnight, though there was no window to judge the night sky. Suddenly the jail shook, an earthquake."

Murmurs and gasps echoed again as everyone looked at each other in surprise. *I didn't feel anything last night.*

Paolo went on. "The stocks on our feet broke open, and all the doors in the prison swung wide. We were free. ... The poor jailer, a good man, he thought we had all rushed out to escape."

Everyone nodded, even as I also did and thought, *I would have run like a maenad.*

"He drew his sword to fall on it, but I called out to him, 'We're all here. Please, don't harm yourself.'" Paolo smiled as we broke into applause. "The jailer took us to his house and called for Jehan. He cleaned our wounds, wrapped us up, and eased the pain. Thank you." He looked to Jehan.

"Yes, thank you, Jehan," Silvanus said. "Then the jailer asked how this came to be, why we wouldn't run, and we told him about Jesus and how he didn't run away from tough times either.

"He had listened to our singing and prayers, and he knew there was something going on, so he asked about Jesus ... and he and his entire household were baptized last night."

We all cheered and applause filled the garden. Songbirds startled from the potted trees and flew straight up to the dark blue sky above. The light was full morning now.

"After they were all baptized," Paolo said, "we agreed to go back to the jail to wait our sentence. As the day began to break, the magistrates came to the prison to ask us to go in peace. They found out we're Roman citizens, and they became frightened.

"We agreed to leave, but we wanted to come here first. We wanted to make sure you met your new brothers and sisters and that you would hold nothing against them." Paolo motioned toward a middle-aged man and his family. "So now we will leave, but don't worry friends; we'll be back one day."

*You must submit to supreme suffering in order to discover the completion of joy.*
~John Calvin~

# CHAPTER 33

FUZZY BUD NUBBINS BROKE OPEN on the trees along Spring Street. The sun shone brightly, melting the dirty snowbanks. Trickling water sang of new hope, new possibilities.

Rachelle showed Frank into the parlor before the noon meal. Mariette sat at the writing desk while David and Clement practiced their lessons.

"Sorry to interrupt your schooling, Mademoiselle Graves. I have a letter." Frank blushed and held the envelope out toward her. "Do you have time to read?"

"Of course, Frank. Boys, why don't you go ahead and wash up for lunch. You can finish this afterward and then we'll take a walk. Please, Frank, come have a seat."

Frank crossed the room and sat on the edge of a chair near the window. He handed the letter to Mariette. "I haven't heard from Ethel since her Christmas letter. I was getting worried." He wrung his hands, then crossed his arms over his chest.

Mariette smiled at his nervousness. "I'm sure she's just been busy. She loves you, Frank. You know that." Mariette opened the letter and began to read. "'*Ma chère, Franc,*'" she read. "See, Frank, nothing to worry about. *Je suis très malade'*—'I am very sick.' Oh, Frank." Mariette looked at the big man whose heart beat in faraway Quebec.

"Continue." Frank pulled his arms tight across his chest and rocked back and forth.

"She must be well now or she wouldn't be writing. We mustn't jump to conclusions." Mariette looked back at the paper with the delicate handwriting. "'*Il a été un long hiver, mais le printemps arrive bientôt'*—'It has been a long winter, but spring is coming soon.'" Mariette smiled at Frank. "It's been a long winter for all of us. Oui?"

Frank nodded and waved Mariette to read on. His lovely Ethel had been very sick, sick enough to not write for several months. He listened to the letter like a desperate sailor clinging to driftwood. The shore was too distant; his love too far away.

"… '*tu me manques tellement. Ethel*—'I miss you so much.'" Mariette folded the letter and slipped it back into the envelope.

"And I miss you, mon cherie," Frank whispered as he wiped his eyes with a coarse handkerchief. "Thank you, Mrs. Graves. It is very kind of you to read for me again."

"Anytime," Mariette said as she handed the envelope back to him. "I'm glad Ethel is feeling better. She should only get stronger and stronger now that the weather is warming."

Frank smiled and stood. "Yes, well … thank you, again." He put out his hand and shook hers. "I need to go now. Lunch."

"Of course." Mariette rose and showed him out the front door. She stood on the porch, watching the back of the man as he walked toward the mill houses. *Why do we want love so badly when it hurts so much?*

The screams were broken by brief bouts of unconsciousness. The young girl was sixteen at best, Increase guessed. Morphine was the only thing that could help right now. He filled the syringe and plunged the needle into her vein.

The bloody bandages wrapped around her head attested to the horror that she had, so far, lived through. She was a loom worker. She watched hundreds of bobbins, making sure each was filled and thrumming along in unison with the others. The thread was running low, and fearing getting behind in her quotas, she pulled over a large spool of thread. The spool was every bit as heavy as the girl, and it caught on her dress. She struggled to free herself, and the long braid that ran down her back caught in the pulley overhead. The braid twisted around the belt and up into the machinery. The poor girl was scalped while the long dress held her body to the floor.

Increase had never seen a scalping. He had meticulously stitched the skin back, but the swelling made the girl's visage grotesque. *A bride for Frankenstein's monster*, Increase thought, shaking his head. *If the mills would only hire more workers, recognize that a child can't be expected to do the same work as an adult ...*

Jean appeared in the recovery ward, his hands in his pockets. "Is it okay to come in?"

Increase glanced at the older man, the one who always seemed to have the answers. "Yes. She's unconscious now. I gave her more morphine."

Jean walked to the bedside and sat on a chair. "Father, protect this, your child, from pain and fear. Guide her mind to your beauty and your perfection," Jean prayed.

"A little late for prayers, isn't it?" Increase huffed and glared at Jean.

"Never."

"Where was your God when she was being scalped?"

"The same place he is now. Right here with her."

"Hmm. Well, that didn't seem to do her any good, now did it? So why does she need God to help her now?" Increase stood to leave.

"God protected her from death, Increase. And he gave her a good doctor, with excellent skills. More importantly he has protected this child every day from things worse than death."

"What could be worse than death?" Increase's mind flashed back to Annie in the coffin, her eyes closed to him forever.

"I've told you before, many things are worse than death." Jean stroked the stubble on his chin. "Living alone and having no one to check on you, no one to care. That's worse, don't you imagine?"

"Hmph," Increase grunted.

"This child's parents are outside now praying and weeping for their daughter. She is loved and she knows it. She'll survive because of it."

"Love doesn't keep you alive."

"Doesn't it? How did you manage to get through Annie's death? Wasn't it the love of your sister and your love for David?" Jean took the girl's hand. "It was love that overcame death's sting. Even when death is the result, because of love there is no true death."

"If you say so." Increase turned and walked from the room.

*Everybody lives; not everybody deserves to.*
~Prudentius~

## CHAPTER 34

"YOU HAD NO RIGHT TO call them." The hardness in Mr. Sheppard's voice slammed into Increase as soon as he walked in the
door. The Public Health Board and the Hospital Board members were
assembled around the wooden conference table. "That girl was at fault
for not tying up her hair properly. Now all of our mills are in jeopardy
because of you."

"*That girl* should never have been working in the first place," Increase
shot back. "She's fourteen!"

Increase had been meeting daily with Francine's mother to help change
her dressings and give her regular shots of morphine. The nurses were
capable, but Increase felt a need to watch her himself.

"She should have been in school," Increase went on. "She's just a child
who—"

"No one forced her to work," Mr. Hoop interrupted. "She chose to be
there. But you, you've started something you can't finish. Now the state
has gotten involved, checking for violations and—"

"Good!" Increase broke in. "It's about time the mills were held accountable."

Mr. Hoop's face was red and his thick eyebrows furrowed into a line
of contempt. "But they aren't just checking the mills. They want to see
the mill houses. Those're private property. These bay pigs are living better
than any of their family back in Canada. What do they have to complain
about?"

Increase clenched his jaw and almost slammed the table with his hands.
"And why should their living conditions be compared to those in Canada? Shouldn't they be compared to your own? I've seen entire families

living in damp cellars with no light and little heat. Workers—your workers!—who freeze all night because the doors and windows don't close properly. And don't get me started on the rats and vermin. Typhus will start back. It'll be every bit as bad as last year's epidemic, even with the new bath houses."

Increase pulled out a chair at the table and sat down. He took a handkerchief from his breast pocket and wiped his forehead. A mouse in a cat's claws would have more fun than he was having tonight.

"Good evening, Increase," Mariette said when she heard the front door click closed. She stayed in the chair by the low fire; glowing red and orange embers tinted her face. A skein of wool yarn wrapped around her skirt as she knitted. "How was your meeting?" she asked, never lifting her eyes from the sweater that was beginning to form.

Increase poured a full glass of brandy and slumped in the chair next to hers. "Same as always. But now the mill owners are grumbling because the state is coming down on them. They think it's my fault." He threw back a swig of liquor and wiped his lip with the back of his hand.

"Why do they think that?" Mariette stopped her knitting and stared at the glass of brandy. She chewed on her bottom lip, then went back to the knit-and-purl pattern.

"I don't know. They think I turned them in after Francine's accident. I should have, with the way they treat people. Christians—humph." Increase threw back another draught, then set the empty glass on the table next to the chair.

"We're Christians," Mariette said quietly as she continued knitting.

"You are." He stood and stared into the coals.

"Alright … I am." She set the knitting aside and looked at her husband. The gray temples were shaggy and his shirt rumpled. Maybe this wasn't the right time, but when was? "I try to treat people right. Not all Christians are money-hungry vultures."

"I'm glad to hear you say that, because I plan to invite several of the mill workers to live here for a while." He turned and smiled down at her when she gasped.

"What?" She set the knitting aside.

"Typhus is starting to make a comeback, and I convinced Hoop and his lot that getting them out of the houses until they can be cleaned up is the only way to stop another epidemic."

"Are you insane? How can we? … Where? … What? …" Mariette tried to comprehend.

"We'll get the priests to take the kids out of town, a camping trip of sorts. The adults have to work, so they can stay in our houses until the issues are cleared up." Increase smiled at his ingenuity.

"I don't want those filthy people in my house. Why do you think there is a typhus problem to start with? They don't keep themselves clean." Mariette stood to face her husband.

"They try to, Mariette, but the cards are stacked against them. You see how well Rachelle and Clement are doing here, where they have a chance. And what about your friend, Frank?"

"Rachelle and Clement are children, and Frank …" *Frank is my only hope that love will grow, perhaps even win.*

"Rachelle is hardly a child, and if you've been able to befriend Frank, you can certainly make more friends."

Increase's voice was low and calm. He had obviously thought his argument through. Mariette had tried her hand at persuading Increase before, so she knew he wouldn't give in. She retrieved the brandy glass from the table and went to the sideboard.

"Where will we put everyone? We'll have to lock up everything, including your whiskey." Maybe she could discourage him by circling the camp. There had to be a weakness somewhere.

"We can make pallets on the floor if we have to. I can lock the cupboard in our room; valuables can be held there. And it might be nice to have someone to share a drink with for a change." There was an accusation hidden in the folds of conversation. "Besides, all of the board members agreed to house workers at their homes too. They're all headed out of town for the summer anyway. The managers will keep an eye on things and make sure all is well." He sunk down into a chair and spread his long legs out in front of him. "It will all work out. The community's health is my concern."

"Please sit and rest." Rachelle motioned toward the soft chair in the corner of the room. "You look worn out. I can prepare the rest of the pallets."

Fifteen men and women already filled the upstairs guest room and

David's room. David had spent the last week bunking with Clement and Rachelle. He thought it was a great adventure, but Mariette found it chaotic and unsettling. Now five more young ladies were moving in after work today. Mariette felt like a twisted piece of laundry, heavy and wet, being wrung out at someone else's discretion.

"Good afternoon, Mrs. Graves." Jean tipped his hat as he stopped on the sidewalk.

Mariette halted and offered a brief smile.

"How are things at your home?" Jean asked. "I hear you and Increase have taken in quite a few."

"We're adding five more this evening," Mariette said, stressing the *five* more than she intended.

"Is it too much for you to bear?" Jean looked at her curiously.

"No." Mariette paused, searching for the reason of her irritation. "Actually they take care of themselves. Rachelle says they clean up after they cook their meals, and they are up for work so early that we don't notice them too much."

"So it's working well. Your husband had a good idea, yes?"

"I suppose." Mariette wasn't willing to admit that she found the whole situation vexing. She didn't want to berate her husband to this man, but the whole thing had gotten out of control. The town leaders' wives were talking behind her back, and some to her face.

"I know the workers appreciate it. I saw Rose Janelle just yesterday, and she had nothing but praise for the good doctor. She and her cousin Marie had planned to go home for the summer to avoid another outbreak, but now they can stay here and make some extra money to send home. Rose's brother needs some new spectacles."

"I'm glad it's helping her anyway." Mariette looked up at the sky. The sun was slipping behind a fluffy white cloud.

"Do you not like the workers? Have they done something to offend you?"

Mariette looked quickly at Jean's face. Sincerity, not condemnation, peered at her. "No, of course not. It's just that they are such an inconvenience. David is sleeping with Clement. The parlor is about to be overrun with young women. The men spend the evening on the porch, talking and carrying on." Mariette raised her arms and spread her hands. She had no more words.

Jean nodded. "I had a patient once who was very ill. He was always tired and irritable. Sometimes he was so tired he would get dizzy and faint. He couldn't go long without eating or he would shake and tremble so that he couldn't hold anything. When he finally came to see me, it was almost too late for him. He had diabetes and needed help to learn to eat for his condition."

Mariette wasn't sure why Jean was telling her this. "Hm. Did he get better?" She moved to the side of the walkway and nodded to a passerby.

"Yes. Once he knew what the problem was, he could deal with it. He didn't like having diabetes, but in the end diabetes taught my patient how to take care of himself." Jean held Mariette's gaze. "Perhaps your current situation can teach you something about your real problem."

"I'm back," Mariette called as she entered the kitchen and set her shopping basket down. "The store brought in new potatoes from ..." Her voice trailed off as she looked across into Rachelle and Clement's room.

The door stood open and Rachelle hovered over the bed. Increase sat on the side with the stethoscope pressed to Clement's chest. David was cross-legged at the foot of the bed, his eyes as big as saucers.

Mariette walked to Rachelle's side and took her hand. "What's going on?" she whispered.

Increase held up his hand for silence.

Alongside Rachelle, Mariette stood over the black cooking stove, stirring a pot absentmindedly. "I'm sure Papa won't mind. Walter and Evelyn always keep the cottage ready. Increase said three weeks, a month at the most, will have Clement fit as a fiddle. Good salty sea air. That's what he needs. You'll see."

Rachelle wiped her eyes with the back of her hand. "But how will Dr. Graves manage without us here?"

"The workers will help. Clement is our concern right now."

Maurice had agreed to let Mariette and Rachelle take the boys to Martha's Vineyard for a month. "Perhaps I can get some time to join you," he said over the crackling phone line.

Trunks were packed with warm clothes and plenty of blankets. Rachelle filled the cupboards with food and instructed the young women how to cook for Dr. Graves. She hated that he would have to eat canned vegetables for a month, but the girls didn't have time or energy to cook from scratch.

The train was pulling into the station as Increase pulled Mariette to his chest. "I'll miss you, but I think this trip will be as good for you as it is for Clement. You've been looking so worn out lately. I'm sorry if having so many boarders has exhausted you. I just thought we could help."

Mariette raised her eyes to look into Increase's face. He was a good man. He had his faults, but then so did she. "I'll come back a new woman." She smiled and put her hand to his cheek.

David pulled at the edge of Increase's jacket. "I'll bring back a seashell for you, Daddy. One that lets you hear the ocean."

Increase laughed. He let go of Mariette and scooped up his son. "I look forward to it. Take care of Clement and your mama."

"And Rachelle too." David grinned.

"Rachelle too," Increase said.

*Suffering! We owe to it all that is good in us, all that gives value to life; we*
*owe to it pity, we owe to it courage, we owe to it all the virtues.*
~Anatole France~

# CHAPTER 35

SUNLIGHT POURED IN THROUGH THE thin lace curtains, waking Mariette from a deep sleep. Her whole body ached from the journey. A ship passed by the island, and the wash of waves against the rocks was soothing. She stretched and yawned, thankful that her stomach had finally settled after yesterday's crossing. She hated not helping Rachelle more with the boys; she hadn't ever been seasick before, not even on the long journey to Paris and back again.

Increase refused to be intimidated. He had been kept waiting in Mr. Hoop's office for half an hour. The large mahogany desk was fitted with gold leaf on the outside edges. A stained-glass lamp sat on the corner of the wooden monstrosity. A silver pen set and ink blotter were nestled in an olivewood holder in the middle of it all. There was no doubt that Mr. Hoop was successful.

"Sorry to keep you waiting," Mr. Hoop said as he opened the heavy oak door. "Business calls, you know. What can I do for you, Dr. Graves?"

Increase stood to shake hands with the older gentleman, but Mr. Hoop walked behind the desk and took a seat. Increase slid his hands on his pant legs and then sat again himself. He cleared his throat.

"Well, sir, I was hoping to talk to you about the health of your workers." He looked across the desk as Mr. Hoop raised his eyebrows.

"Everyone seems healthy to me. No complaints," Mr. Hoop said before Increase could say more.

"Yes. It seems moving the workers into more suitable housing has had an effect, a positive one. The construction workers in the mill houses have nearly completed their updates. Food cupboards have been installed in all of the apartments, and new doors are being fitted to all of the buildings. I guess the last step is to caulk the windows and then Public Health can do their inspections." He leaned forward in his chair. "But I have seen a few cases of typhus recently. I know we can't completely avoid it, but I'd like to be able to control an outbreak."

"It seems you already have." Mr. Hoop turned his palms up. "I can't see what else you can do."

"I would like to check your workers as they come to work in the mornings." Increase was on the edge of his seat now as Mr. Hoop set his jaw. "If I could just do a quick check every morning before they begin work, I should be able to isolate cases and keep it from spreading. We can quarantine them in the hospital."

"I'm not running a nursery, Dr. Graves. This is a business. I can't spare the time that would take."

"But you see, sir, if you spare the time now, just a few minutes really, then you save yourself lost time later. Remember all of the lost hours last year when the workers were dropping like flies?"

Mr. Hoop leaned back in his leather chair and clasped his hands together in thought. He had lost several weeks' worth of labor last summer at the height of the epidemic.

"If you agree to let me check your employees before the morning shift, then I could check workers at the other mills at shift breaks, during lunch, and before the last evening shift. The other mill owners respect you, Mr. Hoop. If you allow it, I know they will follow suit." Increase gave what he hoped was an encouraging smile. "It's a wise business move, really."

"Perhaps." Hoop's fingers danced against each other with indecisiveness. "Where would you do these, mm, checkups? I don't have space for a doctor's office."

"Oh, no, sir. I could station myself at the bottom of the spiral stairs. I just need to ask a couple of questions and check the pulse. Catching it in the incubation period is difficult, but if I see them daily, well, I hope I can spot the sick ones." It wasn't a strong argument, certainly not definitive, but it was the best he could do.

"Alright, Doctor. I'll give you fifteen minutes to check the workers as they come in each morning."

Increase stood and extended his hand across the desk. "Thank you, Mr.

Hoop. You won't regret it."

*Three days in and no signs of typhus. Good news for all.* The letter was harder to write than Increase expected. His medical school letters to Annie had flowed freely across the paper, full of romance and statements of undying love. But now, with Mariette—*his wife*, he reminded himself—he felt reticent to reveal his feelings. He hadn't expected to miss her so much. Her quiet presence was a balm to him after a long day's work. He poured another glass of brandy and headed out to the porch with the men.

Clement and David seemed immune to the frigid waters of Squibnocket Pond. Once Clement found that he could float with great ease, he spent the days kicking and paddling in the water. Mariette and Rachelle rowed the boys out in the blue painted dinghy Maurice kept tied to a docking post, and then watched the boys as they wrestled in the water.

"Careful, David. Don't be so rough." Mariette's voice echoed across the water.

"He can't hurt me," Clement called back. "I'm bigger than he is!"

David took the challenge and ducked Clement. The taller boy came up spluttering and laughing. The chase was on.

"It's so good to hear him laugh." Rachelle smiled ear to ear while she watched the boys. The paddles rested on the edge of the boat as the two women floated in the afternoon sun. "Thank you for bringing us here. It means all the world to us. Papa said he wants to meet the family who treats his children so well." She paused and glanced toward the sandy shoreline. "I just hope he gets to see Clement again. It's been so long."

"When did you see him last?" Mariette shifted her weight in the small boat and it tipped side to side. They both reached for the gunnels to steady themselves.

"It's been over three years. Mamere was not able to travel once the sickness started, and then last summer … Well, it hasn't been possible." She rearranged her skirts and pulled her hat closer to her head. "Maybe next summer Clement will be strong enough. That is, if you are well enough to let us go." Rachelle turned pink.

"Of course I will be well. The typhus isn't going to get us." Mariette looked at Rachelle with surprise.

"It isn't the typhus I meant," Rachelle said, patting her stomach. "The baby will still be nursing."

Mariette covered her abdomen with the light shawl she always kept nearby. "Is it that obvious?" She stared at the floor of the boat.

"Only to those who know the signs; you aren't showing any. Honestly I'm surprised Dr. Graves let you come on such a long trip in your condition."

"Clement's health is very important." Mariette smiled and looked across the water. The boys were swimming toward shore. "We should start rowing. They'll be ready for supper."

The gonging of the first work bell burrowed into Increase's mind like a millstone sinking in a murky lake. His head ached and his mouth was dry with cotton. A shaft of sunlight cut across the bedroom like a scalpel plunging into his eyes. He covered his face with his hands and wondered if there was any coffee left over from the morning rush.

He threw the thin sheet off himself and rolled onto his elbow. The walls spun, the bed shook, and a wave of nausea forced his head back down. He wouldn't be checking for typhus this morning.

There had been a time, after Annie's death, when he couldn't control his drinking. Lively hid the alcohol from him and forced him to talk, to hold David, to be sober. As time went by, the pain lessened, but not the memory. Whiskey had helped, but time had been the healer.

So why did he get so stinking drunk last night? *Mariette. A letter.* That was it. Mariette's letter written in flowing script. He could see her soft hands writing the simple words that plunged him into the abyss: *David loves watching the whaling boats ship out in the mornings. Clement is growing stronger by the day. You were so right to send us here. Rachelle is taking care of me, but I miss our evening talks.*

Increase turned to his side and caressed the pillow that would have been Mariette's. Alcohol couldn't erase her absence forever. *She will be back.* The thought was smoke from an unknown fire.

The ringing phone sliced through the clearing fog of his mind. Increase wiped the drool from his cheek and sat up. He must have fallen back to sleep. The clock on the mantle said it was nearly noon. Increase swung his feet over the side of the bed and reached for a robe. *Why does the phone have to be at the bottom of the stairs?*

"Coming, coming," he mumbled as he shuffled barefoot into the hallway. The stairs loomed ahead and he grabbed the rail. The spinning lessened.

"Hello. Dr. Graves speaking." His voice rasped the greeting.

"We need you at the hospital. Now, Doctor. Mr. Gaines has a broken leg." Nurse Hall's voice belied her composure. Something wasn't right.

"Go ahead and give him a bed. I'll set it when I get there."

"He needs more than a bed, Doctor. It's bad." Her voice was low. "Come quickly." He heard the receiver click.

"I put him in the surgery, Doctor."

Nurse Hall's eyes swept Increase from top to bottom. He rubbed the two days' stubble that paraded across his face. He looked down and pulled the trouser leg out of his sock.

"Thank you, Nurse Hall."

Increase crossed the reception area and pushed open the door to surgery. The cold coffee he had downed before leaving home sloshed in his stomach.

"So, Mr. Gaines, you've broken your—" Increase stopped abruptly, taking in the sight. The librarian was unconscious on the operating table. The tibia was protruding halfway down the left shin, a clean compound fracture.

"He fell off a ladder in the library and caught his leg in a rung." Jean stood at the corner of the bed. "He comes to occasionally, but it's been ten minutes or so since he was last conscious." Jean looked from Increase to the librarian and back again. "Perhaps you would like me to assist?"

Increase bit his lip. He had performed surgery on compound fractures before, but not in such primitive circumstances, and never after a night of drinking. "That would be good, yes. Thank you, Jean." His voice cracked and he coughed to cover up the fear swimming in his stomach.

"I'll wash up with you," Jean said. "Nurse Hall, will you and Helen prepare Mr. Gaines while Dr. Graves gets ready?" Jean nodded toward the nurse and her young student.

"Of course." Nurse Hall began cutting away Mr. Gaines's trousers.

"Hope it holds," Increase said as he unscrewed the metal and rubber tourniquet. The blood flow seeped into the wounded leg. "I'll prepare a camphor compound for you to clean the wound. Teach your student …" He paused, looking at the young girl and then back at Nurse Hall.

"Helen, sir."

"Teach Helen how to dress the wound and apply the camphor. Infection is his greatest enemy now."

Increase turned for his office. Jean followed.

"You did well," Jean said. "Considering." Jean seated himself in a side chair while Increase poured a shot of brandy. "Is that wise?" Jean tipped his head toward the amber bottle.

"Deserved, I'd say. You want some?"

"No, thank you. Why do you drink so much, Increase?"

Increase sat in the wooden office chair and exhaled. "I don't need a lecture, Jean."

"A simple question."

Increase looked at the older man, concern etched on his face. "I drink for many reasons. It tastes good. It calms and relaxes me. After a long day, or a stressful operation …" Increase shrugged. "It helps."

"Are those the only times you drink, then?"

"Well, no." Increase shifted his weight and crossed his legs. He picked a piece of lint off his pant leg. "Sometimes I drink at parties. Often we have wine with dinner."

"So you use alcohol to celebrate, to accompany good food, and to relieve stress. Is that right?"

"Yeah." Increase nodded and sipped the brandy.

"So for which of those reasons were you drinking last night?"

Increase blanched. He set the glass down on the desk beside him. Mariette's letter and the empty pillow came racing back. "I suppose … I suppose celebration. The men were out on the porch drinking and talking. I joined them."

"Mm. And did any of them show up at work late or drunk?" Jean's gaze pierced Increase.

"I told you: no lectures, Jean. Thank you for assisting me with the surgery. I'll make sure you are compensated by the hospital. I better get that camphor compound going." He rose and extended a hand toward Jean.

Jean remained unmoved. "People are prisoners of time." The Frenchman looked across the dim room toward the half-opened door. "Living in the present, but never able to fully leave the past." He rose, unbending until he stood his full height. "How long do you suppose Mr. Gaines will regret climbing that ladder to reach the books that he loves?"

Increase watched as Jean crossed the room and pulled the door shut behind him.

"Do you think Daddy will like this shell?" David held it to his ear. His collection spilled across the porch.

"He'll love it," Mariette said, lowering herself to sit on the step.

The sunset streaked the sky, shimmering on the first evening star. *If only I could be sure he will love all our presents ...*

*Death gives us sleep, eternal youth, and immortality.*
~Jean Paul~

# CHAPTER 36

PAOLO AND SILVANUS LEFT LUDIA'S house quietly, not wanting to create any more trouble. They were concerned that the men who owned the slave girl might cause problems if they found out the two were let go so quickly.

Jehan and I left soon after to check on the marsh community. The children were doing better; only a few were still expelling the worms. The recovered children assured us they would not play in the water this summer, and I believed them. *Pain and suffering are excellent teachers.*

"I think I'm starting to understand why the gods ... I mean, God ... allows us to suffer. At least when there is an opportunity to stop the suffering—make it right."

Jehan and I walked up the stone-paved road busy with travelers, local farmers, and merchants. The sky was beginning to cloud over, affirming my earlier prediction.

"With time you'll understand many things, but, Loukas, you will never fully understand everything, not even suffering. God thinks thoughts that you could never fathom. He makes plans that you cannot comprehend." He looked over at me as we walked under the cover of the large cypress. "He is God, Loukas, and you must be satisfied with that."

I nodded and walked on in silence. The road became busier as we neared the city gate. Carts of fresh fish passed us on their way to the marketplace. *Pater would like some for dinner.*

"I'm going to stop and get some fish for Pater, Jehan. I'll meet you back at your house this afternoon?"

"Sounds good. Say hello to Aegeus."

I waved and headed for the fish vendors. The streets were crowded with people, selling their wares, calling to friends, sharing news. Last night's earthquake that no one else felt seemed to be the talk of the town.

"Revolt! Revolt!" Two youths came running into the market. "At Asyla. The slaves revolted. The soldiers put it down, but not without losses." They panted from the run, and their voices shook. "We saw the whole thing, people beaten and even killed."

I dropped the fish back onto the pile and took off for Jehan's place. *Another "earthquake," and this one we'll all feel.*

Jehan was turning into the garden when I got there.

"Jehan, there's trouble at Asyla, a slave rebellion. We might be needed."

"Let me change my bag," Jehan said as he hurried into the hut.

Silence. No sounds came from the normally busy gold mine complex. Four guards stood at the gate to Asyla, their crossed arms presenting heavy spears.

"We heard there was need of medical help," Jehan said. "Where should we go?"

The chief guard pointed us to the officers' barracks. Jehan nodded and led the way. Three slaves slumped in the dust next to flogging posts where they were tied. Their raw backs lay open to the sun, and flies buzzed around them, gorging themselves on fresh blood.

Jehan passed without stopping, but his lips moved in silent prayer.

Pausing at the barracks' door, Jehan said to a sentry, "We've come to treat the wounded and injured."

"This way."

We walked down the long aisle of officers' beds. A few men were sleeping fitfully, probably loaded up on strong wine. I followed Jehan and the official to the bed of a centurion.

Red blood soaked through a bandage on his head. His eyes were closed, his face set, taut.

"Sir, the doctor has come."

The centurion opened his eyes and looked at Jehan. "A gash is all, Doctor. It will heal."

Jehan walked to his side. "Let me check." He began unwrapping the cloth plastered to the man's dark hair. "Loukas can look after your other men."

The centurion winced as Jehan unwound the bandage. He waved a hand toward me, so I pulled the medical bag off my shoulder and turned toward the next occupied bed. A knife had sliced this soldier's shoulder open. Stitches would be necessary.

I threaded the needle while he sucked on a wine-drenched cloth. The pain of stitching would be nothing next to the actual wound.

I tugged the thread through the tough skin, each pull causing the man to inhale deeply. His back began to spasm as nerves and muscles awoke from their stupor. I told the officer with me to douse the cloth again with wine.

The next patient had a dislocated shoulder. I rolled him on his back and prepared for the physical and emotional strain it would take to put it back in place. It was a common injury after gladiator fights, but I never got used to it.

I distracted the soldier with questions about the bruising on his cheek. While I grasped his hand and elbow, I rotated the man's arm, raising it until the shoulder could pop back into place. The familiar clunk, and the man's cry of surprise, assured me it was relocated.

Standing up, I began fashioning a sling for him out of a sheet.

"Hey! I know you," came a voice from behind me

I turned and saw the guard I had questioned several days ago. He was lying in a bed a few feet away.

"You're the troublemaker who started all this." He raised himself on his elbow. "Yeah. You told those dogs they needed breaks, and—"

The centurion interrupted. "Enough. Varius, take him into custody."

An officer with me grabbed my arm.

"He's a doctor, not a troublemaker," Jehan said. He held a bottle of vinegar. "Perhaps what he said stung." Jehan poured the vinegar on the centurion's stitched head. "But it was meant to clean and heal your camp, not to damage."

The centurion jerked on the bed as the vinegar penetrated the torn flesh. Jehan wiped the running fluid away from the man's eyes.

The injured soldier spoke again: "It's true, sir. He's the one that said the slaves need shorter shifts."

The commanding officer eyed me.

"That's true." Jehan nodded, putting the cork back in the vinegar. "But have you not noticed the way your workers cough and spit? It's miner's cough—deadly."

The guard holding my arms looked to the centurion.

"Medicine comes in many forms," Jehan said. "Some is used as seeds;

some is best harvested as sprouts. Still other plants provide health in their mature leaves. Most medicinal plants, though, are used at the end of their life, dried."

I stared at Jehan. *Really? This is the best time for an apothecary lesson?*

The centurion held his hand in the air, but listened to Jehan's ramblings.

"A good doctor must care for the plant at all the stages," Jehan went on. "Otherwise the usefulness of the plant is severely limited. A little care early on makes the plant produce greater results. And so it is with workers."

Jehan put the bottle of vinegar back in his bag and pulled the drawstring tight.

"Take him to the magistrates." The centurion closed his eyes.

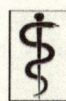

The air was heavy and humid as we descended the hill to town. *Pater will be furious.* I stumbled over the lip of a paving stone. The soldier jerked me back up. *I was helping soldiers.* Sweat dripped in my eyes and trickled down my back. I swiped at my eyes with my tied wrists.

Walking through town felt humiliating. Everyone in the busy streets gawked and stared. I was marched up to the magistrates, who were talking to the slave girl's owners.

"They were Roman citizens," the head magistrate said. "We had to let them go or it would have been trouble for us."

"Trouble? There'll be trouble alright." Their words dripped like henbane. "The gods will fall upon us. This girl was their messenger, and now she's been silenced."

Varius pounded his spear on the pavement and the magistrates turned.

"This man has been accused of inciting a riot at Asyla. The centurion sends him to you for trial."

He pushed me forward and the slave owners caught their breath when they recognized me.

"The gods have rescued us," one of them said. "This man was with the others who expelled the spirit. You've been given another opportunity to do the right thing. He must be punished."

Varius stepped between the men and the magistrates. "He has expelled no spirits. He's accused of inciting a rebellion of slaves at Asyla."

"What do you say?" the head magistrate said. "Did you incite the rebellion?"

Silence echoed for the second time that day. *Am I responsible for the insurrection? Did my prescription of fresh air cause the slave workers to attack their jailers? Are the gods—Is my God at work in this?*

"I did not suggest rebellion or encourage the men to revolt."

The two slave owners spit at my feet.

I went on, "Many of them are sick with miner's cough. I suggested that they would heal more quickly with fresh air and shorter shifts inside the mine."

"He's a traitor and a troublemaker." The men raised their arms in the air and began chanting. "Traitor … Traitor … Traitor."

The head magistrate took control. "Seize these men until we can speak to this one alone."

Varius took the slave owners by their arms and dragged them from the platform. I turned to the magistrates, bowed in a show of respect and humility, and waited.

A roll of thunder echoed from Mount Pangaion.

The head magistrate eyed me. "Were you at Asyla?"

"Yes."

"What were you doing there?"

"I was attending sick soldiers with Doctor Jehan."

"Why are you accused of starting an insurrection?"

Lightning flashed over the mountain and the returning call of thunder turned eyes heavenward.

"While we were looking in on the soldiers, we also treated several slaves. I noticed that many suffered from a cough—miner's cough. It's preventable if the workers are given time between shifts in the fresh air to clean out their lungs. The air in the tunnels is rancid, poisonous."

I paused as raindrops fat as figs plopped onto the warm pavement.

"Go on."

"I suggested to the officers on duty that they would get more done with healthy workers. As you know, Philippi is an important colony because of our rich gold supply. I wouldn't want anything to tarnish our reputation or rank as a colony."

"What he says is prudent," one of the magistrates whispered. "The workforce must remain healthy or we all will suffer."

The men conferred together as the crowd ran for cover under the marketplace booths, in the public baths, and beneath the eaves of houses. The magistrates gathered under the climbing vines in the public forum. I stood drenched in the pouring rain.

After several minutes I was called over to them.

"You are Aegeus's son? Studied in Rome?"

"Yes, I'm Loukas, son of Aegeus. I studied medicine in both Athens and Rome."

"There is wisdom in what you say. You will attend to the workers in Asyla from now on. Make health code requirements as you see fit. We will send you to the centurion tomorrow with a letter."

I walked home, showered by God's blessings.

*Cure sometimes, treat often, comfort always.*
~Author Unknown~

# CHAPTER 37

MARIETTE FOLDED THE LETTER AND placed it back in its envelope. Increase's letters were faithful even if they weren't romantic. She pushed the envelope into her handbag. Someone tapped her shoulder and she turned.

"Papa! We weren't expecting you yet." Mariette crushed Maurice in an ecstatic embrace. "I thought you were coming in two more days. Your telegram said Wednesday." She stepped back and looked across the dock. "Where are your bags?"

"I sent them on with Walter. He happened by when I arrived." Maurice kissed Mariette's cheek. "It's good to see you, ma chère fille—my dear girl. Comment allez-vous—How are you?"

"I'm fine, Papa. Just fine. David will be thrilled you're here early. Are you ready to go? We'll get back just in time for lunch. Rachelle made strawberry shortcake, a special treat. The strawberries were sent in all the way from Georgia." Mariette wrapped her arm in the crook of her father's elbow and inhaled the fresh sea air.

"How is David? And Clement too, of course. Was Increase right to send you here?" Maurice had suggested they go first to Boston and get checked by the doctors there, but Increase had insisted there was nothing they could do that wouldn't be solved by rest at the shore.

"Salts are good for the body. That includes sea salts," Increase had said.

"Clement is making wonderful progress. Yes, Increase was right. He's a magnificent doctor, you know." She smiled up at her father and winked. "Even if he doesn't always recognize it."

The afternoon sun warmed the sand along the pond's shore. Maurice and the boys pulled off their shoes and socks, and the older man indulged them in a game of chase. When his cheeks were red and sweat ran down his temple, Mariette rescued him by sending the boys in for a swim.

"Show Pepè how well you swim, David. You too, Clement. He'll be so impressed."

"Pepè," Maurice said. "I love the sound of that. I've missed the boy. Has the move to Dunstable Plains really been a good one?"

"Papa, you were there at Christmas. You know we're very happy there." Mariette placed her arm on Maurice's.

"Hm. I watched you read your letter today at the docks. Maybe you would be happier to return home. You miss Increase?" He covered her hand with his own and smiled.

Mariette looked down and pulled her hand away from her father. "Increase is a good man. He cares about his patients deeply." She sighed and looked across the water.

"But?" Maurice stared at his precious daughter. His mouth was dry.

She smiled at him and then looked away again. "I don't know. There are suspicions there. It was getting uncomfortable when I left."

"What do you mean?" *If there's another woman, I'll skin him alive.*

"The other wives. They look at me, but it's like they're looking through me. I went to a library meeting and no one spoke to me. They think Increase is causing trouble for the mills."

Maurice breathed easier. "How could he be doing that?"

A seagull perched on a rock just offshore and watched them. Mariette tossed a pebble and it flew away.

"Increase complained to the Public Health Board that a terrible accident could have been avoided. He used that situation to remind the mill owners of last year's typhus outbreak. He wanted to see each mill's workers for a quick daily checkup as they file in to work."

"Very responsible."

"Yes, well. They agreed to it, but at the same time the State Board of Health showed up and started looking around the housing that is provided. It was, shall we say, inadequate. The millers thought Increase called them in, but he didn't, Papa." Mariette took a few steps closer to shore and waved as David surfaced from a jump off the rowboat where Rachelle watched the boys. "In order to pass the inspections, and to save us all from another typhus outbreak of course, Increase somehow managed to get the wealthier townspeople to house the workers." Mariette looked at Maurice as he drew in his breath. "I know. It's temporary, just a few weeks while repairs are made to the housing, but a lot of people think Increase went too far."

"I'm so sorry." Maurice wrapped his arms around Mariette and pulled her close.

She sidestepped out of his hug. "It's not your fault, Papa. It'll blow over with time." She tried to smile.

Maurice clapped along with her as Clement and David raced to one of the islands. Then he looked at his daughter.

"Yes, it actually is my fault," he said. "I called the State Department of Health back in January when I returned home. I saw the deplorable conditions those poor people were living in. I had to do something. I'm sorry I made it difficult for you and Increase."

"Don't be. A lot of people will be better off because of it."

She motioned for Rachelle to tie up the boat. Mariette was ready to go home.

*Absence and death are the same—only that in death there is no suffering.*
~Walter Savage Landor~

# CHAPTER 38

"THAT LINE NO LONGER EXISTS. I can try to reach your husband at the hospital," the operator's voice said.

"Yes …" Mariette said. "Please… of course, the hospital." She covered her mouth and tried not to worry. *How could the line no longer exist?*

"Hello, Mrs. Graves. This is Nurse Lindelof. Dr. Graves and Helen are making a house call. Is there something I can do for you?"

"Oh." *Who is Helen?* "No. Well, yes. Can you please tell him there's been a delay? Rachelle and the boys and I will be a day late. There was a storm and the ferry had trouble in the harbor. We're staying at Papa's. Everyone is safe."

"That's good news. The doctor shouldn't be much longer. They left at the shift change. I'll make sure he gets the message."

"Merci. Thank you." The line went dead in her ear, and she hung the heavy receiver on the iron hook.

"Daddy!" David ran to his father and jumped in his arms.

Increase twirled the boy around and laughed. "You've grown, by George. Did you have a wonderful time?" He kissed the boy's cheek and set him down.

"We went swimming and watched the whalers and had picnics and I flew a kite and Mama and Rachelle rowed the boat and Clement can walk!" David's eyes gleamed as he tried to share everything at once.

"He can walk?"

Mariette joined the two on the station platform like a fawn entering a meadow, unsure and frightened. Her lips trembled as she smiled at Increase. He bent to kiss her cheek.

"I got the message from Nurse Lindelof. I'm glad you're all safe."

"Thank you so much for letting us go with Mrs. Graves and David," Rachelle said, breaking the couple's gaze.

"You're most welcome, but what's this about Clement walking?" Increase turned his attention to Rachelle.

"David spilled the beans," Mariette said as she also turned to the girl. "There was a storm off the coast and it was difficult to get into the harbor. We ended up missing the train, and we were so tired." She sighed and smiled at Rachelle. "So we spent the night with Papa."

Mariette placed her hand in the crook of Increase's arm and looked up at him. "You were so right about sending us to the island. When Papa visited and saw how well Clement was doing, he went back to Boston and had braces made. Papa planned to ship them to us later, but since we ended up there …" She shrugged her shoulders as Clement and a porter climbed down the train steps.

Clement smiled ear to ear. The metal and leather braces held his legs sturdy and he leaned on two canes for support. "Dr. Graves! Look!" The boy was robust and tanned. Gone were the signs of sickness and impending death.

"You were right, Increase," Mariette said again. "Salt air … and swimming in Squibnocket Pond … did the trick."

The crickets chirped in the deepening dusk, mixing their tenor with the bass of a bullfrog under the porch. Mariette's feet barely skimmed the floor as the porch swing creaked on its metal chains. Increase put his arm around his wife's shoulders, letting his hand rest on her upper arm. There was worry in the way she held herself.

"Are you alright, Mariette? You've seemed tense ever since you got back."

She continued looking ahead at the street. The glow of the dining room light made a speckled pattern on the hedge. "Mm-hm. I'm fine."

"I missed you. I'm glad it was good for Clement, but I like having you home."

Mariette glanced at Increase and fluttered her eyes just as quickly back to the street. "What happened to the phone?"

"Well …" Increase pulled his arm back and clasped his hands. He had known this was coming sooner or later. "I didn't feel it was proper to have a phone when so many of the people who were staying here could never afford one. This big house is already uppity enough."

"But what if there's an emergency, some emergency that isn't announced with mill bells and fire sirens? What if a baby comes in the middle of the night and you're … needed?" Fear and doubt swam in her eyes as she tried to look at him. Instead she focused on the whiskers that darkened his chin.

"Good evening." A familiar voice interrupted them.

Increase stood and grabbed hold of the porch pillar. "Good evening, Jean. Mariette is back. Won't you come say hello?"

Jean's soft-soled shoes brushed the stairs, whispering his welcome. "Good evening, madame. Did you enjoy your trip?" He tipped his hat and smiled down at her.

"Oui. Merci. Won't you join us? Increase, bring out a chair."

"No need," Jean said. "I won't stay long. I'm sure you'd like to be alone for a while to catch up. I was just out for an evening stroll and saw the two of you back at each other's side once again." Jean smiled at each of them. "The Father gave a blessing to the world the day you met."

Mariette blushed and looked at the floor. Increase pushed his hands into his trouser pockets. "Hmph," he snorted. "The day we met, I left her house in a huff. I don't think there was a blessing that day."

"Ahh, but there was. Oui, ma'amoiselle?"

Mariette jumped as a door banged shut somewhere in the house. David had to be up.

"I'm sorry, Dr. Giatros. I think David is out of bed. I need to check on him. Won't you excuse me?" She stood quickly and the blood rushed to her head. She grabbed the swing chain to steady herself.

"Are you well, Mrs. Graves?"

"Yes. Fine. I'm fine." The porch came back into focus and the floor was solid once more. "It was good to see you again. Good night."

Increase jumped ahead of her to open the door.

"Good night, Mrs. Graves," Jean said.

Mariette looked over her shoulder and nodded at the older man, then stepped across the threshold into the house. Increase closed the door behind her.

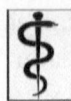

"A mother and child. Actually all of the pictures were in some way."

Increase sat on the wooden swing while Jean leaned against the white porch post. The crickets and frog had ceased their chorus, and the men spoke in hushed tones.

"Mariette had so many pictures of mothers and their children."

"And you … were angry about that?" Jean stroked his chin.

"No … not that they were mothers and children." Increase bent his toes to stop the swing's rhythm. He looked across the street where shadows moved across the curtains, like memories blowing in a breeze. "I was angry that Mariette and Maurice so easily accepted God's role in their loss." He brushed his hair back with his slender fingers, fingers that held a scalpel with such deftness. "I remember saying God is cruel to separate mothers and their children, and Maurice said, 'No, God is kind.' That … That made me angry." Increase could feel the fire kindling again in his chest.

"Why do you think Maurice isn't angry about the death of Mariette's mother?"

"I don't know. He should be. He had to raise Mariette alone; at least I had some help."

"Your sister?"

"Lively … yes. She came right away. She'd been living with Mother in Concord, but she stayed with me for years. Then Mother had health issues and Lively had to leave. That's when Mariette started helping. Jumped right in actually. David loved her right away."

"And you? You loved her right away?"

Increase drew in a deep breath and slowly exhaled. "She was a friend when I needed a friend. Rumors started and …" Increase started the metronomic swing again. "The marriage was to save her reputation. It didn't need saving." Increase looked at Jean. "She was always a lady, and I … Well, I never had eyes for anyone but Annie."

"So it is you who are cruel to Mariette, not God." Jean's voice floated on the evening breeze.

Increase snapped his head up, looking at the older man in shock. "Me? I haven't been cruel to Mariette. I give her everything she wants: clothes, furniture, this house." He raised his shoulders and swept the porch with his arms. "No. No one can say I am cruel to her." Increase pushed the swing so hard the chains rattled.

"Do you love her?" Jean could stare through a brick wall.

Hot acid flooded Increase's stomach and his chest grew warm. "We're married. I've done right by her and saved her reputation. What do you think?" He spat into the hedge, a long arc of venom reaching across the porch and into the darkness beyond.

"I think you're afraid."

Increase blew out a quick puff of air and stood up to look at Jean. "Afraid of what?"

"You're afraid of loving Mariette, because you don't want to experience the pain of losing her like you did Annie." Jean looked Increase in the eye.

"No." Increase took a deep breath and then walked to the porch pillar. He leaned against it for support and ran a shaky hand through his hair. "I still love Annie. That … That's the problem."

"Do you love David?" Jean walked to the edge of the stairs and teetered on the top step, staring out at the stars.

"Of course I do. He's my son."

"And Lively? You love her?"

"What are you getting at? Of course I love my sister, and my mother as well." Increase shoved his hands into his pockets and watched the older doctor.

"So you are capable of loving more than one person?" Jean raised his head and stared into the distance.

Increase remained quiet.

"Of course you still love Annie. That's as it should be." He turned to face Increase. "But the reason you're cruel to Mariette is that you fear losing her, not that you can't love her." He reached across and placed a hand on Increase's arm. "There is no fear in love. Love casts the fear out. Put aside your fears, Increase."

Increase watched Jean's back as he descended the steps and disappeared into the blackness beyond the walkway.

The sounds of sleeping people breathed through the dark house. The last step creaked as Increase climbed the stairs and entered the hallway. He paused outside David's room and listened to the men's snores. Soon the mill houses would be ready to move back into and David would return to his own bed. Increase smiled to himself, thinking about the fuss David would surely make. He enjoyed being with Clement.

Increase crossed the floor and pushed open the door to his own room. Mariette lay with her face to the wall, the light quilt draped across her with one foot sticking out. He had missed her; that was true.

He slipped out of his clothes and into the bed. He lay on his back, hands clasped under his head. *Is Jean right? Is it fear that keeps me from Mariette? Can I really love her and not forget Annie?*

"Who is Helen?" It was barely more than a whisper, wetted with the croaking of crying.

Increase turned on his side and Mariette rolled over. He looked into her face, lit by the moonshine coming in the open window.

"She's one of the student nurses. Why?"

"Is she pretty?" Tears overflowed and raced down the curve of her cheek.

Increase swept her hair back and wiped the tears with the edge of the bedsheet. "She is young and pretty and quite smitten with the fool librarian. But she in no way matches the beauty of the wife in my bed." He smiled and kissed her softly on the nose. "Is that what has you so worried, mi amour?"

Mariette reached for Increase and pulled him to her while tears continued to flow.

"I missed you, Increase," Mariette said as she lay her head against his breast. "I was so miserably fearful." His heartbeat lulled her to sleep.

"Miserably fearful," he whispered. "Yes."

*God had one son on earth without sin, but never one without suffering.*
~Saint Augustine~

# CHAPTER 39

*Philippi—AD 58*

I LISTENED TO THE PHILOSOPHIZING TOWN elders as they poured their glasses full of the rich mountain wine. Goblet and gullet both were drenched in the red liquid. The symposium waxed long about the great gift of Dionysus. I sipped from my own cup and mulled over the past year's events.

Pater was old; it was to be expected. But no one is ever ready to lose their father, no matter how much they expect the inevitable. The suffering was short. Not much could have been worse than the phthisis, and we had conquered that—or Jesus had, anyway—years ago.

Pater had never given himself fully to my Lord and Savior. He was always prone to politics and didn't want to be on the wrong side of any party. He worshipped Dionysus during the festivals, made regular offerings to Asclepius, and proclaimed miraculous healing by Paolo and Jesus Christ. *None of them rescued him this time, though.*

The mines were producing more gold than ever for the great empire. Shorter shifts, daily doses of expectorant teas, and good nutrition seemed to make Philippi more profitable. The town was growing.

"To Dionysus, Filler of the Cup."

Everyone raised their glasses and toasted the deity. I excused myself and wandered into the cool courtyard. The spring air was sweet with flowering trees and vines.

"You aren't drinking."

I turned and saw a young servant maid clearing the courtyard tables.

"Wine is a good medicine, but too much medicine can make you sick."

I winked at the girl. "I prefer to worship the creator of the grape, rather than the grape itself."

The girl nodded. "My master will be sick in the morning. ... Aren't you the doctor at Asyla?"

"Yes. How did you know that?"

"Sometimes I make deliveries there. Bread and such." She jerked a thumb toward the host's party. "When the bakery is very busy, my master lets me work there. ... The slaves talk about you."

"They do?"

"Mm-hm. They help me unload in the kitchen. They say you're kind."

"My God is kind to me. I try to share that with others." I smiled. There was something about the girl. "Have you heard of Jesus Christ?"

"I have." She nodded. "He's why I work here."

I cocked my head to one side and looked at the dark curly wisps that showed under her head covering.

"I used to be a slave to some men. A spirit possessed me. I told futures."

"Ahh." *So this is what happened to her.* "I remember you."

"They sold me here when I couldn't present messages from the gods. I never saw them again. I thought ... I thought they loved me, but I was just a tool." She looked down.

"I'm sorry. So much happened that day—those days...."

She shook her head, unable to look at me.

Ludia met me at the door, her face shining. "Come in." A giggle escaped her faded lips, a little girl's laugh in an old woman's face.

The church was gathered for the weekly meeting. Ludia's large court-yard was the only place that could hold all of us now. Every week someone new joined us. A lot of them were my patients.

I always did my best with the knowledge I had, but often my prayers were as potent as my prescriptions.

A familiar form stood at the table visiting with friends. How long had it been ... five years?

"Paolo?" I said.

He turned and I knew it in an instant: he needed me.

"All over the empire," Paolo replied when I asked him where he'd been. "Lately, though, I've been in Macedonia. I had several friends with me, but I sent them on to Troas. They'll wait for me there." Paolo popped an olive in his mouth. "Ludia has asked me to stay for Passover."

His eyes again looked red and swollen.

"Good," I said. "That will give me time to treat your eyes. You're not using Phrygian powder, I take it?"

"No." Paolo smiled, but it was a smile of fear and fatigue. "My eyes won't get better."

"Not if you aren't taking care of them," I said.

Paolo shook his head and looked at his plate. "I asked God many times to heal me, but he assured me he is the only balm I need. He will not heal them." He glanced up at me. "But perhaps you can give me some relief." He patted my hand across the table.

"I'll do my best."

Ludia celebrated Passover every spring. This year would be extra special.

"I've never had a Pharisee to lead the ceremony."

She seemed giddy as she chose the vegetables for dinner. I had agreed to accompany her to the market. Arthritis was claiming more of her days, and the spring rains made her joints ache. I carried the heavy basket filled with leeks, broccoli, parsnips, cabbage, and turnips.

"Jehan said he'd bring the herbs to me this evening," Ludia said. "The lambs are already roasting. ... Fish. We still need the fish, Loukas. How could you let me forget?"

She picked up her skirts to walk faster. I followed, taking in the sights and smells that said *home* to me. Mount Pangaion played with the white clouds that danced in the sky. Two brown cuckoos jumped in the branches of the fishmonger's tree, calling their breathy song.

"Watch out." Ludia scooted around a group of children kicking a ball through the busy street. "Where are their parents?"

"Ludia?" I picked up a parsnip and examined it.

"Yes?" She poked the fish and then took a deep breath, sniffing for freshness.

"Just brought from Neapolis today." The fishmonger sniffed along with her.

"Five of the biggest," she said. "What did you want, Loukas?"

"I was just wondering about the Exodus ... Passover ..."

"What about it?" She paid for the fish and put her purse back in her skirt.

"Well, some of the Jews wanted to return to Egypt. It was what they knew. ... It was home."

We headed out of the center of town and the noise quieted.

"Their whole lives had been spent in Egypt," I went on. "They ... buried their families there."

Ludia nodded.

"What if they hadn't gone?"

"Things were very bad in Egypt," Ludia said.

"Yes." I shifted the heavy basket. "But things were very bad on the journey too. It was almost another time of oppression to some of them."

Ludia looked across at me. "What are you asking, Loukas?"

"Sometimes ... Sometimes God asks his people to do things, and then it doesn't seem like it is working out right. How do you know if it is right?"

"If God asked it, then it is right."

The evening drew late. The Feast of Unleavened Bread was a long ceremony punctuated by good food and good wine. I preferred this celebration over the symposium at the town elder's house. Good friends made the food and wine even better.

"How are you feeling?" I asked.

Paolo raised his fingers to his eyes and gingerly pushed the swollen lids. "Better. Thank you, Loukas. ... And how are you? Jehan told me your father sleeps."

I sighed. "Yes. Casper is still at the house, but it's lonely at night."

"You'll find a wife soon."

I shook my head. "I think—"

"Yes?" Ludia jumped in, her eyes sparkling in the candlelight. She had suggested many village girls to me.

I smiled at Ludia, but then I said, "I think ... I'd like to ask you a question, Paolo."

"Certainly." He leaned back on a cushion and took a handful of almonds. "Anything."

Ludia gave me a playful frown, then refilled our glasses. She wiped the pitcher lip with a cloth, staining it red like blood in the Nile.

"You said Pharoah's suffering hardened his heart. Why did God make him suffer so much? It seems like an easier life would've softened Pharoah's heart."

Paolo nodded, chewing almonds like a ruminating cow. "I've had to tan a lot of leather in my life, Loukas, and one thing I've learned is that pounding, beating, stretching, and scraping can soften or harden leather. Our hearts are a lot like leather. We can let the pounding and stretching soften them or make them hard." He pulled apart a fig and dipped it in his wine glass. "But even the hardest leather can be made soft again if you oil it. Pharaoh never applied the oil."

I sipped my wine and thought. The room was quiet in the glow of flickering lights.

"Please," I said, "allow me one more question. … When God led the Hebrews out of Egypt, he didn't take them straight to the Promised Land. I know they disobeyed and were being punished, but if Canaan was meant for them, and they were doing what God asked, why did they have to wander for forty years? It seems such senseless suffering."

"They learned to rely on the Lord during their time of suffering. They learned that God would lead them through dangerous situations: wars, snakes, famine, the flooded Jordan. Their suffering made them stronger because they relied on God instead of themselves." Paolo leaned forward on his elbow. "My eyes, Loukas, are painful and you know well that they cause me to suffer. But God has continued to be my strength."

"Yes, I can see some sense to that. Like children in the marsh …" I looked over at Jehan, who nodded approval. "The young ones learn each year a very important lesson through their suffering.

"But, Paolo, I don't understand why you don't heal yourself. You have so much power. You healed Pater when nothing else and no one else could." I studied his face, waiting like a hunter waits for a prize ram.

"You don't understand because you don't recognize the power, Loukas. I don't have power, except what is given to me for each task. Sometimes the Father gives me power to heal; sometimes he doesn't. He is the one who decides, not me."

"Surely if anyone deserves to be healed, it is you. I can't understand a god who would deny such healing to his servant." I smacked the table in anger.

"Actually, Loukas, none of us deserves to be healed—not me, not your father, not anyone. God chooses to heal those who will respond to the healing."

"But Pater didn't respond."

"Perhaps not … but you have. Healings aren't only for the sick." Paolo smiled. "And as for the sick, sometimes it's better not to be healed. Should we expect to live an entire lifetime free of pain? That seems very arrogant, doesn't it? Are any of us so holy that we don't deserve to suffer sometime?"

I thought of the times I cursed in my anger, hurting people with my words and my actions. I had murdered with my tongue, stolen in my heart, committed adultery in my mind. No, I did not deserve a life without suffering.

*What really raises one's indignation against suffering is*
*not suffering intrinsically, but the senselessness of suffering.*
~Friedrich Nietzsche~

# CHAPTER 40

"C'EST L'HEURE," FRANK'S VOICE BOOMED as Mariette welcomed him in. "It's time—to ask Ethel to marry me."

He picked Mariette up and spun her in a circle. Mariette laughed and hugged Frank as he put her back on the floor.

"Pardon, ma'am. I shouldn't have done that." He looked at the floor, his face red as a jar of pickled beets.

"No, Frank. It's fine. I'm so excited; please come in and sit." She walked into the parlor and Frank followed.

Frank sat in the chair by the window and looked at Mariette. His eyes shone and no less than six crooked teeth appeared in his broad smile.

"I've been saving money these last few years. I didn't go home so I wouldn't have to pay the train fare, even though it meant not seeing her." He scooted forward in the chair. "Last week I was able to move back into the mill house, and you should see it." He shook his head in wonder and raised his hands above his head. "The Lord provides."

"When will you get married?" Mariette asked as she handed him a cup of tea.

"As soon as possible. You will write to her for me?" He took the offered cup.

Mariette sat at the desk and pulled a sheet of writing paper from the top drawer. "How shall we begin?"

"There's a fundraiser at the church tomorrow evening." Rachelle stirred pancake batter and poured it onto the griddle. The hot grease crackled and popped. "It's to help the farmers back home."

"You already send most of your pay to your papa," Mariette said as she pulled plates from the cupboard.

"Oui, most people do." Rachelle shrugged her shoulders and flipped her long blonde braid over her back. "But not everyone has family working in America to help them. There's been a drought for years now and times are hard."

"Why don't they just leave? You didn't seem to have any trouble finding work." She pulled the pitcher of milk from the icebox.

Rachelle looked up from the griddle. "It isn't always so easy. There are taxes to pay, people are sick, some live too far away from the trains to make a trip. I was lucky that Mamere could come with me and Clement." Her voice choked at the mention of her grandmother.

She flipped the pancakes and continued. "So would you like to come to the fundraiser? There'll be music and a cakewalk. Maybe Dr. Graves would buy your cake." Rachelle giggled and glanced at Mariette. "No one else would."

"Such impertinence." Mariette laughed and threw a towel at the young girl. Then she bowed her head and fell serious. "I remember when Papa sent me to France to stay with his parents. I was so nervous and … frightened. Has it been terrible for you to be away from your papa?" Mariette looked up at Rachelle, a girl who had grown up faster than her years.

"I knew I would have to go after Mama passed away. My sister could take care of Papa and my brothers, but we needed money to pay for the medical bills. It helped that Mamere came too, and Clement was a reason to not complain."

She smiled at Mariette and reached for a platter. Mariette handed it to her from the counter. Rachelle slid the pancakes off the turner onto the dish. Steam rose from the crusty, golden-edged cakes.

"I'm sorry." Mariette took the pile of pancakes from Rachelle. "I didn't realize."

Rachelle turned back to the stove and poured another batch onto the griddle.

The beds were not so full now that summer was coming on. Increase sat in the office reading the latest copy of the *Boston Medical and Surgical*

*Journal.* An article on recent discoveries in gynecology absorbed his attention.

"Doctor."

A light tapping at the door penetrated his consciousness. Increase looked up as Nurse Hall knocked again.

"Sorry. Yes, Nurse Hall?"

"There's a phone call for you. It's the hospital in Lowell."

"Thank you." Increase stood up and followed her back to the registration desk. "Hello. Dr. Graves speaking."

"Dr. Graves, this is Dr. Warren over at Lowell General Hospital. How are you?"

"Fine, thank you. How can I help you, sir?" Increase shifted his weight and mentally ran through his list of patients. Which one would have gone to Lowell General?

"Well, Dr. Graves, we are a fairly new hospital, but we've been growing. There's lots of opportunity and need here in Lowell, you know."

"Mm-hm."

"Well, we are adding to our surgical unit and your name came up as a possibility to head the new department." The voice on the other end sped up: "Other doctors in the area have noticed your work in Dunstable Plains, and we think it is a shame to have your talents wasted out there. We'd like you to visit our hospital and consider the position of chief surgeon."

"That's very kind … Dr. Warren, did you say?"

"Yes."

"But I haven't been in Dunstable Plains very long. They're depending on me."

"There are other doctors who can work there. But you … you have so much education and experience that is needed here in Lowell. We're a larger hospital and I'm sure we can pay you better than Dunstable Plains can."

Increase thought about the many times Mariette had spent the day in Lowell. *It would make her happy.* "I'll talk to my wife and get back to you."

"I look forward to hearing from you. Good day, Dr. Graves."

Increase placed the receiver back on the hook and turned to see Nurse Hall staring at him. She turned away like a child from medicine, disdain written on her face.

"Fresh spinach, and Rachelle got her hands on some young hens. New potatoes too." Mariette wrapped her arms around Increase's waist and buried her face in his chest. "Doesn't that sound wonderful?"

Increase laughed. "Yes, and it smells wonderful too. When do we eat?"

She let go of him and stepped back. "Soon as David and Clement finish making the dessert." She pushed him toward the stairs. "Go clean up and I'll get everything ready."

Five places were set around the dining room table when Increase walked in. "Are we having company?" he asked Mariette as she folded the last napkin and set it next to the plate.

"It's a celebration dinner. I asked Rachelle and Clement to join us."

"What are we celebrating?" Increase sorted through his memory for any forgotten occasion or holiday. Nothing.

"Listen."

Increase cocked his head to one side. "Seems quiet to me."

"Exactly." Mariette winked. "All of our house guests are gone."

"So we're celebrating an empty house?" Increase chuckled.

"No ... we're celebrating that people have homes. And very nice homes at that. Frank has even asked Ethel to marry him and move here." She clapped her hands like a child being handed a peppermint stick. "Isn't it wonderful?"

Clement held the kitchen door open while David carried the cake into the dining room. The boys looked very proud of their angel food cake with strawberry glaze. They had worked hard stirring and whisking the light cake batter.

Glasses were filled with fresh milk for the boys, and Rachelle poured coffee for the adults. Mariette cut the cake and passed the pieces around.

"To homes ... and home," Increase said as he raised his cup.

"Home," everyone echoed.

Mariette and Increase held hands on the porch. The boys had finally quieted down and faded to sleep. They could hear Rachelle preparing dough for a nighttime rising. Her soft singing drifted out the open window.

"It's such a nice evening," Mariette said as she rested her head on Increase's shoulder. She paused as the bullfrog assented with a deep croak. "Increase." She squeezed his hand. "There's something I want to talk to you about."

"I have something to tell you too," Increase said.

"You first," Mariette said, twisting a little so she could look at him.

"Well ... I had a phone call today at the hospital." He couldn't read anything in her eyes. "It was a Dr. Warren in Lowell. He asked me to be the chief surgeon at Lowell General Hospital."

Mariette's eyes widened. "In Lowell?"

"Yes, in Lowell." Increase chuckled. "I told him I would have to talk to my wife about it." He squeezed Mariette's hand. "So what do you think?"

"Well, it certainly would be a step up from Dunstable Plains. But ..." She looked away into the street and thought, *But what?* "We haven't been here very long, I know, but it's already starting to feel like a home. I guess, after the years abroad in France, and then all of the ... well, you know, I just would sort of like to stay at home, I guess." She looked back at him and smiled uncertainly. "What do you think?"

"I'm not sure. I guess I like it here if you do. I thought you might like the larger city life of Lowell." He put his arm around her shoulders and drew her close. "Now what did you want to tell me?" He rested his head on top of hers.

"Out! Out!" Rachelle screamed from the kitchen.

Increase jumped from the swing and threw open the front door. Rachelle came running out, chasing a mouse with the broom.

"All the guests are gone, and you're not welcome," she yelled as she smacked the broom hard on the rodent.

Increase laughed and took the broom from her. "I'll handle this, Rachelle. I'm glad I own the house." He winked at Mariette and swept the mouse off the porch and into the bushes.

Mariette giggled and rose from the swing. "I'll leave that to you. I'm feeling tired. We can talk later." She turned and followed Rachelle into the house. *I'm being a coward. I know.*

"Good night," Increase called after her.

The afternoon sun bore down on Increase's shoulders like a hot iron. The walk to the parish house had brought a salty sweat to his brow and his eyes burned under the wide-brimmed hat. He knocked on the door and then opened it.

"Good afternoon, Father," he called.

The glare of the outdoors blinded him in the dim light. Muted voices came from the back room.

"It's Dr. Graves," Increase said as he started toward the bedroom.

"Increase." Jean popped his head into the hallway. "Come on back."

The priest was lying on top of the bedsheets, his leg propped up on a pillow. A large poultice was wrapped around the slender calf.

"Dr. Graves," the priest said as he tried to straighten himself in bed. "Come in, come in. Medic Giatros has been plying my wound with his secret herbs." He smiled at Jean.

"Not so much secret as they are forgotten," Jean said, patting the man's hand. "Perhaps Dr. Graves would like to look at your leg?" Jean looked up at Increase from his seat by the bed.

Increase walked into the room, taking off his hat and placing it on the bureau. "That's why I came," Increase said, catching a glance of himself in the mirror. *The gray is starting to show.* He turned to the two men. "It was looking better last week. Perhaps Jean's herbs have done the trick by now. Let's have a look."

He crossed to the bed and gently unwrapped the leg. Acidic vinegar struck his nose and then the sweet citrus of lemon verbena. "What all have you put in this, Jean?"

"Some antiseptic, some healing, and some care." He winked at Father Cartier, then studied Increase. "What's your prognosis, Doctor?"

The ulcer was closing and the striated signs of poison were completely gone. "I say Father Cartier is a lucky man. Another week or two and he'll be back on his feet." He wrapped the poultice around the man's leg again.

"Not luck," the priest said. He looked at his caregivers. "Three physicians, Medic Giatros, Dr. Graves, and ..." He pointed to the ceiling. "The Great Physician. I couldn't help but get better with that cord wrapped around my leg."

"I'm glad you're doing so well. I'll swing by in a couple days and check on you again," Increase said, ignoring the reference.

"I'll walk out with you," Jean said. "I'm glad you're feeling better." He nodded to the priest. "I'll send some more paste over in a few days."

"Merci, Medic. You're a blessing. Thank you too, Dr. Graves. Thanks for coming by." The lame man waved from the bed. "Just pull the door shut behind you."

The air outside felt thick, and a dark cloud boiled over the mills. "Looks like a storm is coming." Jean pointed to the sky. "The evening bell might ring before it hits, though."

"Have you been in the new rooms over at Lytle's?" Increase asked as he shut the gate to the parish picket fence. "They look great. No more cracks, new windows, quite an improvement."

"You've been a blessing to the people here. Thank you for your work." Jean extended a hand.

Increase shook his hand. "I'm glad I could make a difference." He paused, then exhaled and turned.

"But?" Jean fell in step with Increase.

Increase fixed his eyes on the horizon and headed toward the hospital. "I had a call a couple days ago. It was an offer, actually. To be chief surgeon in Lowell."

"Mm-hm." Jean nodded and kept walking.

Increase's steps were heavy in the growing soup of an early-summer haze. Jean slowed his pace and Increase followed suit. The cloud neared the bright sunshine, casting a shadow over half the town.

"I thought Mariette would jump at the chance to leave, but she didn't seem to want to go."

"And you? Do you want to go?"

"Well, it would be a lie to say it isn't flattering, but I'm not sure it would be right to leave so soon." Increase stopped in the shade of an elm and fanned himself with his hat.

Jean stood beside him, unreadable. "Have you done everything here that God has called you to do?"

"I've done what I've seen to do," Increase huffed. "I didn't get a call from God." He stopped fanning and smashed the hat back onto his head.

"Whether you heard it or not, the line was ringing. You have come to heal the people. Have you done that?" Jean's voice was steady, like a sailboat on a lake, gliding effortlessly.

"Some have been healed, but I've lost a lot of them too. I don't get to work my magic and then pass the buck on to someone else. Someone has to be blamed for failures."

"Is it a failure if a patient dies?" Jean looked into Increase's eyes.

"Of course!" Increase said. "The doctor's job is to heal. If the patient dies, of course he's a failure." He started walking again.

Jean kept up without any trouble, his soft-soled shoes whispering on the brick walkway. "Not really. If the patient doesn't die, the doctor has only delayed the inevitable."

Increase stopped short. "What do you mean?"

"Only that everyone has a life and everyone has a death. The death will come no matter what." Jean motioned toward his house. "Every herb in my garden has a time frame. Some are harvested as small plants. Others are clipped when they're in full bloom. Still others provide healing through their death or even through their fruit or seeds. But eventually all of them die."

"So if we're all going to die anyway, what's the point of helping anyone?" Increase's eyes flashed lightning.

Jean stood tall beside him, a smooth boat on a placid lake. "Every plant grows, but some live longer than others. You don't get upset or stop gardening. A little fertilizer, some weeding and watering, perhaps even some vinegar to discourage the pests, but eventually the plant still dies."

"So again I ask … what's the point?" Increase squared his shoulders and set his jaw.

"The plants that live for a while have a purpose. They grow, give food, shade, even wood for fires or buildings. Each of us has a purpose, and yours, Increase, is to help those plants to grow."

"I'm not a gardener," Increase spat. "I'm a doctor. If one of my plants dies, it's a major loss. Annie was not a flower or a tree. She was my wife." Increase's eyes grew wide and he took a jagged breath. "I've got to get to the hospital."

"Stay a minute," Jean said, the wind in his sails strong and steady. "You're right that Annie wasn't a plant. She was more than that, to you and to the Father. She did, however, have a time frame, a lifespan, just like all people. But, Increase, you can't keep smelling the same flower. That one is gone, a pleasant memory of a happy day, but now there are other flowers scenting your garden, offering their healing powers. Don't cling to the dried flower and leave the garden untended, or you'll miss your purpose." Jean nodded his farewell and crossed the street.

Huge, heavy raindrops splashed on the walk. Increase was soaked by the time he made it to the hospital.

*Man cannot remake himself without suffering, for he is*
*both the marble and the sculptor.*
~Alexis Carrel~

# CHAPTER 41

MARIETTE STOOD ON THE HOSPITAL porch, her eyes red and swollen.

"What is it?" Increase asked as he took the last step. Lightning flashed near the street.

"Oh, Increase," Mariette choked. "I … I …" Tears rolled down her cheeks.

"What?" He held her close.

The heavy hospital door opened. "There you are," Nurse Hall said softly. "Clement is going to be fine."

"Clement?" Increase said. "What happened? Did he have another attack?"

Mariette looked at him through blue pools of despair. "No. He and David decided to go swimming in the canals. Some other children were with them. They said Clement was struggling …" She broke into sobs.

Nurse Hall came out on the porch. "You should come inside, Doctor. There's been an accident." She gathered the couple like a mother hen and moved them inside. "In your office, Doctor."

Increase walked toward his office, wondering what could be the matter. *An accident? Why go to my office?* He turned. "You said an accident? Shouldn't I go to the surgery?"

The tall brunette shook her head and shooed him on to the office. She closed the door behind them, leaving Increase and Mariette alone.

"What's going on?" Increase's voice rose above the thunder outside.

"David … he's drowned." Her shoulders racked, withholding the sobs that threatened.

Increase stepped back. "What?" he whispered.

*Drowned?*

"No … No, it can't be."

*David is an excellent swimmer.*

Mariette only looked at him through teary eyes, her lips quivering, confirming the reality of what she'd told him.

Increase shook his head. "No," he said, louder than he'd intended.

*He's just a boy! There … must be a mistake.* Now Increase felt tears forming in his own eyes. *No. He's all I have. Drowned?*

"How? … How?" Increase whispered.

Mariette drew a deep breath. "He and Clement asked to go down to the canals with the other children. I thought it was okay; they both swim, and it was so hot and sticky. I don't know…." She reached out for him, but he took another step back, staring at her. "The children said Clement was struggling. David was trying to help him, but he went under. The kids ran for help. They beat on the door."

Mariette sat down on one of the office chairs. Increase felt himself turning ashen, but he stood there, just staring at her.

"Rachelle and I ran for the canal. Clement was on the wall crying when we got there. Some men were pulling David out."

Increase watched as Mariette sank into the chair like a shadow. He blinked, feeling a hundred emotions churning within. She was telling a story—explaining a bad dream. It had to be.

A knock on the door drew her attention, but Increase stood, unmoving.

"Medic Giatros is here," Nurse Hall said using her hushed, professional tone. "Would you like him to come in?"

Mariette looked at Increase, questioning.

Increase turned to the woman. "No … David. Where is David?"

"He's in the surgery, Doctor. We've laid him out now. You can see him."

She held open the door, but Increase turned to the decanter on the file cabinet. With shaky hands he poured a full shot of whiskey and downed it in one gulp. He walked past Mariette and into the hospital waiting room. A crowd was starting to form, but he only saw Jean.

Increase pushed through the room and entered the surgery. He shut the door on the storm outside as he entered his own hurricane.

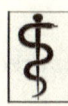

The sweet smell of peonies and irises filled the church. Increase sat on the front pew with Mariette and Maurice, an automaton without emotion. Lively was in the row behind. He could see her holding Rachelle's hand and caressing Clement's hair.

Father Cartier led the service that Mariette had planned over Increase's objections. *Why give God any more attention? He certainly hasn't done anything helpful for me thus far.*

He looked at Mariette from the corner of his eye. She held some salts in a lace hankie and sniffled into the cloth.

*Women get to be fragile. What do I get to be?*

"Tell Dr. Graves to take a week off. The doctor from Nashua has agreed to come over and help during this tragedy."

Increase could hear Mr. Neal's voice from the front door. Visitors from the town were dropping by to leave food and flowers for the family. Lively and Maurice met each at the door and politely refused entry. Mariette was in the bedroom, but Increase sat in the front room, staring into the empty fire grate. A bottle of whiskey dangled in his hand. He didn't bother with a glass.

"This won't make it stop," came Maurice's voice.

Sunlight stabbed Increase as he opened one eye. A blurry haze danced around Maurice on the divan. Increase closed his eye and moaned.

"Drinking isn't going to bring him back." Maurice was matter-of-fact.

"But it will help me forget."

"No, not really. You should know that, losing Annie and all."

Increase had always liked Maurice; he was straightforward and pragmatic. But Increase wasn't in the mood for honesty right now. He sat up in the chair and ran his hand through his hair. An empty bottle sat by his feet.

"I have to go back tomorrow," Maurice said. "I have some surgeries scheduled and the orphans' board is meeting. I'm sorry I can't stay longer."

He went to the sideboard and poured a cup of coffee, then brought it back to Increase.

"I loved David as my own grandchild, Increase. We all are hurting—Mariette too. Grieve together. Don't let this pull you apart from each other." He sat back down on the divan. "There are lots of people who will help you through this. Rachelle and Clement need your forgiveness, but they'll be a boon to you."

Increase glared at the good doctor. "The last thing I need is another child around here."

A muffled cry came from the entryway. Increase turned to see Mariette and Rachelle hurry to the kitchen hand in hand.

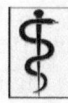

The bricks tripped him as he headed for the church. The last work bell had rung hours ago and the little town was quiet. Increase stumbled over a bat left by some neighborhood kid.

"Little brats," he slurred.

He walked on, reviewing the argument he'd had with Mariette at the house. There was no need for Rachelle to stay with Lively there to help Mariette. Increase had dismissed Rachelle and sent Clement with her. He hadn't expected Mariette to be so furious.

The church was silhouetted by the half-moon that slid now and then behind scraggly horse-tail clouds. A loose brick caught his toe and Increase went down in a heap. He grabbed the errant brick and rose to his feet.

"Why do you taunt me?" he shouted and lobbed the brick toward the church. It fell a few feet away. "Why was I ever born if all you do is kill those around me? You're so smug. You sit up there in your heaven and plan all the ways you can torture me."

"You sound like Job."

Increase swirled around to see Jean standing by the gate to his herb garden. "Well, Job had it right. Nothing but turmoil and despair all around, and it's all God's fault."

"Explain." Jean leaned against the fence.

"He's supposed to be a God of love, who cares for us. Funny way to show it if you ask me." He kicked at the curb and then plopped down on the sidewalk, his back against the fence. "I never have peace. No rest."

The street swam in murky darkness. *Is this what it was like for David?*

"My boy … my son … David." He broke into sobs that made his stomach heave the bile and alcohol that churned there.

Jean went to him and held his head while the last of his retching splattered on the walkway. "Come in the house," Jean said when it ended.

A kerosene lamp sat in the middle of a rough-hewn table, its glow shimmering on the pine walls of the small apartment . Increase could see his reflection mirrored on the windows, the dark night beyond casting a mournful shadow to his face. He wiped his mouth with a hanky and stuffed it back in his trousers. Jean motioned for him to sit.

Increase sat on the wicker-bottomed seat and crossed and uncrossed his legs. "I should go," he said and started to stand.

Jean put his hand on Increase's shoulder. "No, you should stay a little while. Let me make some coffee."

Jean threw a handful of beans in the grinder and turned the handle. The strong smell began penetrating the fog that drifted through Increase's mind. He dropped his head into his hands and rubbed his hair and face, trying to make sense of it all, of any of it.

"I just don't get it. I do good things. I save people. Not all people, but some of them." He rested his elbows on his knees while he looked at his reflection in the window. "I even do good things in the community, like getting the mill houses cleaned up. I just don't get why God hates me so much."

"Why do you think he hates you?" Jean poured the grinds into the percolator container and set it on top of the coal stove.

"I think it's pretty obvious," Increase said. "My wife died and now my son. I try …" He waved his hands in the air, reaching for words or ideas to fill the empty space.

Jean took two cups from the sink and rinsed them out. "Go on."

"I try to be a good doctor, a good man. I think I was a good father, but I got rid of the phone. Maybe I shouldn't have been so stubborn about the phone. Mariette could've called for help." His words wandered with his mind. "But whom would she have called? I was with the priest. The priest!" The irony of it struck him. "I was helping a man of God when God was failing to help me." He caught Jean's eye. "Now how is that righteous?" His words were hard and bitter.

Jean added a little sugar to the cups and stood near the stove. "How did God fail you?"

"How did he fail me?" Increase spat the question back. "He let my son die."

"Perhaps." Jean took the pot from the stove and poured a dark stream into each cup.

"Perhaps? David is dead. Of course he let him die."

"David saved Clement. David chose to love his friend and brother. I could give you answers to all of your questions, Increase, but they wouldn't make you feel better, would they?"

He carried the hot cups over to the chairs and handed one to Increase.

Jean sat down. "You see, you don't want answers. You want your son back." He took a sip of the coffee and exhaled. "But if you had your son back, he would still die."

Increase growled. "I would keep him safe."

"Yes, you would do your best to keep him safe from disease, and knowing what you know now, you would probably never let him near canals or ponds or even the ocean." The older man took a long sip and then set the cup on his knee. "But David would never be free from death; it's the one thing no one escapes, no matter how careful they are." He looked at Increase. "But there are worse things than dying."

"You keep saying that. But … I just don't understand." Increase shook his head. His hand trembled as he held the hot cup.

"Living while you're dead is one of the worst." Jean took another sip and watched Increase.

Increase raised an eyebrow and cocked his head. "I've yet to see that," he scoffed.

"You've looked in that window all night and you haven't seen the dead man who stares back?"

Increase looked out the window over Jean's shoulder. Death was looking back.

The full heat of summer wilted the pansies Mariette and Rachelle had planted in the spring. Mariette watched Lively tipping the watering can over the purple and blue heads.

"Water can't save them now," Mariette said from the porch. "Seems water kills when there's too much and when there's not enough." She blew out all of her air and turned for the front door. "I'm going to lie down. If Increase comes home, tell him I'm asleep."

She pulled the door shut behind her.

Lively was setting dishes around the table when Increase walked in. "How are things at the hospital?" she asked.

"Busy as ever. They're talking about buying another property, a bigger one. The hospital is always full, it seems." He loosened his necktie.

"Well, that's something. Maybe you'll get a promotion or a raise." Lively smiled at her brother.

"Don't think so."

"Why ever not?"

"I quit. Just now."

"What?" Mariette came charging down the last few steps and into the dining room. "How could you do that without talking to me?"

"Don't worry. I took the job in Lowell. I called this afternoon and talked to Dr. Warren. He said the position was still available." Increase pulled the necktie off and headed for the stairs. "I'll be back down in a minute. Dinner smells good, Lively."

Mariette focused on the vegetable soup swimming in her bowl. Lively was a huge help to her, but she was still angry that Increase had dismissed Rachelle without her knowledge. Now he had quit his job and taken another in a different city without so much as a "How do you do." She took a sip of water to squelch the fire that burned in her throat and warmed her cheeks.

"Tell us what happened," Lively said as she passed the butter to Increase. She glanced across the table to Mariette, but Mariette stared into her bowl.

"The board director, Mr. Neal, came in this morning and told me that the plans to purchase a larger building have been approved. There are plans to expand the current mills and the town is growing. They need a bigger space, more beds." He finished buttering the bread and took a bite. "Mr. Neal wanted me to head up the project."

Mariette looked up. "Surely that's a promotion, a raise, a good thing." Her voice trembled, a city wall threatening to fall under enemy attack.

"It would be," Increase said as he lifted a glass of wine to his lips. He took a long drink and set it back down. "But I can't, Mariette." He looked at her, pleading. "I can't stay here where all I see is David. We'll move as soon as I can find a place. You'll come too, Lively."

"No," Lively answered. "I'll go back home. You and Mariette should make a home together. It's time you were a family, not just friends."

"I'm not sure we're that … anymore," Mariette mumbled and got up from the table.

Increase rose early to catch the train to Lowell. Mariette tried to occupy herself with the housekeeping, but she still knew so little. She was unsure what to do.

Rachelle had kept most of the perishable produce in the root cellar. Mariette descended the dark stairs looking for something she could use for dinner—a dinner for one most likely.

Behind the potatoes a box hid in cobwebs and dust. Mariette pulled it out and smiled. Her paints hadn't been touched since she returned from France. Time had seemed in such short supply before … before it all. She sighed and opened the lid.

The smell of oil and kerosene filled her nostrils. Brushes, rags, tubes of paint … All were rolled together. It was a flash, a glimpse of a forgotten memory: happiness. Happiness, peace, calm. That was why she painted.

She rifled through the other boxes stacked under the staircase until she found a half-painted canvas. She struggled up the stairs with the box of supplies under one arm and the canvas flung across her shoulder.

*The light in front of the parlor window ought to be just right.* She headed back down the cellar stairs to search for the easel. Back up again. Was her heart pounding from the exertion or the excitement?

Midmorning light poured through the filmy drape. Light bounced off the wooden floorboards. Yes, this would be perfect. She set up the canvas, spurted a bit of paint onto the palette, and sat with brush in hand.

Squibnocket Pond. Those were happy days, as a child and as a mother. The blue water reflected red cliffs. Darkness marched across the picture, but was it advancing or retreating?

A knock came at the door. Mariette set the paints aside and wiped her fingers on a rag. She walked to the door and opened it.

"Dr. Giatros, how good to see you." Mariette's smile played at the corners of her mouth, unused to the expression of late. "Please come in."

Jean removed his hat and walked in.

"Increase isn't here. He's working in Lowell now. I thought you would have heard by now." Mariette led him into the parlor.

"Oui. I heard. I thought it might be good to check on you." He followed behind.

"Please have a seat." Mariette motioned toward one of the chairs. "Would you like a sandwich for lunch? I can make something really quick."

Jean laughed. "No, I had lunch a couple hours ago."

Mariette glanced at the clock. *How did that happen?* "Would you like something to drink? I have some lemonade in the icebox."

"No, thank you. Please, sit with me."

Mariette sat across from Jean and breathed deeply. "Thank you for dropping by. I do get lonely, especially now that Lively has gone away."

"It looks like you've found something to distract yourself. You're painting again?"

"Oui." Mariette colored a little.

"Increase told me about your paintings. He said you like to paint mothers and children." Jean rose and walked to the canvas.

"Yes, I got in trouble for that at school. Funny, there's no mother or child in this one. ..." She joined him to stare at the landscape.

"It's a dark picture, but I think there is hope ... perhaps in the water." Jean pointed to the light that played on the surface of the pond.

"Mm." Mariette contemplated her work. "I'm not sure if there is hope ... or light. Maybe there is an approaching storm. I can't decide."

"You'll have to keep at it to see."

"I don't know." Mariette's shoulders drooped. "It may be too difficult to complete."

Jean turned to look at the young woman. "An artist must never give up, even when it hurts. The stone trembles at the strike of the mallet, but when the statue is finished, there is nothing but rejoicing over its beauty." Jean put his hand on Mariette's arm. "Keep at it. You'll find the joy again."

"Increase should be home soon. Would you like to stay for dinner? I'm not sure what we'll have, but I can figure something out." She colored at thinking what a poor hostess she was.

"No, merci. Tell Increase I'll drop by another time. Perhaps tomorrow evening?"

"That would be lovely. I'll have coffee and cookies ready."

Increase stumbled up the steps. An empty bottle fell from his pocket and clattered on the porch. Mariette opened the door.

"Where've you been? I was getting so worried." She held the door open for him.

"I stopped by the tavern for a drink and dinner. I knew I wouldn't get anything good here."

His words punched her in the gut, and tears jumped to her eyes. "I held some cornbread and beans on the back of the stove. I'll go put them away." She left him in the foyer holding his jacket.

*He's hurting,* she tried to console herself. *He lost a son.* She put the coffeepot on the stove and cleared up the dinner things. She set the bowl of beans and bread in the icebox, and got out the coffee mugs from the cupboard. She liked her coffee with sugar and milk, but Increase would need his dark and strong.

She stood by the counter and prayed. *Father, you lost a son, too. You know how he hurts. Please help Increase to feel your comfort and peace. Show me how I can help.*

She poured the cup and sighed. It was a prayer said more than felt. She was tired.

"I brought you coffee," Mariette said as she carried a tray into the parlor.

"What's this?" Increase stood at the canvas, staring at it, frowning.

"I thought I would try painting again." She placed the tray on the sideboard and poured the coffee. "What do you think?"

Increase was silent. Mariette brought the cup of steaming coffee to him. He never looked at her.

"I'm going to bed." He stumbled across the room and pulled himself up the stairs using the banister.

"Good night." Mariette contemplated the painting. *Is the darkness waxing or waning?*

Increase stared at the clock. Not even the dark room could make sleep come. Mariette lay at the edge of the bed. *I don't blame her for wanting to stay away.* Pain shot through his head as he sat up and slipped his feet into his house shoes. He grabbed his trousers and shirt, and headed for the bathroom. A night walk was what he needed to clear his mind.

The fading moon cast shadows across the street. Houses stood with their windows wide open, hoping some cool refreshment might blow in on a breeze. A horse nickered in the stable and an answer came drifting back through the dusk. Lights glowed in the mill houses as the tenants rose early for work. A crack of light glowed in the bathhouse door as Increase passed by on the other side.

He stopped in front of Rachelle's house. He could make out her shadow. *Probably making breakfast for Clement before she heads out for the day.* He moved on down the sidewalk and neared the church. The morning work bell clanged.

Across from the church Jean stood against the fence to his herb garden. Increase raised a hand in greeting.

"Good morning, Increase," Jean called out. "Come on over and visit a minute."

Increase looked down the street as he crossed. Rachelle and Clement were closing the door. They turned toward the mills.

"What are you doing out so early?" Jean asked as he shook Increase's hand. "How're things in Lowell? Got your hands full there, I expect."

"Yeah, it's busy alright. It's got Dunstable Plains beat, though—up-to-date equipment, no surgeries in bedrooms." He shook his head and leaned on the fence.

"We miss you around here. I stopped by yesterday to see you and Mariette, but you were still gone. She's started painting again." Jean looked down the street, watching the workers streaming out of their houses like salmon in springtime. "Maybe it'll help the pain."

"Wouldn't do anything for me. A fifth is about all that can numb it." He sniffed and rubbed his face. "Doesn't last long at that."

"Some pain has to be felt to heal." Jean continued looking down the street.

"Huh," Increase snorted. "I've felt enough pain for a lifetime and there's no healing. I might as well cut my arm off and be done with it."

"I've told you before, Increase. Bleeding is just a different kind of death." Jean turned to look at the doctor. Orange clouds tinted the horizon just over his shoulder. "You, Doctor, are very nearly dead. Your marriage, your career, your soul. Increase …"

"Don't start your preaching, Jean. Save it for someone who'll listen." He struck the air in disgust and walked off. "I've got to get to work."

"He's an oil boy at the mill now." Mariette was talking as she finished setting the dinner table.

*Only two places,* Increase thought. *What happened to the full table?*

"I'm really concerned. She didn't look well at all."

Mariette sat down in her place and looked at Increase. He startled from his thoughts and joined her. She said the prayer and continued.

"Maybe I should take some dinner over after we eat. I know it won't be as good as her own cooking, but it's the thought that counts." She gave a halfhearted smile. "Will you go with me?"

"Where?" Increase felt like he'd been caught, a child with his hand in the cookie jar.

"To see Rachelle, of course. Maybe you could make sure she's okay. I really didn't like the look of her today."

"It's been a long day, Mariette. Maybe tomorrow."

He got up and went into the parlor. The bourbon was all gone. "I'm going to the store." He was out of the house in a flash, but not before he heard her muffled sob.

The train swayed like a boat on the high sea. The summer storm blew rain sideways into the glass windows that peered out on the New Hampshire countryside. The gray light that broke over the ridge matched Increase's mood. He took another swig of bourbon and stuffed the flask back into his pocket.

The smell of gangrene penetrated the hallway. The young man had been wasting away in one of the basements of a Lowell mill house. Increase took a deep breath and then headed into the surgery.

The youth had mangled his foot and tried to doctor it himself. Infection had spread as far as the knee. The leg would have to be removed mid-thigh. He was already anesthetized. Three nurses and another doctor stood ready to assist.

Increase clamped off the leg, his hands shaking with the effort.

"Are you alright, Dr. Graves?" the assisting doctor asked.

"Yeah." He cleared his throat.

*I've performed this surgery before. What's wrong with me? ... You can't help this boy; you couldn't take care of your own boy. ... Annie! Annie, I'm so sorry. ...*

*Scalpel. Cut a fish mouth from the skin. … Fish. Did he see fish as he drowned? … Tie off the vein. The lifeblood. … My life's blood is gone. Dead.*

Clattering metal on the tile floor filled his ears.

Increase felt himself slipping off the narrow couch. He opened his eyes and slammed them shut again.

"I sent a message to your wife. She said she'd come on the first train." Dr. Warren's voice was disapproving, like Increase's fifth-grade teacher in Concord who had not enjoyed a frog in his desk. "I know you have had a trauma recently, but you cannot continue to work here. You put a young man's life in danger and could have ruined the hospital's reputation."

Increase sat up. "Is the patient okay?"

"Yes, the assisting was able to cover for you while the nurses dragged you from the room. Really, Dr. Graves, you should know not to drink on the job."

"Yes. Of course. I'm … I'm sorry. I'll go now." He rose and shook the other man's hand, then turned to leave. "You said you called my wife?"

"Yes. She's on her way."

Increase walked toward the train station, light and sound pulling the hairs from his head. People stared at him as he stumbled over a flowerpot near the dime store. *A cup of coffee.* He went in and ordered at the counter. The strong black liquid washed away the fog and mist that drifted through his head. He left a nickel for the waitress and headed again for the train station. *What will I tell Mariette?* He was a disgraced man.

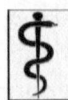

Mariette sat stiffly beside him. She had bought their tickets home without saying a word to him. He had expected tears, yelling, anger, and disgust. Instead she was quiet, distant, and withdrawn. The sun was sinking over the green rolling hills as the train traveled back again to the scene of his crime—a crime no father should ever commit: losing a child on his watch. A single tear slid silently down his cheek, wedging itself between two days' growth of whiskers.

Increase and Mariette walked through the blue dusk of evening.

"I'm sorry," he whispered. "I know I've let you down. I've done nothing but bring disgrace on your name since the day we met."

She took his hand. "My name is Graves, and together we'll resurrect it." She half-smiled at him and kept on walking.

A little boy sat on the top step of the porch.

"Clement? Is that you?" Mariette called as they neared the corner of the hedge.

Clement raised himself on his braces and shuffled down the stairs as fast as he could. "It's Rachelle. Please, Dr. Graves, you have to come. She's sick—very, very sick." The boy's eyes pleaded with the man. "I'm so sorry about David, sir. But … please help Rachelle." He grabbed Increase's hand.

The three of them hurried through the darkening streets.

"Appendicitis," Increase announced after checking the feverish girl. "She has to go to the hospital now. Call a cab, Mariette."

The horse hooves clattered on the stone road, echoing Increase's fears. *It's late. The doctor from Nashua will be gone. I'll have to complete the surgery. What if I botch this one too? What will become of Clement? How will I live with myself?*

His hands were shaking as he jumped from the cab. He cradled Rachelle in his arms and climbed the stairs to the hospital. Mariette swung open the door and greeted Nurse Lindelof.

Increase headed straight for the surgery. "Appendicitis, Nurse. Get prepped right away. It'll burst soon if it hasn't already."

"Yes, Doctor."

"She should be fine," Increase said as he entered the waiting area near the front desk. "We'll have to take her home in the morning, though. There aren't any beds left for her according to Nurse Lindelof."

Mariette nodded. "She's right; they're full. Clement and I have been visiting with the patients while we waited for you."

"She's going to get better? Oui?" Clement held Increase's fingertips in anticipation.

"Oui." Increase looked down at David's playmate. Oh how it hurt to know this child lived because his child died. "Let's go home." He turned to Mariette.

"Come on, Clement. You come stay with us and we'll get Rachelle in the morning."

Increase didn't have the energy to argue.

Mariette entered the bedroom with a tray of breakfast food. The pungent coffee permeated the air.

"Rise and shine, you sleepy old bear." Mariette set the tray on the bedside table and then went to pull open the drapes. "You've had a very long sleep. I already brought Rachelle home."

Increase sat up in bed, shielding his eyes from the bright sunlight. It had to be nearly noon. He picked up the cup of coffee and looked at the clock—11:30.

"How did you get her home by yourself?"

"Dr. Giatros—Jean," Mariette said, "was there when I arrived. He helped to get her situated and even came to the house with us. He said not to disturb you, so I left you alone." She smoothed her skirts and pulled on her shirt waist. "I want to thank you for helping Rachelle. I know it was a bad time for you."

"I should have checked on her when you asked. I'm sorry." He sipped the hot coffee. "How is she?"

"The medic said she is doing well, that you saved her life, but I won't rest easy until you look at her." She smiled down at him. "So finish your breakfast and get a bath. You need a good shave too." She brushed his cheek with her hand and then left the room.

"Shouldn't he be outside?" Increase asked from the dinner table.

Clement was in the parlor building with David's blocks.

"He wants to be near Rachelle, but she needs to sleep," Mariette said. "It does my heart good to see a child."

"Hmph. The last thing I need is another child around here."

Mariette wrapped her arms around herself. "I'm sorry you feel that way. I know you're hurting for David, but, Increase, you can't blame Clement."

"Whom should I blame? You were supposed to be watching him." His lip curled in an ugly snarl.

Mariette cried like a wounded animal and left the table. The kitchen door swung shut behind her. Increase kicked over the chair as he hurried out of the house. If ever he needed a drink, now was the time.

*Suffering passes, while love is eternal. That's a gift*
*that you have received from God. Don't waste it.*
~Laura Ingalls Wilder~

# CHAPTER 42

SCREAMS PIERCED THE NIGHT LIKE broken-necked conies waiting the slice of the knife. Wailing women poured into the dark streets, pushing, crying, falling on their knees. Blood oozed out the doors, staining the sandy road red.

I stood in the center of town as a couple raced past me; a child wrapped in robes was tied to the man's back. Their eyes were white, searching the road in fear.

"Hurry. Hurry." The man urged the young woman on. "He'll be next."

I held the medical bag to my side and followed the couple to see where they would hide from the plague. The night turned gray as the dawning sun began to rise. The couple stopped beneath a dead tree to rest.

"Why?" the woman asked. "Why did they have to die so he could live?"

"I don't know." The man held her close as the child slept in the sling on his back. "But there is a reason. Now, up. We must keep moving."

A plume of dust rose on the horizon. The thundering hooves of a Roman legion pounded the air. The couple looked at each other, then, untying the cradle of robes, they handed the child to me.

"He's dangerous … and he's in danger. Take him. Go!"

I grabbed the child and raced in front of the horses. The boy woke and embraced me, his arms circling my neck, his legs wrapped around my waist. Power surged through me and I ran like Hermes, outpacing the Roman cavalry.

I ran into a canyon and flung the boy into a crevice. I jumped in next to him and watched as the horses ran on. My lungs ached and the muscles in my legs quivered. My heart began to slow. I turned to the boy.

He was gone. Sitting on a rock was a man dressed all in white, his face glowing like the rising sun. Tears trickled down his cheeks, glittering in the bright light.

"For me the children died." He looked at me, piercing my soul. "They didn't do anything wrong. It was so senseless, and yet so necessary. Comfort them, Loukas. Give them relief."

A cock crowed outside as I opened my eyes.

The early light filtered through the misty fog, catching sunbeams and turning them into colorful rainbows. It was a promise that God would go with me. *With me is all I ask.*

Jehan's gravelly humming filled the stone hut. I knocked on the door.

"Come in."

I pushed the wooden door and entered the room that didn't change. I was never sure if the smell was last year's flowers or the year before's. The odor of herbs, flowers, dirt … *Earth, I suppose* … penetrated the walls and clung to the very presence of the home. *Not earth, but heaven.* I took a deep breath and sighed.

"Hypíaine. Good morning, Jehan."

"I was expecting you. Join me." He poured hot water into two bowls on the table.

I raised my brows. "You were?"

"Mm-hm. You've made a decision." Jehan nodded and sat down at the bench.

"How?" I sat across from him.

"A good doctor anticipates his patient." Jehan tapped his temple. "Now tell me."

"I'm going to travel with Paolo." It was the first time I'd said it aloud. I hadn't even told Paolo yet. "He needs me, and I … I think I can learn from him."

"You'll be good for each other. A doctor for the body, and a doctor for the soul." He smiled and sipped his tea. Then his face changed. "You'll be called on to watch a lot of suffering, Loukas. You might be tempted to turn from the Father. Remember this: to live in a world where you get what you do not deserve is to live in a world with great suffering … and great mercy. Trust, believe, and obey."

The sun was up and hot. The fog had lifted and the dewy drops on the tall grass by the roadside would soon be gone. A magpie flew back and forth, carrying food to a juvenile cuckoo in its nest.

The sounds of the city drifted up the hillside. The Aegean Sea sparkled on the horizon. *Where will it take us?*

People brushed past me in the busy marketplace. I stopped for pastries from Ludia's favorite baker. I would miss her so much.

Ludia was coming out her door as I walked up to the house. We stopped in the shade of a spreading cypress.

"Hypíaine, Ludia. How are you this morning?"

"Loukas, it was a fine Passover, wasn't it?" She lifted onto her tiptoes and kissed my cheek. "I was just heading to the marketplace. Paolo will be leaving today and I want to give him a special—"

I lifted the cover from the pastries. "I already took care of it." I grinned as her girlish giggle wiped away the years.

"You know me so well. Come in, then, and join us."

The courtyard table was filled with fruit breads and cheeses made by Ludia's wonderful cook.

"You don't need these pastries, you know." I winked as I pulled them out of the basket.

"It's good to keep up relations in the city." Ludia smiled back. "Makes business sweeter." She giggled again. "I'm surprised to see you this morning. I thought you'd be heading to Asyla by now."

"Mm, well. Can we sit?"

Ludia moved to the bench under the potted trees. I sat beside her, half-turned to look in her face.

"I'm not working at Asyla anymore."

She pulled her head back in surprise.

"I'm going to go with Paolo."

"Oh, really?" Paolo's voice made me jump.

Paolo walked in from a side door and stopped in front of the bench. He crossed his arms in front of him and spread his feet.

*My first struggle.*

"You need a doctor." I stood up and faced him, eye to eye.

"You can't heal me," Paolo said. "I told you God has denied this particular healing."

"A cure has been denied; relief has not. I believe there'll be a lot of suffering in your future, Paolo, and you will need me then too." I placed a hand on his arm. "I don't know why, brother, but your suffering is essential. Most suffering ... the suffering I see ... seems indiscriminate—maybe it is, maybe it isn't. But your suffering ... yours ... is part of a plan."

"Who told you this?" Paolo's voice cracked.

"I had a dream, a dream about the children who died in Bethlehem when Mary and Joseph escaped with the Christ child. So many people suffered, and they didn't know why. But, Paolo, the suffering had meaning. The suffering meant we would have a savior. I think ... I think you're like another Joseph—Jacob's son."

Paolo furrowed his brow at me.

I continued. "Yes, he didn't know what was going on, being cast aside, sent to Egypt. He didn't know why he had to go to prison; he just believed that God had a purpose to the pain. It took many years before he could see how his pain was meant to save his family, even to save me."

"You?"

"Had Joseph not gone along with God's plan, the Israelites would not have been saved from the famine. There would've been no Messiah. You wouldn't be here to tell a Gentile like me that I could be saved." I pulled my hand back and turned to Ludia. "Tell him, Ludia. Tell him he needs me."

Ludia's eyes filled like the marsh in spring. She drew us to her.

"I'll miss you both."

*Death's unavoidable; let's have a drink.*
~Seneca the Elder~

# CHAPTER 43

"I HEARD YOU WERE HERE." JEAN placed a hand on Increase's shoulder and sat on the stool next to him. "What are you doing?"

Increase looked into the shot glass sitting on the counter. "Drowning my sorrows. I guess you've heard about Lowell."

"Oui. But you've already lost one Graves to drowning. Don't lose another."

Increase looked at Jean. "I don't know how to stop. Death is my curse."

"Physical death is not a curse, Increase. It's a passage, a journey you haven't been called to take just yet. Spiritual death—now that's a curse you don't want to fall under. Let's get you home."

They walked into the evening. The sound of children playing stickball in the street made Increase cringe.

"Physical or spiritual, it doesn't matter. I just want to die with them." Increase leaned against a storefront, catching his breath. *When did walking home become so difficult?*

"Layer by layer your life has been stripped from you, Increase." Jean leaned against the wall, close enough to feel but not so close to touch. "You've found your meaning in earthly things: your family, your job. You are a good man, Increase. You've helped a lot of people because you have a heart that wants to heal ... to heal others ... and to heal itself."

The sound of Jean's voice was soothing. Increase rested a foot on the brick wall and crossed his arms.

"Don't mistake your pain for punishment, Increase. The joys of this world should lead you closer to God, and when they don't, then perhaps he removes the obstacles. Annie was not what you needed, neither was David, nor will Mariette be. What you need is God. He alone is the Great

Physician."

"Papa has invited us to Boston," Mariette said.

She had a letter from Maurice inviting them to visit for a while. There was to be a medical conference in Boston and he had two tickets to attend.

"A lecture on ancient medicines used in Gaul during the first century. Huh, that sounds interesting." She looked up from the letter.

Increase sat across from her, despondent.

"It might be good for you to get out of town for a while, change your surroundings."

"I can't go to Boston. … I can't stay with Dr. Shevenell." Increase hung his head.

"Maurice. And Papa wouldn't have invited you if he didn't want you to go." Mariette watched a bird swoop to the ground outside the window. "I'll go with you. Rachelle and Clement will be fine. Dr. Giatros can check on them while we're gone." She struggled to stand.

"Are you feeling well, Mariette? Your hands have been swollen lately."

Mariette examined her hands. "Must be the dog days of summer. I'll go to the post office and call Papa that we'll be there."

The bustle of Boston was surprising after so long in Dunstable Plains. More people were driving the new automobiles, honking horns and speeding through the streets.

"Someone's going to get hurt," Increase exclaimed as another auto hurried around their horse and buggy. "They should ride the trolley."

"Oh, Increase, stop being a stick in the mud. Times are changing." Mariette waved to Maurice on the front stairs. "Pay the driver and get our things." She lighted from the carriage and flew up the stairs.

"You have news," Maurice said, taking in the picture of his daughter.

"Not yet," Mariette said quietly and hugged her father.

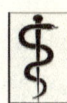

"I thought a day out would do you some good," Maurice was saying. Increase and Mariette looked up from their oatmeal. "I've heard Revere Beach is a nice escape from the city. We'll ride the train up and take a picnic. How's that sound?" He smiled.

"Oh, Papa, that would be lovely. Wouldn't it, Increase?" She squeezed his hand next to hers on the table.

Increase tried to smile back at her. "Yes. That would be nice."

He knew it was a halfhearted attempt, but for Mariette and for the old friendship of his mentor, Maurice, he would try.

The acrid smell of coal soot floating through the crowd mixed with the salt air. Friends calling salutations on the platform mingled with the steam's hiss and the clatter of the train wheels slowly pulling away.

The sun was strong enough to make wading a desirable activity. At least the humidity was low, and Maurice had brought large umbrellas for shade. Mariette spread some old blankets on a grassy spot near the sand and began hauling out the goodies that Cook had packed for luncheon. She clapped her hands when she spotted her favorite chicken salad and cucumber sandwiches.

"Shall we eat first or try the water?" Maurice asked.

"How about a nibble, a walk, then the real chow-down?" Mariette suggested with a grin.

"I know what you'll be nibbling first," Maurice teased.

Everyone sat on the blankets, though Mariette looked uncomfortable. Increase watched the father and daughter enjoy their visit. *They must have been very close without a wife and mother. Like me and David without Annie. Or maybe not. I was working all the time and Lively took care of David.*

"Why the sigh, dear?" Mariette was staring at him.

"Did I sigh?" Increase was surprised. "I was thinking of you as a child. You must have had your father wrapped around your little finger."

"She did at that!" Maurice said. "And what a perfect place to be. I guess you've taken my place now." He chuckled and took a bite of a peach. "Won't you have something to eat?" He passed a bowl of grapes to Increase.

Increase took a few and then stood up. "I believe I'll walk around a bit."

"I'll join you," Maurice said and stood.

"We won't be long. You'll be alright?" Increase asked Mariette.

"Yes, of course. I might head down to the water and cool my feet," she said as she kicked off the slippers she had chosen for the foray.

The men wandered through the crowds and around the shore to watch the little sailboats skirting the edge of the small harbor. Rowboats were anchored a little way out and men dangled fishing lines over the blue-green water.

Increase couldn't help thinking of little David pulling Clement up and then pushing him toward the canal wall. How the friendly water changed—a snarling enemy strangling his son.

"The boats glide so gracefully, never recognizing the danger that lies below," he murmured.

"Hmm. Thinking of David. He was a brave boy, so selfless to help his friend." Maurice threw the peach pit out into the water. It floated on top. "You must be very proud of him." The older man looked at his son-in-law.

"I guess I should be … but I'm angry that he saved Clement and not himself. It isn't fair that Clement lives and David doesn't." His voice cracked. He cleared his throat and scuffed his shoe into the sand.

"You're right. You loved your son and you wanted to see him grow into a man, to do great things and make his mark on the world." Maurice looked across the water. "Clement should have died."

Increase jerked his head up. "No, they both should have lived."

"But they didn't." He paused. "Is it possible to be happy for Clement and still mourn David?" Maurice asked. "Mariette is worried about you, Increase. She fears your anger and your desperation."

"So do I, truth be told. Time is supposed to heal all wounds, but I never got over Annie and I can't imagine ever getting over David. There's no healing a broken heart." He followed the path of a boat with his eyes. The wind filled its sails and pushed it along.

"There will always be scar tissue, yes, but the heart still beats."

A commotion in front of the lemonade stand caused them to turn. Some men were helping a woman across the sandy shore. It was Mariette—soaked from head to toe. Maurice and Increase took off running.

"I'm okay. I'm okay." Mariette was laughing and pushing her hair away from her face. "Just lost my balance is all."

Increase and Maurice reached her.

"Mariette, are you—" Increase pulled up short. The shape of a large cantaloupe nestled under her clinging skirt. "Are you alright?"

His eyes darted up and down from the swollen abdomen to the blue eyes that questioned his reaction. He took her arm and thanked the men.

"I'll help her now," he said as he picked her up and carried her toward the blankets.

Maurice followed behind.

"Why didn't you tell me?" Increase whispered in her ear.

She leaned her head on his chest. "I tried before … and then after … I was afraid."

Increase kept his gaze on the blankets ahead. "I'm sorry."

He placed her gently on the blankets and started feeling her limbs. "Are you sure you're okay? Nothing sprained or broken?"

"Only my pride. I lost my balance and ended up on my derriere. How embarrassing." She looked up at her father, who was anxiously watching the husband-and-wife exchange. "Well, there's no hiding it now, Papa. You're going to be a grand-père again."

Maurice smiled and sighed. "I look forward to being called 'Pepè' once more. And when will this happy event take place?"

Mariette looked at Increase and colored. "November, I believe."

"You will come with us, won't you?" Mariette asked. "It's been so long since I was at church. Papa wants you to come too."

Increase rolled over and looked at his wife. She was dressing for Mass. How had he not noticed the swollen belly? Surely it didn't just appear this morning. *Am I really that neglectful?*

"Yes. I'll go with you." He swung his feet over the edge of the bed. "I'm sorry, Mariette."

She stopped buttoning the shirtwaist and looked over at him.

"I've been self-absorbed. I've let you down, and a lot of other people too. I'll do better; I promise. But this …" He pointed toward her midsection. "This is going to take time. I'm happy for you, I think. But … it's hard."

She crossed the room in a second and stood holding his head to the burgeoning life that grew inside her. "I know it's hard. I'm sorry you found out like you did. I tried, really I did, Increase. I didn't want to hurt you. I know how you feel about having another baby, but you mustn't be afraid."

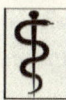

The church bells rang, calling them to worship. Increase helped Mariette from the automobile and then Maurice drove around to park on the street. The couple waited on the front steps for him to return.

They walked in as a family and found their seats. Maurice's eyes shone and his chest was two sizes bigger as old friends and acquaintances waved from their spots. Maurice led the way and Mariette followed. Increase sat on the aisle.

The organist pounded out the processional as the priests and acolytes paraded to the front of the church. Then the choir began singing. Deep bass filled the church and echoed the haunting lyrics:

> Brightly beams our Father's mercy,
> From His lighthouse evermore,
> But to us He gives the keeping
> Of the lights along the shore.

*David. I should have been there. I should have done something. I let the lights go out. Now another child is coming.* Increase glanced at Mariette. She listened to the choir, looking up at the expansive ceiling.

> Dark the night of sin has settled,
> Loud the angry billows roar;
> Eager eyes are watching, longing,
> For the lights along the shore.

*I couldn't save Annie. I couldn't save our child. Now what will happen to Mariette? I can't lose another one.* His hands shook and his breathing became erratic.

Mariette looked at him and took his hand. "Are you okay?"

He nodded his head. *When will it stop?*

> Trim your feeble lamp, my brother;
> Some poor sailor, tempest-tossed,
> Trying now to make the harbor,
> In the darkness may be lost.

Sweat broke out on his forehead. *The darkness closed in on my poor boy. Death's dark hand gripped Annie and tore her from me. There was no one to rescue. No one to save.*

> Let the lower lights be burning!
> Send a gleam across the wave!
> Some poor fainting, struggling seaman
> You may rescue, you may save.

*Hmph, how could I ever rescue someone? I'm a doctor who kills, a father who deserts, a husband who neglects.*

The song was over. The priest stood for the sermon.

"Today's word of encouragement comes from Isaiah 43. 'But now thus saith the Lord that created thee, O Jacob, and he that formed thee, O Israel, Fear not: for I have redeemed thee, I have called thee by thy name; thou art mine. When thou passest through the waters, I will be with thee; and through the rivers, they shall not overflow thee: when thou walkest through …'"

Ignoring the words that followed, Increase rose and stormed from the church. The doors loomed far from him. The nearer he drew to them, the farther away they moved. Finally he spilled out into the bright sunlight of the street, like a man thrown overboard. He turned and fled to the cemetery. *Annie. I need to see Annie.*

Her grave was familiar. He had visited it daily the first year after her death. Gradually it became a place of refuge. He met her here, to talk and remember.

"I'm sorry it's been so long, Annie."

He held his hat and looked at the stone marker: *Annie Graves. Forever Loved.*

"I haven't forgotten you. I've let you down. David …" His voice cracked. A sob broke from him, a beast without designation or understanding, tearing him apart, ripping joints and marrow.

He fell to his knees and cried.

Mariette joined him, timidly holding his shoulders. Tears slipped down her cheeks as she watched him grieve and mourn while the nameless dread filled him, always, with darkness.

"Don't tell me you are there, God!" Increase shouted. "You weren't there when the waters rushed over my child. You weren't there when the fires of pain devoured my wife. You haven't been with me. You deserted me ... left me...." His stomach churned and bile filled his throat. "You are cruel and hateful! You taunt me and take all I love. Why?"

Mariette sobbed next to him, feeling the awful pain that lived inside his soul. *Will I ever understand him? Do I really want to understand? The agony has driven him to drink, to lose his job, to abandon all happiness. What if something happens to this child, or to me?* She felt the warm roundness flutter and kick. *What will happen to this man I have chosen to love?*

She rubbed his back and let him cry. Wordless prayers echoed in her heart.

*For it is one of the acts of life, this act by which we die....*
*~Marcus Aurelius~*

# CHAPTER 44

"I DON'T KNOW WHEN I'LL RETURN ... if I'll return."

Casper nodded his bald head. He was family to me, part of my life since birth. He held me tight, tears mingling with the rain beginning to fall.

"I'll take care of everything," he said. "You'll return."

Ludia and the church that met at her house, that had surrounded me in my time of grief, now stood at the city gate to say good-bye. They joined Casper, hugging, crying, and calling blessings and assurances.

Passover week was over. Paolo and I carried light packs on our backs. We turned down the Via Egnatia as everyone waved good-bye.

"Hypiaínete! Good-bye." The last parting cry was cut short as we left the city walls.

The morning was gloomy; the northeast winds were blowing, predicting difficulty in the straits. *I was warned it wouldn't be easy.* The knot in my midsection pulled tighter.

"Where will we go first?" I asked.

"We'll catch a boat to Troas. Friends are waiting for us there."

I nodded. Troas was a couple days' sail. "That will give you time to rest."

Paolo grinned. "You're not going to be a mother hen, are you?"

"If I have to be." I smiled back. "You may need a sheltering wing. I'm sure you don't take care of yourself."

I watched as the rocky coast of Neapolis shrank from view. The harbor turned, curving out to sea. The outline of Mount Pangaion blended into the gray clouds. I inhaled the salty wind that whipped the chilly mist against my face. *Help me, Lord.*

The Hellespont currents were against us, and the Etesian winds fought our progress. The bread was dry and crumbly on the fourth day. The taste of Ludia's favorite pastry was sweet in my mind, though it would have made me heave.

Paolo slept well on the ship, tucked into a crevice of cargo cushioned by my roll and his. I treated his eyes each day. They were much improved over his arrival in Philippi. *I relieve his eyes and he helps me to see.* I shook my head at the paradox. *Which of us is the doctor?*

Finally on the fifth day we neared the port. I was made for the shore, not the ship. My stomach lurched again. I chewed calamus and anticipated the solid ground fast approaching.

"Paolo." I shook his shoulder. "We'll be getting off soon."

"Good. The fish have had enough of you." He grinned and sat up. "You go on and wait above. I'll pack for both of us."

We stayed with Ignatius again. Names and faces blurred. I thought I was here for Paolo, perhaps even for myself, but the relief I was asked to provide wasn't intended for two alone. Paolo gave miraculous healing; I administered drugs and remedies. We became a team for the body and the spirit.

I visited local doctors, sharing the medical knowledge I had gained in Athens and Rome, but also teaching about the healing power of Jesus Christ. Some listened; others pointed to the Asclepion, a day's walk away in Pergamum. The special waters and the rooms of snakes there administered a healthy dose of competition.

"Come and see. There's no pool, but living water flows," I said.

We stayed a full week, long enough for my land legs to feel strong again.

"We leave tomorrow," Paolo said.

My stomach flipped.

The upstairs room where we assembled was filled to capacity. A small church already met in Troas, and Paolo's nightly preaching had swelled the numbers. So many ached for the Great Physician that nightly we trekked down to the coast and baptized people.

Tonight no less than five doctors had gathered to witness the healings that were discussed all over town. Their own house calls had proven that some powerful medicine was at work in Troas. Candlelight flickered on the upturned faces as Paolo spoke late into the night.

*He'll wear himself out, but at least he can rest on the ship tomorrow.*

Small children leaned against their mothers, their mouths hanging open in gentle, breathy snores. The room was nearly silent now as Paolo got to the truth.

"There is one God, who is over all and in all. He is the creator and provider of all that was and is and ever will be. You have heard of him. You know the stories of Abraham and Moses and the mighty escape from Egypt. It was the prophets of this same God who forewarned of the fall of Babylon and the rise of the mighty Roman Empire."

Paolo paused, then said, "Yet this God is not satisfied."

A gasp of fear echoed around the room. I knew the question in their hearts: *What would it take to satisfy a god who could do such things?*

Paolo continued. "He wants each of us to be his child."

A burst of laughter broke out.

"No, no. Now listen. He wants us to be his children, but none of us knows how to be a child of a god."

Heads nodded.

"So he sent his Son, Jesus, to show us how a child of God behaves."

"Oh go on!" one of the doctors cried out. "A child of the gods has great powers. I don't see any power here in these myths and stories."

The crowd began to jeer, and then a scream from the back of the room. "My son! My son!"

Everyone turned. A woman leaned out the window. Children began to wake and cry.

"He's dead," came the call from the street.

The woman fell to her knees sobbing.

"Stay calm," Paolo said.

I was the first to the stairs. A couple doctors followed me, while the others headed for the woman overcome by her grief.

A crowd had gathered on the street, and the boy that had fallen lay battered in the arms of a stranger.

"Let me. Here …" I helped clear a space on the street. "Lay him down."

The other doctors and I watched carefully for any sign that the boy had survived the three-story fall, but there was none.

Paolo pushed through the crowd. "Loukas?" he said.

I looked up at him and shook my head. Paolo fell on the boy, covering the youth with his own body. He embraced the lifeless body, breathing deeply. The crowd stared at each other, whispering that this must be the young man's father.

"Don't be afraid." Paolo sat up, holding the boy against his chest. "He lives."

The boy moaned, grabbed his head, then opened his eyes.

The doctors with me jumped back. "What is this?" they asked each other.

"This is a child of God," I answered.

We helped the boy upstairs to his mother's cries of delight. The doctors checked him out and found him to be whole and healthy. Paolo asked that we take a break and eat together, then after the midnight snack, he went to preaching the good news again.

When the sun slipped above the eastern mountains, we said our farewells and headed for the port.

Paolo pulled me aside and spoke in my ear. "I'll meet you in Assos." I drew back, but he pulled me close. "I need to be alone for a while."

"You need rest. I know what happened last night. … You don't need a long walk across the mountains."

Paolo hugged me tight. "You're good to care for me, Loukas. But I know what I need. … I need to withdraw, like Jesus used to do." He looked me in the eye. "I promise I'll see you there and then I can rest."

I nodded and returned his embrace. "We'll wait for you there."

*Until recently, Diaulus was a doctor; now he is an undertaker.*
*He is still doing as an undertaker, what he used to do as a doctor.*
~Martial~

# CHAPTER 45

THE LECTURE HALL WAS FILLED. Increase recognized some former colleagues from St. Patrick's in Boston. Had it only been a
year since he'd left? He waved from across the room and sat down with
Maurice. The hum of voices subsided as the speaker took the stage.

"It's been so long since I heard a medical lecture. Thank you for inviting me," Increase whispered to Maurice.

Maurice patted Increase's arm. The speaker was from France, and the
accent and broken English required concentration.

"The ancient city of Lugdunum was important to the mystical medicines.
Artifacts have been identified, revealing many surgical advancements. ..."

Surgery had been Increase's interest since he was young. The body
fascinated him. It had the power to care for itself, to recover and heal,
without much help from the doctors.

"Religion was a part of the process. ..."

Religion had been important in the beginning. His mother had empha-
sized God's role in the doctor-patient relationship. *Never forget that you are
not God,* she had said at his medical school graduation. But God had not
intervened, not when it was important, not when Annie needed him
most. Increase should have been able to do more, could have done more,
if he had only known what and how.

"The herbalist was most important to the healing process. Ancient
journals describe a tea that was especially helpful to stop bleeding in the
kidneys."

*Jean is a good herbalist. And a good friend. He's tried to help me and I've
pushed him away. He's smarter than I've given him credit for.*

"The herb was native to the area, though now it has traveled the world. In France we call it 'bourse de pasteur'—shepherd's purse, I believe you say. Midwives combined bourse de pasteur with bearberry and comfrey to ease the postpartum bleeding."

Increase squinted in the bright sunlight. "Thank you again for inviting me, Maurice. I enjoyed it."

"You're very welcome. A doctor should never stop learning, even from the past." He steered the Stanhope through the busy Boston streets. "What especially piqued your interest?"

"It all seemed so pertinent. We really know so little, have made so few advancements since ancient times. It's a shame we've forgotten some of the knowledge we once had." Increase lifted his hat to a passing group of ladies. "The herbalist seemed especially fascinating to me. Jean Giatros, back in Dunstable Plains, has been a big help to me."

"Yes, I spoke with him during my Christmas visit. He reminded me of a doctor I knew once a long time ago." Maurice slowed down for a dog crossing the street.

"How's that?"

"I don't know. He seemed to have a deepness about him. When Adelaide died, he helped me grasp hold of life again."

Increase raised his brows and looked at Maurice. "I didn't know you lost your grasp on life. You always seemed so ... vibrant. I never understood how you moved on."

Maurice nodded. "You've had difficulty. I know." He pulled up to the brownstone. "I think the best thing my doctor friend ever said was that I couldn't live for Adelaide or Mariette or even for my job as a doctor. They would never fulfill me. I had to learn to live for God." Maurice clapped Increase on the knee. "And he was right."

"That sounds like Jean, alright."

Increase climbed out of the auto and headed into the house. *I just don't know if I want to live for God. He's so cruel at times.*

"I thought Paris was so much better than Boston, always busy and at the center of art and fashion," Mariette said. "Then when I returned to Boston, I thought nothing could be better. I liked it quieter, calmer. And I met you." Mariette smiled over at Increase, who was watching the scenery as they neared Dunstable Plains. The train's whistle signaled they were past Nashua. "But I think I like Dunstable Plains even better than Boston. Isn't it amazing how we change over time?"

"Hmm. Well, I hope you can manage another change. I'm going to have to find a job and soon." He looked at her midsection, the growing belly still hidden beneath the large skirt she wore. "I'll get our bags. You wait on the platform." He rose from his seat as the train slowed.

Mariette grabbed his hand. "We'll change together. It'll be okay."

Increase looked down at her; a child's trust gleamed in her eyes. If only he could be so sure.

"That certainly is good news. Enjoy your time in Boston," Mariette said as she waved to Mrs. Sheppard.

Increase carried their bags, his arms loaded like a pack mule. "What's good news?" he asked as he neared Mariette.

She turned to him. "Everything is cleared up from the fire. Sheppard Mills even expanded their lines. She's headed to Boston to look for new furniture for the house. She says the bay pigs ruined everything while they stayed this summer."

"Mariette!"

"I didn't say it; she did. You don't see me wanting new furniture, do you?" She smiled up at him. "Let's get out of here before you fall over."

The house felt stifling after being closed up for nearly a week. Mariette opened windows and then checked the icebox. She would need to make an early order for ice. A knock sounded at the front door.

Increase emptied out the heavy bags from their trip and stored them in the attic. A man's voice echoed up the stairwell. Increase walked down the hall.

Mariette was hugging Frank Viollette. Frank was blushing red and grinning ear to ear.

"Increase! Increase, come down here," Mariette called. She turned and waved an envelope at him from the bottom of the stairs. "Increase, wait till you hear. Ethel said 'Yes.' Isn't it wonderful?"

Increase started down the stairs. "Good news. Good news, Frank," Increase said as he made it to the foyer. "And when will the wedding be?" He reached out to shake Frank's hand.

"Soon. I've been waiting for Mrs. Graves to come home so she could read me Ethel's letter. Ethel wrote it weeks ago and said she will be on the train tomorrow. I'm glad you got back in time." Frank's voice boomed in the tiny foyer. "I would have missed my bride."

"And where will the wedding be?" Mariette wiggled up and down on her toes, like a little girl waiting for birthday cake.

"At St. Anne's of course. I need to go speak to Father Cartier. Will you … Will you go with me?" He looked at the two of them. "You've been the best of friends to me." He twisted his hat and looked from one to the other.

Increase looked at Mariette. "I'll go with you. Mrs. Graves should stay home, though. We just had a long trip … and I don't want her getting too tired."

Mariette blushed and put her arm around Increase. "I'll look through the pantry and see what we can have for dinner." She smiled at Frank. "Dr. Graves will give me all the details when he gets back. I can't wait to meet your Ethel." She leaned up to kiss his cheek.

"Vous allez l'aimer—You will love her. She's wonderful," Frank said.

"No doubt about it," Mariette said as she opened the door for the men to leave. "Tell me everything, Increase." She stroked his arm as he walked past her.

"I'll remember it all." *I love her*, he thought to his own surprise.

"Dr. Graves. Frank. Come in, come in." Father Cartier greeted them at the door. The smell of fish permeated the house. "The children brought back a bucket of fish for their old priest." He chuckled. "I remember spending all day on a creekside when I was young."

He led them into the sitting room and motioned toward the chairs. "It's good to see you back, Dr. Graves. My leg is cleared up thanks to you and Medic Giatros." He sat down across from the men. "How was your trip?"

"It was a good trip, thank you. But this isn't really a social call." Increase looked over at Frank.

"Oh, I think I know why you're here," Father Cartier said. "It's a little sooner than I expected, but I figured you'd be by." The priest grinned, clasping his fingers and raising the index fingers together.

"You know about Ethel? How?" Frank furrowed his brow and stared at the man's knowing presumption.

Father Cartier tilted his head. "Ethel?"

"We're getting married. She'll be here tomorrow," Frank said.

"Oh." Father Cartier cleared his throat. "Well, that's quite the news, Frank. Congratulations. Tomorrow, you say?"

"Yes. She said she would be on the morning train. Mrs. Graves ..." Frank paused to look at Increase and then scooted to the front of his chair, focusing on the priest. "She said she would help Ethel get ready. She's been reading Ethel's letters to me, you see, and well, we want to get married at the church."

"Of course, in the church, of course." The man scratched his head as he realized the change of direction the conversation had taken. "Well, that's awfully kind of Mrs. Graves to help your lady. What time were you thinking?"

"Seven? I can miss the evening shift at work. That'll give me time to bathe." Frank blushed and looked at the wooden floor.

"Seven it is, then. Will there be guests?"

"Some of the people from the mill might come. ..." Frank's voice softened. "I wish my mother was still alive."

The men sat in silence for a moment.

Frank looked up, a glimmer of hope shining in his eyes. "I guess she'll be there in spirit, looking on from above. Don't you suppose, Father?"

"I imagine so, Frank."

"See you tomorrow, a happy groom." Father Cartier shook Frank's hand at the door.

"Thank you," Frank said and stepped out into the twilight.

"You go on, Frank," Increase said. "I want to talk to the Father a minute."

Frank waved and floated out to the street.

Increase turned back to the priest. "You didn't expect us to be here about a wedding. So why did you think we were here?"

Father Cartier gave a small smile, but said nothing as Increase searched the priest's face. The cleric stepped out on the porch and pulled the door closed behind him. He took a deep breath.

"Well, I don't know that I ought to say just yet." The man looked at Increase, sizing him up and down. "Did you find a job in Boston?"

Increase bit his lower lip and shook his head. "I went there to stay with my father-in-law and attend a lecture. I didn't look for a job."

Father Cartier chuckled. "That's not what the town thought. They were sure you were headed back to the big city for good." He walked to the porch railing and leaned on it, looking Increase full in the face. "The mill workers went to the city meeting about it."

"There was a meeting?" Increase drew a sharp breath. *What in the world is this about?*

The priest nodded. "It caused quite a stir. They told the city board members all about how you helped them, making this a better place to live. Some of them said they'd leave for New Bedford if you didn't stay here."

Increase licked his lips, watching the minister. "I don't understand. They know I … that I … That is …"

"Yes, they all know you gave in to grief. You lost your child, Increase." His voice was tender. "It was wrong for you to go into surgery after drinking, but these are people who know loss. They know pain. They forgive you." He looked straight into Increase's eyes. "They want you to stay here, to be their doctor."

"But the board …"

"I believe they have agreed to it. I thought that was why you were coming to talk to me, that perhaps Mr. Neal had been to speak to you already. The board wants to bring you back at the new hospital, but only if you'll agree to meet with me and keep a check on your drinking. What do you think?"

Increase moved to the porch railing and looked out on the street. The church bell chimed the half hour. *The bells are always ringing, calling me to work.*

"I … I'll think about it." He turned toward the priest, but he couldn't look at him. He stared over his shoulder. "I need to talk to my wife. There's a lot of pain here in Dunstable Plains."

"Yes, I'm sure there is. But pain will follow you wherever you go. Talk to Mariette and see if you can ease the pain here. So many of us want to help you."

Warmth radiated from Increase, the pink glow of sunset. *Or was it the sunrise?*

The church was filled with well-wishers who had raced there as soon as the first evening work bell rang. Frank was a hero to many, and to see him happy was cause for a community party.

Mariette had twisted Ethel's hair and filled it with the last of summer's flowers from her garden. A bouquet of roses had been fashioned and tied with a ribbon. She was a beautiful bride.

Mariette held Increase's hand during the ceremony, remembering her own wedding. The tiny life inside her flipped and fluttered.

The ceremony ended and everyone gathered outside to kiss the happy couple.

"Dr. Graves, Dr. Graves," a voice called from the edge of the crowd.

Increase turned and spotted the young man. It was Michael Flint from over near Rocky Pond. Increase maneuvered through the wedding guests.

"Michael, what is it? Is something wrong?" Increase recalled it was nearing time for Mrs. Flint to deliver.

"She's bad off, Doc. Her mama said to come get you right away. The baby isn't turned." Sweat beaded on his forehead and worry etched fear into his face.

"How'd you get here?" Increase looked around the grounds.

"Rode my horse fast as she'd go," the young man answered.

"My bag's in the buggy, but I've got to take my wife home. I'll meet you there."

"I can get myself home. You go on," Mariette said. She had followed Increase through the crowd.

Increase looked at her with worry. "You shouldn't spend too much time on your feet. I'll take you home."

"I'm fine. I want to be here with Frank and Ethel. Please, Increase. Go on and help them," she said. She put her hand on his arm. "Really, I'm fine."

"I'll go with you, Dr. Graves," Jean said as he walked into the little circle.

Increase nodded, gave Mariette a peck on the cheek, and headed toward the buggy.

The baby hadn't turned and the mother was struggling. Jean got the family out of the bedroom and shut the door. He sat on the bed near the young woman's head.

"Dr. Graves is here now," Jean said as he turned her attention to himself. "He's going to check on the baby. It'll be uncomfortable, painful perhaps, but you'll forget it as soon as this baby is born."

She nodded and relaxed under the hypnosis of his gentle voice. Increase pushed on her expansive belly to turn the child. She cried out.

"Keep looking at me," Jean directed. "Keep your eyes on me." He began singing an old hymn.

Increase kneaded the womb to the rhythm of the song and the baby moved a quarter turn. The mother-to-be breathed heavily, but kept watching Jean, listening to his song. He smoothed her hair and nodded encouragement while he sang. Another quarter turn and the baby was in position.

"Good job, Mrs. Flint," Increase said. "The baby is turned. You did great." He beamed at her. "Now we just have to wait for this little guy to descend. It shouldn't be too long."

Her breathing steadied and she was able to doze between contractions. Increase went out to the family and told them the news. Now it was just a matter of waiting.

Soon the whistle of the night train called long and lonely through the dark. And then the cry of a baby sounded. The wait was over.

Increase stumbled into bed in the wee hours of morning. A successful birth for both mother and babe; it was deserving of deep rest.

Gentle and calm as ever, Annie lay supported against the pillows, her face twitching with the occasional contraction. *She's so beautiful*, Increase thought.

"Hold my hand," she said. "It will be awhile, I expect. What do you think it'll be, a boy or a girl?"

"There's only way to know for sure." Increase frowned. "And that time will be here very soon. You're nearly ready for the hard part."

"No," she replied. "The hard part comes after this. The diapers, the sicknesses, the colic. The hard part is living life. Living requires pain." She relaxed her head on the pillows and a soft smile played with her lips. "I think beautiful, exciting pain is my favorite."

Then she grimaced. The contractions were getting stronger. "Increase, I need you." Annie bent over, bracing herself against the flood of anguish that crashes over every mother. "It hurts," she gasped.

"I know, Love," Increase whispered as he stroked her hand. "It will pass soon."

"Send for the dressmaker," Annie commanded with a new urgency. Sweat broke out on her forehead and her delicate hand trembled in Increase's own grasp.

"The dressmaker?" Increase didn't understand.

"For David. He needs new clothes—bright, white clothes. I can't wait to show him to the Father." Her voice was only an echo in the room.

Increase looked at his wife lying motionless in the bed; David lay at her side. Increase fell on his knees sobbing and clutching at them, begging them to speak.

His tears flowed unchecked, the salty taste catching in the corner of his mouth. A knock at the door caused Increase to turn. There stood the dressmaker with Annie, a bolt of white silk fabric in his arms.

"No—no, w-wait," Increase said. "Not yet. I'm not ready."

But Annie turned, holding David's hand, and followed the dressmaker out.

"You're going to love it here," Increase heard her say.

David smiled up at her, skipping by her side.

Increase sat up and looked around. He was alone in bed. The shades were drawn and light filtered around the edges of the white curtains like a halo. Annie was there. She was there to meet David. Increase wiped the tears from his cheeks as he breathed a peaceful sigh.

"Potato soup," Increase said as he sniffed the air. "But I smell something else too."

He put his arms around Mariette and caressed her swollen tummy. "You're not working too hard, are you?"

She smiled and put the last bowl on the table. "Not even close. I spend most of my time knitting for this new little person." She turned and wrapped her arms around his neck. "But you're right: there is another smell. Sit down."

Increase sat at his place while Mariette went back into the kitchen. She came out carrying a frosted cake.

"I made it early this morning. It's for David's birthday." She looked at him like a naughty puppy looks at the newspaper.

Increase startled. "David's birthday."

"I'm sorry if it upsets you," Mariette said. "But I just don't think we should stop celebrating him. He's an important part of our lives."

She placed the cake on the table and sat catty-corner to her husband. She took his hand and looked him in the eye.

"David will always be a part of our lives," she said. "He was your son, and, I like to believe, mine as well. I don't want you to think this baby is a replacement. This is our second child, David's brother or sister."

Increase started to speak, but Mariette hushed him. "Let me finish. I know Mr. Neal has asked you to come back to the hospital. I'll go wherever you decide we should go, but, Increase, I think we ought to stay here. This is where we became a family. I can never replace Annie. I know you still love her, and I'm glad you do. That means that you can love deeply and forever. I want you to love me like that as well."

"I …" Increase began.

Mariette put her free hand over their clasped ones. "Listen, please. It's David's birthday, but I think we're the ones with a present to open. You know … when we first came here, I was disgusted by the French Canadians. They were dirty and ignorant in my eyes. But when I got to know them, I could look past their circumstances and see what a blessing they are to me."

She looked at the cake at the end of the table and gathered her thoughts. "Everything that happens in life is a blessing. If you don't receive the blessing, then you probably aren't opening the package the right way. I don't want you to forget Annie. I want you to remember how much you loved her, so you can try to love me that much. I know I'm not the girl who waited for you all through medical school. I'm not your sister's childhood friend. I'm not your first love." Teardrops glistened in her lashes. "But do you think you could try, in time, to love me?"

"I've already started." He slid out of the chair and knelt beside her. "Forgive me for taking so long."

*We are healed of a suffering only by experiencing it to the full.*
~Marcel Proust~

# CHAPTER 46

*Rome—AD 68*

"LET HIM PASS," THE CAPTAIN instructed the guard. I nodded my thanks and entered the coolness of Tertulliam. Torches lit on the walls cast shadows as I walked toward the opening in the floor. A belt was wrapped around my waist and I was lowered into the second floor of the prison.

"Loukas … my faithful friend. You've come back."

Paolo sat along the wall, his back resting against the cool stone wall. Light from above filtered through the hole in the ceiling, but my eyes still needed time to adjust. I walked with hesitation, feeling along the floor with my feet.

"Of course. I couldn't leave you alone like this. The bandages will be wet through by now. Here, lie down on your stomach." I spread the blanket I carried with me and Paolo slowly uncurled himself and stretched out on the rough wool. "Were you able to sleep any?"

"Not too much." Paolo moaned as I unwrapped the bandages that held the lacerated skin together. "But you'll have me better soon and then I can sleep."

"I brought some chamomile. Sleep is the best medicine for you. Let me finish this and then we'll get you settled."

"You know this is the end," the guard said.

*Was that a question … or a statement?*

The guard stood next to me, watching the doctor watching his patient. I nodded my head and inhaled deeply. Paolo was resting quietly now, his breathing coming in short puffs.

"Why won't he just say it? It would be so easy to spare his life. ..." The guard stared at Paolo and shook his head. "I just don't get it."

"I've been at sea in a terrible storm, shipwrecked." I never broke my watchful gaze. "In the middle of the storm, the waves crash. They look hundreds of feet high, pounding ... pounding one after another, over and over." I looked over at the guard and offered a half smile. "It's very frightening; you can't breathe it's so terrifying. The ship tosses and pitches. You can't hang on to anything; you're bloody and bruised. ... And then, shhh ... it stops. The wind dies down; the waves become calmer. You can start to breathe again." I lifted my shoulders and hands. "What had been terrifying becomes peaceful. The water that threatened your death now conducts you on your journey."

I nodded my head. My old friend slept peacefully.

"Paolo knew long ago that the time would come for the waters to lead him home. This storm looks to you like a bitter end, but to him ... it's safe travel home."

"Senseless suffering," the guard scoffed.

"No," I answered. "A wise friend once told me that the herbs we doctors use are most productive in their death. Paolo's suffering ... death ... is also productive. Without it I wouldn't be here to tell you about Jesus."

*One must learn to love, and go through a good deal of suffering to get to it …*
*and the journey is always towards the other soul.*
~D. H. Lawrence~

# CHAPTER 47

"I HAD A DREAM THIS MORNING," Increase told Jean as they passed through the countryside in a carriage. The first of the leaves were turning golden after the cool night air.

"Oh?" Jean watched a flock of geese overhead. Their honking calls sent the front guard dropping to the rear and another took his place.

"It was about Annie and David." Increase looked sideways at Jean.

"Mm-hm."

"It started like all of the other dreams. She was struggling in labor, but then it changed. David was with her. There was light and … something … like serenity, I think. She was there to meet David, to take him home." He took a deep breath. "Do you think that's right?" His sweaty hands trembled on the reins.

"I have no doubt that David was met by his mother. God is very much like a mother, comforting her children." Jean looked back at the road ahead.

"If God comforts his children, why don't I feel comforted?"

It was an earnest question, free of the hatred and anger that had so plagued him the last eight years.

"Have you not seen a child stiffening his back in his mother's arms, refusing to be comforted?" Jean asked. "All of the love and tenderness a mother offers cannot comfort a child who refuses to be comforted, and neither can God's loving tenderness comfort you when you refuse it."

"I think some pain is too much for God to comfort." Increase's chest tightened as he remembered the dark, lonely nights when bourbon was his only friend.

"No pain is beyond the Great Physician's healing touch, if only you will take the medicine."

They traveled on toward Rocky Pond, deep in thought. The horse slowed on the curving road.

"Then why didn't God answer me when I cried out to him?" Increase's voice cracked.

"A mother hears all of her children's cries in the nursery. Happy noises often go unnoticed, but you can be sure she is alert at the first cry of pain or trouble. God the Father is more ready with help than the most attentive mother. But just as the child doesn't always see the mother's response, so you too might not always hear your Father." Jean looked over at Increase. "That doesn't make him any less present and concerned."

Increase remembered the times that he had stood in the corner of a room watching David overcome a difficulty. He was ready to grab David if he needed to, but the boy hadn't known that.

They pulled up to the Flints' house, and Increase jumped from the carriage. He wrapped the reins around the post and grabbed his doctor kit. Jean was already at the door with one of his jars.

"Good afternoon, Medic. Please come in." Michael Flint held open the door and stepped aside for Jean. He waved to Increase as he climbed the stairs. "Good afternoon, Doctor. Thank you for coming."

"And how is the new mother?" Increase shook hands with Michael.

"She's doing well. I think. Mama says she's bleeding heavy, though."

"We'll have a peek at her." Increase knew the look of hidden fear.

Jean was in the kitchen with the women. "Steep it for several minutes," he was saying.

"Mrs. Flint," Increase interrupted as he walked in. "Would you come in the bedroom? I'll have a look at you and see how everything is healing." He smiled encouragement.

She looked at the floor in embarrassment. "I'm sorry about all of the fuss. I don't mean to be any trouble." She walked to the bedroom.

Increase checked her and was pleased. There was a good bit of swelling, and the bleeding heavy but not too concerning.

"Stay off your feet for a week. Let your mother take care of things in the house. Your body needs to heal. You just take care of yourself and feeding the baby."

"Yes, Doctor." She smiled as she sat back up. "And Medic Giatros made a tea for me. He says it'll stop the bleeding pretty quick. Says it's made from a shepherd's purse." Increase tipped his head at her and she laughed.

"He's such a nice man. I really do appreciate you two coming all the way out here to help me when my mama couldn't."

Increase smiled and opened the door.

"You gave the Flints some tea?" Increase asked as he drove toward home.

"Yes, it ought to help with the bleeding."

"Oh yeah? Raspberry leaf?"

"No, it's a little stronger—bourse de pasteur. I grew it back home, but I have some in the garden here now."

"You know, you never told me where you studied in France." Increase looked over at him.

"Didn't I? Well, my father is a physician. He taught me the healing arts." Jean smiled and started humming.

*November 1900*

Rachelle opened the door. "Medic Giatros. Come in. Mariette will be so happy to see you. She has the baby with her."

Rachelle closed the door on the brisk wind that scattered dried leaves on the porch. She took Jean's coat and hat and hung them on the coat tree.

"Jean, my friend. Come see the most beautiful little girl you'll ever meet." Increase laughed from the top of the stairs.

Jean climbed the steps and shook Increase's hand. "All went well, then?"

"Yes, thank God. There were no difficulties."

They walked together down the hallway and into the bedroom. Mariette lay in bed, holding the baby. She looked at the doorway and beamed.

"Come meet Annie," she said.

"Annie?" Jean said.

"It was Annie who brought us together in a way," Mariette said and looked down at the baby. "And Annie will keep us together. It just seemed right."

Increase walked out on the porch with Jean to say good-bye. The wind spoke of frost that night. The men rubbed their arms for warmth.

"She's perfect, isn't she?" Increase said.

"Perfect. And you? How are you?" Jean looked at the worry lines etched around Increase's eyes.

"Trying not to worry." He smiled faintly. "Trying to remember that God hears me when I call out."

"Trust that he does. Believe that the Father hears you during the long, lonely nights as well as the bright, clear days. It will take a lot of effort; he knows that. But all of the effort will pay off. Trust will become a natural habit. Every act of trust will make the next act less difficult, until finally, trusting will be as natural as breathing."

Increase nodded. "I believe you."

He looked off to the horizon that was disrupted by the town mills. Jean followed his gaze.

"I've lived so long in fear: Annie's death, raising David and then losing him, and all of the times I failed as a doctor." He blew out a breath. "I don't have to tell you, Mariette's pregnancy had me nervous. It's this name, you know?"

"What name?" Jean turned toward him.

"Increase Graves. It's always seemed a curse to me. I just seem to make people die, like my name says. It's my Midas Touch." He shrugged his shoulders, uncertain how to explain his lifelong fear.

"Why did your parents name you 'Increase'?"

"My sister, Lively, and I are twins. Mother knew it was too soon for us, but we were born anyway. Lively was strong and healthy, but I struggled to live. Mother named me Increase hoping I would get stronger and live. … I guess she never thought about our last name." He sighed softly.

"But you lived up to your name. You increased in life and health."

"And I also increased in deaths and graves." Increase flipped his coat collar up and dug his fists into his pockets.

"You know the story of Jonah, right?"

"Yeah." He wasn't sure what Jonah had to do with any of it.

"God asked Jonah to go down a road he didn't want to travel, so Jonah ran away. He got on a boat and set out in the opposite direction. Then a huge storm blew up and death was in sight. Jonah believed he was going to die."

"But...?"

"The sailors threw Jonah into the sea and he sank. He sank under the water, black and treacherous. ... But he didn't die. Instead a fish swallowed him.

"Certainly Jonah had every right to expect to die then, but he still didn't die. Not in the fish, anyway." Jean reached out and placed his hand over Increase's heart. "Death doesn't have anything to do with a name, or a touch, or a curse. Only God knows the right time for people to die. Until that time comes, Increase, you should choose to live."

Jean clapped his hand on Increase's shoulder and walked down the stairs. The final work bell rang as Increase opened the front door.

# OTHER BOOKS BY TRACI STEAD

**FICTION**
The Potter of Paradox Volume 1 in the Spirit Series
The Shepherd of Shoton Cross Volume 3 in the Spirit Series coming
in 2017

**NON-FICTION**
Devotions of a Gerbil
With Love, John coming in 2017

# ABOUT TRACI

TRACI STEAD IS A CHRISTIAN wife, mother, volunteer, and all-around mountain girl. Transplanted from West Virginia into the sandy soil of the North Carolina coastal plain, she often escapes to the mountains by train or by brain. Sipping a cup of tea, visiting with family, and rocking in the porch chair is her idea of living the high life.

Traci believes stories of real life are the best tales to tell. Though she often writes fiction, the stories are all true.

You can get to know Traci better at **www.TraciStead.com.**